CHOSE
HELL

THESE MEN CHOSE HELL

WILLIAM W. JOHNSTONE
AND J.A. JOHNSTONE

PINNACLE BOOKS
Kensington Publishers, Inc.
kensingtonbooks.com

PINNACLE BOOKS are published by

Kensington Publishing Corp.
900 Third Avenue
New York, NY 10022

Copyright © 2025 by J.A. Johnstone

PUBLISHER'S NOTE: Following the death of William W. Johnstone, the Johnstone family is working with a carefully selected writer to organize and complete Mr. Johnstone's outlines and many unfinished manuscripts to create additional novels in all of his series, like The Last Gunfighter, Mountain Man, and Eagles, among others. This novel was inspired by Mr. Johnstone's superb storytelling.

All Kensington titles, imprints, and distributed lines are available at special quantity discounts for bulk purchases for sales promotion, premiums, fundraising, and educational or institutional use.

Special book excerpts or customized printings can also be created to fit specific needs. For details, write or phone the office of the Kensington Sales Manager: Kensington Publishing Corp., 900 Third Avenue, New York, NY 10022. Attn. Sales Department. Phone: 1-800-221-2647.

PINNACLE BOOKS, the Pinnacle logo, and the WWJ steer head logo Reg. U.S. Pat. & TM Off.

First Printing: July 2025
ISBN-13: 978-0-7860-4962-2
ISBN-13: 978-0-7860-4967-7 (eBook)

10 9 8 7 6 5 4 3 2 1

Printed in the United States of America

The authorized representative in the EU for product safety and compliance is eucomply OU, Parnu mnt 139b-14, Apt 123
Tallinn, Berlin 11317, hello@eucompliancepartner.com.

Chapter 1

"Bad news, Captain?" Sergeant Major Saul Olinger said.

"Does Fort Misery get any other kind from Washington?" Captain Joe Kellerman saw the question form on Olinger's face and grimaced. "Here, Saul, see it for yourself."

Olinger took the dispatch and read:

To Captain Peter Joseph Kellerman.
You are hereby requested and required to end
the conditions of banditry, plunder, and murder
that runs northerly from the Rio Grande and
between the Arizona Territory south of Yuma
and the Mexican state of Sonora. When caught,
the perpetrators, be they white men, Apache, or
Mexicans, must be dealt with severely.

Then, in a different hand:

Joe, I want something done to stop this
lawlessness. Go ahead on your own plan of
action and your authority and backing will be
myself and President Grant.
  William T. Sherman, General of the Army

"I thought Uncle Billy was a friend of yours," Olinger said. "You helped protect his left flank during his March to the Sea." He laid the orders on Kellerman's desk, reverently, as though they were pages torn from the Bible.

"So did I," the captain said. "Once he slapped me on the back and promoted me to full brevet colonel, and now he changes hands, stabs me in the back, and gives me an impossible order."

"You can't put your trust in generals, and you're dealing with two of them," the sergeant major said.

Olinger had treated the orders like a holy document, but Kellerman had no such reverence. He took two glasses and a bottle of bourbon from a desk drawer and slammed them down on the papers.

"A drink with you, Saul," he said.

"Don't mind if I do, Joe," Olinger said. He and the captain had fought in the war together, and the familiarity came naturally to him, but only when there were no enlisted men around.

Kellerman poured the drinks, downed his in one swallow and refilled his glass. "All right, Saul, give me the rest of the bad news."

"Three officers and twenty-eight enlisted men, four of them in the infirmary and one of them, Private Shanks, is running a fever and isn't likely to live."

"What does Mrs. Zimmermann say about him?"

"That he isn't likely to live."

Kellerman looked as though he was trying to put a face to the name and the sergeant major said, "Small, even for a cavalryman, blue eyes, black hair, a Reb, he fought in John Bell Hood's Army of Tennessee . . ."

"I remember now," Kellerman said. "He knifed somebody . . ."

"Two people, a lady of the evening and her pimp. The woman lived but the pimp died."

"So the Army offered him a choice, the noose or Fort Misery."

"Yes," Olinger said. "He chose Fort Misery."

"Bad choice."

"Joe, all of our enlisted men made the same mistake and then realized what they'd done was to arrive in hell early. It's a fact of our existence."

"Look out the window and see another fact of our existence," Kellerman said.

"I don't have to. I know what's out there," the sergeant major said. "The view never changes."

Thrown deep into the Arizona Territory's vast Yuma desert, the post's official name was Fort Benjamin Grierson but seldom used. It looked like a ramshackle shantytown that had fallen from the sky during a great storm and landed on a sea of sand. Fort Misery was manned by a sweating, understrength troop of cavalry composed of deserters, thieves, malingerers, mutineers, murderers, and rapists. "A grubby bunch, the scum of the earth," Lieutenant James Hall called them. Officially, the troop didn't exist. It had no regimental affiliation, wasn't allowed to carry a guidon, and in Washington, any inquiry into its rumored presence was met with blank stares. Since it was somewhat of an embarrassment, the Army had been quick to sweep the fort under the rug and there it stayed, the silence surrounding its formation unbroken.

The post was such a pariah, supplies from Yuma

were dropped about two miles north of the fort at a place called Devil's Rock, a ten-foot-tall granite monolith shaped like a crouching human being. The civilian teamsters would come no closer to Fort Misery and its evil reputation, and wasted no time throwing off their load before hightailing it away from there. Withal, the officers and men of Fort Misery were on a voyage of the damned on an ocean of sand . . . and death would be their only port of call.

Kellerman rose from his desk, and stepped to the window, looking down at the parade ground that had never seen a parade. Triangles of dust had collected on all four corners of the glass panes, one of them marred by a bullet hole and never replaced. Like the fort itself, repairs were not a high priority, though the carpenter, Tobias Zimmermann, did his best to keep the buildings hammered together, just as his wife, Mary, the post's cook, nurse, and laundress strived to keep the soldiers fed and reasonably healthy.

"Second Lieutenant Cranston is coming in with the supply wagon," Kellerman said. "I wonder how the army plans to starve us this month?"

"There's one way to find out," Sergeant Major Olinger said. He stood to attention and saluted. "Permission to inspect the supplies, sir."

Kellerman returned the salute. "Make sure Lieutenant Hall's snuff arrived safe and sound from his dear mama. He's been as worried as a frog in a frying pan about the stuff for weeks."

CHAPTER 2

Mary Zimmermann was already overseeing the unloading of the supplies when Sergeant Major Olinger arrived. He looked at the piled-up sacks and crates and said, "How is it, Mrs. Zimmermann?"

"Looks no better and no worse than usual," the woman said, frowning. "At least they remembered the raisins this time. I can't make plum duff without raisins, sergeant major."

"No, indeed, ma'am," Olinger said. "And I'm glad they arrived safely."

Mrs. Zimmermann was surrounded by salt pork and salt beef in barrels, sacks of beans, coffee, hardtack, salt, brown sugar, and vinegar and molasses in jugs. There were bottles of bourbon packed in straw for the officers and jugs of cheaper whiskey for the other ranks, General Sherman aware that the fort had no sutler.

"Hey, you scoundrel, easy with those crates," Olinger yelled to a clumsy private. "The officers' bourbon is in one of those."

"And Lieutenant Hall's brandy," Mrs. Zimmermann said.

"From his fond mama," Olinger said. And then to Lieutenant Cranston, "An uneventful trip, sir?"

"At sundown on our second day out, Private Ritter and myself heard drums in the distance of the night. Corporal Lockhart couldn't hear them, and neither could the other private, but they were there all right."

"Apache?" Olinger said.

"That would be my guess. I'll let Captain Kellerman know." Suddenly the young officer looked like the bearer of bad news. "By the way, sergeant major, there are three wagons coming in behind us."

Olinger was stricken. "Don't tell me, sir."

"Yes, I'm telling you, three professors all dressed up in safari clothes, boots, and pith helmets are here to dig up our parade ground in search of Spanish treasure. According to the gentleman who spoke to me, Professor Oliver Berryman, they're fresh from a British Museum expedition to the Valley of the Kings sponsored by the Department of Egyptian and Assyrian Antiquities. Apparently, they discovered a royal scribe's tomb with a curse on it and are eager for more triumphs."

"After all the Comanchero trouble we had last year, Captain Kellerman didn't think they'd come."

"Well, they're here, sergeant major, or they will be in about an hour or so."

"And they're bringing a curse with them. The last thing Fort Misery needs is another curse."

"It's just a piece of superstitious nonsense written by some pencil pusher three thousand years ago," Atticus Cranston said. "I wouldn't worry about it."

The second lieutenant was a tall, slender young man with earnest brown eyes and dark red hair showing from beneath his kepi. His top lip was fuzzed with the hopeful beginnings of a cavalryman's mustache, and like everyone else in Fort Misery, he was covered from hat to boots in gray dust. He wore his revolver and saber well and had given a good account of himself in the previous year's battles.

"Sir, if this was Fort Concho, I'd agree with what you just told me," Olinger said. "But this is Fort Misery, and therefore, I'll worry about it." A deep sigh, then: "We're already cursed, but I guess another one won't make any difference."

CHAPTER 3

Lieutenant James Hall was officer of the day when the sentries reported that the mule-drawn wagons were coming in, two covered, the other open, each with a driver at the reins, three older white men and an Asian fellow in a brocade robe walking solemnly behind them.

"Those are the perfessers by the look of them, sir," the sentry said.

"By the lord Harry, they look like a grim lot," Hall said. "There's not a general hidden among them, I hope."

"Sir, they don't look like generals," said the soldier, a tow-headed youngster with freckles. "More like them perfessers that are always talking about strange stuff."

"Ah, yes, the prodigal professors! Well, show them in," Hall said. "It will be a nice change to talk to my intellectual equals. And be respectful, you ruffian."

The drivers, three rough-looking muleskinners, parked the wagons on the parade ground, and the occupants, three skinny older men wearing tan clothes and pith helmets, staggered toward Lieutenant Hall.

The apparent eldest of the three was a tall, cadaverous man with long gray hair, rough-cut beard, staring hazel eyes that Hall at once decided were half-mad, and a sharp, pointed nose that was red in color, peeling and sunburned.

"Officer, oh, officer," the man said, in a grating, whiny voice replete with a posh English accent, "what a dreadful journey, what an ordeal we've suffered. Sun, heat, little water—and for the past three days, only disgusting dried meat and ship's biscuit to eat. I swear, we are almost dead from the horror of it all."

One of the wagon drivers, a rough-hewn character whose expression bordered on the villainous, said, "Perfessor, the trials of your journey was no fault of ours. We only drive the wagons. We don't control the weather or the vittles. Which, it was all explained to you afore we left Yuma."

"Yes, it was, Mr. Belcher, but we did not anticipate its severity. Many of my countrymen have voyaged to these lands and spoken nothing but praise upon their return."

"And what is your name, and why are you here?" Hall said to the whiny older man.

"My name is Paul Fernsby, *Professor* Paul Fernsby, and these are my associates, Professors Julius Dankworth and Oliver Berryman. Oh, listen to my voice. My throat's as dry as dust in a mummy's pocket."

"We anticipated your arrival and we're glad to have you here, sir," Hall lied. "Private, pass around your canteen to the gentlemen."

After tilting the canteen to his parched mouth, water running down his chin, Fernsby wiped off his patchy beard with the back of his hand and said, "Young man, you have a right to be glad since you'll have a front seat at the greatest archaeological triumph since the 1813 discovery of the Temple of Ramesses the Second by the circus strongman turned archaeologist, the incomparable Giovanni Battista Belzoni. Walking in the great man's shadow, I'm here to uncover the remains of the lost army of the Spanish Conquistador Don Esteban de Toro and—and this should be of interest to you—his rumored treasure chest."

"Where is all this?" Hall said.

"'Where is all this?'" Fernsby parroted. "Do you hear that Professor Berryman? Professor Dankworth?" He smiled and said, "Why, young man, if my map is correct, and I'm certain it is, you may be standing on it."

"So where do you want us to dump your stuff, perfesser?" Belcher said. "If it ain't too much to ask."

"Right on this spot, my man," Fernsby said. "The dig begins right here."

"I can't allow you to do that until I speak to my commanding officer," Hall said. "Army protocol, you understand."

"Which is of no concern of mine," Belcher said. He turned in his seat and said, "Bob, get that stuff unloaded, and let's get out of here." He looked at Hall, shook his head, and said, "Which he's the laziest of my lazy sons."

"Halt!" Lieutenant Hall said. "As I told you, you need the permission of Captain Kellerman."

Fernsby reached into his coat and produced a sweat-damp, lank envelope. "Right here is all the permission I need. It gives me and my archaeologist colleagues permission to dig at Fort Benjamin Grierson without let or hindrance." He held up the letter inside as though it was a sacred scroll. "Look at the signature, young man, and prepare to be impressed."

Lieutenant Hall read, and then, shocked, said, "It's signed by President Grant."

"Indeed, it is. The president is a close personal friend of mine. One of his cousins is wed to my cousin Gertrude, and that makes us almost family."

"Close enough for me," Hall said. "I'll take you to Captain Kellerman."

"Julius, Oliver, stay with the equipment," Fernsby said. "I'll be right back." Then, "Mr. Belcher, after you finish unloading, you are dismissed from my current employ. You may take one of the wagons and provisions and water enough to get you back to El Paso." He dug into his pocket and produced a gold coin. "Here's a little extra for all your trouble."

Belcher smiled and said, "Which is the act of a true gent as ever was."

"Now get busy, man, finish the unloading, and be off with you," Fernsby said.

The president's letter in mind, Lieutenant Hall decided to be ingratiating. He said to Berryman, a man as gaunt as his boss but two feet shorter and possessed of hollow eyes and temples to match. "During the war I served with a captain named Oliver. We called him Ollie." He smiled. "Does anyone call you that?"

Berryman spaced out the words, stressing their severity: "No one—ever—calls me—that."

Deflated, Hall said, "Ah, then Oliver it is."

"No, Oliver it isn't. You will address me as Professor Berryman. Do I make myself clear, Lieutenant?"

"Clear as a bell, sir," Hall said. "Would you care for a pinch of snuff?"

"And what did he say when you offered him snuff?" Captain Joe Kellerman said.

"He said it was a wicked substance used only by barbarians," Lieutenant Hall said. "I must say it hurt my feelings a little."

"You'll get over it. The professor changed his mind and decided to remain outside. Any idea why?"

"He wants to show you where he'll dig his trench."

"His what?"

"His trench. Apparently, it's what archaeologists call a hole in the ground."

"You can't dig a trench in sand."

"Begging the captain's pardon, but I think you should tell him that."

"All right," Kellerman said. "I'll go talk to him. What's the name again?"

"Professor Fernsby."

Groaning, Kellerman stood, broad chested and handsome despite the bags under his eyes from overdrinking and undersleeping, thanks in no small part to being in charge of the godforsaken fort and the disgraced soldiers within it. He buckled on his .45 Colt Single Action Army revolver and grabbed his hat off the rack, settling it on his head. In contrast to the rugged captain, Lieutenant Hall looked fresh and well-rested, his black hair falling in shiny ringlets to his shoulders and blending into his magnificent beard, the very model of an officer.

"All right, Lieutenant, lead me to him."

CHAPTER 4

"Finger or toe?"

"Neither! Let me go you—you lunatics!"

"If you don't pick one, I'll take 'em both. So, I ask you again, finger or toe?" The man waved a knife blade perilously close to the young soldier's face, and the soldier whimpered and blanched white under his tan. The knife wielder was U.S. Army Private Jack Nelson, a hard case who had landed at the hellscape of Fort Benjamin Grierson for a list of very good reasons. Given the choice of the fort or twenty years in Yuma prison for the rape and murder of a prostitute in Dallas, he chose Fort Misery—a choice he often regretted, since Yuma might have at least had better food. His current wrath, focused on the teenage soldier he knew only as Private Wesley, secretly filled him with a rare glimmer of joy, violence being his most treasured hobby.

Nelson was rather unremarkable as a gunman and a soldier, and so it was for his looks: his only defining feature was a giant beak of a nose that paired with his beady eyes and balding pate gave him the appearance of a demented vulture. The squirming Private Wesley meanwhile had the face of an altar boy, flushed rosy cheeks and a soft curve to his chin, that made him look very much like a child. Innocent, though, he was not, as Wesley had ended up at Fort Misery for thievery and being a general nuisance across several towns, crimes that would otherwise have stuck him in the pen for a decade if he'd chosen prison.

But currently, young Private Wesley was held firmly by two feral-looking men, one old and fat, one young and thin as a beanpole, and both grinning like crocodiles while they waited for the show to begin. All four men were sweating buckets in the wooden storage room that had become an oven beneath the blazing desert sun, dark circles in the armpits of their faded blue shirts.

"Puh-puh-puleeze just lemme go. I gave it back to you, didn't I? It ain't count as a crime no more when you got it back," Wesley yelled, terror giving him a stutter and high, keening voice.

"Puh-puh-puleeze tell me which you'd rather lose, boy. I'm at the end of my patience with you," Nelson said, sneering, the mocking stutter drawing guffaws from his accomplices. When no reply but sputtering came, he said sharply, "Right, well, time is up. I'm taking them both. Say, Johnson, help me get one of his boots off."

Nelson squatted and began to untie the brittle boot in question, which was caked with dust and cracked from lack of attention with a polish and brush to preserve the leather. At this, young Private Wesley started to squeal like a stuck pig, his fearful voice so loud it carried across the barren parade ground outside the shack. Nelson had just managed to remove the boot and a holey sock and was trying to select a toe when the door flew open with a bang. The four men flinched, and Nelson accidently cut a slice across the arch of Wesley's foot, making him shriek even louder.

Joe Kellerman, followed by Lieutenant Hall, stormed into the room. "What in the hell is the meaning of this?" he demanded in a stern voice.

"They're tryin' to kill me!" Wesley cried, sinking to his knees as the two men holding him were forced to let his arms go so that they could snap off halfhearted salutes to their commanding officers.

Nelson pointed at the young private with his knife. "Sir, he's a thief. He took two—that's two!—whole double eagles from beneath my mattress, and then a photo of Johnson's favorite gal from beneath his. We're teaching him a lesson. I told him he could choose a finger or a toe to be cut off. That way he'll always have a reminder why thieving is an unsavory path unless performed with the dignity of an outlaw. Can you see Jesse James stealing from beneath a fella's mattress? It's indecent!" He stopped to draw a breath. "Sir."

"I see," Kellerman said. "Did you hear that, Lieutenant Hall?"

Hall made a "tut-tut" noise and shook his head at the teary young private, "I heard, Captain. Shameful, you villain, how could you steal from your own comrades?"

Private Wesley sobbed. "I gave it back. I gave it all right back." He moaned in terror.

"Is this true, did he return the booty in a prompt fashion?" Kellerman asked of Nelson, who looked unsure, but replied, "Well, yes—but that don't make him no less of a thieving rat, do it?"

"What say you, Lieutenant Hall, does that make him any less of a thieving rat?" Kellerman said, stepping further into the room and glowering down at Wesley.

"No, sir, it does not—especially if the photo of the gal was of fine quality," Hall replied earnestly.

Johnson reached behind him and took the photo from where it was tucked in his suspenders, being too large for a pocket. "It's of real fine quality, sir. Her name is Daisy Mae and she said she loves me, and I love her." He handed the photo over to Kellerman, who studied it before passing it to Hall.

"Well, she's . . ."

The photo showed a woman with a face like a hatchet, who'd clearly come to an age when her best days would soon be through, heavy rolls of fat around her belly stretching the ruffled satin dress she wore. Hall looked at Private Johnson, a man who reminded the lieutenant of the Yuma's black-footed ferrets that popped out of gopher holes to study humans curiously: thin, long, and pinched about the nose and mouth.

"She's a perfect match for you, private. Bully for true love!" He handed the photo back with a smile and ignored the bemused look Kellerman shot him.

Kellerman stroked his majestic calvary mustache. "So you think the suitable punishment is to amputate a digit, is that correct?"

Before Nelson could answer, Hall interrupted, "In Arabia when they catch a thief, they take the whole hand clean off. Or so I've heard."

"Thank you for that tidbit, Lieutenant," Kellerman said, glaring daggers at Hall. The last thing any of these men needed was fresh ideas. "And how do you plan to stop the bleeding, once the toe is chopped off?" he asked calmly.

Nelson scratched the frizzy ring of thin hair still holding on by a thread to his scalp, frowning. "*Finger* and toe, sir—he wouldn't choose, so it's gotta be both. I dunno. We didn't think about that, I suppose." Then, brightening: "Oh! We can get a hot bit of iron and press it against the stump, I've seen it done afore. They call it caut—caulk—cawter . . ."

"Cauterizing," Kellerman said.

Nelson snapped his fingers, "Yep, that's the one! I can ask Tobias to heat us up something real good! Let me go tell him." He made for the door, and Kellerman stopped him with a firm hand on the chest. While looking into Nelson's beady and nervous eyes, Kellerman addressed Lieutenant Hall.

"Tell me, Lieutenant, do you agree we should mutilate Private Wesley as a reprimand for theft?"

Hall stroked his beard, "Well, it would be fair, sir, yes." At that Wesley began sobbing again. "But there are roving bands of Apache to deal with, and a man with a missing finger *and* a missing toe will be, at the very least, quite wobbly when he walks, and it may make it hard to shoot straight, too. I imagine it would be difficult to file the papers if requested, as well. Sir."

"An excellent observation, Lieutenant Hall. However, we certainly can't tolerate thievery under our roof, can we? Private Nelson, please give me your knife." Kellerman held out an expectant hand. Nelson hesitated and then passed the knife over handle first, being careful not to cut himself or the captain on the sharp blade.

Wesley was the color of curdled milk as Captain Kellerman approached him and knelt. "Are you right-handed or left-handed?" he asked, his face and tone placid, as if he was having a conversation about the weather. "Sir, left-handed, sir. Oh, please don't take my fingers, I need 'em!" Wesley blubbered.

"Is that so, are you good with a gun?" Kellerman asked.

"Kind of . . . I mean, yes, yes, I am excellent with a gun!"

"You're lying. Give me your right hand. By the way, I've heard left handedness is a sure sign of a devilish nature. I'm sure father Stac—Sacks—"

"Staszczyk." Lieutenant Hall supplied the name.

"Yes, him—I'm sure he could tell you about your wickedness. You should visit him for an act of contrition." Kellerman took Wesley's hand and singled out the pinkie finger, as the young soldier turned his face away, not wanting to see the carnage.

"Sir, begging your pardon, didn't we need to cat'er'ize him?" Johnson said, consternation clouding his face.

"No need, I have a better solution to this dilemma," Kellerman said, and then without warning he dropped the knife and snapped the bones in the screaming Wesley's poor little finger. The digit, having had no part in the crime and undesiring of being cracked back and forth, made a sound like breaking twigs. "See here, you scoundrel, you'll have a month's worth of healing, and that should be enough to remind you of your misdeeds. I will leave your toe alone. If I get a report that you have returned to your evils, then I will see to it myself that your hand is chopped off like an Arabian, fighting the Apache be damned. Is that fair, Private Nelson and Private Johnson?" Kellerman stood, his back aching as his morning bourbon began wearing off, exacerbated by the heavy sweating brought on by the insufferable heat.

"That's fair, Captain, I reckon," Nelson said, disappointed but still pleased by the young private's howls.

"Can't say fairer than that, sir," Johnson agreed.

"Crackerjack!" Lieutenant Hall declared. "Well, now that this grisly business is done, would anyone care for some snuff?"

CHAPTER 5

"Professor Frenzy . . ."

"Ah, that's Fernsby, Captain."

"Right. I appreciate you taking time out of your busy schedule to snitch on my soldiers—you saved that boy's digits and perhaps life. However, I am still unimpressed by your insistence about digging a hole in the middle of my parade ground"—Kellerman looked at a pile of shovels, picks and mattocks, and pith helmets, and grimaced—"for two months." He hesitated a moment, then said, "And it may behoove you to understand that there are roving bands of Apache, Chiricahua, and possibly Mexicans ready to strike at any moment. If that happens, you and your fellows will be expected to pick up those tools or anything else nearby and use them in defense of the fort, do you understand? This is not a territory for weak men, and quite frankly the lot of you strike me as weak men. Are you?"

The tall, cadaverous Professor Fernsby's sunburn had spread and turned him a boiled bright red beneath the relentless Yuma sun, sweat streaming down his face from beneath his pith helmet. At the accusation of being an inferior male specimen, however, he turned downright purple.

"Intelligence is strength, Captain Kellerman. We may be older and perhaps weaker—physically I mean—than the boys you oversee, but I can guarantee that our brains work much faster. It may not take us two whole months, either. That parchment map I acquired was discovered in a hidden vault in the ruined castle of Vozmediano, situated halfway between Castile and Aragon in Spain," Fernsby said, agitated.

Chan, the Chinese servingman who traveled with the professors, approached and bowed reverently to Kellerman before placing a palm on Paul Fernsby's shoulder, "Remember your heart. Yelling's no good. Calm breaths."

The discourse was interrupted by the Belcher youngsters, who laid three heavy boxes, a large steamer trunk, and spare tan canvas pants, shirts, and pith helmets beside the tools already unloaded. At last, their pa, the elder Belcher, said, "That's it, perfesser. Which is everything we brung." He lit a clay pipe that belched black smoke.

"Thank you, my good man," Fernsby said. "Go now, but come back for us in two months, mind."

"Which I will do," the man said. He nodded to Kellerman, gave him a wink, and climbed onto the wagon while his sons piled their heavy corn-fed bodies into the back with grunts, making the wood creak.

"Two months," Kellerman said, agitated. "You can't stay here that long."

"Oh yes, I can." Fernsby pulled the now limp envelope out of his coat and said, "Read it, Captain. Last paragraph." Then, after a few moments: "Well?"

"It says I am to render you all possible assistance because the uncovering of Don Esteban's treasure could be one of the most important archaeological finds in our nation's history," Kellerman said. He lifted his hat and ran his fingers through his hair, a sure sign of his disquiet. He watched the wagon leave with a heavy sigh.

"And again, our map indicates the treasure is . . ." Fernsby pointed downward. "Therefore, we must dig . . ."

Joe Kellerman impatiently cut him off midsentence. "Yes, yes, I already heard about the treasure map. Yet I am still questioning why you're certain X marks the spot on my parade ground even though I've explained how quickly the desert shifts. This all sounds like nothing more than a fool's errand. If the truth is that you plan to burgle us in the night, I am sorry to say you won't make away with more than rations of questionable quality and a belly full of lead."

"Ah, you make so many little jokes," Fernsby said, brushing away Chan's hand and lowering his tone. "Anyway, since the map is dated 1540, it could hardly show Fort Benjamin Grierson parade ground, now, could it? Let's just say that after adventures in Mexico, in 1538, the conquistador Don Esteban de Toro marched this way, and his army, suffering from thirst, starvation, and exhaustion, was soon wiped out by local attackers and—based on surviving notes—some sort of dreadful gut affliction. But one man escaped, and he later returned to Spain and drew up the map, secreting it in the castle vault alongside a brief diary that shared accounts of the exploration and fate of de Toro. He was very sick, of course, and no doubt died from the bloody emesis before he could return and search for the treasures that

Don Esteban was rumored to have carried with him. That the army chose to build a fort over the top of buried treasure and the remains of lost souls is inconsequential to the pursuit of history and knowledge."

"Professor Frizzy, for the tenth time, this is a desert," Kellerman said. "Mile after mile of flat sand and dunes that shift in the wind and, when God chooses, become rivers as rain fills the arroyos. A true map needs coordinates and landmarks, and you appear to be fresh out of those."

"Fernsby! And yes, but there is that rock shelf about three miles to the west of us and that's as clearly marked on the map as any coordinate might be."

"Yes, I know that shelf very well, but it is yet another feature that would come and go in the desert. We see it now, but not too long ago it may have been hidden, meaning your conquistador could have been referencing something else entirely. The sandstorms can be miles long and thousands of feet high, and they cover everything. The floods that plague this region wear down rocks and change their appearance, and I am quite certain this has happened often over the past three-odd centuries. If you're unfortunate, maybe you will get to experience it once during your stay and learn a thing or two. All the rocks you see today might not be there tomorrow." Kellerman shook his head. "Professor, I am telling you plainly as I can that your map is worthless."

"Ah, but that's where you're wrong, Captain. I spoke to a gathering of Yuma Indians who know the desert, and they, too, remembered the rock shelf. Apparently, there is a trickle of water atop the shelf that flows from an aquifer and collects in a natural tank. That's why the natives know it so well, a location passed down in their oral traditions for generations."

"Did I mention that in addition to the Apache being out, there are armed Mexican troops making repeated excursions this way, across the Rio Bravo, to cut the Indians off before they reach Sonora? And that this fort happens to fall right in the path of both parties, who, on account of being irritated already, will not hesitate to make their conflicts our problem?" Kellerman said, knowing it could be his last desperate appeal to reason and suspecting that it fell on deaf ears. He badly needed bourbon and pinched the bridge of his nose, willing away an increasingly sharp headache that throbbed behind his right eye.

"Well, sure, you just said it, Captain. And oh, we heard word of that as we were leaving Yuma," Fernsby said. "Rumors, mostly. Though thusly, I must say our encounters with Americans in the West have been less than—pleasant. I was a few times told to take a ship back to where I came from, and there were very harsh words used in the delivery of that message. Quite rude!"

"They're not rumors, professor. I've had a letter delivered, signed by the noble William T. Sherman and endorsed by President Grant, instructing me to somehow put a stop to it all. The Mescalero and Chiricahua are both out and have their blood up, so they're searching for trouble. I suppose the X on your booty map may mark the spot of a lot of deaths, in the end. Keep those pickaxes handy, as your lives could be in—hell, *are* in imminent danger."

Paul Fernsby waved a hand that encompassed his colleagues. "I'm sure I speak for Professor Berryman and Professor Dankworth when I say that we don't fear the natives and Mexican bandits. Our work here is much too important to be derailed by such simplistic emotion."

"Quite so," said Professor Berryman.

"Hear, hear," said Professor Dankworth, though he looked less certain about the sentiment than his compatriots.

"Then don't say you weren't fairly warned," said Captain Kellerman, defeated for the moment.

"Thank you, my good man," Fernsby said. "I look forward to proving you quite wrong about the wisdom of us archaeologists in the near future. I say, I wonder what is keeping my dear Constance. Has anyone seen her wagon? She was only a day or two behind us."

Kellerman had turned to leave, eager to be away from the blazing sun and primed for salving his soul with whiskey, but halted in his tracks. "Constance? Who the blazes is Constance?" he said querulously.

Lieutenant Hall frowned, having returned after delivering the still squalling Private Wesley to Mrs. Zimmermann's loving care and generous laudanum at the small infirmary that held no true army surgeon. "That's a woman's name! Good God, man, you haven't sent a woman here, have you?" Hall said, alarmed.

Fernsby smiled, "My niece and ward, Miss Constance Courtenay. I assure you she will be no trouble. She's a fine archaeologist, and when she was just a slip of a girl, she traveled to Cathay and trained in the martial arts—the Wing Chun style of kung fu—at a school founded by the female Buddhist nun, the immortal Ng Mui." His smile was as warm as a snowy day in winter. "Constance can take care of herself. She knows a hundred different ways to disable an attacker. Even Mr. Belcher and his large sons were terrified of her." He paused thoughtfully, "I do worry that she hasn't arrived yet, however. Could you send a dispatch to look for her, perhaps?"

Kellerman and Hall exchanged glances, and without a word the lieutenant handed a silver flask to Kellerman who took a heavy pull. "You must be joking. How was she to arrive, your martial artist niece?" the captain asked, lifting his hat and wiping sweat from his forehead with the back of his hand. His blond hair laid heavy against his neck and forehead, clinging to his skin with the dampness of sweat. The manifestation of these archaeologists in his fort was piling insult upon insult onto the barely tethered sanity of a man trying to wrangle some of the worst men in the country while maintaining some semblance of military dignity and order.

"Mr. Belcher—who delivered us here?—he recommended a chap by the name of Stanley, who was to bring her along with a delivery of your rations after she'd finished wrapping up a few administrative tasks in Yuma. We foresaw no trouble. They do bring the accoutrements straight here, do they not?" For the first time Fernsby had the good sense to show a bit of concern, a slight frown puckering his sun chapped lips.

"Oh, for the love of—Lieutenant Hall, get Second Lieutenant Cranston to lead a party to Devil's Rock right this instant," Kellerman barked. "Make sure they take extra canteens. If the girl is half as a dumb as these lot, she'll already have died from thirst—which may be a blessing if the Apache found her first."

Hall quickly darted away to follow his orders, and

Kellerman turned back to the archaeologist. "No, Mr. Friendly, they do not deliver the supplies here. On the rare occasions they deliver them at all, they're left at Devil's Rock, that large formation over there," he pointed to the north, but the giant boulder was lost in a shimmering horizon of heat and dust. "The civilians won't set foot near this place, they think the land is cursed, and they're quite right. I hope your girl is still there, and if she is, pray that she is alive and in one piece. Now, pardon me, I have fort business to attend to."

Chapter 6

Second Lieutenant Atticus Cranston removed his kepi to wipe away the sweat that streamed from his scalp and dampened his copper hair, the rivulets stinging his eyes. He peered into the distance at Devil's Rock but found that all he could see were the shimmering mirage waves of heat rising above the bright sand. "Ahiga, can you see?" Cranston asked, and the Navajo scout looked at him with a flat expression, the man's coal black eyes still unnerving to the lieutenant even after months working together.

"See what?"

Cranston frowned, irritable from the heat and the unnecessary trip. "The baby Jesus. Good God, man, Devil's Rock. Can you see if the woman is there?"

Ahiga looked ahead and then silently took off on his paint horse, until he disappeared into the glare. Cranston laughed. "I guess that was a no."

Corporal John Lockhart grinned.

Cranston took a swig from his canteen. "This heat is brutal. I thought I'd get used to it after some time. But I don't believe Lucifer himself could tolerate it for long."

"This remind you of your arrival, Lieutenant Cranston? Abandoned on the rock and waiting for salvation, if I recall the story correctly," Lockhart said.

Cranston shook his head with a wistful smile, reminiscing. Having graduated second of his class at West Point only a month or so before being unceremoniously dumped in the desert, Cranston had originally been granted a posting at Fort Concho. Then, some harried clerk crossed his mental wires badly enough to send the young lieutenant first to Yuma, whence the quartermaster, happy to see the back of the smart young second lieutenant who seemed a stickler for rules, had organized things such that he be bestowed upon Captain Joseph Kellerman alongside a transport of rations to Devil's Rock, where he could wait for a patrol to collect him. The teamsters had dropped him off with nothing but a pair of full canteens, hardtack, and a half-hearted prayer. Only later did he realize they assumed he was a criminal being sent to the fort as punishment and were therefore none too concerned about his well-being.

Not knowing any better Cranston had had no complaints. He assumed it would be easy enough to transfer back to Fort Concho and planned to do so at the first opportunity.

Things changed when the peasant *bandido* Miguel Lozado set up camp near the fort with the nerve to claim himself a wealthy hidalgo, dozens of Mexican slaves under his control, and recruited Comanche and Comancheros to his camp of ruthless men hell-bent on taking control of the army post. During a fierce fight with the desperados, Cranston, vengeful over the suicide of a young woman Lozado had raped, gutshot Lozado, leaving him to die a lingering death in the desert. And the young lieutenant knew in that moment that the optimistic shine of his West Point officer training was far removed from reality. Captain Joe Kellerman was a drunk and damaged, but he was the smartest, most reliable man Cranston had ever met during his time in the army. When given a chance to leave, he had chosen to stay at the fort.

Atticus Cranston shook his head again, clearing the memories. "I wouldn't have it any other way, Corporal. Fort Misery is where I was meant be, and the hands of fate knew it."

Corporal Lockhart just nodded.

Private Wesley had spent the journey sulking in a most pathetic fashion over his wounded hand, bound in a white wrapping and splint, supplied by Mrs. Zimmermann, that stretched from finger to wrist, but suddenly he sat bolt upright, excited. He raised his spyglass and saw a gathering of men to their east. "Lieutenant," he shouted, instantly forgetting his pain and blue mood.

"Men at our east, say, four clock, with horses and a wagon, too. Should we approach to see what they're about?"

Cranston pulled his horse even with Wesley and lifted his spyglass to his eye, observing the men briefly, "No, Private Wesley, I have already met with them. Ahiga was there, seemed to make them nervous seeing an Indian up close and personal-like." Cranston grinned, the freckles softly scattered across his nose were darker from sun and made his eyes shine. "A hunting party is what they claim to be, out of Yuma. Led by a fella named Lucas Dean. They seem relatively harmless, for now.

We shall see what the future brings. Good looking out, Wesley."

Still on horseback, Wesley snapped off a salute, his stutter returning, "Yes si-si-sir, th-th-ank you, suh-sir!"

The ambitious young private had returned to a less sullen silence when Ahiga reappeared, covered in dust, and looking strained. "Man at the rock with her, one I don't know. I don't trust him, Cranston. We need full speed ahead. This—white man, he seemed to be encouraging her to go with him to the Spirit only knows where." An imposing figure, a yellow bandanna holding his braids in place, his flint eyes steely, the scout looked intently at Cranston, awaiting an order.

A long moment, then neatly replacing his kepi at a jaunty angle, the second lieutenant sheathed his right hand back into a butter yellow leather gauntlet that he raised high in the air as he said, "We will ride as if the lady's life depends upon it. Indeed, boys, it may!"

Private Wesley, Corporal Lockhart, and Ahiga, watched for the gauntlet to fall, and then, with many a *huzzah* and *yeeeee*, spurred the horses into full speed ahead toward the unusual monolith known as Devil's Rock. Great clouds of sand surrounded them, and Lockhart thought what a sight they must be to anyone watching— a biblical sandstorm filled with the glints of shining weaponry.

CHAPTER 7

To the delight of all, supplies had been conveniently left at Devil's Rock once more, far ahead of schedule, though the pickings were sure to be slim. Sitting amid the crates of coffee, tinned milk, dried beef, whiskey, and salt, a rumpled and dusty, yet still strikingly beautiful, woman spoke with a tall dark-haired man in tense tones. Both parties immediately hushed and looked at the approaching soldiers, the man forcing a smile that looked unnatural as he tipped his hat.

"Good afternoon, gents, I was just offering to bring this little lady to your doorstep, but she did not trust me to protect her honor. Good thing. It looks like you've saved me a trip and a lot more convincing." The man studied Ahiga warily.

Atticus Cranston grinned. "Well, we are sure glad to find you, Miss . . . ?"

The woman stood and wiped the dust off her trousers, "Constance Courtenay. I'm looking for Fort Benjamin Grierson, I suppose that is where you've come from?" Sweat and grit plastered tangled dark hair to her sunburned forehead, and she scowled irritably at the soldiers as though they'd offended her ancestors. Her clipped English accent was endearing, and Atticus was taken in by her beauty, despite it being masked by a layer of grime, but his thoughts rapidly drifted to the hazard she'd pose among the men of Fort Misery.

"Yes, ma'am, your uncle thought you may be here, and we came as quickly as we could. Terribly sorry to keep you waiting in this heat. I'm Atticus Cranston, second lieutenant, right pleased to make your acquaintance. And Mr. Lucas Dean, what a surprise to see you here as well. Still searching for those bighorn sheep?"

Cranston's time at the fort had dulled the edge of his natural optimism, West Point having left him well trained in the tactical side of warfare yet unprepared for the darkness of reality. Being surrounded by criminals had helped the young lieutenant develop a keen sense of danger, and there was something about Lucas Dean that didn't sit right with him. The way he held his body, and the tone he used with Miss Courtenay seemed off-putting, and vaguely threatening.

Dean smiled again, his broad lips chapped and ruddy. "Yep, but we saw the wagon come by and I thought to investigate a bit—and I'm sure glad I did. This little lady didn't have any water. We only wanted to watch out for your fine gentleman at the fort in case hostiles or thieves were staking out the territory. Still no luck with the hunting, but we haven't really put our backs into it yet on account of resting from our travels. The Yuma desert sure does take the vigor out of a man, it seems."

The first time Atticus Cranston had encountered Lucas Dean he was with a group of other men who had made camp suspiciously near the fort without having stopped by to introduce themselves, a glaringly odd behavior, considering the barren territory meant they would surely have noticed the Union Army landmark. They had declared their intentions to be purely that of a hunting party enjoying some solitude together in the wild. What the other fellows were up to now, he had no idea, but the second lieutenant suspected it was nothing good, and he felt watched from afar.

Ahiga had not taken his obsidian eyes off the man, his bronze face mistrustful and alert as he cradled his .44-40 Henry in tense arms.

"Anyhow, thanks for coming, officer, now that you're here I can get back to my men and prepare for the climb. I only wanted to make sure Miss Courtenay was safe and sound. Enjoy the whiskey. I promise we didn't drink a drop." Dean tipped his hat again and made a hasty retreat toward his horse, uncomfortable beneath the gaze of Ahiga.

"Sure thing, Mr. Dean. Good luck hunting," Atticus replied, but he couldn't shake the queasy feeling in his belly that the man imposed. He'd talk it over with Kellerman later. He turned to the woman and picked up her carpetbag. "Now, let's get everything loaded up and bring you to the fort. I'm sure you'd like to be out of the sun."

Constance harrumphed as a reply and began gathering her remaining belongings about her, waving her hand at the gathering flies that buzzed around her face. "I'm famished. I have been abandoned here nearly ten hours, you know. I could kill that wagon driver and his dopey sons for suggesting the delivery drivers." Her tone was sour, but a slight smile played at the corner of her lips, relieved to be protected from what she, too, had read to be Lucas Dean's ill intent.

Atticus Cranston and Ahiga shared a look. If the little lady thought Fort Misery would bring a relief to her suffering, she was in for a terrible surprise.

"Well, madam, I hope you have a taste for green pork and stale biscuits," Corporal Lockhart said cheerfully, as he began moving crates onto the flat wagon.

Constance shielded her eyes from the sun and stepped forward to offer Captain Kellerman a handshake, which he accepted somewhat grudgingly—and found his fingers in a steel vice. "As my uncle told you, Captain," she said, squeezing even harder, "I can take care of myself."

Kellerman disengaged, discreetly shaking his hand to ease the pain throbbing in his fingers. He made a quick assessment of her appearance and her apparent intent to break his fingers. The woman was beautiful, but he would bet all his bourbon on the fact that she would prove as deadly as a riled-up she-wolf if the occasion was presented for her to lash out. It soothed his concerns for her safety slightly, but no matter how fierce, one small woman against a troop of scoundrels was not good odds. He smiled at her politely and then turned to a private who stood nearby, gaping open-mouthed at the woman's sun flushed décolletage, and said, "Soldier, go fetch Mrs. Zimmermann. Tell her I know she's busy, but I've got a crisis on my hands." A pause, and then more sternly: "And keep your eyes to yourself."

"I suppose I'm the crisis?" Constance said with a grin.

Kellerman said, "Yes, you are, Miss Court—Court—"

"Courtenay."

"Miss Courtenay, an attractive young lady taking her holiday at Fort Benjamin Grierson is not a well-laid plan. For that matter, a withered old one-eyed grandmother would not fare much better. Most of these men have chosen hell over confinement, and on top of their sins, that choice alone should give you an idea of who you'll be dealing with. Mrs. Zimmermann is the only woman here and she remains safe purely out of spite and the graces of the good Lord above, as you will see—plus the protection of her husband, a great man who suffers no insults."

"I'm flattered," she replied, "but please note that this isn't a holiday. I am here on an important archaeological mission to unravel the secrets of Don Esteban de Toro's lost treasures. It will be quite the discovery when we have unearthed it. They say it is cursed, you know. I suppose we will find out soon."

Kellerman ignored that little tidbit of more bad news and said, "Your uncle has already given me the entire tale, but maybe you can enlighten me further, Madame Professor, about what you expect to find. God help us all."

"Of course, Captain. I am not a professor yet, though— please just call me Connie. According to the map—"

Kellerman lost it a little. "Damn the map! I meant how long does your party plan to engage my fort in these reckless shenanigans, and how can I best encourage you to leave? Leave right away, instead of sixty days from now."

"My uncle didn't give you the score?" she said, frowning.

"He tried, but now I have more questions. Such as, how did the map lead you here?"

"Because, as I believe I already told you, Captain, the mapmaker wrote that the site of the massacre was a league to the east of the shelf. And then there is the matter of the bones and other artifacts." Professor Fernsby appeared at their side and embraced his ward with a warm hug and kiss on the forehead.

"What bones and other artifacts?" Kellerman demanded. "Except for the sorry remains of dead soldiers, there are no bones and artifacts at Fort Misery."

"Quite, quite wrong," Fernsby said, enthusiastically. "It's common knowledge in Yuma that human bones and metal antiquities were dug up when the foundations of Fort Benjamin Grierson were laid. It's the opinion of myself and my colleagues that those specimens were relics of our lost Spanish explorers."

"I never heard anything like that," Kellerman said. "It's nonsense."

Lieutenant Hall spoke for the first time. "Sir, Tobias Zimmermann was here around the time the fort was constructed. I know he worked as a carpenter on the headquarters building and officer's quarters. Maybe he knows something about the artifacts."

"Then bring him here, Lieutenant. Tell Mr. Zimmermann I want to ask about digging up bones."

"And metal antiquities," Fernsby said.

"Yes, and those, too," Kellerman said. "And Lieutenant Hall, be quick about it."

* * *

"Well . . . yes, Captain, when we worked on the foundations of the headquarters building, we did dig up what we took to be human bones. It was hard to tell, since there were no skulls found," Tobias Zimmermann said.

"And metal artifacts?" Fernsby said.

"We came across a knife blade and a brass buckle, both badly corroded."

"A brass—probably bronze—buckle from a sword belt?" Fernsby said, his creaky voice hopeful.

"From some kind of belt. Probably the bones were Indian, and the knife and buckle were trade goods."

"More likely the bones were Spanish," Fernsby said.

"I couldn't say," Zimmermann said. "One human leg bone looks like any other human leg bone." Then to Kellerman, "I'd like to return to my duties, Captain."

"Still patching up bullet holes?" Kellerman said.

"No, I'm repairing Mrs. Zimmermann's stove that was badly shot up during the battle with Juan Ramirez and his Comanchero trash."

"Then don't let me detain you. Right now, the stove is more important than old bones."

"Quite so, sir," Lieutenant Hall said. "We can't take any chances on Mrs. Zimmermann's stove, or her entire kitchen, come to that."

"That is also Mrs. Zimmermann's opinion," her husband said. "Oh, and look, she's walking this way."

After a long, appraising glare at the professors and

a more critical one at Constance Courtenay, Mrs. Zimmermann said, "You wished to see me, Captain?"

After making the necessary introductions, Kellerman said, "Miss Courtenay will be our guest for a couple of months or until I can convince her to leave . . ."

Mrs. Zimmermann didn't try to conceal her surprised alarm. "Two months!"

Kellerman shrugged, then, "That seems to be the case. She'll need suitable accommodation, Mrs. Zimmermann. The professors and their servingman insist on using their tents, but when they tire of that in a day, have them take up the remaining empty officers' quarters as you see fit."

"Mrs. Zimmermann," Constance said, "I've slept in a pup tent in the Valley of the Kings in Egypt, on a hard wooden bed in a Tibetan monastery, and on rocky ground in Syria with a Krag rifle at my side. I'm not hard to please."

"I think we can make you a little more comfortable than you were in those heathen places," Mrs. Zimmermann said. Then to Kellerman, "Captain, I can put a cot in the doctor's office, and there's a lock on the door."

Constance smiled. "Captain Kellerman, I know we are a nuisance to you, but tell me fairly, am I truly in such terrible danger at Fort Benjamin Grierson?"

"At Fort Benjamin Grierson, as declared on paper by politicians, you'd be safe," Kellerman said. "But this is Fort Misery, and it's a different story. Yes, Miss Courtenay, so long as you're here you're in danger."

"Connie, call me Connie. What sort of danger?

Explain your meaning so that I can prepare, Captain Kellerman."

"Assault, insubordination . . . Do I really have to spell it out in a four-letter word?"

"The man who tried to outrage me would not live long enough to boast of it."

"Don't underestimate the men under my command. They're the worst of the worst. My officers are tiptop, and there are a few half-respectable men among the rest of the rabble, but a lot of the others are scum. You will notice our permanent scaffolding, and I can tell you this is the only posting across the Union to boast of having one."

"As I said, I'll take what you've told me into consideration," Constance said softly, searching Kellerman's handsome face for any hint of deception. Surely soldiers in the mighty Yankee army could not be so bad, she thought to herself.

Kellerman nodded, not believing she would. "I will count on it, ma'am."

Sighing deeply, he stalked back to his office with legs and back stiff and cramping from stress. The bourbon waited, and at least he could always reliably count on that, if nothing else.

CHAPTER 8

"So, what is the upshot of all this?" Sergeant Major Olinger said, as he sat in Joe Kellerman's office.

"The upshot is that the professors are digging a trench in my parade ground," Kellerman said. "The president of the United States is sponsoring them and has even supplied taxpayers' money to finance what Fernsby calls"—he made quotation marks in the air—"his 'expedition.'"

Olinger sipped his whiskey, shook his head, and said, "I have some bad news, Joe. Well, at least worrisome news."

Kellerman's smile came and went. "Saul, Fort Misery is the worrisome news capital of the republic. Don't you know that? Let me have it."

"Corporal Pierce came in with his patrol about thirty minutes ago. I can't say it was uneventful."

The captain's attention instantly became more focused. "Was he in an action?"

"No, nothing like that, but he reconnoitered as far as the rock shelf the professor was talking about."

"You mean raving about, him and the other two lunatics. What about the rock shelf?"

"It does have a spring."

"I know that. Go on."

"Pierce said six men are camped there. Hard cases, by the look of them, and one goes by the name of Nicky Barnes."

"I've never heard of him," Kellerman said. He stared hard at the sergeant major. "Should I have?"

"Yes, according to Pierce. He'd seen Barnes before, but mercifully, the man didn't recognize him."

"Seen him before, where?"

"At a saloon in Abilene, when Pierce was still cowboy-ing. Barnes killed two men that day. He drew down on them and gunned both. *Bang! Bang!* Two shots, two kills. Pierce says the men had reputations as fast-draw pistoleros and were bad hombres to cross. Well, Barnes crossed them."

"What was the quarrel about?"

"The corporal doesn't rightly recollect, but he thinks it was something about a stolen horse."

"It could've been self-defense," Kellerman said.

"It could've been. But Barnes dragged the two dead men to a table and hauled them into chairs. He shoved lit cigars into the mouths of the corpses and then or-dered drinks all round. He sat and casually talked to the men about this and that for an hour."

"A one-way conversation," Kellerman said.

"But not what a sane man would do. Corporal Pierce says Barnes was real odd. Kind of dead-fish eyes. And he was a might unfriendly, and his compadres were the same."

"Did they say why they were there?"

"Yeah, to set up a hunting camp. Bighorn sheep. Joe, I have a bad feeling about these rannies. And I think— nah, you'll reckon I'm crazy."

"Of course, you're crazy, Saul. Why else would a man with the Medal of Honor elect to serve in Fort Misery after he was offered a cozy berth in Washington? So let me hear what you have to say."

"Well, let's just suppose that the professors did some loose talking in Yuma about digging up a treasure, and let's suppose those six hard cases heard them and decided to—"

"Rob the professors on their way back to Yuma."

"It's possible," Olinger said.

"Anything is possible. I'll send Lieutenant Hall to talk with them tomorrow, have them state their intentions."

Second Lieutenant Atticus Cranston knocked on Kellerman's office door and waited, the afternoon sun shifting to the west and reinforcing a growing headache behind his eyes. "Yeah, yeah, come in," came the gruff reply, and Atticus stepped into the dark quarters with a measure of relief, snapping off a salute, then rubbing his forehead with the back of his hand.

"Sir, Olinger says he apprised you of the hunting party based on Corporal Pierce's information. I thought I might fill in the rest, if you have a moment."

Kellerman looked at the young officer and thought he seemed peaked. "You look peaked, Lieutenant, sit down."

Atticus sat. "Thank you, sir—just a headache from the sun. Downright blinding out there at this time of day."

Kellerman poured a shot of bourbon into a chipped glass and slid it across the desk before pouring his own. "Take it. You can speak to Mrs. Zimmermann if you need a headache powder."

Atticus tossed the shot back. "Thank you, sir."

"Watch your drinking, Atticus," Kellerman said, as he poured a second round.

"Yes, sir."

"All right. The hunters, are they actually out in this hellscape searching for game, or is a plot afoot?"

Atticus thought, absentmindedly spinning his glass on the desk. "Well, that's just it, sir. The first time I ran into them they seemed all right enough, but today when we went to pick up Miss Courtenay the encounter was— tense. The man in charge is Lucas Dean, and he was the one who had shown up at the rock. There are the other five, as Pierce probably said, who were off at a distance today, and didn't say much on the first encounter. You ever—" He paused, choosing his words carefully, taking a delicate sip of the bourbon, wishing it was water. "You ever meet a man who hasn't done anything threatening that you can put your finger on, but he just comes across as real, real bad?"

Kellerman looked at him blankly and then erupted in laughter. "You're asking me? Every man—well, most of the men—out there in my fort right now are those types of bad hombres. Good God, man, they're the only kind I ever meet!"

Atticus flushed and he nipped the rest of his drink. Seeing that he'd embarrassed the young lieutenant,

Kellerman softened his tone. "And that's what makes a fine officer, Cranston, the intuition of mind to see a character for what he is. If you say the man is bad news, I trust you."

The young officer grinned, relieved. "Thank you, sir! Yes, I say he's bad news, but I can't tell you exactly why. At least, not yet. I think we need to keep an eye on them during their stay. Should I send Ahiga out again tonight?"

Kellerman stretched his back against the wooden chair until his spine popped, then lit a cigarette before replying. Watching the blue smoke curling toward the ceiling for a moment, he then returned his gaze to the young officer. "Not tonight. Let the scoundrels sink in a bit and get comfortable. They'll know we are curious, but let them think we forgot about them for a day. That'll be all, Lieutenant, tell Sergeant Major Olinger I need to speak with him, instanter."

CHAPTER 9

Captain Joe Kellerman had relayed Second Lieutenant Cranston's report on the hunting gang to Sergeant Major Saul Olinger and now had bad news of his own.

"This just arrived from Yuma," he said, passing Olinger a dispatch. "The Apache are out."

"Well, we knew that was bound to happen," Olinger said. "Yuma's already warned us that there's recently been much coming and going among the wickiups, and the young men are dancing every night. Joe, my guess is that, at a minimum, the Chiricahua and Mescalero plan to raid into Mexico, and maybe others will join them."

"General Sherman wants us to put a stop to it," Kellerman said. "Easy for him to say."

That got no reaction from the sergeant major, and the captain sighed and then said to the soldier sitting at a desk outside the door, "Orderly, officer's call. Sober up the bugler."

"Maybe Lieutenant Hall will have an idea," Olinger said.

"Stranger things have happened," Kellerman said.

* * *

"I have no idea," Lieutenant James Hall said, waving a vague hand. "I haven't a clue, sir." He opened his snuffbox, took a pinch, and sniffed deeply. A sneeze, then: "But I'll study on the matter."

"Do that, Lieutenant," Kellerman said. "Well, here's how things stand. But first help yourselves to a drink."

He waited until the glasses were filled. Even strait-laced, spit-and-polish Second Lieutenant Atticus Cranston chose to imbibe again, tarnishing a little of his West Point sheen with every passing day. "Right. Drink up and listen up," the captain said finally. "The latest intelligence coming from Washington is that General Sherman and President Grant request and require us to keep the peace between the Rio Bravo to the south and Yuma to the north, and thus end the conditions of banditry, plunder, and murder now existing in that area."

"Bully!" Lieutenant Hall said. "Give each man a brace of pistols and a sharp saber and we'll soon rid ourselves of that frontier scum."

"Lieutenant, I haven't reached the interesting part yet," Kellerman said, slightly irritated.

"Please proceed, Captain," Hall said.

"Thank you. The Chiricahua and Mescalero are out, and I agree with Sergeant Major Olinger that they'll do what they've done in the past, head south and raid into Sonora. In other words, they'll come this way—and, no doubt, will stop by to say howdy."

"And we'll be ready for them sir," Hall said, refilling his glass. "Darn right, we will."

"And as though that wasn't enough, of course, we're

playing host to the professors—with General Sherman's blessing—who plan to dig up Fort Misery in search of dead Spaniards and their treasure. One of the said archaeologists being a beautiful woman."

The infirmary was stucco and had dark and dingy crossbeam hallways that led to twelve beds, a surgery, such as it was, a linen closet, and a small locking office with a bed for a post doctor who never had arrived. Four men lay in iron beds quietly moaning in their sleep. Private Shanks was white as the sheet he lay beneath, sweat dampening the blankets and pillow to a dark gray. Mary Zimmermann touched his forehead with the back of her hand and pulled away as if burned, shaking her head sadly. The boy wouldn't last the night.

Constance Courtenay took in the sad sight as she made her way toward the surgeon's office under the watchful gaze of Mrs. Zimmermann. The office had never hosted a surgeon. Though an occasional doctor might pass through and leave in a hurry, Mrs. Zimmermann was the nurse and did most of her healing by prayer. She was unimpressed by the younger lady's assurances about how easily she would survive the fort.

"You mustn't leave this room unlocked while changing or sleeping, and you certainly must not go anywhere unarmed. We may be the fairer sex, but God has seen fit to give us Colts that make us equals. The men here are the worst of the worst, so you may prattle on about Pharoah's tombs and mountainsides until Kingdom come, but I am telling—no, *demanding*—that you be armed and vigilant. Understood?"

Constance smiled, "Completely understood. I'll be on my best behavior the entire time we're visiting, and most of that time will be spent in the company of my uncle and his colleagues. They'll keep me quite safe." She had shaken the dust out of the top layers in her trunk and was doing her best to find a way to hang them in an empty armoire half-filled with medical gear. "Will we have supper quite soon? I'm starving."

CHAPTER 10

The officers' mess was afforded a slightly cleaner, more spacious hall for meals than the rabble had, and as the sun sank into the rolling waves of sand to the west, painting the sky lavender and blue. The generous oil lanterns, all three of them, made glitter on the dusty air that sparkled like fireflies. Professor Paul Fernsby sat toward the head of the table beside Kellerman and across from Major Olinger, who, with Lieutenant Hall flanked Constance, as though her personal bodyguards, as they all approached the table. "Miss Courtenay you'll need to relocate Major Mouser carefully—he's mean. Tip the chair and he'll take off. He knows that isn't his seat," Kellerman said.

Constance looked down at the huge orange cat and smiled. "Oh, poor thing." She began to reach out to stroke him and pulled her hand back as if burned when the cat hissed like a teakettle. "Oh!" Constance tipped the chair slowly, and Major Mouser plopped to the floor with a huff, slowly stamping his way out of the mess on white-mittened feet.

Mary Zimmermann entered the room brandishing

heavy platters and quickly placed them on the table. "One more coming, and we will have suet plum duff for dessert." Then to Constance she explained, "With raisins. The Army has yet seen fit to send me plums, though I ask." Then she glided to the kitchen again in her long black skirts. Hall took in the spread with a jolly grin, "Braised beef, beans, potatoes. I daresay, professors, maybe with you lot around, Mrs. Zimmermann will take to fattening us up."

Mary returned and laid plates piled high with fresh biscuits, examined the table, and then left again. "You've outdone yourself. We thank you, Mrs. Zimmermann," Kellerman cried cheerfully toward the woman's back. She flailed her hand at him without turning in reply.

"Now then, professors, I assume you find your lodgings quite satisfactory," Kellerman said, downing his whiskey before diving into the beef.

Oliver Berryman spoke first, his grating voice carried a whining tone that at once set the officers on edge. "We've prepared our tents. It seemed preferable to the quarters you've offered. Cleaner, at least." He sniffed.

Olinger and Kellerman shared a look, then the sergeant major spoke, "You've taken over our parade ground with canvas tents, then?"

Fernsby smiled. "Why, yes, right next to the dig site. I promise we won't be in your way too much at all. I say, this beef is quite delicious."

Lieutenant Hall poured himself a snifter of brandy, sent by his beloved mama, and with all seriousness said, "And what of the ghosts, professors?"

Fernsby stopped with a forkful of beans half to his mouth. "Ghosts?"

"Yes, ghosts. I can't imagine that the warriors of the 1500s, being dug up out of their resting place for you to poke at, will be quite thrilled with the operation. Have you never encountered ghosts on a dig, before, then?" Hall's tone was light and it was impossible to say how serious he was about this new worry.

Oliver Berryman scoffed, but Professor Dankworth happily intervened. "I daresay, I have seen a few ghosts in my time, Lieutenant. We were on a dig ten years ago, an ancient Roman battlefield—I won't bore you with the details. We dug up quite an impressive mass grave, and as we worked, the sky grew dark and filled with thunder. We had just begun to clear the trench when the heavens opened and rain like you've never seen came down in heavy sheets. Our team retreated to our tents, and we could do little but watch as the floodwaters rose. When the sun set and the rain carried on, there was little to be done, so we all bedded down for the night, damp and freezing. I took third watch, for you know archaeological sites are a hot target of rogue thieves, and I was awakened at three in the morning by my colleague. The rain had slowed some, and I took my oil lantern in hand and sat beneath the little flap of my tent to watch. I was quite lost in my own thoughts about the work we'd have to do to get the trenches dug out again, when I began to hear a strange sound. A distant—*howling*, not quite that of an animal, but not entirely human either. And then . . ." Dankworth trailed off, swirling the whiskey in his glass before downing it in one gulp. Then, with a haunted expression on his face, he continued, "And then these shapes came, great swirling gray shapes of men that moved like animals. Slinking and slithering, with glowing yellow eyes. I admit I was not brave. I watched, then doused my lantern and fell back into the tent and closed the flaps. From outside I heard the sounds of a cat screeching and the low moaning and anguished yelps of a man in pain. When, all at once—"

SSSCREEEEECCCHHHHHH!

Kellerman leapt from the table, as did Hall and Olinger, Dankworth frozen in place midsentence. "What was that?" Kellerman barked.

Constance saw and she too leapt from the table. "Oh you poor thing. Look, Major Mouser got his tail caught under the chair leg." She pointed to where Atticus Cranston had shuffled his chair back onto the outraged cat's great fluffy orange tail, a tuft of fur stuck beneath the leg and the tail itself now freed but being angrily licked by the owner.

Atticus leapt to his feet, "Oh no! Oh, I feel terrible. Poor Major Mouser, you all right?" He knelt in front of the cat who hissed like a baby dragon and glared with menacing yellow eyes. Constance bravely put her hand out to stroke the cat's head and this time he allowed it. She gently petted the soft space between his ears and was rewarded with a deep purr. "There, there, you're all right now, good kitty."

The officers all stared at the woman as she continued calmly stroking the cat, all four men momentarily speechless. Finally, Hall said, clearly impressed, "That cat has hated everyone here since the day and hour he arrived. You must have a special gift, Miss Courtenay."

After a final stroke of the feline from nose to the tip of his tail, Constance stood, and as she returned to her chair, the heavy orange cat followed. She sat and the cat leapt into her lap, curled into a ball, and began to purr. "Well, I say! I have made a new friend, it seems."

Joe Kellerman cleared his throat of surprise and said, "Miss Courtenay you're under no obligation to eat with Major Mouser on your lap. There should be at least some dignity in the officers' mess, if nowhere else."

"Oh, it's fine"—she smiled at the captain—"quite soothing really, and perhaps he will follow to my bed-chambers tonight and keep me warm. The room is very sparse, and I know the desert temperature tends to drop quite low overnight."

The men grumbled that this was true, and then Dankworth tried to recover his story. "Well, as I was saying, the ancient Romans seemed unsettled by our presence that night, and I hid behind my canvas flaps shaking in my boots, yet everyone else slept through the noise. After an hour had passed and the night slipped from three a.m. to four, the commotion ceased all at once and I fell asleep. In the morning, everyone else insisted I'd had a nightmare, but not I. I know exactly what I witnessed, and it wasn't a sight right for a Christian man to set eyes upon."

Hall clapped his hands gaily. "Jolly good, Dankworth. Have a pinch of snuff, will you? I appreciate a good ghost story from time to time. Everyone around here gets a bit stodgy." Lieutenant Hall passed the small bone box that held his snuff to Dankworth. Professor Berryman scowled at the trinket as if it was a gilded cat turd but was duly ignored by everyone around him. Jules Dankworth took a hearty sniff, and then his face turned several interesting shades, before he exclaimed, "I daresay, that's quite good! Clears the mind!"

From across the table Constance reached out her dainty hand, palm up. "Let me try, Jules." The man hesitated, then proffered the box. She took a dainty sniff up each nostril and smiled at Hall. "Excellent quality, Lieutenant. Your dear mama must love you very much."

Hall beamed, the lamplight making his carefully coiffed black curls shine as bright as his white teeth. "Here, you must try the brandy." He slid a snifter to the young lady, who reveled in the taste. And so, the night went on with lighthearted conversation made all the more mirthful by the appearance of Mrs. Zimmermann's plum duff, which was given a rousing round of applause by all.

Outside the warm little room, made hazy with smoke, a darkening on the horizon was growing. Thunderheads formed and shot lightning across the desert like the signature of a demented God, but it was the earthly eyes gazing upon the fort from a great many vantage points that held true danger. The merrymaking wouldn't last, and Fort Misery was soon to be caught in the crossfire of a bloody battle that would shape the terrain of Western history.

CHAPTER 11

"**D**ang this rain." Lucas Dean spat, scowling as the wind tried to take off both his hat and the Mexican blanket wrapped around his shoulders. He and his assembly of shootists and outlaws, who called themselves the Trey-Treys, huddled by the fire, backs against their wagon in a feeble attempt to stay dry. The small piece of canvas they'd draped off the wagon as a lean-to offered little protection against the relentless rain, and the men were soggy, unhappy, and on edge.

The bonfire burned high and bright, casting dark shadows across the men's faces, and though the warmth was welcome, the flames made their periodic attempts to gaze into the black-as-pitch desert futile, as their eyes struggled to adjust between light and dark. Six mounts circled the camp, and a Morgan restlessly stood beside the wagon. A red tin oil lantern blew back and forth in the wind with creaking squeaks, an ominous sound that was getting on draw fighter Frank Abilene's nerves. Despite his chosen occupation, the man was by nature spooked in wide open spaces.

The men's range clothes were dusty and well worn,

but quality, and they were well heeled beyond the conventional garb of average hunters. They sat in various stages of unrest, only Adam Louis was sound asleep and snoring in a sleeping bag, contented by a belly full of beans and whiskey, oblivious to the rain.

"Them soldiers. They'll be keeping an eye on us, Lucas, you know that," Frankie said, struggling to light a cigarette against the raising wind.

Lucas Dean nodded, "Oh yeah, maybe watching us tonight. They have them sneaky scouts in their ranks who could be eyeballing us right now. Listen, let's be on our best behaviors for a few days and keep quiet, that's all we need to do. Take ourselves a bighorn sheep tomorrow and prove that we're mighty hunters, and I bet that naïve little fella—what's his name?—Cranston, will shove right off for a while after that."

"He's not the one I'm worried about, Lucas. Joe Kellerman is a hard man, and that pretty-boy lieutenant he has with him ain't no bargain, either. I got a bad feeling about all of this, mark my words."

Lucas yawned and rolled down into his bedroll, bracing himself against the whipping wind and following Adam's example by keeping his head and shoulders beneath the lean-to. "Frankie, you ain't never come across a moment in life you don't have a bad feeling about. You're as nervous as a maiden aunt on her wedding night. Go to sleep."

He looked across the fire to Dick Freedman, the old man he kept around out of a sense of loyalty. The former bounty hunter had saved Dean's hide when he was fleeing from a cuckolded husband in New Orleans, and besides, he was a fine trail cook. "Tell the man one of your stories, Dick," he said. "Put nervous Ned here to sleep. Maybe tell us how you plan on a-roasting that sheep tomorrow."

Dick grunted and coughed, "Heck no. I'm too old and too tired and too sick. Go to sleep Frankie, sweet dreams." He pulled a blanket around his shoulders and coughed deeply, rolling over to ignore the men.

"Sweet dreams of sheep, Frankie." Dean grinned. "And gold."

As the storm picked up across the desert, Private Nelson and Corporal Lockhart began hearing things, or so they thought. "Drums?" Lockhart said, nervously. "Could be," Nelson replied, the hair on the back of his neck standing up.

The three professors had arranged canvas tents smack dab in the middle of the parade ground, and the lanterns within were dark, suggesting the men were asleep. On the wind the sounds came again, *drum . . . drum . . . drum . . .* spaced out like a funeral dirge.

"Should we sound the alarm?" Nelson asked, nervously. The pair paused to listen . . . the drumming had stopped. They scanned the distance frantically but saw no sign of movement.

"No, not yet, just keep listening."

Inside the infirmary Constance Courtenay had settled Major Mouser onto her bed, then stepped out to aid Mrs. Zimmermann and the priest who stood alongside Private Shanks, who was at any moment to take his last breath. Constance sat beside him and took the man's thin, white hand in her own. It was cold and clammy as the grave already. She smiled. "I'm terribly sorry I didn't have a chance to know you, Private, but I hope you won't feel so alone now."

Private Shanks rolled his eyes toward her, the startled whites showing with a bovine quality. "Sister? You came all this way?"

Mrs. Zimmermann gave Constance a look and nod, so Constance replied, "Why, yes, brother, all this way just to see you again. Are you very glad?"

Private Shanks smiled and foam-tinged pink with blood smeared his teeth and mouth, as tears ran down his face. "Betsy Sue, my sweet Betsy Sue, how is Mama?"

Father Staszczyk stood alert and began to pray quietly, his holy water clutched in his left hand and a Bible open in his right, the beautiful purple stole draped around his shoulders until he lifted one edge and wrapped Private Shanks beside him.

"Mama loves you very much, brother," Constance said sweetly.

"Even after all I done?" Shanks asked, turning gray.

"Even after all you done, yes," Constance said.

Mrs. Zimmermann swept in then, "A mama will never stop loving her children, don't you worry, Percival. Close your eyes now. The nice father will give you your last rites, so you can rest."

Constance took her hand away as the priest began with the sign of the cross, then the anointing, and then mumbling of mysterious sacraments and confessions and creeds, until at last Private Shanks shuddered out a final breath and became still. Mrs. Zimmermann and

Father Staszczyk pulled the white sheet over the dead man's face with reverence, as Constance, with a shiver, opened a window, then returned to the surgeon's quarters and locked her door. Thunder boomed and the room lit with a white flash of light making her jolt with fright, but she had soon settled into her flannel nightshirt and cuddled the cat underneath her arm atop the hard mattress, and was quickly lost in sleep beneath the soothing rain musically pounding on the tin roof above.

Outside the men on patrol grumbled beneath their wet kepis, as the great whirling storm soaked them to the skin, even through their slickers. The horses across the fort neighed, sighed, and tramped with agitation, their eyes wide enough for the whites to show, though there was nothing obvious to spook them. Again, came the sound of the drums, carrying in on gusts of wind and rain that stung like pins of ice, yet again they faded out quickly. The young private Charles Parker peered into the shadows but saw nothing, yet a feeling of doom was rising in his chest.

Inside, Joe Kellerman poured a double from an earthenware jug of whiskey and slammed it quickly. There was darkness in the desert tonight, he could feel it, a great menacing storm that had little to do with mother nature's bad temper. They were in for a bloody battle, soon, and he wished he had a crystal ball and knew where it would come from—or how to stop it.

CHAPTER 12

Despite the bad feelings and fitful sleep the night had brought for both men and beasts at Fort Misery, the dawn broke as usual with little fanfare. The storm had eased, and the warmth of the desert was rising quickly, as the sun kissed her lover the moon good night in a display of orange, pink, and cobalt blue. Slowly the stars faded out of sight as the sun rose to full splendor, a glowing orb that sent shadows running. There were a few spots of damage to the wooden structures from the heavy wind gusts, and Tobias Zimmerman made a list. After breakfast he would set right away to repairs.

The professors exited their tents and stretched, looking about busily, and eager to get to work. The chow bell chimed, and Berryman rubbed his hands together excitedly, "Jolly good. I'm starving. A bit damp in those tents last night, wasn't it?" he said, as he made his way to the mess hall.

Professor Fernsby nodded, "Yes, if this weather becomes a routine, I'm afraid we may need to beg solid quarters until it passes. I'm too old to sleep in the damp and cold all night. I can barely move from the rheumatism this morning. It's hell getting old, boys, remember that."

"Perhaps, but it is better than the alternative," Berryman said sagely.

"I'll bring the white oil, Professor, to make your joints new again. One moment." Chan, the Chinese man who traveled alongside the roving professors, and acted not only as a valet but medic, ducked into the nearest tent on silent feet.

"He's a good lad, our Chan," Fernsby said, rubbing his hands together to relieve the ache in his knuckles.

Lieutenant Hall, hair shining gallantly, greeted the professors warmly. "Good morning, old chaps. Please join us in the officers' mess again." He stretched a leather gauntleted hand to guide them in the right direction, and they scurried ahead as he walked behind. The room was bustling with life as platters of biscuits, beans, and ham and eggs were laid out. Kellerman sat at the end of the table, looking haunted and poorly with dark circles under his eyes. He smoked a cigarette and watched the curling blue smoke twirl to the ceiling. His mood dropped when the professors sauntered in, yawning and overdressed for the occasion. Constance made her appearance last, clad in men's tan pants and boots and a buttoned shirt. Even dressed in the common garb of a working man her beauty shone like a spot of gold in a dark river, and it made Kellerman nervous. "How was your first night, gentlemen? And gentlelady," Kellerman asked, discreetly taking a nip of bourbon that he washed down with scalding hot coffee.

Paul Fernsby made his way to a chair, walking bow-legged. "I'm afraid the chill and rain has left me a bit stiff this morning. Hopefully that was a one-off event. I hear the desert is meant to be dry. We don't want floods washing away our treasures as we dig them up, either." He offered a halfhearted smile, then poured a hefty cup of coffee for himself and settled delicately onto the hard wooden chair.

"Ah, Professor Frenzy, she holds many mysteries, our desert, you'll soon find. Whatever you expect her to do, prepare for the opposite. Since you are taking up my entire parade ground, I'd be quite content to offer you quarters indoors instead of those tents. All you need do is ask. I will say that they tend to have rats, leaks, and spiders, but they keep the worst of the chill away and have a fireplace."

Fernsby grimaced, "That's Fernsby, Captain. Yes, indeed a solid wood structure would suit me well. However, some of the canvas drapes staked above the areas of our dig must remain, you do understand. Great treasures take sacrifice, be it the tombs of Egypt or the lost conquistador gold of Yuma."

"And how about you, little lady, were your quarters to your satisfaction?" Kellerman turned his attention to Constance, her tumble of black hair shining brightly in the morning sun but doing little to hide the purple bruises of insomnia from her eyes.

"Oh yes, thank you. It was the strangest thing, I kept thinking I heard war drums in the night. Each time the sound woke me, they'd stop. Perhaps it was merely nightmares, since I know the Apache are afoot nearby," she said thoughtfully, chewing a biscuit dipped in bacon grease.

The professors all opened their mouths to chime in

with their own stories of the drums, but a sharp rap came at the door of the hall first.

Saul Olinger and Kellerman shared a look of concern. "Well, come in!" Kellerman barked.

Corporal Lockhart looked dead on his feet but snapped off his salute and stood, swaying, at the entrance to the hall.

Lieutenant Hall looked him up and down and said, "Good God, lad, take a seat before you fall."

A less sympathetic Kellerman sternly asked, "Where is Nelson?"

"He is to bed, sir, but I thought we should make a report to you about the—the drumming in the night." The corporal even in his exhaustion spared too long a glance at the gleaming beauty of Constance, again setting Kellerman on edge.

"Well, out with it, Corporal Lockhart. Civilized people are trying to drink their coffee in peace," Saul Olinger said testily.

"Yes, sir—well, it seemed all night we heard drums, like war drums, but they'd only do it a few times, then stop for an hour. Never seemed to get closer or farther away."

Kellerman rubbed his mustache with the back of his hand, "And you didn't report this to me because . . ."

Lockhart paled a bit, an impressive feat for a man who already looked half-dead. "Well, we thought by the time anyone came it would have stopped again, and it seemed that way. Is it—is it hostiles, sir? Threatening the fort?"

"Could be. Could also be a lot of other things. Tonight, we will send the Navajo out with you and Nelson and a few others. I want you to track down the source. Could be a white man who's traded for a skin drum and thinks himself a virtuoso. There is another concern, the so-called hunters. I need a better look at what they're really up to out there."

At this Second Lieutenant Atticus Cranston stiffened, feeling naïve in the lack of Kellerman's trust. Cheeks pink, Cranston said, "Let me lead, sir. If these men are not hunting, it is my responsibility to get to the root of their misdeeds."

Kellerman and Hall shared a side-eyed look, "Maybe, Cranston. If you take Hall with you. Let's see what the day brings, first."

Further discussion was cut short by the appearance of Chan, who applied a strongly scented oil to Fernsby's hands and massaged it in as the old professor grunted a withheld shriek of pain.

Lucas Dean loaded the Trey-Treys with their appropriate hunting regalia after a quick breakfast of salt pork and coffee. "What exactly are we doing?" asked an agitated Adam Louis, already sick from the heat of the day and a whiskey hangover.

Dean didn't look up from adjusting his saddle. "Hunting," he said plainly.

"We ain't here to hunt, and it is too hot, anyway." Adam spit at his boots.

Dean slowly stopped fiddling with the saddle and turned to Adam, his hand going for a Colt on his hip that was drawn and against Adam's forehead in seconds.

"We told the soldiers we are here to hunt. If they

notice we ain't hunting, what do you think is going to happen? Those men at that fort, they ain't like others you've met, the ones you've taken advantage of. They're the worst selection of men around, and they're protected by the authority of the entire U.S. Army. We don't want them on our tails. Now I will gladly eliminate you right now and right here if your intention is to refuse to play along a little while. Tell me, Adam, you want to play or die? Makes no difference to me."

A thin stream ran down the right pant leg of Adam Louis's trousers, making Dean curl his face up in a cruel smile. "I always knew you were a coward at heart. All bullies are. You gonna play?" He cocked the revolver.

Louis threw his hands up. "I'll play! For God's sake, I will play. What are we s'posed to be hunting again?"

"Bighorn sheep. Need to bag one, at least. Or maybe a mule deer." He looked at Dick. "Good eating either way, eh, Dick?"

The rest of the Trey-Treys were dressed and ready, working hard at looking every inch the hunters they pretended to be. "Boss, what do we do with the wagon?" Dick Freedman asked, his cough deep.

Lucas Dean studied the old man. The son of a Georgia slaver and his lady's maid, Dick's complexion was the color of pale coffee that intensified his startlingly sky-blue eyes. Today, his skin had taken on such a pallor that the constellations of mahogany freckles across his broad, flat nose stood out like drops of ink, and his eyes had become rheumy and plain. The man was not well, and Dean knew the day ahead would be strenuous and hot. After a long moment he said, "Unhitch the Morgan. It can carry our sheep. But you stay here, Dick. You never know who might show up." Dean was uneasy about leaving the old man behind, and he added, "Keep your Winchester close. If the army comes poking around again, ask if they have a doctor at that fort. You don't look too well."

Dick began to protest but fell back into coughing and sat down breathlessly and exhausted. Ready to leave, Dean looked around—Frankie was nowhere to be seen. "Frank," he shouted, testily.

Frank Abilene was no bargain, though on first meeting him, based on his stature and cadence, people wrongly assumed he was a mild-mannered man. A strange, tweedy little man with cold round eyes like dead fish, perhaps his mama had called him handsome from time to time, but it mattered little. The ladies who encountered him kept their eyes closed or downcast as he passed, while Frank stuck to dark taverns and never even tried to win a lady's heart. He was a man of the West and always would be, hoping to die with boots on and Colt cocked. He'd joined up with the Trey-Treys after Luke Short had run him and Lucas Dean out of Fort Worth, and it had been a happy coincidence to overhear the prissy professors speaking about the gold dripped trials and tribulations of some lost conquistadors in the desert, and an even happier fate when one of them, Fernsby, got drunk and began to share details of his map.

The Trey-Treys' hunting trip had followed shortly after the professors left, and then to their advantage, the little lady involved in the project became stranded at Devil's Rock—a lucky stroke for the Trey-Treys, but perhaps not so lucky for the talkative professors.

Lucas Dean, the least threatening of the men, had seized the opportunity to pry out more details about the dig for treasure. But he was disappointed, getting little out of the woman, who looked harmless but seemed cleverer than the gossipy professors. Still, the mission was clear: Keep apprised of the dig, and when the time had arrived, sneak in, strike hard, and retrieve the treasure. Then escape, which might prove the hardest part, but he had a plan. First, however, they needed to track down a bighorn sheep to prove themselves to the Army who seemed to have no intention of leaving them alone anytime soon.

Sighing, having thought it over and come to no new conclusions, Frank stood from his desert latrine and pulled his pants up, shambling back to the camp.

"All right, let's go find us a sheep."

The sun was hot and cruel, and Kellerman was eager to be anywhere but his current spot, watching a group of lunatics digging up his parade ground.

"You need a parasol, Captain." Constance grinned up at him, pausing in her work of shoveling out layers of compacted sand and shale. The hole had grown to her knees, and she was drenched in sweat, her hair plastered to her scalp and the armpits of her white linen shirt soaked right through. "I daresay you'd look rather fetching in a pink one. In fact, if you would care to borrow mine . . ." Her eyes sparkled with mirth, a thick streak of putty colored mud creating a muttonchop on the right side of her face.

Kellerman scowled but quickly found the corners of

his mouth tip up against his will at the vision of himself twirling a pink lace parasol. "I could order you into the hole for that remark," he said gruffly.

Constance looked down and then waved her arms to show her current predicament. "Good thing I'm already in one, then!" She laughed lightly and went back to her work, the shovel making an unpleasant clang against the hardened bits of shale.

"Find anything yet?" Kellerman called.

"Lots of dirt, Captain, if you need it."

Rolling his eyes, Kellerman made his way toward where the three older professors huddled, a drawing board and charcoal in hand as they animatedly demonstrated something for an increasingly disgruntled looking Tobias Zimmermann.

"What are we having here, do you do spirit drawings, Mr. Frenzy? Saw that once at a traveling show," Kellerman interjected, and Tobias shot him a look filled with daggers.

"Fernsby. Oh no—something else quite entirely. But please, tell me what the medium saw at the spiritualist show, these things fascinate me so."

"She drew a man and revealed it to be my brother who had been lost to sea. Real neat depiction with seaweed clinging to his hair and the whole bit. Cost a nickel."

Fernsby clutched his chest and went pale, "And? Its accuracy to your long-lost brother below the waves?"

Kellerman unscrewed his flask and took a sip. "It was the likeness of someone, I'm sure. But I never had a brother. I think I recognized the model, without the seaweed of course, selling candy floss across the way."

Fernsby frowned, but before he could speak, a cry came from ten yards away. "Found something!" Constance held a gleaming metal object in her hand, the tip extending now just an inch past the hole entrance.

The other professors scurried to her side, and Kellerman picked up the drawing, it was a blueprint for a wooden box with a fine grid of wire and a wooden spout in each corner.

"What's this they want you to build?" he asked Zimmermann, who stood wiping away sweat with a red bandana and frowning deeply.

"Something for when they've dug deep enough to hit water," he said.

"Water? Out here? How deep do they plan to dig? And do they know this is my parade ground, and they better leave it as they found it."

Zimmermann shrugged. "Keep an eye on them. I'll build the thing just to shut them up. I also need two men to help me patch some fence on the east quad. Who do you want me to take?"

Kellerman handed the drawing over and twisted his mustache in thought, "Private Wesley and Private Johnson."

He began to walk away. "And Tobias? Make them miserable."

"Aye, aye, Captain." Zimmermann offered a half-assed salute and shambled off toward his workshop.

"Well, it could be Spanish but it's hard to say with the damage here, and here, blue could be lapis you see—" Julius Dankworth was cut off as Joe Kellerman snatched the scrap from the professor's hand. "Careful, you lout! That's a priceless artifact," he yelled, spittle flying from his purple lips.

"Priceless? See here, this U? and S—and that MI? This is an old standard-issue United States milk ration. Your ancient relic is some soldier's saving grace for hardtack or Arbuckle's." He tossed the can to the ground and Dankworth scrambled to pick it up. "I wouldn't lie to you, Professor, and I am telling you it's rubbish. Trash."

Kellerman was too hot and irritable to continue supervising what he knew would be a pointless dig, and with a wave of his arm he sauntered off to his office where at least there was whiskey, coffee, and shade. Let them dig up the whole cursed Yuma desert, he thought. Just keep them out of my hair.

CHAPTER 13

Private Wesley nervously held on to the fence post while Private Johnson hammered it into the ground, the heavy mallet landing erratically with substantial thuds. "Say, be careful there. You're about to swing off the edge," Wesley said, the pain in his broken finger flashing as he imagined having the mallet smash into his hand.

Tobias was busily unrolling barbed wire from a small spool, battling with the sharp burs getting stuck in the wood of the wagon it rested in. Lost in his own grumbling thoughts, he pulled the wire to the fence, glancing up at the sand and scrub that stretched away from him beneath a sky darkening with thunderheads. A bright flash of red caught the corner of his eye, and he snapped his attention to it while reaching for his Colt. It was gone, but a heavy wind gust revealed it once more along with something black. "Privates," Tobias said, steel in his voice, "Stop what you're doing, we have a problem."

The two men reached for their own guns and followed Tobias's gaze, seeing the flashes of unnatural color twenty yards away. "What it is?" Private Johnson whispered, eyes narrowing in his pinched face.

"Don't know, but we're going to go find out." Tobias drew his gun and stepped over the fence slowly, cautiously watching for any indication of an ambush.

Johnson, and then Wesley, followed over the fence, and the trio had made it ten feet before *boom!* followed by *bang!* As Private Johnson fired into the desert, prompting curses from Tobias and a yell from Wesley. Tobias barked, his heart racing, "Did you leave the mallet balanced on the post, you idiot?"

"Maybe," Private Johnson said sheepishly, doubly embarrassed for having fired his gun.

"Scoundrel," Tobias said. "Try not to shoot us this time, you madman."

Shaken and less confident now, the men moved on light feet until they drew near the red, but halfway there they knew what would be found. The sweet, cloying stench of death assailed them as it was carried on the wind, growing stronger with each step and making their stomachs roil.

Holding their breath, Wesley pulling his bandana over his nose, they climbed a small dune and came upon a terrible sight. Sprawled on the sand, his black hair and red headband swirling in the wind like an angry serpent, lay the decomposing remains of an Indian, and past him, near the remnants of a fire, a young girl lying on a gray-and-blue woven blanket stared unblinking at the sun, open mouthed and still. Beside her a stiff, still form lay rolled in a blanket, only thick, braided black hair showing.

Tobias rubbed his chin and contemplated the scene.

Three dead Indians at a makeshift camp. Why were they out here and what killed them? Then he took a closer look at the boy—he cried out, backing away carefully. "Back, back, get back!" He yelled at Private Johnson who had gone into the campsite ready to loot what he could find. Johnson glared at him and began rifling through the clothing, kneeling to get a better look.

Tobias roared in fury, "Smallpox—look at them! Stay there. Don't you dare come near me. One step and I'll shoot you in the gut. You, boy"—he turned to Wesley—"go fetch the captain. Tell him we came across dead Indians covered in smallpox. Be quick now!"

Captain Joseph Kellerman stood and took in the scene before him. Private Johnson sat sulking to the north of the dead Indians, his elbows crossed on his knees and his rat face pinched into a scowl. Tobias Zimmermann had a Colt leveled at the little man from a far distance, suggesting Johnson had already tried to bolt. At a casual glance the dead looked to be in a state of decomposition, but a closer look showed that they were ravaged by the angry blisters of smallpox, the huge opaque swellings dented in the middle. The young girl had suffered the worst, her small face was a monstrous mask, and it tugged at Kellerman's heart. "They must have left their people, willingly or not, but there's no reason to believe it has done any good. No horses?" Kellerman asked Tobias.

The man replied without taking his eyes off Johnson,

"No horses. Sand shifted around enough I doubt we'd find a trail."

Kellerman frowned. "Don't think we want to find them, Zimmermann."

His eyes wandered over the dead, searching and found Johnson. "Private, I should kick you into the desert for this, but I can't trust you to not expose innocent men should anyone find you. Since God sees fit to torment me like he did Job and saddle me with you lot, I will make arrangements for you to have shelter, but you'll be under guard. If you're not dead in a reasonable amount of time, we'll decide your fate. I'll have Ahiga and Mrs. Zimmermann say a prayer for the dead Indians, and then you'll haul them out into the desert and let the scavengers have them."

The man balked, "But they have smallpox," he yelled.

Kellerman narrowed his eyes, "Watch your tone, Private. You're already exposed by your own foolishness and greed, and your tent will be right here, so if you want to sleep next to the coyotes eating the remains be my guest." With that the captain left, calling over his shoulder, "I'll have you relieved momentarily, Mr. Zimmermann."

CHAPTER 14

The night had come on swift and cool, and Ahiga left to make his usual patrol. All was quiet but for the occasional murmur of words or tinkle of glass that faded the farther Ahiga rode out from the fort, the moonlight and stars lighting the desert sands an eerie white. He headed in the direction of the hunting camp and had been riding for ten minutes when a coyote stepped out from the night. Ahiga stopped, staring at the animal as it stared back at him with piercing yellow eyes. His people believed that if a coyote crossed your path, it was taboo to continue, that you must turn around or stop to make offerings and prayers. Yet the coyote did not cross, it sat down on its haunches and made no signs of aggression or fear. Ahiga did not move, waiting to see what message trickster coyote would send.

After a few moments an owl swooped down on silent wings, letting out a mournful hoot as it passed and quickly disappeared into the night. At the same time, the coyote had darted across his path and dissolved into shadow. Ahiga shivered—bad medicine, but for who? Him alone, or the fort behind? During his time as a scout, the Indian had been forced to set aside his customs, he had come to ignore taboos often as dealing with dead men and eating whatever food was provided were part of army life, but this was too much to shrug off. He dismounted quietly and took the pouch of tobacco from his shirt pocket, sinking to his knees in the desert sand and beginning a prayer. The mournful notes spiraled toward the dark sky as the wind caught the tobacco and made it dance above his head. When it was done, he returned to his horse and continued ahead, keenly aware of his surroundings and keeping his Henry at the ready.

There was no fire where he knew the men's camp to be, and Ahiga slipped into the sand and became a snake, approaching the camp quickly, feeling the warm earth glide beneath his belly. A man lay in a slump, blood staining the pale ground beneath him. The wagon remained, but there was no mule in the traces and there were no horses in sight. Ahiga scanned the area and saw footprints trailing all around the area then off to the east. There were no scents but the stink of the dead man and the cloying odor of his emptied bowels carried on the slight breeze. Ahiga slithered back to his horse, and this time approached the camp, looking down at the dead. The man's scalp had been taken; blood soaked his face. Yet . . . he had been shot just once, in his head. This was not the Apache way, but white men don't scalp—most of the time.

Frowning, Ahiga made his way to the wagon and saw that all the supplies had been emptied. As for the other men, there was no sign. If they'd left possessions behind, it had all been taken. With a grunt, Ahiga turned and took off toward the fort, scanning the cliffs for signs of life and seeing none. Something terrible was coming, the spirits had warned him, and the message scrawled in flesh and blood. Alongside the corpse, one word was traced by a blood-soaked finger into the packed sand:

CURSED

"Captain, the Injun has a report," Corporal Hawes said sleepily, interrupting Kellerman at his desk where he wrote in a logbook by lantern light.

"The 'Injun' has a name and a role, Corporal. We are all soldiers here, and you'll do well to remember it. Send him in."

Kellerman watched Ahiga as he came in and immediately became alarmed. The scout was a stoic man, rarely showing fear or pain or any other emotion with much vigor, but he looked pale and ill at ease in the flickering light. "This won't be good news, will it? You look like you saw a ghost. Tell me."

"I scouted the gang camp and found only one man. Dead. Scalped. The rest are missing along with the horses and mule. Many tracks in the sand and the wagon empty of cargo. Nothing but an empty coffee pot on a dead fire, no bedrolls."

"Damn it, Ahiga, that's close. We knew a fight was coming per my orders to start one, but I thought we had more time. What direction did they depart in?" He opened his desk drawer and took out a bottle of whiskey, downing a shot then pouring a second.

"East, Captain." Ahiga pointed toward the whiskey. "Might you offer me one of those, sir?"

Kellerman's eyes widened in surprise, knowing his scout to be a teetotaler as a rule, but he pulled out a second glass, filled it and slid it across the desk without a word. Ahiga drank it in one gulp. "Watch your drinking, Ahiga."

"Yes, sir. The dead man is not why I am looking like I have seen a ghost, sir."

Kellerman waited, then, "Well?"

"On the ride there, I witnessed bad omens. Then at the camp, beside the dead white man, someone had drawn an English word in blood. It said only CURSED."

The men sat in contemplative silence for a moment, as Kellerman weighed his options. They'd survived the attack on the fort by Comancheros and Comanche led by Santiago Miguel Lozado by the skin of their teeth, with help from a few named guns and Second Lieutenant Cranston's Mexican hussars. Now, Sherman expected them to put a stop to the roving bands of Apache on their way into Sonora, but between the smallpox family and the attack on the hunter's camp, the captain had a feeling they'd be fighting the warriors on their own turf. "What say you, Ahiga, give me your opinion. Was this an Apache kill? Will they strike the fort?"

"Apache are what white men call 'notional,' sir. Hard to guess what they will do. The men have been making reports of hearing drums at night, yet we see no fire. There were many tracks at the camp, but the man had been shot before they took his scalp. They did not give him an honorable death; it was a quick business and would bring shame to the warrior who killed him. I think that, yes, the ones who did it will likely attack, but . . . I suspect a white man attacked the hunters. They looped their footsteps making it seem like many red hands, yet they did not perform as Apache would. I do think Indians will attack. When that will be I cannot say, and maybe not the fort. But they will attack somewhere."

Kellerman stood, "Let's hope it won't be us, or tonight."

"Well, we knew it was inevitable. Poor timing to have civilians digging up our parade ground I must say." Sergeant Major Saul Olinger sat behind his desk, having been apprised an hour before by the Navajo scout of the bad tidings. He and Kellerman had given their orders, then retired to Saul's office for bourbon. "Look on the bright side, Joe, letting them come here saves us a trip. We've fought off tougher villains than a few roving Apache."

Kellerman took out the makings and rolled a cigarette. "Yes, at a cost."

"There's always a price to be paid for the honor of defending our great nation against the heathens." Saul smiled knowingly and Kellerman returned it.

"I pity the nation if our troops of raggedy-assed scoundrels are the thin line between salvation and a fall into the hands of the heathens."

The sergeant major grinned, clean white teeth bright in his florid face. Then he called, "Come in," to a knock at the door. Lieutenant James Hall stepped in, with a crisp salute, his magnificent beard gleaming in the light of the oil lamp. "At ease, Lieutenant," Kellerman said,

"Pour a bourbon—soldier's rotgut since we don't all have loving mamas like you. But you'll need it."

Hall didn't need to be told twice. "Thank you, sir,"

Another *rap-rap-rap* at the door. "Yes, come in," Kellerman barked.

Second Lieutenant Atticus Cranston stepped inside and saluted his commanding officers. The normal spit-polished West Point shine was off him. He looked as though he'd been rudely awakened.

"At ease," Kellerman said, gesturing to the bourbon.

"You scoundrel, you scallywag, were you asleep, Lieutenant?" Hall said, pulling his snuffbox from his pocket.

"Yes, sir. Sorry, sir." Cranston took the bourbon and drank it in one gulp.

"Watch your drinking, Cranston," Olinger said.

"Yes, sir."

Kellerman sighed, "The situation is thus: the Navajo scout found one of the Bean men scalped, the word CURSED written in his blood in the sand."

"That's Dean, sir," Cranston supplied.

"Thank you, he found one of the Dean men scalped, their wagon emptied, the word CURSED, and no trace of the rest of the Fey-Feys."

"That's the Trey-Treys," Olinger said, suppressing a laugh.

Kellerman waved his hand, "Yes, them—no trace. Ahiga tells me that it seemed like the attack of a white man, staged to incriminate the Apache. I tend to agree, but our troops report drums in the night, so we know the Apache are close. A decision must be made on how to handle the Apache threat, and it needs to be made now.

General Sherman is confident in our ability to cut them off at the pass as they head into Sonora, but I admit that I think he overestimates our resources, and I suspect they plan on attacking us before they head to the Rio Bravo. Scalping the hunter is a warning, the bloody word was meant to trigger off superstitious nonsense, and we can be sure that white or red, they're testing the waters. Eight-and-forty men here, how many can fight well and stand firm in the face of Apache warriors?"

Saul poured another round, "Thirty or so solid men, Captain, the rest . . . They're not gunmen, that is certain. But they are hard, and ready to fight. And they've taken a shine to Cranston it seems. The legend of his hussars has gone down in the annals of Fort Benjamin Grierson as a true achievement that saved our hides."

All eyes fell on the young lieutenant, "That was a one-off, sir, and I am short now of Mexicans. I can try, sir, but—"

"But nothing," Hall interrupted. "Never have I seen a man take rabble and turn them into the kind of force that you did. Bully for young Cranston! Hero of the day! We sent those lowdown dirty Comancheros fleeing—the few that survived, that is. You can do it again, no doubt."

"Very few survived," Cranston said.

"Exactly! Huzzah!" Hall cheered, and the rest raised their glasses in toast.

"Sirs, those were Mexicans with a reason to fight. What have we now?"

"Well, for a start you have men who likely don't

want to die, scoundrels though they may be," Olinger began.

A *rap-rap-rap* came at the door again, and the officers exchanged a glance before Kellerman blared, "Enter."

Tobias Zimmermann entered, his movement stiff and tired. "Begging your pardon, sirs, at this late hour."

Kellerman waved a hand. "Cranston, give Mr. Zimmermann your chair."

The young lieutenant scampered up and made way, and Zimmermann nodded his thanks.

"Snuff? Anyone?" Hall stood and offered. Tobias accepted with a caveat: "Thank you, but one word of it gets to Mrs. Zimmermann and I'll shoot off your big toe. Understood?"

Hall blanched and shifted uncomfortably. "Understood."

"Cranston pour this man a bourbon, he looks peaked," Kellerman commanded. Tobias Zimmermann did look drawn and tired. He carried the warm scent of sawdust, and a patch of tar clung stubbornly between his left thumb and forefinger. He downed the bourbon in one shot and then sighed. "I had an idea, Joe, but you're not going to like it. Well, two ideas, both that you won't like a bit."

A moment of silence passed and then: "Back in the days before I became a noble carpenter for the United States Army, I used to sell my gun. One shootist is equal to ten of the rabble you have out there. We need men who can shoot, accurately, and fast, and what you have is a group of hard cases. Yes, they'll fight, most of them anyway, but you need men who can shoot."

The room was warm and smelled of sweat, leather, and bourbon, yet underneath it the waxed shine of Saul's desk gave off a clinical odor and shone brightly in the lamplight, its glow reflecting on the tired men, turning their faces shiny and red. Not a speck of dust could be found on any surface, and Kellerman often wondered how Olinger managed to keep the stink of the stables out, declaring Olinger's office clean enough to eat off the floor. It made him a bit shamefaced that as captain, he managed to maintain a certain grubby charm in his own quarters, but he was far too busy for routine tidying, and Mrs. Zimmermann rarely made it a point to shine up his office the way she favorited those who in her estimation were decent Christian men—primarily her husband and the sergeant major.

"Well, give it to me, then, Tobias. I may not like it, but I want to hear it."

Tobias rubbed at the tar stain and took a deep breath. "First, the civilians. Old and frail though they may be, we need to train them up as good as we can. When the attack comes, it'll do us no good to have three men, no, four, counting the Chinese fella, plus a woman, squealing like pigs while Apaches run through us like a tornado. Especially the woman—you know what will become of her. My wife would go down swinging but the girl . . ." Zimmermann poured a drink. "Then, and this is the part you'll really hate—"

Kellerman was growing impatient and tapped his glass as he glared at Tobias. "Get on with it."

"We beat back Santiago and his Comancheros by a hair, and we had the Mexican hussars, but we also had gunfighters. If they're still alive, we have access to shootists again, bad men, but good with a gun. Do you understand what I'm suggesting?"

Groaning, Kellerman closed his eyes. "You want to bring in the Fey-Fey men, to this fort, as if I don't have enough to worry about?"

"That's the Trey-Treys, sir," Hall said.

"Thank you, Lieutenant. You are right. I don't like it one bit, Tobias. If they're still alive, I doubt their intentions were ever truly hunting sheep. And we can't spare the men to go find them in the cliffs. They could be anywhere."

Atticus Cranston perked up. "Sir, they've lost all their supplies and their camp was raided. I don't think we have to find them. They'll find us."

The room fell silent, as a fierce wind picked up outside, the howling echoing through the room like souls crying out from purgatory and sending a chill down Kellerman's spine.

"That's what I'm afraid of, Atticus."

CHAPTER 15

The night had come on cold, a stiff wind in the cliffs that froze a man to the bones, but Lucas Dean forbade a campfire for fear of attracting unwanted attention. A dead bighorn lay stiffening alongside the rocky outcropping the Trey-Treys huddled under, providing a buffer against the worst of the icy wind gusts but adding a ripe, gamey odor to the scene. The five men sat with their backs against the rock, grumbling about wanting a fire and hot coffee, but their complaints fell on deaf ears.

"Cold camp, and that's final," Dean said.

"Boss, you gotta let us have a small fire or we'll die up here," Adam Louis said, through chattering teeth.

Dean looked around at his gang. The men were miserable and freezing, whining like schoolgirls. Yet, truth be told, Dean was also suffering, and as the temperature kept plummeting, he wondered if they'd be able to survive the night without a fire. He'd watched from up high as a pistolero had taken out Dick Freedman, then paused to scalp the old man. The shootist had wanted it to look like an Indian attack, but Dean saw a man oddly dressed in finery that stood out against the landscape like a sore thumb and he knew it wasn't an Apache attack. They had come, though, and seized all the belongings left in the wagon and supplies scattered about before scurrying away. The Trey-Treys had heard the war drums at night like everyone else and were on alert, but the attack on his camp seemed targeted, intentional, far removed from an Indian raid. The half dozen Indians who had stolen the supplies were mostly women in their long-skirted clothes, though their mates were liable to be nearby and waiting, a fact that made Dean wary of giving away their mountaintop location. He had also watched as the army scout surveyed the scene and performed some sort of dance before he left in a mighty big hurry.

Scanning the horizon, he could barely see Fort Benjamin Grierson. Its flickering fires and lanterns rose from the gloom like will-o'-the-wisps above the bogs of his father's Irish homeland. Occasionally, a light would be enveloped by shadow. It seemed the soldiers were wide awake and preparing for a battle, against whom he couldn't say.

Sighing, Dean flicked his green eyes from man to man and knew they were right. The temperature was dropping rapidly, and their shelter provided only a slight windbreak. A fire would warm the stone walls behind them, and they could cook some of the sheep to fill their bellies with warmth.

"Fine, a small fire, close enough to warm the cliff face—and one of you skin the legs on the sheep and let's roast them. Chances are the men who raided our camp are to bed and won't be bothering us at this god-forsaken hour. But you're gonna have to take turns on guard duty. I catch you sleeping then, you'll never wake again as I'll put a bullet in your brain as easy as dotting an *i*. You savvy?"

Nods all around, then Adam Louis, a tall, thin man who moved like a coiled snake, rose to his feet, saying, "Get the fire lit fast before we freeze." He pointed to another man. "Ike, help me find more wood."

As the two men headed off to a deadfall that looked promising, Nicky Barnes studied Dean with his cold black eyes, then went to work skinning the sheep. Frank Abilene said nothing and selected a long piece of wood to carve with his heavy hunting knife, fashioning the spit.

They made short work of building the fire and soon had a bighorn leg roasting on the spit, the fat drippings making the fire pop and hiss. The cliff walls warmed and became cozy enough to keep the chill away, and drowsiness set in after the men had eaten their fill.

Dean was lost in thought, taking slow drags off a cigarette and watching the smoke curl into a cobalt sky that looked like velvet sewn with diamonds and pearls. Finally, he sighed deeply, and said, "We need help—there's little choice in the matter. That fort is our only salvation. You all need to be on your best behavior and continue pretending to be mild-mannered hunters, although the hard, clever men posted up there won't buy it. Think on it some tonight. Create your stories and learn how to grin like you're greeting kissin' cousins."

Adam scowled. "You want to run scared from a man who gunned down an old drunk and a few thieves?"

Lucas Dean scowled back. "You really are an idiot—anyone ever tell you that outside of me? We can defend against pistoleros and squaws, but they raided our supplies, and we'll starve to death out here long before the time comes to retrieve any treasure. And them squaws likely have mates—I feel like they're watching us right now." He shivered and took a deep drag off his burning cigarette. "Unless you want to try surviving off of sheep meat, or robbing a Union fort filled with criminals and madmen, I suggest you get yourself in line and at least try to behave human. It's an easy in. The scout saw the state of things and will have reported it back, so they know we ain't making up stories for the sake of an invitation to the mess hall. Shut up and sleep. I'll take first watch. Keep one ear open, boys. This ain't a casual camping excursion anymore."

CHAPTER 16

Two nights after the word CURSED had been scribbled in blood beside a dead man, the darkness had come upon the fort heavy and thick with the scent of creosote. Traversing through the dark terrain with lantern aloft, Private Grimes carefully made his way toward the small campfire flickering in the distance. It was his turn to relieve the man guarding Private Johnson, and the duty spooked him through and through. "Rather be on latrine duty," he muttered, the cool evening breeze raising a chill on his flesh that made him shudder. He approached the site to find no guard. Kellerman would tan the man's hide if he found out. "Hello?" he called, but there came no reply. Unnerved, he stepped over the fence and went to the edge of the pit Johnson had dug to serve as a quarantine zone. Johnson looked to be sleeping, his feet stuck out from the canvas pup tent alongside the warm fire. A cooking pot sat by the fire's edge, half filled with a murky looking salt-beef broth. Not far from the barebones camp, Grimes could see the shallow graves that covered the dead Indians and hastily crossed himself. Why the odd little man hadn't just dragged the corpses all the way out into the desert Grimes couldn't fathom, and he wondered if the coyotes had sniffed out their own buried treasure yet. "Johnson," he called, not so loud as to wake the man from a sound sleep on account of not wanting to listen to the long list of grievances Private Johnson had been reportedly droning on about to his other watchmen. No reply. With a grunt, Grimes backed up to sit against the fence, his rifle laid across his lap, and he pulled open a scary book called *The Woman in White* to read his night away until his relief would arrive at dawn.

Two hours had passed when at a particularly thrilling moment in his novel, a sound came that set his hair on end. "*UuuhHhhhnnnn*" came the sound, out of the darkness in the direction of the dead Indians. Grimes dropped the book and snatched his lantern and rifle, pushing the light over toward the pit with a shaking hand. "John—son—?" he called, hating the crack in his voice.

"*Mooaauuuuuuhhhnnn*" came the sound again, then even louder, "*MooOOAAHHHHHHHNNnnUUUNnnn.*"

Private Grimes gulped, then carefully tiptoed through the loose sand to get as near the tent as he safely could. He used his rifle to push aside the flap and his jaw dropped at what he saw inside. Private Johnson was broken out in boils, black centers leaking fluid that reeked of decay. His eyes were slits, pushed down by the vile afflictions that covered his face and grew across the edges of his mouth and nostrils. Torrents of sweat poured across the man's face and muddled with pus to drip like tears upon his chest. Each breath produced an odd whistling noise as the air drew in around the bulbous pox. "Kuhll . . . *Kill* me," he begged, staring intently into Grimes's eyes. "Can't take the pain—dying anyway—just kill . . . me." Johnson began crying, gasping with pain as the salt of his tears fell into the weeping sores across his face. Grimes stepped back.

"I— I should get the captain. I can't just kill you or he'll hang me for murder," he said, a tremor in his young voice.

Johnson slapped his hand on the soaked and soiled wool blanket, "Damn it, boy, it ain't murder when a man is begging it. Please don't let me die over days like this. Mrs. Zimmermann sent me laudanum, and it ain't made a spot of difference. I'd do it myself, but that is a grave sin—I'd be sent to hell. If you do it my soul is clean—don't you see, boy?"

Johnson grasped for his Colt and with a shaking hand weakly pointed it at Grimes, the boils on his hand making the cold iron burn like fire against his palm.

"Here, look here. If you ain't kill me, I'm gonna kill you. So, you shoot me now and it was self-defense, Kellerman can't take offense to that."

When Grimes made no reply nor motion, Johnson cocked the hammer and released another wail of pain before leveling the revolver at the young private's head with what was left of his strength, "All right, then, you asked for it . . . Ten—nine—eight—seven—"

Blam!

It took a single shot to the head to end the lifetime of misery that had cumulated in throes of unbearable suffering before death, as though Johnson was sent to hell on earth while still alive. Grimes had never shot a man at close range before and sank to his knees, sick in the sand. Somewhere out in the distance the mournful call of an owl swept through the night, and Grimes scampered to his feet and ran to inform his captain of what had occurred.

Captain Kellerman was unhappy to be rousted from his bed, where enough whiskey had finally pulled him down into a fitful sleep. Wide awake and ornery, he now took in the shaking, pale private who had come to interrupt his slumber. "And who was it you were to relieve, Private Grimes?"

"I—I don't know, sir. My orders were to supervise Private Johnson at gunpoint until dawn when my relief would arrive. There was nobody but Johnson when I got there."

"I see. I'll find out. It's the middle of the night. We will leave the corpse where it lies until dawn and then a detail will burn the body and all the bedding. The last thing we need is a smallpox outbreak in this fort. Did you touch Johnson, or any of his belongings, be truthful because if I find you lied, you'll hang."

"No! No, I didn't touch anything, sir."

"Good lad," Kellerman put a comforting hand on the young private's shoulder and steered him to the door. "Go see Mrs. Zimmermann, she will give you prayers and perhaps a sleeping draught. First man you've killed, son?"

Private Grimes nodded. "Yes, sir, and I did not want to but was given no choice."

"There is small choice in rotten apples, Private. Sleep it off and forget. I need you at full strength tomorrow."

With that the young private left, allowing Kellerman to collapse back into his cot, the straw mattress lumpy and itchy, yet still comfortable enough to allow his spine to decompress with a pleasant burning ache. Groaning, he rolled onto his left side and closed his eyes, praying sleep would return.

Chapter 17

"In the name of the Father, and of the Son, and of the Holy Spirit. Amen."

Father Staszczyk stood at the edge of the sand-filled pit, where a funeral pyre had been quickly put together by Tobias Zimmermann. The high desert winds whipped his cassock and made him look like a vulture lingering above the dead. A small gathering joined him, forming a circle and keeping their distance from the pox-covered corpse of Private Johnson. Mrs. Zimmermann had carefully covered herself from head to toe, a scarf wrapped across her face, and thick gloves protecting her small hands, and had wound the dead man in a white sheet. Two young soldiers, also covered well, had carefully grabbed the ends of the sheet in spots that had not made contact with the body and gingerly lifted Private Johnson to the short pyre, where he now waited, still and cold.

"I am the resurrection and the life, says the Lord: he that believeth in me, though he were dead, yet shall he live: and whosoever live and believe in me shall never die. Let us pray:

"Grant us, with all who have died in the hope of resurrection, to have our consummation and bliss in thy eternal and everlasting glory, and with the blessed Virgin Mary and all thy saints, to receive the crown of life which thou dost promise to all who share in the victory of thy Son Jesus Christ; who lives and reigns with thee in the unity of the Holy Spirit, one God, for ever and ever. Amen."

Staszczyk motioned to Mrs. Zimmermann, and she handed him a small glass bottle of holy water. He sprinkled the water atop the shrouded corpse, flinging the water from a distance, "With this water we call to mind—uh, what was the name of this man?"

"Jebediah Johnson, Father," Second Lieutenant Cranston said.

"With this water we call to mind Jebediah Johnson's baptism. As Christ went through the deep waters of death for us, so may he bring Jebediah Johnson to the fullness of resurrection and life with all the redeemed. Amen."

"Amen," murmured the graveside mourners.

"Like as a father has pity on his own children: even so is the Lord merciful unto them that fear him. For he knows whereof we are made: he remembers that we are but dust. The days of man are but as grass: for he flourishes as a flower of the field. For as soon as the wind goes over it, it is gone: and the place thereof shall know it no more. But the merciful goodness of the Lord endures forever and ever upon them that fear him: and his righteousness upon children's children.

"Rest eternal grant unto them, O Lord: and let light perpetual shine upon them. Amen."

The priest nodded to Kellerman, who opened his lantern and lit the soaked rag top of his torch, turning to light the funeral pyre and the ends of the sheets. He tossed the torch into the base of the pyre as flames began to flick high into the sky. Kellerman then went to the tent and lit it ablaze, noting that the well-loved photo of Daisy Mae, Johnson's beloved gal now began to curl at the edges and dissolve. Kellerman was eager to get back to his office and shot a meaningful glare at the priest, but the man studiously ignored him and started up again.

"Ashes to ashes, dust to dust. May almighty God have mercy on us, forgive us our sins, and brings us to everlasting life. Amen."

"Amen."

The crowd seized their moment to escape and began to wander off to their duties. Only Mrs. Zimmermann remained, kneeling with her rosary, and praying for the soul of Jebediah Johnson with all the love and charity she could muster, which, were she honest, wasn't much. The flames began to roar up into the sky, spurred on by the wind, and with that the whole ordeal was over.

"It was a crackerjack funeral, I'd say. Johnson sent off like a Viking! Jolly good show," Lieutenant Hall said brightly, taking a pinch of snuff.

Professor Fernsby frowned at him. "Actually, the Viking funeral was a more elaborate—"

He was cut off by Hall. "Professor, let me enjoy my imagination. Pinch of snuff?"

Paul Fernsby considered. "You know what? Yes,

please. I shall consider it an anthropological study." He took the snuff and inhaled it sharply, sending him into a coughing and sneezing fit until his cheeks turned purple. "Interesting," he managed between coughs.

Kellerman scanned the archaeologist. "This morning, Lieutenant Atticus Cranston will take you under his wing and teach you to shoot. You'll have to set the digging aside for a day. This is far more important than lost gold."

A few murmured protests came from the men, but Constance's eyes lit up with excitement. "Me too, Captain?" she asked hopefully.

"Especially you. Women can become ruthless shootists, given the chance, and I do hope you're one of them." He left off the details of what would become of her if the Apaches took her alive, knowing her only salvation would be a self-inflicted bullet to the brain.

Julias Dankworth spoke up. "I was at one time a fine hunter, I'll have it known. Deer, rabbit, once even a grizzly bear. I'm ready."

A loud, unpleasant snort filled the room and brought silence, as heads turned to look at the offending party, Berryman, snooty as always. "My dear soldiers, I am a man of great intellect. I am here to seek out historical artifacts that could change the course of history, yet you dare to tell me I must drop my work to become part of your defense against the hostiles. I say not. It was promised to me that I would be well defended at this fort so as to better complete my highly scientific studies in peace. Men of my caliber do not participate in bloodshed and battle. The rest of you may go on without me, but I will continue my work alone until the rest of this team comes to their senses. Taking up arms was not part of my plan, and I steadfastly refuse."

A deep stillness filled the room at this display of insubordination to the post commander, with wide-eyed glances exchanged by heads that did not move. Young Atticus Cranston's hand froze halfway to his mouth, a biscuit dripping honey. Only Lieutenant Hall looked positively gleeful and indulged in his snuff yet again.

Kellerman wiped his face carefully with a napkin, then slowly pushed his chair out, the wood dragging across the floor sounding like a terrible demented train engine in the silence. He stood to his full height. Carefully he made his way to Berryman's chair with a smile that did not reach his eyes. He placed his hand on Berryman's head and turned the man to face him, pinning him hard enough that the man's cheeks turned ruddy purple. With a wolfish grin he stared into the professor's eyes. "Do you see me, Professor? Look me in the eye. Yes, yes, right in the eye. If you refuse to take up arms training with the lieutenant, then you will have found your archaeology career cut terribly short. You see, right now, I could snap your thin bird neck as if you're one of Mrs. Zimmermann's chickens about to be fried up for supper. We have plenty of sand dunes out here. Your frail corpse would receive the full mummification experience—scientific—a glimpse at the Egyptians, wouldn't it be? Oh, you'll be dead and unable to write the understanding of it down, but I suppose fifty years from now some ranny may stumble across you and look. Why, he'll sell you for a small fortune, I'd say, Professor, and they'll display you in a traveling show. But"—he pretended to rethink the matter—"a snapped neck would be too kind. I may instead stake you to an ant hill and let them eat you down to bones—a new, clean, specimen I can send off to a museum. You'd like to be in a museum, would you not? Given your superior intellect and determination."

Kellerman squeezed harder, causing uncontrollable tears to fall from the man's glaring eyes as his lips puckered unnaturally from the pressure. "I am Captain Peter Joseph Kellerman. Nothing happens in Fort Benjamin Grierson unless I bid it done, and nothing I bid done doesn't happen without grave consequence. Now I bid you join Second Lieutenant Atticus Cranston, our shiny West Point graduate, who has proven his worth time and time again. He will teach you, you will listen, and if I find that you are ignoring his commands, he will return you to me."

Kellerman released his hands and Berryman gasped for air, his muddled face pale against the dark red imprints of the captain's hand. Kellerman clapped his hands sharply. "Atticus, keep special watch on this one. At the first sign of trouble release him to me."

Atticus nodded. "Yes, sir."

Berryman drew in a breath as though he were about to unleash a fresh tirade, but a swift kick beneath the table by Dankworth stopped him and he closed his mouth and pouted with eyes lowered. The tension over, the room erupted into sound, as biscuits were passed and coffee was sipped. Mrs. Zimmermann apologized for a lack of plum duff but delivered a tray of very welcome corn cookies to cheers.

"Training begins at dawn, Cranston. You will mold these men, and this lady, into fighters. If the trouble passes, they are welcome to return to their dig in my parade ground, but I expect a full report by dusk about your progress."

Atticus Cranston poured a bourbon and downed it. "Yes, Captain, as you wish, sir."

Hall made a *tsk-tsk* sound. "Watch your drinking, Atticus."

Cranston snapped off a salute. "Yes, sir."

CHAPTER 18

At dawn, Second Lieutenant Atticus Cranston had assembled not only the professors and their servant but a few of the weakest members of the fort troops, lining them up and teaching them military authority. Berryman wore a sour expression, but Constance was aglow with excitement, as Fernsby fidgeted nervously beside her.

Cranston handed each man an unloaded rifle with a bayonet. "Rifles and guns are convenient for long range, but most fighting will come in fast and close, and the bayonet is to discourage an approach or to be used as needed. I've set up these sacks of straw, I want you to spend the morning charging dummies with your bayonet as though your life depended upon it. Indeed, in a real fight, it may just be so."

With the assistance of Mr. Zimmermann, Atticus had built fifteen bad men fighting dummies. They looked rather like scarecrows in the morning light aside from the sloppily painted red circles upon their burlap straw stuffed middles.

"I will count to five," Cranston called, "then you attack. Ready? 1—2—3—4—*Five!*"

Constance charged with her bayonet, quickly dispatching three strikes in a row. Berryman approached and stuck a dummy once in the middle of the red circle, then stood there, looking around with his lip curled into a sneer. Fernsby, despite all his hesitation about violence, charged the dummy with war cries and stabbed so violently, the straw began leaking out. Dankworth took a few attempts to hit the target, while Chan stabbed the dummy with slow precision. The twelve soldiers did their duty and charged swiftly before retreating, bayonet still pointed ahead as though the scarecrow might attack at any moment.

"Excellent first attempt. Again."

Atticus's troop began again, and so it was for thirty minutes, until he finally called for them to halt.

"Now, we will try your marksmanship." He led the troop to a long table and had them lay out their rifles. Tobias Zimmermann set to work adding canvas sack heads to the dummies, painting smiley and frowny faces in black before circling the outline in red.

A storm was blowing up, the desert not done with being fickle just yet this season, and Ahiga watched from his post in deep thought. Great billowing black clouds formed ridges in the skies as the fierce wind picked up, throwing dust and debris across the spot where Atticus Cranston commenced his training. Bad medicine, Ahiga thought, but said nothing.

As the heavens opened, Cranston and his troop were soon soaked to the bone, and when Berryman loudly squawked his protest, the second lieutenant pointed at him and quickly said but two words: "Ant hill." Soon silence fell once again.

"The enemy cares not about weather, or that your Meemaw has just died, or that your knee is sore. The enemy is ruthless and cunning, and now you will become ruthless and cunning yourselves. Rifles loaded, men and lady? Good. Fire at will.

"Not bad. Again!"

CHAPTER 19

Lucas Dean was cold, wet, and ornery. "We go to the fort, now, today. Anyone got a problem with it?" he said, stretching his tight limbs, as the rising sun struggled to peek through in shades of pink and orange that the gathering steel clouds fought to keep hidden.

"Yeah, I got a problem. What if they open fire?" Frank said coldly, surveying the unfriendly landscape.

"They won't. The Army doesn't make a habit of opening fire on civilians without asking questions first. They may still believe we are but mere hunters who have been met with an unfortunate attack at the hands of outlaws. Let's try to hit a mule deer or another sheep on the way down. We collect the wagon and horses and load poor old Dick into the back, so the soldiers can see how unjustly we have suffered. Then we simply ride in hands up and smiling, no trouble at all."

Blam!

"Good grief, a little warning," Dean snapped.

"Got your sheep—you may as well be a bit grateful," Nicky Barnes said.

Dean rubbed his head with both hands. "I got a

headache and need coffee. Least I have these." He took out the makings and rolled a cigarette, inhaling with a satisfied sigh.

"All right, let's get rolling. Put the sheep, and what is left of the other on a horse. I'll walk down. We approach the wagon with caution and then light a shuck, no farting around."

The trip down the cliffs and valleys was treacherous, the mud making for slick surfaces and unexpected slips. Nicky ended up sliding down on his rear twenty feet, yelling all the way, and he wasn't letting anyone hear the end of it. But finally, the men reached the desert floor and, with guns drawn, approached the site of their old camp. The stench of death was overpowering, and they pulled bandanas over their noses, as Dean toed over the rotting corpse to see his bloodstained face. "Guess he got the death that he deserved. None of our concern now."

"You still want to load him up, boss?"

"Shoot, no, I don't want to, but . . . I don't trust the scout's report—and remember, we are seeking sympathy here. So, sorry, boys, go on and load the wagon with the sheep, and slop Dick in there far away from them as you can, and get your horses harnessed. Scoundrels took everything we had, and Dick probably had it coming, but what did I ever do to deserve such an outrage against my own soul?"

"Well that one time over in—" Ike began.

"Oh, shut up, Ike—that was a rhetorical question. Now remember, we ride in grinning like we are recruiting for church. Nice and slow."

Nicky Barnes obliged, unbothered and calm despite

the swarming buzz of fat black flies and cloying odor, but Ike frowned, mulling over the meaning of the word *rhetorical*.

Wagon loaded with their game and former gangmate, the Trey-Treys took off in the direction of the fort feeling a bit apprehensive. Dean was more optimistic, since this was to be their destination ultimately, anyway, and though it was coming on a bit sooner, maybe the incident had made for the perfect excuse to get in and out without being shot at.

"Riders coming." The watchman on duty, Private Steve Silversmith, called out, the message quickly spreading down the line. Soon, Kellerman's door banged open with a thud, and he sauntered out to take in the sight of the men on horseback and their wooden wagon.

"Looks like Saul was right, sir," Hall added helpfully, earning him a glare from Kellerman.

"That's Sergeant Major, to you, Hall."

"Looks like Sergeant Major Saul Olinger, hero and gentleman, was right, sir."

Kellerman briefly ducked back into his office and downed two shots of bourbon in quick succession, lighting a cigarette as well. A doctor had told him this was the cure for his chronic headaches, and he clung to the belief like a life raft.

The men pulled their wagon to a stop and dismounted, all of them grinning and being careful to keep their hands away from their guns. Kellerman walked to Lucas Dean and eyed him suspiciously, while the rest of the Trey-Treys hung back near their wagon. Their black clothing mixed with the horrific smell and cloud of black flies that surrounded the wagon made the men look like riders come up from Hades against the background of an angry dark sky.

"You the boss man?" Dean said pleasantly, his eyes crinkling at the corners with a bright smile as he tried to sell the appearance of an innocent man met with misfortune.

"Captain Joseph Kellerman, yes. I heard you may have had some trouble at your camp."

"That's a word for it, all right. We left a man to watch our supplies while hunting for bighorn, which we successfully snagged two of, you may be interested to know. Poor fellow was shot dead and scalped, and our wagon emptied. This isn't a hospitable territory for men with no accoutrements, and we are worried the savages might return, so I wisely thought the noble U.S. Army might be willing to help."

Ahiga had approached, a .44-40 Henry cradled in his arms, his bare chest gleaming bronze in the sun and his eyes narrowing as he took in the group. Dean flicked his eyes toward Ahiga with an unsettled look before returning his attention to Kellerman.

"How many are you?" Kellerman asked.

"Five now that old Dick is dead, and I promise we won't be any trouble."

"I doubt that very much. However, if you're willing to earn your keep, we will take you in as refugees—but understand that we have little by way of provisions, and I'm already burdened by another set of—*guests*. We expect Apache trouble, and I need shootists with sand, and you'll be thrown in with a hive of villains—although the intelligence I've received tells me that you're not upstanding citizens yourselves."

Dean feigned a frown, but his green eyes sparkled with humor. "I am hurt by your lack of faith, Captain. We are merely humble men searching for a bit of recreational enjoyment and have fallen upon hard times. We do have skills with a gun, though, and are happy to assist. As for provisions, I've got fresh meat in the wagon if you're not picky." He thumbed over his shoulder toward the sheep. "I'm afraid that what you're smelling is old Dick Freedman, now deceased. We didn't think it would be right to leave his corpse to rot out in the desert on account of how he is a fellow Christian and all."

As though God took offense to the sentiment, the heavens split open with a roar of thunder and the rain began pouring heavily in sheets, as lightning danced across the sky. At once the gathered audience began to disperse back to their duties, teeth chattering from the shockingly chilly raindrops.

"Mrs. Zimmermann will be pleased to have mutton, I'd say. Private Silversmith will show you where to drop off your dead to the care of Father Sta—Stac—"

"Father Staszczyk, sir," Private Silversmith supplied.

"Thank you, Private. Take your game to the kitchen and then we will see about getting you settled. Private, make sure the father informs Mr. Zimmermann of the need for a box."

As the men left for the kitchen, Ahiga quickly stepped in to speak to Kellerman. "They are bad men, Captain.

No good," he said, watching their retreating forms with narrowed eyes.

Kellerman followed his gaze. "I agree, but I do need men who can shoot. Watch them, report straight to me or Sergeant Major Olinger if you find out to what length of 'no good' they are."

CHAPTER 20

Day passed into night, as the sun sank like a hot iron ball into the steel gray horizon, and the still-leaden clouds that lingered above the fort made the air muggy and thick. Kellerman prepared himself to head for supper with a splash of water onto his sweaty face, plucking the damp and uncomfortable fabric of his shirt off his skin. A sound of thundering hooves approaching outside sent a prickle up his neck in the darkness of his room, the lamps yet unlit, shades of orange and yellow, like fire cast through the windows from the falling sun, in erratic patterns that danced with the heavy shadows. "Now what," he grumbled, patting his face dry with a scratchy towel and stepping out into the sunset.

A rider in crisp uniform approached with a salute. "Captain, new recruits for you."

The young soldier stepped down, and Kellerman eyed him warily. "Who've they sent me this time?"

The soldier pulled a neatly folded sheet of paper from his pocket and began the rundown, as behind him, under the watchful eye of two Buffalo Soldiers cradling their rifles and a white whiskered old-timer with pistol drawn, a ragtag group exited two wagons with iron-barred windows and looked around curiously.

"Sir, Corporal Wilhelm Stockton. Assault." The young soldier gestured to one of the men, continuing, "Private Billy Burt, that's the yellow haired fella, petty theft. Private Howard Smythe, desertion, possibly more but not proven. Corporal Edgar Wayne, assaulting an officer. And—well, Frederick Mann, sir. Dereliction of duty. You should know something about him, though. He calls himself 'Jesus.' Won't reply to any other name and—well, that is where the dereliction part came in—refuses to take up arms. Something about refusing violence. We have had a helluva time with getting him here, sir. At one point he claimed to see an apparition in the clouds and wouldn't eat for two days."

Kellerman appraised the men and immediately picked out "Jesus" from the lineup. The man was young and had long flowing hair that draped his shoulders and a beard that reached his chest. His uniform appeared generally unwashed, and he had a dazed look in his eyes that reflected insanity.

"Welcome to Fort Benjamin Grierson. I'm your captain, Peter Joseph Kellerman. You men have chosen Hell, and I can say no more plainly than that but to warn you that, scoundrels though you may be, I run this fort fairly. In the interest of that fairness, let it be known here and now that I have hanged five men and have no qualms about adding"—he paused and counted heads with a wave of his finger—"five more to the tally. I do not tolerate acts of villainy on this ground. Be on your best behavior, and you might just survive long enough to serve your time here and live out the rest of your life in peace. Understood?"

With little enthusiasm the men replied, "Hear, hear! Sir," and "Yes, sir!"—though their posture revealed disquieted minds.

"Very good. Private Jacks will show you to your quarters and make certain of your provisions. Put your kit away quickly as you're just in time for supper. Jacks." Kellerman waved his hand toward the private, who saluted crisply and then got to the work of settling the men into their new home. As they retrieved their bundles from their transport, the men spoke in hushed, disturbed whispers. A terrible storm was once again gathering to the east, and now the thick black roiling waves in the sky turned into gales that threatened dust storms and heavy rains.

Kellerman turned back to the young soldier. "I must insist your party bunk down here for the night. You fellows head out into a dust storm and you'll never be seen again—and believe me, if you lose against nature, the Army will decide from the start that it was all my fault. Come along, let's find you a place to rest, and then you can head out once the weather is clear."

The young soldier, having heard tales of the horrors of Fort Misery raised his hand to protest but a fierce glare from Kellerman knocked away that idea. "Thank you, sir, that is most generous of you."

Kellerman smiled. "Thank me in the morning, if you feel the same."

* * *

Great billowing clouds carrying sand swelled and bloomed across the horizon, from time to time picking up a dust devil that ripped rocks and dry grasses from the earth. The troops frantically latched windows and closed hatches, ushering horses into their stalls, where the panicked beasts stamped hooves and neighed with distress. Dust storms could flatten a building in seconds, and the men ate in shifts so that from all angles they could be ever watchful of the storm in its terrifying approach—though what precisely they would be able to do against the storm, besides die, they had not a clue. Inside the hot kitchen, Mrs. Zimmermann said "Hail Marys" as she put the finishing touches on supper, happy for once to be serving fresh meat that wasn't a hen who'd outlived her purposes.

Bang! Bang! Bang! The heavy shutters slammed fiercely against their strappings and made her jump, but she paid no mind, other than an occasional glance to make sure no dust was getting through the cracks. As a small gust of sandy air whipped through a crack, she frowned and stuffed the offending hole with a dishrag, then returned to thinking about the drippings of the sheep legs and the excellent gravy they'd make for her soda biscuits, and what a welcome addition to the morning gruel it would be when breakfast came. The sound of a steam engine began roaring across the desert, and Mrs. Zimmermann's heart sank. "Heavenly Father," she said quietly, "protect us in the name of Jesus Christ our Savior against the snares of this storm." Wiping sweat from her brow, she turned to retrieve a pan and shrieked, clutching the small silver crucifix at her throat. A soldier stood in her kitchen, barefoot, ragged, unexpected, and unwelcomed. His long brown hair was twisted from wind and his beard needed combing. His large honey eyes were wild. Mrs. Zimmermann grabbed up a cast-iron pan and, in a stern voice, called, "What are you supposed to be? Get out of my kitchen, demon!"

The soldier raised his open palms in a gesture of peace, his soft smile and voice pleading. "Forgive me, ma'am, I thought you may need a helping hand with the sheep. They're heavy creatures, I am told."

Mrs. Zimmermann studied the soldier, just a boy really, and something about him was familiar, yet she couldn't place him. She lowered the pan only two inches, then: "Do I know you?"

The boy smiled and revealed surprisingly clean white teeth. "No, ma'am, I've come today. I am Jesus."

Mrs. Zimmermann, pan still clutched, swooned a bit against the cupboards. "Mother Mary, intercede on my behalf. Am I dead? Pray for me, oh, pray for me if I am dead."

The young soldier's eyes softened and lost their feral shine to a look of compassion. "Ma'am, I assure you, you are not dead. I am just here to help with the dressing of the sheep, if you need it." He raised his hands to reach out but thought better of it and once more raised them in a placating gesture.

Constance came out from the small locked room adjacent to the kitchen, pretty as a picture in a silk shirt and canvas skirt. "What in heaven's name has happened, did you burn your—" She paused and took in the scene, then, fiercely: "Are you bothering Mrs. Zimmermann? I will scream, we will both scream!" She reached her hand into the pocket of her skirt and kept it there, grasping something unseen.

The man began to speak again just as Steve Silver-smith came bursting into the kitchen red in the face and puffing. "For God's sake, get out of here, you lunatic. Leave these ladies alone and come with me. You can't have supper barefoot and filthy—the captain won't allow it. Come on, out with you!" The private placed a firm hand on the clearly crazy soldier's shoulder and spun him around, shoving him out of the kitchen.

"Terribly sorry about all that, Mrs. Zimmermann and Miss— Miss—?"

"Constance Courtenay"

"Miss Courtenay. It won't happen again. If you could be so kind as to not, uh—" he cast his eyes downward.

Mrs. Zimmermann sat the pan down and righted herself, "We won't mention it to the captain. Or anyone else. But do see to it you keep track of your charges, Private. Next time we will sound the alarm."

Private Silversmith nodded and made a hasty exit, leaving the women to retell the story to each other several times over.

"You can't terrorize the women, Mann," Steve Silver-smith said, scrubbing his face with a look of sheer exasperation. "You may terrorize some of the men, as needed, but not the officers, or they'll hang you if you are lucky and do worse if you ain't." He looked Frederick Mann over carefully, then: "And why in the heck are you so shabby? Army has standards—you look like a pirate."

Mann stroked his beard and thought a moment, "'Cause I was once terrorized, to use your word. And I ran to hide, but they caught me sure enough and dragged me back in chains, so now here I am like this on account of how it is hard to groom yourself properly while manacled. I even went to court like this, and I reckon it did me no favors, but in keeping with my father the Lord, I chose to embrace my suffering. You see, sir, I am Jesus returned, and I suppose this is how my papa wanted it, so here I stand before you clothed in rags and humble of heart."

Silversmith blinked like an owl in disbelief at the lunacy before him and struggled to find the words needed to share his full opinion on this alleged ragged incarnation of the Second Coming. Finally, after a few false starts, he gave up, throwing his hands in the air in defeat.

"I am not even going to acknowledge what you just said, for the sake of my own sanity. No matter, we need to get you cleaned up and in boots, because if the captain sees you like this, all the blame will fall to me, and I ain't taking blame for a madman raving lunatic—'Jesus' or not, no, sir. I get in enough trouble already. Water is scarce, but we can wash you up and put you right. Come on."

Silversmith first guided Mann with a gesture of his hand, but when the man did not move, he roughly grabbed him by the ear and dragged him like a badly behaved child. To his surprise the action generated no complaints. "We will make a real soldier out of you yet, if'n you can keep it together. It seems a mighty funny thing for a fella who believes he is Jesus incarnate to choose a sentence in hell, so lay off that nonsense and you may have a better time. What did you do, anyway?"

Mann did not reply, so Silversmith tried again, still holding the man's ear. "See, mine ain't too bad. I only beat down my lieutenant on account of how he said something I didn't like, but I can't remember what it was he said since I were drunk at the time. Of course, he says he never said nothing to me, and they believed him."

Mann still didn't reply as he was dragged to the quarters and swiftly cleaned, trimmed, and dressed with, at times, unnecessarily rough handling. After being shined up, his entrance to the mess hall caused no stir, and though his blistered feet ached in the stiff boots, he uttered no complaints and conducted himself quietly. However, anytime his name was asked by his fellows his reply of "Jesus" set off a hooting and hollering round of laughter that made the company of bored men repeat the question at intervals. Mann, for his part, just smiled meekly in a way that inspired violence. The gentle reply provoked a desire to harm him in the way a pack of wolves single out an injured deer to take down, enthralled by obvious weakness, even if they weren't particularly hungry.

The man who called himself "Jesus" was surrounded by men lathering at the thought of cruelty toward his gentleness, but he didn't know or recognize the gleam in their eyes. He would.

Chapter 21

"Flooded! Why, this will take another day of the same work to get where we were before. What are the chances of rain in this wasteland? We are cursed, cursed by Don Esteban de Toro—but I daresay that means we have indeed come across his cache!" Professor Fernsby wiped sweat from beneath his pith helmet and sighed, his narrow shoulders slumping as he stood at the sloshy mire that had been his dig site. "Down, but never defeated, that's what I always say, isn't it Connie?"

Constance glanced at him with a sidelong look. "Yes, I suppose you do, uncle." She had never heard him say it before but saw no point in arguing.

He clapped her cheerfully on the shoulder, "Quite right!" he said, then: "Right. Let's get our backs into it again. I'm sure the lieutenant will be demanding more of our time this evening."

Berryman clutched his lower back and scowled. "My back is out of it and will not be getting into it again anytime soon. That infernal lieutenant is a brute, with little understanding of true might existing in the mind. I'll supervise while you work. Perhaps time to rest will heal me." He settled into a small wooden chair at the edge of the dig pit with a contented sigh. Chan sidled up to him and passed him a canteen. "Professor, I have a balm to help your back. If you will allow me to—"

"Get away from me, Chan," Berryman snapped, and the servant bowed before joining the other professors.

Constance and Fernsby ignored Chan, while Dankworth muttered a few oaths under his breath, and they got to their work. The stretched canvas that had been laid out and hammered down had been ripped by the wind and sand of the night prior, poking in and out of the dirt like the sails of a sunken ship.

Sergeant Major Saul Olinger and Second Lieutenant Cranston strolled over to the dig and surveyed the scene. Olinger shook his head. "I have an idea, but the captain isn't going to like it much." He rolled his shoulders, and the bones of his neck clicked in a way that made Cranston flinch. "Yep, you'll be old someday, too, son, if you're lucky. Say, that gives me a thought that hadn't occurred to me before. As I said, I have an idea that the captain won't like much coming from an old goat like me, but if you tell him . . . Well, he may think a fresh young mind like your own is sharper. Build you up some confidence, too."

Atticus Cranston narrowed his eyes, "It hadn't occurred to you, huh? What is this sharp idea I am supposed to propose?"

The sergeant major grinned. "Naw, hadn't occurred to me, but now I see it, my plan is the best way to win him over. In fact, coming from you, there is no way he could possibly say no."

* * *

"No," Kellerman snapped from behind his desk, eyes darting in bewilderment between Saul Olinger and Lieutenant Cranston like they were a never before seen species of desert bug. "Lieutenant Cranston, have you lost your mind?"

Atticus Cranston frowned and shot the Sergeant Major a withering sidelong look. "No, sir."

"You think that I should give my men over to the lunatic treasure hunters, now, in the midst of"—he gestured toward the south-facing window and the desert beyond—"outgoing patrols, incoming attacks, God knows what else. I don't have enough soldiers here of any quality to begin with. The last thing I need is any of the bunch becoming distracted by hole digging. You must be joking. Sergeant Major, is he joking?"

Olinger stepped forward. "No, sir. I believe despite the outlandish nature of his suggestion, he is quite serious." A sentiment that may have been left alone by the irritated Cranston, if the sergeant major had not followed it with a shake of his head and a "tut-tut."

Cranston turned pink and balled his fists until the knuckles blanched white. "Permission to speak freely, Captain?" he said tightly.

"You've been speaking freely—too much for my liking."

"Well, permission to speak freely in a potentially unflattering manner about the Sergeant Major, sir?"

Olinger made a small choking sound in his throat that may have been a suppressed chuckle, and Kellerman raised his eyebrow at the older man, who kept his face neutral, the creases in his sunbaked skin placid and un-moving, though he glared at the lieutenant.

Kellerman smiled. "Oh, by all means, Lieutenant, do go ahead. This ought to be good."

"You see, sir, I must confess, this was not my idea at all. However, the sergeant major suggested it to me, and I then agreed to raise the topic with you. So, I am most at fault for agreeing to be the messenger but would rather not accept full blame and any accompanying ire for . . . all the rest of it."

Kellerman nodded and fumbled with a match as he lit a cigarette. Speaking from behind a twisting cloud of blue smoke, he said, "And why, Lieutenant, would the sergeant major foist this task upon you?"

Cranston shifted his weight, and the floorboards creaked beneath him. Sweat ran down his throat in heavy rivulets and dampened his collar to the color of cobalt. "I believe he said it was more likely to be ac-ceptable to you if it came from me, and that posing such a suggestion would build my confidence."

"I see," Kellerman said. "So in good faith your com-manding officer sought to boost your confidence and present his highly imaginative idea as your very own bright-minded and inspired thought on the matter, and yet here you are, ratting him out because my reply dis-pleased you. Whereas, if the plan had gone well with me and received my joyful acceptance, you would, no doubt, have taken full responsibility."

Olinger once again released a sad "tut-tut."

Kellerman took on a disappointed tone. "For shame,

Lieutenant. I expect more honor from a graduate of West Point."

Stuttering and wide-eyed with befuddlement, Cranston tried to recover. "No, sir! I—I would have happily confided the idea was not mine—and I just thought the burden of any harsh repri—"

"No, no—speak no more on this matter. I will have to consider this cruel act of derision carefully after I have spoken with Sergeant Major Olinger privately." He indicated the door. "You are dismissed, Lieutenant. Please return to your duties until called." He snapped a salute that Cranston returned before swiftly, and sulkily, exiting.

Once the door closed behind him, the men waited a ten count before Olinger burst into a laugh. "You're torturing the poor lad, Joe."

Kellerman grinned broadly and retrieved two glasses and a jug of bourbon from his desk. "Bah, it's good for him. Builds up character and wit. Look how far he has come already beneath our wise guidance. But Saul, I see why you sent him to take the fall for your lunacy. Tell me why you are suddenly possessed of a passion for archaeology and cursed Spanish gold, at the worst possible time?"

Olinger sat with a heavy sigh and took out the makings, rolling a tight, crisp cigarette and lighting it. "I am most certainly not impassioned, sir. This is a nuisance. However, three old men, one of them, as far as I can tell, useless as teats on a boar, another who spends most of his time running about fetching God knows what, and a girl, will take years to finish their work. Especially in this weather—which, I have been informed, is the result of said cursed treasure, by the by. Anyhow, it seems to me that a unit of misfits, who stand little chance of being the most valuable in a gunfight, will prove their strength with a shovel quite easily and give us a chance to get the roving archaeologists out of the way in a hurry.

"Now, I see no reason to change anything else in the routine, and these soldiers will be expected to live, and conduct themselves, in a manner always befitting the United States Army. They are to understand that we—er, you, Captain—will be of a mind to select two patrols who can switch each day. Monday, first group gets up, does their business, then spends the day in the conquistador trenches unless bugled to readiness in defending the fort. Tuesday, second group does the same, and so on and so on. Young Lieutenant Cranston can choose the hours for his training as he sees fit and make the archaeology work around the dictated times. You'll only be short men in rotation in the sense of immediate readiness, since we will have them keep their arms handy, and we will select from the weakest links, men for whom all the training in the world won't make of them brave warriors. Get the digging work done, they won't find gold, they'll leave, and we can move on with our lives."

Kellerman thought, staring into the dying embers in his small iron belly stove. "Let me sleep on it, see if I feel of a mind for it in the morning. I'll give you an answer then."

The evening thunder crashed, as if providing an omen. "First thing in the morning I will declare my official decision. Now you scat and go find the lieutenant to make peace, since I suspect he has a lot of unhappy thoughts toward you, and I don't need even more curses thrown around this place. I have a lot of contemplating to do, alone." Kellerman yawned and stood, saluting the man across from him and watching him exit into the stormy night before he settled into the silence interrupted now and again by creaking wood and low rumbling thunder. Tiredness rested heavy in his bones, but he would not sleep yet, as he pondered the struggles he must soon overcome.

CHAPTER 22

Dark clouds provided cover from the moon and stars as a shadowy figure skulked through the quiet fort like a stray cat, pausing at the corners of structures and listening attentively for inorganic sounds loud enough to be heard above the rumbling storm. The night patrol was easily enough avoided with care and dexterity, but tonight the figure was on the hunt for the men, much like a wolf stalking a deer. On the southeastern corner of the fort, a lone soldier stood beneath an open wooden structure made simply of four boards that held up a slanted roof, a small guard post meant to ward off sun and rain while the man on duty shifted his weight uncomfortably atop the flat floor. Beyond him lay the empty building that had been built as a sutlery and never filled, the area just beyond it settled by Lipan families who would sometimes draw near the fort to pick up odd jobs and make trades. Tonight, a half dozen or so had set up camp and huddled inside a pair of tipis, the dwindling remains of a fire shining dully and casting dancing light upon the deserted sutlery. This was an unfortunate addition to the fort's population, but it was the reason for the test, the shadowy figure thought, and if the exercise failed, then so be it. There was a carefully constructed backup plan, after all.

The shadowy figure slowly crept up behind the soldier, footsteps easily blending into the sound of the whistling wind. By the time the soldier began to stir with the sense of being watched, it was too late, and light glinted from a bowie knife as it slashed the man's throat before he had a chance to yell. Hot blood fell from the wound and the figure stepped back with a grimace, as the soldier toppled forward onto the wet sand. A brief glance toward the Lipans showed that they had seen and heard nothing, and the shadowy killer grinned with success. Kneeling just out of the light cast by the soldier's lantern, the killer scalped the man with brutal strokes, then, hand coated in blood, traced a message onto the sandy wooden floor of the guard post—so that the rain would be less liable to wash it away—and, satisfied, slipped back into the darkness without a sound.

"I think it says . . . 'Custer Old' . . . ? That can't possibly be it." Lieutenant Hall squinted down at the blood that stained the weathered wood of the guard post, clearly left as a message but proving ineffective, as it was one nobody could decipher.

Captain Kellerman stroked his mustache in contemplation. "I don't believe so, Lieutenant, I don't believe so . . ."

A small crowd had gathered at the scene, though Kellerman and Hall had made short work of dispatching men to their posts in doubles to prevent a reoccurrence of the murder. The predawn hours had come on heavily clouded and windy, but warm. Kellerman and Hall had covered the dead soldier with a shroud in a last attempt at dignity for the deceased. Lanterns provided enough light to see the grim tableau, and the flames flickered gently against the strongest gusts of a storm gathering once more. A woman's voice rang out from behind, demanding to be let through to the scene as gruff male voices tried to hold the lady back. At last, Constance made her way to the guard post looking outraged by the inconvenience of her classification as the fairer sex.

"Miss Courtenay you really don't need to—" Kellerman began, his voice stern.

"Oh, for heaven's sake, Captain, all I have heard are rumors, and it sounds as if you are unable to identify the warning, such as it is. Let me see—I specialize in matters of archaic script." She confidently marched past the covered body without a flinch and joined Hall and Kellerman at the post, first inspecting the roof and then casting her eyes to the small square floor where the words were scrawled.

Hall caught Kellerman's eyes and shrugged with indifference—if the lady wished to investigate, so be it.

Constance knelt into the sand and moved a lantern nearer, then traced the letters delicately with her finger hovering an inch away from the surface, careful to not touch the cryptic lettering as she did. "Quite simple, gentleman, it says CURSED GOLD and looks to have been written"—she paused and peered up at the roof of the post and the slowly brightening sky outside it, then the sandy terrain now starting to dance under the ever-growing wind—"oh, I'd say no more than eight hours ago, if even that long. It is really quite fresh. Your trouble is coming from the grit blowing across the surface and whatever was there when they wrote this. You see, there are marks here"—she pointed—"and here"—then used her left hand to show a gap in the letter R while her right index finger remained over the G—"that show the sand was in the way." She smiled at the officers with a knowing expression, before standing and brushing off her hands on her trousers.

"I see," Kellerman said. "And I suppose this attack would be related to your quest for the gold of the famous conquistador, what is his name again, Don Estepan la Hembra?"

Constance laughed, and Kellerman all at once realized her voice sounded like bells rung by angels in heaven, a thought he quickly shook off.

"Close, Captain Kellerman, but he was Don Esteban de Toro. *Toro*, the bull—I daresay he'd be very insulted to hear the name *la hembra*, the cow! Perhaps named for the legendary Battle of Toro, though nearly half a century too late. That is not my field of study, I am afraid, but my dear uncle will know. At any rate, yes, this is likely a warning against the cursed golden treasures." She paused and looked toward the covered corpse, her face clouding with consternation. "And this man was punished for our sins. But I cannot see why, or by whom, can you?"

Lieutenant Hall looked to Captain Kellerman and then back to the young woman, and was surprised to see a longing expression cross the captain's face that had nothing to do with solving this mystery. Hall smiled, until Kellerman looked his way and he rearranged his face to appear suitably dour for the current predicament.

"Perhaps, perhaps, Miss Courtenay. I have an inkling that may grow into an explanation once coffee has been served. For now, I request that you return to your chaperones and remain safe. Mrs. Zimmermann may require a hand in the kitchen while we clean this up. I lost a good man today and must think on it. Corporal Pierce had not been a champion of decency outside the fort, but he was a darn good soldier, and I am sorry to lose him."

Constance frowned, though she had grown used to being dismissed by men despite her talents. "Of course, Captain, I will return to the kitchen as you wish." She strolled away without urgency and rolled her eyes skyward once out of sight, mulling over the murder in her mind to piece together clues if she could. Cursed gold certainly met with the legends attached to Don Esteban de Toro's lost treasure, but what on earth would drive a person to murder before the treasure was even found? Surely, an answer was there to be found, and she would find it.

Once the young lady had rounded the corner, Lieutenant Hall spoke up, his tone light and cheery as ever. "Why I say, she sure is purty, Captain Kellerman. I dare declare she may be as beautiful as an autumn sunrise, don't you think so?"

Kellerman flushed. "She's a nuisance to me and to this fort, Hall. Stop mooning over the girl and get Corporal Pierce to the father so that we can plant him and send news back to his family. Chop, chop."

Hall grinned and took a pinch of snuff, watching Kellerman march stiffly into the morning glare. "I knew it," he said to himself, then. "All right, boys, you heard the captain. Let us clean up this poor devil and allow Father Staszczyk to send his soul to heaven."

CHAPTER 23

"They're trying to make an impression, but upon whom? Us? The U.S. Army? Why would we care about the presence of alleged cursed gold," Sergeant Major Saul Olinger said, his face wan and tired after the rude awakening he'd received upon the discovery of Corporal Pierce.

Joe Kellerman rolled his neck until the bones cracked, then sighed deeply. "That is the question supreme, Sergeant Major. But more importantly, who is the murderer at large? If it is a member of the Fey-Fey clan, we must boot them out instanter—or better yet, hang them as villains. Yet something deep in my gut tells me it isn't them at all . . . Saul, if you told me I would be speaking to the honor of a lawbreaking gang of gunmen but a week ago, I would have declared you insane, yet"—he shook his head obstinately—"I don't see it, do you?"

Saul pondered for a moment, before he replied, "No, I don't see it. They'd have had to kill and scalp one of their own, make away with their rations, then come here and immediately murder a soldier and write the threat, or whatever it's supposed to be. What end would that serve? I don't trust the buggers—that much is certain—but this crime simply doesn't fit the men."

A comfortable silence fell over the two officers as each ran through the list of possibilities in their own minds.

"What about the girl?" Saul said, a smile playing at his lips.

Kellerman scowled and took to focusing on the makings as he rolled a cigarette. "What of her?"

"She seems quite adept at investigating, wouldn't you say? Her thoughts on the subject as pertains both to the two murders and the gold might bring about ideas beyond the minds of Union men like ourselves."

"Humbug," Kellerman said sternly. "She sorted out the words, that was all. I am quite sure any one of us would have done the same in due time. But it is a helluva thing to drag a man off his bunk before dawn to look for evidence. Besides, the last thing we need is a woman roving around the fort like a Pinkerton man. She would get herself killed—best case, and—and—"

"Raped and killed," Saul supplied.

"Yes, that—at worst. Let her stick to the bone hunting and kitchen assistance while we sort the rest."

The Sergeant Major shifted in his chair, crossing his legs to relieve an aching pain in his left hip. "She won't be sweet on you any longer if you try to pretend she's just a kitchen wench, you know." He stretched his arms above his head and let the hard chair back pop his spine, casually, as if he were picking flowers in a summer meadow.

Kellerman started upright in his chair and his cheeks

turned red. "I am quite sure, Sergeant Major, that I have no idea what you are talking about."

Saul grinned. "Oh, for God's sake, Joe, don't you try to Sergeant Major me. I may be old, but I still have eyes and ears. Even Hall and that Cranston boy have seen the way you look at each other. In fact, I say it might be love. She's a beauty, and better still, she's smart. You need a woman who can keep you on your toes."

Sputtering and now a deep shade of crimson, Joe Kellerman leapt to his feet. "That is quite enough out of you, Sargent Major Olinger! Insubordination! Indecency!"

Saul cackled and pushed back his chair, raising his hand in a salute. "All right, all right. I'll see you at breakfast, Captain." He made his way to the door and hesitated, then decided to risk it. "Do wax that mustache a bit, won't you? You look a bit disheveled."

As the Sergeant Major ducked out the door, the only reply was an empty bourbon bottle, aimed near his head, that burst upon the doorframe and fell in a bright tinkle of shattered glass. Saul shook his head and laughed even harder, gently closing the door behind him as he stepped into the dawning day.

CHAPTER 24

"And then he sent me to the kitchens," Constance Courtenay said, outraged, wiping sweat from her brow with a flour sack towel as she tended to salt pork sizzling in a heavy pan.

Mrs. Zimmermann listened distractedly as she kneaded biscuit dough, her straying focus wandering to the hen in her coop who had not laid an egg for well over two months. The old hen should become a fried treat for the officers, but she had named her Cecilia after her favored saint and could not bring herself to execute the poor dear. "I'm not sure what you expect, dear heart. Even Joan of Arc faced scrutiny by men. And to a point, I must agree that your detective work should proceed only with caution. I'd hate to see you entangled in the affairs of murder and mayhem just to prove a point. Look at the example set by Our Lady, who could but stand back in prayer while her only Son was nailed upon a cross."

Constance paused long enough to glare at the older woman. "She had no other choice. Surely, if a man were to be crucified here, today, we women would intervene no matter the opposition of these men. God made us physically weaker, perhaps, but he has gifted us with Colts and derringers to make us equal."

Mrs. Zimmermann chuckled. "Yes, I suppose that is true. Tell me girl, how are your archaeological pursuits progressing? I am afraid that the professors you travel with do tend to bluster a bit, and I have yet to see one Spanish coin as proof of your efforts. My soul will not rest until you're away from here, no matter your guns."

The younger woman sighed and wiped her hands. "Well . . . My uncle is very ambitious, you see . . ."

Mrs. Zimmermann nodded. "Oh yes, that much I have discerned." Her flat tone drew a giggle from Constance who was dipping her face into the rising billows of steam from her pan in a rather unsuccessful effort to dislodge what felt like a permanent coating of dust from her pores.

"Yes, and I have seen his ambition lead to great discoveries in lands far away from here, time and time again. In fact, he is the reason I chose to study archaeology, though he was quite reluctant to encourage my curiosity about the field in the beginning."

"Is that so," Mrs. Zimmermann said quietly, her thoughts once again resting with the beloved Cecilia's fate.

"Oh yes, he was a very traditional man, you see, in his opinions on women. But he took me in as his ward when I was a girl of six, and I suppose we won each other over in a way. He didn't know the first thing about raising a daughter, and I was so desperate to feel included in his adventures and not be left alone with my boring old governess that I rapidly learned to read and memorized the texts that lined nearly all the walls of our home. Some people keep a library, but Uncle Paul had every room filled with books."

Inside a moderate oven, the biscuits were stacked in layers, each sheet filled edge-to-edge so that the soldiers could have their fill. Mrs. Zimmermann was limited by her supplies, and there were often discreet grumbles about the quality of ingredients, but she saw to it that no man went hungry under her careful eye. Even though nearly the entire lot of them were lowdown derelicts, she simply could not allow an empty belly at her tables.

"What had become of your parents, if you will forgive such a question?"

"Oh, well . . ." Constance removed the pan of salt pork from the heat. "I never knew my mother. She died a few days after giving birth to me."

Mrs. Zimmermann crossed herself, knowing all too well the horrors of maternal sickness and death.

"And then my father . . . Well, I suppose you may find it funny, but my father was a pirate."

"A pirate, raiding on the seas and trading rum?" Mrs. Zimmermann looked aghast. No wonder the girl was such a high-strung little creature.

Constance grinned. "Oh yes, or at least that is what my uncle tells me. He's my mother's brother and has few kind words about my father, as he was far away when I—well, when I killed my mother." Her face fell and she turned to concentrate upon the eggs, cracking each with light taps upon the counter before emptying the runny contents into her sizzling pan.

This would not stand in the presence of Mrs. Zimmermann, whose Catholic devotion made her comfortable with guilt, but only as it was deserved. She quickly made her way to the girl and placed her warm, callused hands upon her cheeks to turn her face upward. "Ah, none of that, little one, for you have done no wrong. The Lord giveth us life, and he taketh away. Your dear Mama is singing among the angels in Heaven and watching over you even now. I can sense her love right through this very roof, can't you?"

Constance pulled away and dashed her tears, gazing up toward the ceiling that held cobwebs in its far corners. "Yes, I suppose I can. She wouldn't want me to weep—I know. But the fact remains that my father was a pirate, and the last anyone heard his ship went missing somewhere out in the Atlantic Ocean, near Florida. So, with him likely dead, and my mother definitely dead, Uncle Paul was all I had left. My grandparents passed away long ago." She smiled, "Please don't pity me, Mrs. Zimmermann. My life has been positively filled with adventure."

Mrs. Zimmermann grinned, "I surely hope you're not under the impression that I pity anyone routinely. If you have a doubt, ask Mr. Zimmermann or Captain Kellerman, they'll set you straight."

At the mention of Kellerman, Constance blushed, her fair skin showing the pink beneath prominently.

"Oh . . . oh, my. I don't imagine a young lady sweet on my husband, dear though he is. You are fond of the captain!"

Immediately Constance returned her full attention to

the eggs. "I have no idea what you're talking about, ma'am. He's . . . rather boorish."

Another rare grin from Mrs. Zimmermann as she forgot all about her favorite hen with a new mission in mind. "Oh yes, boorish indeed. Handsome, though, isn't he, our captain?"

CHAPTER 25

Shortly after dawn the captain sent the prison transport back off to Yuma, with full canteens and a message to pass on, regarding the death of Corporal Pierce. The departing soldiers didn't linger, even though rushing off meant heading into a raging storm. No one could blame them for wishing to make such a speedy exit.

The officers gathered for a brief meeting post-breakfast, and although Kellerman was normally confident and outspoken in his opinions, he had not much of anything helpful to say about how to solve the crime. The murder had unnerved everyone at Fort Misery.

Earlier Kellerman and Lieutenant Hall had been forced to calm down a forming mob intent on stringing up the Trey-Treys. Because the gang had arrived shortly before the murder, the soldiers were suspicious, and in the words of one loud and belligerent young private, "bad hombres." Words were bandied about by a few others who pointed out that the latest group of enlisted men to arrive were equally suspect, but finally, all agreed the latest group of soldiers was perhaps no more suspect than the rest of the killers sent to Fort Misery for their sins.

After Kellerman threatened to shoot any man who took matters into his own hands, the men backed down. He calmly pointed out that it seemed unlikely that the pistoleros would have scalped one of their own just to stage a murder of a corporal they'd presumably never met before.

And there was the rub, Kellerman thought, that kept him from locking up Lucas Dean and his associates until further evidence was unearthed. It could be a lie, but Dean also claimed he had witnessed the slaughter of their own man, old Dick Freedman. He'd sworn it was an oddly dressed person, not in a uniform, who'd carried nothing away after the shooting but the dead man's scalp.

The only thing the captain was certain of was the terrible evil hanging heavy in the air above Fort Misery, and the anger he felt over a vicious killing that happened right under his nose. His nerves were raw as he ran the possible suspects and their motivation through his mind over and over again and sought fresh ideas at the bottom of a bourbon glass.

Justice would eventually come, but for now, he stayed firm in his conviction that he couldn't hang a man for having the misfortune of arriving on this cursed land with very bad timing.

"I am allowing this only by the virtue of my good heart and levelheaded nature," Kellerman said, sparking smiles on Saul Olinger and James Hall, who stood at attention beside him as the captain addressed two dozen enlisted men on the parade ground. "In order to get these professors away from my territory and back to the museums where they belong, you gentleman will assist in the digging, hauling, scraping, and general excavation of my poor parade ground to search for antiquities. If you come across said antiquities, you are not to pocket them, and any man found stealing from the site will be hanged or shot immediately. There are twenty-four of you men chosen for this task, and you will trade off by the dozen on alternating days. Your assignment to this project does not liberate you from other duties, and as I have selected you scoundrels as the worst gunmen we have and, thereby, the ones I can afford to spare, you are to continue training with Second Lieutenant Cranston, who will report to me daily on your progress. If you behave well, I may add a commendation to your files. If you behave badly, the consequences will be dire. Any questions?"

"Sir, ain't it true the treasure is a-cursed? Ain't that why Pierce were killed, cause of the ghosts and cursed ground? An' ain't we gotta be watching for them hostiles on account of how they're drumming and carrying on all night," a swarthy, heavyset man called from the rear line, nervously fiddling with the revolver at his waist like it was a talisman.

The inquiry encouraged others to begin piping up with their own worries, and out of the din came a litany of cries over the notion of cursed gold and angry haints. Finally, Kellerman raised his hand. "Enough! You're acting like frightened children. Superstitious nonsense will not get you off this detail, and as for bogeymen, the truth of it is that the real curse is having three old men and a lady taking over this fort at a most inconvenient time. You can direct further questions to the professors or to the sergeant major, who cooked this idea up. Every man in the front line, your shift starts now. Dismissed."

Muttering, twelve soldiers descended upon the dig site, where the professors were starting their day, rolling back the canvas tarps that covered their deeply dug trenches and glancing skyward at the threatening dark clouds pregnant with heavy rain. After wild gesticulation by Dankworth and stern words from Berryman, the instructions were communicated, and the soldiers began breaking ground with a far more rapid efficiency than the older gentleman had achieved.

Constance Courtenay leapt from a trench and grinning, approached Kellerman. "Thank you, Captain, for sparing us your men. Why I believe at this pace our expedition will be complete in no time!" She wiped her muddy hands on a cloth before slinging it over her shoulder.

"Don't thank me, Miss Courtenay, it was Sergeant Major Olinger who hatched this plan. I do not share his, and your, confidence in the brilliance of the idea, but if it takes you back to England faster, then it was a bargain."

A flash of consternation crossed Constance's face, but she maintained her smile. "I keep telling you, please just call me Connie. And thank you, Sergeant Major, for your suggestion. It is nice to know that at least someone here is supportive of the pursuit of knowledge."

"My pleasure, ma'am, I am indeed a great supporter of the fine arts, history, and antiquities," Saul Olinger said, with a straight face, as Kellerman glared at him intently.

"Quite so," said Hall. "We are all intellectuals of the highest order. That is why we were selected by the Union to be granted the honor of our ranks as officers."

"Hear, hear," Olinger agreed. "Say, Connie, perhaps it would help enlighten the captain about the importance of your work if you tutored him of an evening, when your workday is done."

She brightened. "I would love to! I have some texts you can learn a great deal from. I'll bring them to you tonight."

Flustered, Kellerman simply nodded. "I look forward to it." He began to walk away but turned back. "Sergeant Major, I think you should spend the afternoon overseeing the work. Report back to me at supper."

Olinger chuckled and offered Constance his arm in a fatherly fashion, which she quickly accepted. "Now, please tell me all about your conquistador, so I know what we're looking for."

CHAPTER 26

"This is enough water to drown a frog," Lieutenant James Hall said, watching the heavy sheets of rain bombarding the earth as he stood beneath the roofed walkway that ran the length of the stables. Behind him, Frederick Mann was mucking out a stall, the livery detail being the best place for him until the officers could unwind his thoughts about being the Messiah.

He paused and turned to Hall, glassy eyed but clean and wearing his uniform to the standards. "Yes, sir. It is God angry over the hunt for riches. The gold is a false idol, you see, so the professors have brought wrath upon the land. A flood will come and wash away their sins." He met Hall's eyes, blinked slowly, and then returned to his work.

"That is certainly a theory, private. Jolly clever notion about God and his wrathful floods, quite imaginative. However, I'd keep those thoughts to yourself, as you are surrounded by heathens, and they won't appreciate the sentiment at an intellectual level, as I have."

"Yes, sir, I will."

Hall nodded. "Good man. Now while we're on the

subject of vengeful acts of God, I need to introduce you to someone you'll be working with often during your duties." He stepped back into the building and gestured for Mann to follow him. The private gathered his curry brush, hoof picks, and sackcloth into a bucket and propped the shovel and pitchfork outside the mucked stall.

Bucket in hand, he and Hall made their way to the end of the row, where an enormous black stallion stood glaring over the stall's door with huge coal eyes.

"This is Lucifer," Hall said. "He's the meanest, most uncooperative animal I have ever met, and he's on a mission to take out the entire population of Fort Misery one man at a time. He bites, kicks, bucks, and lives by his own rules when any poor soldier is riding him. He may be quite calm while you saddle him and cooperate with your first commands, but you mustn't trust him, Private Mann. He tends to break into a wild gallop and deliver the rider into the first patch of sharp rocks or creosote bush he comes across."

Frederick Mann studied the horse, wide-eyed, smiling. "Lucifer . . . Yet you keep him, why?"

"Because Captain Kellerman is quite partial to him and insists that he is merely a hyper-intelligent horse who commands respect from humans he finds inferior. And . . . because it is entertaining to watch a man who believes he can soothe the savage beast discover it isn't a talent he possesses. We have no theaters, no amusements . . . No, Private Mann, we make our own fun here at Fort Misery, as we can. Now, if you need to speak about him, just call him Luce if you're in the company of Mrs. Zimmermann. She is adamant that we're tempting Satan by naming a wild horse after Beelzebub."

Confused, Mann studied Hall's face to search for a sign that this was a prank, because since he had enlisted his superiors and peers often tormented him with gags and jokes that were born out of cruelty and little amusing to himself, though they seemed to enjoy it. But the lieutenant's smile seemed genuine enough, and nothing about his manner suggested deception.

Hall clapped his hand on Mann's shoulder. "I don't believe you truly think you're the Messiah, by the by. I believe you're searching for a way to be dishonorably discharged. Unfortunately, now that you're here, your time will have to be served. Don't worry—when your stint at the fort is over, the world will have forgotten all about your grandiose delusions and you can lead a normal life again." Hall spoke without judgment, for despite thinking the man was crazy as a bedbug, he wanted to keep him in an optimistic state of mind and found his presence oddly pleasant.

Although the short lecture was intended to be helpful, Frederick Mann felt a wave of defeat wash over him and stepped away from Hall with a slight shiver, his damp uniform chilled by the stiff breeze that had begun whipping down the stable corridor. They'll find out, he thought, and they'd realize later that he'd been telling the truth, once his purpose was revealed and fulfilled. He set his bucket of tools down, then offered the stallion a hand, his long fingers bony and pale against the shining ebony coat. The horse swung his head to allow Mann to stroke his neck, surprising Hall, who thought for sure the private would be bitten instead. Mann leaned in and murmured something to Luce, and the horse nuzzled him, an action that made Lieutenant Hall's jaw drop.

Mann then opened the stall and slipped inside, calm and fearless, and Lucifer was as sweet and gentle as a newborn kitten.

"Sir, I'll have him groomed and the stall mucked within the next forty-five minutes. That'll be the last of the work until the patrols return their horses in the evening. Is there anything else?"

Hall had retrieved his snuffbox and taken a pinch, setting off a brief sneezing fit. "Yes, after luncheon, you're to report to Lieutenant Cranston's training session today at 1400. Since you're gifted with horses, it seems, I am eager to learn if you're good at handling a rifle, too. Why, you may just become one of our fiercest warriors!"

Mann stopped short, lowering the curry comb and frowning, "I'm sorry, sir, I won't commit acts of violence. I'll attend as ordered, but the effort will be wasted on me if it comes time for a battle."

Hall chose his words carefully. His tone was grave, and he pulled himself to his full height, aware of the intimidating figure he cut. "That is a problem, Private Mann. Insubordination at Fort Misery is a death sentence, as is inability to fight back when we are under attack. I suggest you think on your foolishness and decide if an Apache lance to the gut or a snapped neck is how your story will end."

CHAPTER 27

Lucas Dean stepped into Captain Kellerman's office and removed his hat, "You wanted to see me, sir?"

Kellerman stood and gestured to the chair across from him before sitting back down behind his cluttered desk. "Have a seat," he said, gathering scattered papers into a single pile and taking bourbon and two glasses from his drawer.

Dean did as he was bidden, sending up a silent prayer that the captain wasn't about to accuse him or any of the Trey-Treys for Corporal Pierce's murder on account of it having the bad luck to coincide with their arrival. Kellerman's face was unreadable, placid and cool.

The office was damp, the close air creating a miasma of sweat and leather threaded by stale tobacco smoke.

"Drink?" Kellerman asked, lifting the bottle above the glasses.

"That would be mighty kind of you, yes, sir," Dean said.

"I bet you're nervous as a hen in a fox den right about now, and I must admit there have been many calls from my enlisted men to hang you high for the brutal murder of Corporal Pierce."

Dean paled, his bright green eyes growing dark and wary. "I was afraid of that, but I will tell you true, Captain, the killer wasn't any member of my party. After supper we were in the bunks playing a friendly game of euchre,—not gambling for money, of course, per the fort rules—and there was a young soldier who joined in for a time." He snapped his fingers and frowned, trying to remember. "Billy! Billy Burt. Yellow hair and blue eyes. Told us he's a new arrival and already regretful of his choice to come here instead of sticking with the Yuma prison. That there is an alibi, if we need one. I'm sure he'll be happy to provide you with a report of our whereabouts for the entire evening, since we cheered him up, and his team won two games in a row. Nice kid, but he snores like a steam engine."

Kellerman stood. "One moment," he said, and rounded the desk and popped his head out the door "Orderly!" he called, and Private Silversmith hurried over. "Go find Private Billy—"

"Burt," Dean called out.

"Burt. He was with the new arrivals, and if I am thinking of the right man, he should be helping with the dig right now. Speak to Sergeant Major Olinger. Tell him I need Burt in my office without delay."

Silversmith snapped off a salute. "Yes, sir, right away."

Kellerman returned the salute and then shut the door against the blustering wind and rain.

"Mr. Bean," he began, returning to his seat and reaching for the glass of bourbon.

"That's Dean, Lucas Dean. Please just call me Lucas, if you'd like to."

"Mr. Dean, I do not believe that you or your compatriots murdered Pierce, but to cover my hide and yours, I'll have Burt put your alibi in writing, just as a formality to get the calls for your timely hanging to stop. I told you when you arrived that you'd be expected to earn your keep, and the real reason I called this meeting is to ask for your assistance, since it seems you will be stuck here for a time."

Dean relaxed some, his posture loosening as he reached for the bourbon and downed the glass in one gulp. "Why, I am flattered that you want me to help, Captain, but I suppose my agreeing depends on exactly what it is you want done."

Kellerman locked eyes with Dean, hesitant about what he was about to suggest, but knowing that a storm of violence was on the way to Fort Misery and they had to batten down the hatches with guns and grit to survive.

"First, drop the hunting story. You know you're lying and so do I. I don't know what you're doing here, but it doesn't have anything to do with bighorn sheep."

Lucas Dean started to protest, and Kellerman held up his hand in a stop motion. "Dean, don't bother. I'm not going to trust you, and you likely do not trust me, either, but we can work together under a truce. Listen up, here's what I need from you."

"Hired guns, gents. The Trey-Treys are now special agents for the U.S. Army." Dean grinned. He sat with his feet hanging from a bunk in the cramped sleeping quarters. Somewhere in the corner, a pair of rats were squeaking and nibbling, and the entire structure creaked from wind as though it could fall at any moment. Despite the rundown conditions, the bunkhouse was cozy and dry, and Dean had slept in far worse places.

Nicky Barnes took out the makings and rolled a loose cigarette, lighting it and studying Dean cooly. "What's the pay for this extra endeavor, Lucas. I don't enjoy risking my life if there isn't a reward at the end."

Dean stood and began pacing the room. "Pay is our supplies replaced, a cash sum to be determined at the end of our engagement here, and a commendation given by Sherman if we do our part. But more importantly, Nicky, it gives us good reason to be here at the fort, ready to strike when the treasure is unearthed—hide our intentions in plain sight, so to speak."

From the corner of the room, Frank Abilene snorted. "Have you looked at the hole they claim the gold is in? So far, they ain't found a single thing. It looks like children building a sandcastle on the beach."

"You ain't ever been to the beach, Frank," Adam Louis snapped.

Dean frowned. "Hush. You all need to be on your best behavior until we see this thing through. No fighting, no telling tales about your past exploits, and no thieving or drunkenness. You're as of now temporary special agents commissioned by the captain and will conduct yourselves as gentleman, or I'll shoot you my own self."

Frank stretched lazily with a yawn, "All right, Dean, don't get so excited. You're too high-strung all the time. Someday your ticker is gonna go if you can't calm down. Tell us who to shoot, we'll do it—but if there ain't a pot of gold at the end of our time in this god-forsaken fort, you and me have a problem." He looked around the room. "Right, boys?"

Ike Fletcher, never a man of many words, looked up from the gun he'd been quietly cleaning. "Darn right, Frankie."

Chapter 28

Mrs. Zimmermann was on her way to ring the lunch bell, as the sun rose high above the desert and fought to shine through the stormy clouds, when the parade ground exploded with a noisy cacophony. Alarmed, she patted her skirt, checking for her derringer and marched from the officers' mess hall over to the center of the fort, slipping here and there on the slick mud. The yelling escalated, and soon more voices joined the fray, but she couldn't make out a word of it. Please God, don't let it be another murder, she muttered to herself.

As she turned the corner past the stables, Lieutenant James Hall marched out with long steps and joined her. "What has happened?" he said, scanning the area with narrowed eyes, hand firmly on his revolver. Then, remembering his manners, he tipped his campaign hat. "Ma'am," he added politely.

Mrs. Zimmermann, unimpressed, ignored that and said, "I don't know, Lieutenant, but we are about to find out."

"Maybe you should return to headquarters, lest it is

dangerous, Mr. Zimmermann would be quite angry if I allowed you to get hurt."

Mrs. Zimmermann's eyes slid to his face, and she frowned. "Lieutenant Hall, I have full faith in your ability to protect my honor, should the need arise."

They reached the parade ground and were relieved to take in a festive scene, with no blood or Indians in sight. Jubilant celebration was the source of the screaming and hollering, as the archaeology pits were swarmed by men who peered into the hole and exclaimed, "Huzzah!" and "Crackerjack!"

Professor Berryman was in the deepest trench and only the top of his pith helmet showed over the edge, until at last he reached up for assistance climbing out while cradling something under his arm. Once he was out, he held up a human skull, mummified skin stretched taut across the cheekbones and forehead while the eye sockets were empty pits of black. Lifting the skull above his head he began to loudly cry out, "Hip-hip!" and the entire gathering replied, "Hooray!"

Captain Kellerman had come to investigate and joined Lieutenant Hall and Mrs. Zimmermann. He grinned. "Well, I'll be darned, those crazy old coots actually found something."

Berryman handed the skull to Professor Fernsby, and the crowd gathered around him while he examined it carefully.

"Natural mummification, how remarkable," he said, rolling the skull in his hands gently and exposing the back of the cranium where a large section of bone was missing. Tracing the edge of the hole with his finger he turned to Dankworth, "I say, Jules, this is a wound from a death blow."

Professor Dankworth joined him and pulled a pair of spectacles from his shirt pocket, balancing the thin gold frames on his deeply sunburned nose with a wince. "Hmmm, yes, yes, quite so. It looks like the poor fellow was hit by a rather impressive blunt weapon." He turned the grinning skull to face him. "Sorry, old chap, that must have been a bad way to go."

A white flash of lightning split the sky, accompanying a mighty roar of thunder that rumbled across the desert and echoed off the distant rock formations.

Mrs. Zimmermann jumped and placed a hand over her heart. "I am going back inside. Luncheon is waiting to be served, Lieutenant Hall. Please be so kind as to wrangle up the grave robbers."

Hall stifled a laugh, and said, "Yes, ma'am, right away."

"And so, now we have our first evidence that proves Don Esteban's ill-fated exploration did indeed end right here at Fort Benjamin Grierson. I hate to say I told you so, but I knew the map would prove invaluable." Professor Fernsby was holding court at the lunch table. The mummified skull sat facing his plate, a deranged centerpiece. He picked at his meal of bacon, beans, and thick slices of bread, but downed coffee with enthusiasm.

Kellerman frowned at the morbid table decoration, but only Mrs. Zimmermann seemed to be perturbed, so he let it stay. "Yes, Professor, I must give you due credit, as you were right about the lost dead. But there were Indian wars in this region for a very long time. Can you be sure that your new friend was a Spaniard?"

Fernsby nodded enthusiastically. "After this discovery I have no doubt more will be found this very day and am quite confident in the assessment of origin based on the phrenology of the skull."

"Bully for scientific progress! I considered becoming a physician, you know, but the siren song of the military held too much allure for a man of my brave disposition," Hall declared.

"Why not become an army surgeon, then?" Berryman asked dryly.

"Ah, it is a complicated state of affairs, but I was sent to this arid hellscape before I got the chance to inquire about the opportunity."

"Lieutenant Cranston, how goes the progress of your command?" Kellerman asked.

"Well, sir," Atticus Cranston began, "some are better than others, but I daresay they are ready to fight, sir. The enlisted men, at least, have become quite savvy at shooting from horseback, sir. Mr. Zimmermann has been assisting as he can, and Lieutenant Hall has made strides in teaching fast mounting and dismounting while holding the Sharps."

"And our civilians?"

"Miss Courtenay is a crack shot, sir. The professors are—they are trying. Professor Dankworth is quite adept with blades it seems. And—"

A commotion erupted at the end of the table.

"'Alas, poor Yorick! I knew him, Horatio. A fellow

of infinite jest, of most excellent fancy. He hath borne me on his back a thousand times. And now how abhorred in my imagination it is! My gorge rises at it. Here hung those lips that I have kiss'd I know not how oft. Where be your gibes now? your gambols? your songs? your flashes of merriment that were wont to set the table on a roar? Not one now, to mock your own grinning? Quite chap-fall'n? Now get you to my lady's chamber, and tell her, let her paint an inch thick, to this favor she must come. Make her laugh at that.'"

Nicky Barnes bowed dramatically, the Spanish skull held aloft in one hand, to the reception of a stunned, silent audience. Jaws were dropped, eyes were wide, forks held hovering above plates as the drunk pistolero delivered his monologue with all the dramatic gusto of any actor on a London stage.

"Bravo, bravo!" Lieutenant Hall burst into applause, delighted by the performance. "Quite a tribute to the Bard, a capital recitation."

Captain Kellerman glared at him, then at Lucas Dean, who to his credit looked abashed.

"Nicky, you're drunk!" Dean said, "Give that back to the professor, you scoundrel. What is wrong with you? We're guests here! Conduct yourself like a gentleman for once in your life."

Paul Fernsby watched nervously as Barnes swayed on his feet and balanced the skull precariously on the palm of one hand. He thought about making a grab for it, but the Colt on the drunken man's hip made him reluctant to try.

Nicky Barnes cackled. "Ah, relax, Lucas. I'm just

having a little fun. Here, professor," he tossed the skull to Berryman, who gasped and leapt out of his seat, fumbling the catch but managing to not drop the centuries-old artifact on the floor.

Sighing, Kellerman neatly wiped his mouth and mustache with a napkin and then stood. "Mr. Barnes, I suggest you go to your bunk and sleep it off. Mr. Dean can accompany you there to make sure you don't get lost on the way."

Barnes leveled his gaze on the captain, his eyes glassy from drink and gleaming with malice. His thinning hair fell over his forehead in greasy clumps and tangled in his sideburns, creating a furry helmet that gave him the look of a feral dog.

"Maybe I wasn't done eating," he said.

Thunder rattled the building, and the air grew thick with tension, as everyone braced for a fight. Lieutenant Cranston casually dropped his hand to his revolver, watching Frank Abilene out of the corner of his eye for any furtive movement as the man seemed poised to spring at any moment from his seat. Lucas Dean stood up slowly, stiff and uneasy.

Kellerman stretched to his full height, stern and imposing. "Maybe you weren't, but I am telling you that you're done now."

Nobody moved for an anxious moment until finally Barnes, aware enough that he was outnumbered, smiled and raised his hands. "Sure, Cap'n. Give my compliments to the old broad for a mighty fine meal, will ya?"

The heel of his boot squeaked on the wood floor and emitted a fart sound as he turned to leave, and he giggled childishly, then broke into a whistled tune as he staggered out of the door. Dean followed but paused to address the room. "I apologize to you all for my associate's behavior. It won't happen again. Frank, Adam, Ike, you better come, too."

The men made curt apologies and left in a hurry, as Mrs. Zimmerman was coming in with a fresh pot of coffee in each of her hands. She stopped in her tracks when she saw the strained expression on the faces around the table. "What now?"

Lieutenant Hall opened his snuffbox and took a pinch, "Only a little performance of *Hamlet*, ma'am. It was quite good. They had business to attend to but send their compliments to your cooking, as do I."

CHAPTER 29

"More! Oh, what a glorious day, look at what we've found here!" Professor Fernsby carefully brushed aside the earth to reveal the rusted remnants of a heavy steel armor piece, and beside it the hilt of a sword. Constance leapt down into the trench and took a trowel to a patch she thought held the shape of bones, uncovering vertebrae and parts of a pelvis. "Why, I say, uncle, with the armor present, we seem to have found the burial site for Don Esteban's lost souls for certain. How thrilling!"

Beaming, Fernsby wrapped his arm around his niece and kissed her on the cheek. "We will be the talk of the journals with this find, my dear."

Julius Dankworth joined the celebration and then called to their servant, "Chan, bring me the labels and a pencil so that we can begin moving the finds into the tent."

As Chan went to procure the requested items and prepare tables for the relics to be sorted and labeled on, Berryman surveyed the trenches carefully from above, searching for inorganic abnormalities that might reveal a casket of treasure. Millions worth of gold and silver had been taken by the Europeans over the years, and much of it had been left behind whenever the Spaniards had to leave in a hurry, plagued by Indian attacks, with no access to fresh horses, fighting to find water when their wine ran dry, or taken out by disease to die in the wilderness. There were likely a hundred places in the Americas that held caches of riches, but the maps were long gone, and the oral histories lost to the ages, never to be spoken. This site, however, was known to be overflowing with a river of gold, and Berryman intended to find it for himself, and himself alone. He looked at the silly woman, who thought of herself as his peer, and her harebrained uncle, and smiled unpleasantly. Yes, gold and glory would all be his for the taking soon, no matter the cost.

CHAPTER 30

As the afternoon drew near to a close, the clouds had finally parted and the desert was bathed in a soft lemon light. Birds flitted in the oak burs and perched on the slanted roofs of the post buildings, grooming their feathers and singing, as they looked for spiders to pluck from the eaves. Lieutenant Cranston had reluctantly agreed to allow the professors to have a shortened rifle practice, as they were barely paying attention, anyway, in the state of excitement over finding dead men and their accoutrements deep under the sand. The finds made him wonder if everywhere he stepped there were bones beneath his feet, an entire underworld of the dead that existed unknown.

An ominous sense of foreboding that coiled deep in his gut and would not ease made him unsettled, and after drilling his command on the bayonet charge, he had slipped away for a quiet moment alone, to gather his thoughts and reflect. Recent events had shaken him more than he cared to admit to his fellows, as it always seemed like his superior officers could take on the worst of violence and suffering with little concern. He deeply admired their fearlessness and had learned much about how to be courageous in the face of horror—training not provided at West Point but found easily here, west of nowhere and surrounded by criminals.

He scanned the horizon in search of any hint of a war party, but nothing stirred. It was just the murder that had shaken him, he concluded. Corporal Pierce had been a fine trooper and had earned his promotion a mere three weeks ago, having proven himself after two years served at Fort Misery. He was a quiet, intelligent man and unlikely to have made an enemy who would go so far as to slit his throat in the dark. The bloody message made no sense. Certainly, no link existed between Pierce and the cursed gold of de Toro.

Atticus rolled the tension from his shoulders with a heavy sigh and had turned to head back when a flash of movement caught his eye. Startled, he squinted and shielded his eyes against the dying sun, what was it? There! A rider framed against the bright glare—Apache? A second rider joined the first, then a third, and the fort erupted in noise as the lookouts raised an alarm, and all hell broke loose.

"Hall! Get your command mounted and positioned. Damn it all, where is Cranston?" Captain Kellerman barked orders from horseback, as troopers ran to pick up their rifles and get to their stations. The sound of hooves and drums drew nearer across the flat desert, and though the morning's storm had wet the earth, enough dust was raised to obscure the numbers of the Apache warriors as they made their approach.

"Here, sir!" the young lieutenant called, breathless and flushed. "Sir, I have sent my command to headquarters, but I haven't called on the civilians yet."

"Never mind them. Get your troopers into position. I'll deal with the professors. The pistoleros may all be drunk by now, but drunk or not, they can fire a rifle. Quickly now—no time to spare."

"Yes, sir."

Lieutenant Hall had his command up and ready within minutes, and they made a fine sight as they crossed the parade ground on their way to the headquarters. He held his saber high, "Come on, you ruffians, look alive! Fight with vigor and I'll reinvigorate you with brandy after the fight. If any of you die on me, I'll kill you again."

As soldiers filled their posts and fell silent, waiting for the oncoming attack, Joe Kellerman swung out of his saddle in front of the enlisted men's bunk house just as Lucas Dean stepped outside. "Apache?" Dean said, his green eyes alive with the prospect of violence.

"Seems that way. Has your man sobered up any?"

"Enough to point a gun, yes. Maybe not enough to aim it very well."

"The sergeant major will be at the infirmary. Take your men and meet him there, and I won't be long behind."

"All right." Dean turned to go inside.

"And Mr. Dean," Kellerman said, scowling.

"Yes?"

"Don't give me any reason to hang one of you."

"All right." Dean said, and headed inside to rouse his associates.

CHAPTER 31

The infirmary was dark and quiet. The structure had been rebuilt after the Comancheros burned it down the year before, during the violent battle against Lozarado, the fight that had convinced Atticus Cranston to remain at Fort Misery under Kellerman's command. Tobias Zimmermann had reinforced the building's doors with iron this time around. But it still lacked a surgeon to run it, and the cots were often filled with poorly, coughing men alongside dusty trays of unused instruments that were useless to their afflictions in the hands of their unskilled attendants. Respiratory infections ran rampant at frontier forts, and the threat of tuberculosis was omnipresent.

Sergeant Major Olinger slammed to attention as Kellerman entered, and the captain returned his salute.

"What say ye, Sergeant Major?"

"Sir, Ahiga reports that this is an exploratory attack to test our resilience against the warriors. It isn't a full war band, only a dozen or so 'raggedy Apache bucks'—his words not mine. They are painted and mighty fired up, yipping and yeeing their way to us at a zigzag. I suspect he is quite right, and they want to scout out our numbers to see how easy the fort is to take."

"Then we need to give them fire and brimstone, Sergeant Major," Kellerman said. "Make them think we have a hundred trained troopers eager to shed their blood."

Nicky Barnes rolled a cot to align with a window, and the heavy metal dragged across the floor with an unpleasant screech. He climbed onto it belly first and lay like a snake, pistol in his right hand and whiskey in his left. Lucas Dean and his associates joined in by lining the walls close to the windowpanes, where they could easily shoot out while staying behind a wall.

"Tree-Tree men," Kellerman said.

"It is Trey-Treys," Frank Abilene said.

Kellerman waved his hand. "Yes—you lot. When the Apache are in sight, I want you to open fire like you are raining down the very wrath of God upon the earth. Think of Sodom and Gomorrah, and don't stop shooting until you run out of lead. Don't turn away, or you may become a pillar of salt. You have rifles?"

They did, and to a man they patted the gunstocks to show where they rested, ready to fire. Then Ike Fletcher holstered his revolver and took up a Winchester instead.

"Excellent, by God—we may just survive this. Sergeant Major, I have stashed the professors and the ladies down the hall in the storage room. If we need them to fight this small party, I'd say we're in trouble, although the second lieutenant assures me they're quite proficient after his thorough instruction. If you need one of them, send Silversmith." Kellerman gestured at Private Silversmith, who stood aside the infirmary door with a carbine ready to kill any man who tried to break inside.

And just in time to be a potential target, a small black-haired figure appeared at the door and peered into the square peephole Tobias had constructed as a safety precaution. With a gasp, Silversmith stepped back and pointed his rifle and bayonet as the door swung outward.

"No, no. Do not shoot!" Chan stood at the door with a Henry cradled in his arms and a long sword strapped to a sheath across his back. "I came to help. The Navajo soldier man sent me here."

Kellerman frowned—he had completely forgotten about Chan. "You can go stay with the professors in the storage room. It's right down the hall there and has no windows, so you will be safe, in theory."

"No, no, I will not hide with the old men. I am young enough to join this battle. Your redheaded lieutenant has praised my skill."

The bewildered Private Silversmith looked to Kellerman who shrugged. "All right, Mr. Chan, bring your hind end in here and lock that door up behind you. You should know there is no doctor, and if you're injured, the best we can offer is morphine, gauze, and prayer."

Chan quickly hustled inside, and pulled down the three iron latches. "I do medicine, Captain. Ancient Chinese knowledge of healing has been passed down my family line for centuries. My medical chest is behind in the tent, if we need after killing the Apache." He grinned, oddly chipper about the incoming attack, which he seemed to view as a fun adventure.

Kellerman nodded. "Works for me."

CHAPTER 32

"All right, you scallywags, you scum! The time has come to fight as commanded by our very own Captain Kellerman and the mighty General Sherman. Will you let down the captain today?" Lieutenant Hall bellowed as he paced the line of his command of calvary troopers back and forth astride an enormous red American Saddlebred stud, who held his head high and pranced as if showing off the polished officer—dressed to regulation, and sporting his magnificent beard and curls—who had chosen him for the battle.

"No, sir!" came the reply.

"Will you disappoint General William T. Sherman with the cowardly act of dying in this godforsaken desert instead of in your old age by apoplexy in the arms of a buxom beauty above a tavern?"

"No, sir!"

"I didn't hear you—speak up, you villains!" bellowed Lieutenant Hall.

"SIR! NO, SIR!"

"Damn right! Bully for the mighty forces of Fort

Misery! Forward charge on my signal—they'll be here any moment now."

Inside the headquarters, Second Lieutenant Cranston, joined by Tobias Zimmermann, paced the long corridors, oil lamps flickering in the murky rooms as the sky darkened into dusk and a blanket of clouds returned. He had set his men to their posts by twos and threes and hoped the hours spent trying to shape them into real soldiers had paid off. They looked rough, hair uncut and shaggy, their boots dusty, and the red and blue of their uniforms faded to shades of pink and lavender. Ahiga had joined them after scouting the number of warriors on the move, and he now went from room to room poking and prodding at the men who were lacking in battle form. Private Billy Burt, just seventeen, was shaking like a leaf when the Navajo scout found him huddled into a corner. With a grunt, Ahiga used the butt of his Henry to smack the crouching man in the rear, making him pop up with a shriek. "If you try to hide, Apache will find you before you see them. Don't let them get near you, shoot first, or—" He slid his finger across his throat the way he'd seen Hall do when explaining the possibility of an impending death.

"Yes, sir," Burt said, building his courage to peek out the open window.

"Gun first, not face."

"Yes, sir." Burt pulled back and rested the barrel of his rifle on the windowsill.

"Better."

* * *

"I hate this, it is ridiculous. I am just as well equipped to fight as most of the men out there, and instead, I am stuffed in here with"—Constance glared at the stacks of crates the professors perched on—"canned peaches and flour."

Mrs. Zimmermann clutched her rosary and paused in her prayers. "It isn't that we are weak and as useless as the canned peaches, but if the fort is overrun. the kindest thing would be to shoot each other in the head. The Apache kill slow and keep white women as slaves. I have seen—well, I have seen terrible things that no Christian should ever witness."

Constance paced the small room in a circle. She clutched a Winchester in her hands and, each time she turned the barrel, swept the professors who swayed to the opposite direction in a synchronized move. Right. Left. Right. Left.

Finally, Fernsby intervened. "Dearest, stop pointing that thing at us. You're liable to blow off our heads if you trip."

She stopped and pointed the barrel at the ground, "Sorry, uncle. Ooh, I just want to know what is happening. This is a miserable state of affairs. We didn't even have time to pack the relics into— Oh no, where is Chan?"

CHAPTER 33

"Here they come," Kellerman called, as the Apache rode in on a cloud of billowing dust made red by the falling sun, their faces and bare bronze chests painted in a dazzling array that gave them the appearance of demons rising from Hades. *Thunk*. An arrow hit the exterior, and the festivities had officially begun.

Thunk. Thunk. Thunk. Thunk.

A shower of arrows and bullets assailed the building, but none made it into the windows. Nicky Barnes leveled his rifle and fired, hitting a young warrior with a deadly shot to the heart, the man flying back off his horse with a foot tangled in his Union calvary saddle, a trophy from some other fight.

"That's the spirit!" cried Kellerman. "Take 'em down fast and easy!" He fired, a miss that sent up a V of dirt. A reply came, and hot lead grazed his temple, sending a shower of blood down his cheek. "Damn it, I could have done without that," he said, sending back a spray of wild shots some of which landed, taking down a horse that collapsed on its rider with a thousand pounds of deadweight. The squashed Apache screamed wildly for a solid minute before falling still as his lungs and innards were crushed under the pressure.

Saul Olinger glanced over at Kellerman and saw the blood through the haze of gunsmoke that filled the room. "Joe! Talk to me!" he yelled over the deafening blasts of the pistoleros rapid firing revolvers.

"Hit, but alive, just keep shooting."

Enraged by the injury of a man who Olinger had come to think of as a younger brother over their years serving together, the sergeant major roared, "Damn you all!" and fired again and again, ducking back to avoid the returning onslaught as best he could while still keeping his aim true.

Chan took down an Apache who had gotten himself so worked up he attempted to run at the infirmary on foot, firing a rifle in quick succession and hollering out a war cry that made everyone's hair stand on end. *Bang! Bang! Bang!* Three neat shots to the ambitious young warrior's chest knocked him down, and Chan let out a little cheer.

Lucas Dean let out a slow breath and fired his Colt with precision, and the head of an Apache who had decided to try his luck at riding nearer than the other warriors exploded out the rear in a shower of brain and bone. He stayed upright for a moment, then slid from the paint pony who carried him and hit the earth like a sack of potatoes. Dean grinned. "Got him."

Shwunk.

An arrow whizzed past Dean's head and he heard a terrible squelching *thunk* behind him. He turned to see Ike Fletcher standing stunned with the arrow shaft through his right eye. For a long moment the man tried to form a word, his mouth opening and closing like a fish out of water. Then he fell back as dead as he ever would be with the rifle still clutched tightly in his hands.

Lieutenant Hall dropped his saber with a dramatic flair. "Forward charge!"

With a thunder of hooves and a few cries of "Huzzah!" his troop surged through the gate built into the stucco and timber walls that enclosed the fort and rounded the corner, galloping past the headquarters and rushing the Apache from the rear, reducing the chance of crossfire from Kellerman's troop. A few of the warriors lay dead or dying and the scouts had been correct in their count, so mercifully not many fighters endured. The light was fading, and Hall considered the rapidly gathering shadows to be a worse enemy than the remaining Apache, though he knew the Indians had no quarrel with fighting in the dark.

The Apache split into two groups, and three mounted warriors rushed Hall's men, lances held out as though they were knights on a joust. A man, with red-and-white paint and long braids that fell across his buckskin shirt, charged a private who had fumbled his gun as he fought his sorrel, who had reared with a scream of pain—for a reason the soldier couldn't figure, as there had been no bullet or blood. The horse danced on a hobbled leg, and then the private saw it, a rattlesnake now trampled to death on the white sand. Distraction brought death, as the Apache ran his lance through the soldier's chest with a cry of victory, then ripped the spear back out.

Whooping, the warrior circled back to repeat the

attack on Lieutenant Hall, who saw the charge coming and made short work of a shot to the throat, a pulsing spray of blood rising from the Indian's neck and coating the white hide of his pony as he fell to the side.

Rain began to fall and lightning scrawled across the cobalt sky, the remains of the day now nothing more than a brilliant pink glow sinking into the western horizon. Hall turned to his troop and saw two of his men dismounted and firing shots on bended knee at the retreating backs of three Apaches who rode furiously to the east. *Off to lick their wounds and report our numbers to the rest of the Mescalero*, he thought glumly, but then was cheered by a hit that ripped a warrior in the shoulder. "I say, jolly good shot, Private Wesley!"

"Thank you, sir."

He looked at the remains of the battle with a heavy sigh, then noticed the lame horse trotting in a panicked circle and set off to collect the poor thing's reins.

Corporal Lockhart met Atticus Cranston in the headquarters, and the lieutenant began helping the orderly light and trim the oil lamps, as he gave the details of the battle he had gathered so far.

"We didn't have a chance to engage—shooting wildly around blind corners in the dark would have been a disaster, especially with my troop. I am still not confident that they can reliably hit a target at ten paces away," Cranston said with a small frown. "This works one of two ways, as I see it. Either they come back with a weak effort, since they didn't appear to realize my men exist, giving us the advantage of surprise, or they gather a huge party to take the fort down once and for all, and we end up outnumbered."

"Yes, sir," Lockhart said, shaking out a match that had burned down to his fingertips. "Indians are notional—who knows what they'll cook up next?" He snapped his fingers. "Say, I forgot to mention, the captain was wounded. Only a graze, I think. That Chan fella that came with the professors is patching him and a few of the others up."

"I knew you were going to put me in silk, dang your hide," Kellerman grumbled, as Chan took one of the yellow silk ties from his boot to wrap tightly around the captain's bleeding head.

"Ah, just for now," said Chan. "You be patient, few more minutes, and I get my chest and fix you proper. I have to tie on tight or the bleeding will continue. This will hurt," he added. And it sure enough did.

CHAPTER 34

Gathering the dead was a solemn ritual, and the light rain and distant thunder gave the right ambience to the occasion. In the yellow squares of lantern light, the blood looked black as spilled ink. Father Staszczyk said prayers for the departed, including the Apaches, though they did not worship his God. A mass grave was dug for the Indians, and they were buried quickly in respect of at least part of their beliefs, as they thought the dead must be buried immediately and the lost souls' worldly possessions burned. Kellerman was also hoping to head off any Indians skulking around the fort trying to retrieve their fallen comrade's bodies.

Ike Fletcher and the dead trooper, Sam Daniels, were laid out in the priest's quarters until they could receive burials in the fort cemetery when the sun was up again. Daniels had been serving out a thirty-year sentence for the rape and murder of a young girl in New York, and he was not well liked by his fellows, as even the worst criminals look down on a man who harmed a child. Private Wesley was charged with rolling the dead man onto a litter, and when no one was looking, spit on

Daniels's face. "Good riddance to you," he said before proceeding with his grim task.

The walking wounded filed to the infirmary, and the night grew still once again.

"How is he?" Lieutenant Hall approached the stall where Tobias Zimmermann knelt alongside the sorrel who'd been struck by a rattlesnake, applying a poultice to the small fang wound on the horse's swollen fetlock.

"Not too bad. Won't need to put him down yet," Tobias said. "Looks like the rattling jackass missed part of his strike, so there is only one puncture wound, here." He pulled the poultice away and pointed to the angry red wound. "I think we can pull him through, if the pain doesn't get too much for him—isn't that right, Sergeant Chestnut," he said affectionately to the horse, who nuzzled his shoulder gently and snorted. "He's a strong fella. He'll fight the villain's venom off in record time, I believe."

"He got Daniels killed, so he is all right in my book. Hell, the snake is all right with me, too. He should get a medal, God rest his soul—as long as Sergeant Chestnut lives."

Frederick Mann appeared in the stable hall, the shadows and light dancing across his wild-eyed face as he held a crucifix on a chain around his throat up in one filthy hand and a pitchfork, spikes up, in the other.

Hall recoiled, "Dang, you are spooky! Anyone ever tell you that before?" Then, opening his snuffbox: "Here, have a pinch, Spooky."

Mann smiled and let the cross drop back against his

chest to accept the pinch. His ragged fingernails and ripped cuticles made the lieutenant scrunch his face in disgust but he made no comment. "What do I do with it, sir?" he asked.

"Stick it up your nostril and sniff hard, like you are trying to send it up to your brain. You won't regret it."

The soldier did as instructed, and it set him into a sneezing, coughing fit that took a moment to ease. "Should the room be spinning, sir?"

"For your first time, yes."

"Sir, I do regret it."

"Hogwash! Next, we try brandy. I'll make a fine trooper out of you yet. Pinch, Mr. Zimmermann?"

CHAPTER 35

"Orderly! Officer's call! Get Corporal Lockhart in here, too."

Joe Kellerman sat heavy behind his desk, his head throbbing and unpleasantly coated beneath layers of bandages with strange goo, some of which had dripped onto his calvary mustache on one side and made it droop. He opened the drawer and pulled out the whiskey and laid out glasses, filling his own and downing it, then repeating the action once more. From the left drawer he took out a map of the territory and studied it briefly, wondering if the Chiricahua were on their way or had skipped and headed straight for Sonora. He jotted down a few points of likely attack and then folded the weathered map and replaced it in the drawer. The night was suspiciously quiet. It set his nerves on edge and made the tinny ringing in his right ear seem like a train engine was rushing past his face.

Kellerman drummed his fingers on the desktop just to make a noise and then rolled a cigarette and lit it. Finally heavy footsteps and low conversation neared his door and his officers stepped in and slammed to attention.

The captain saluted from his seat, "At ease. Forgive me for not standing. I'm a little dizzy on my feet for the time being."

Atticus Cranston looked worried, "Maybe we should send a courier to Yuma and try to get a real surgeon out here, sir."

"I admire your optimism, Second Lieutenant, but there isn't a snowflake's chance in hell of convincing a sawbones to ride out here in the middle of Apache roving."

"Sir, what is that smell?" Lieutenant Hall said, sniffing the air with an appalled expression.

"That's me," Kellerman said. "Mr. Chan informs me that the herbs, oils, and potions slathered on my wound is the premiere tonic for healing and has come all the way from the Orient and directly to my head."

"Respectfully, sir, you smell like a hog farm."

"Thank you, Lieutenant." Kellerman hoisted the whiskey. "Have a drink, all of you. We lost one of our troopers and a member of the Fey-Feys and should offer them a toast."

"Trey-Treys, sir," Corporal Lockhart said.

"Thank you, Corporal."

"Sir, I will toast to the dead pistolero, and even to the dead Apaches, who fought well for heathen villains, but I can only raise a glass to the well-deserved death of Private Daniels and not the man's life," Hall said, his tone firm and flat.

Kellerman racked his brain but was dizzy and dulled,

and couldn't recall the trooper's face, never mind his list of offenses.

"Please enlighten me, Lieutenant, as I think the bullet knocked his memory out of my brain."

"Child rapist and murderer, sir. He was shunned by the rest of the troops, and quite frankly, I am surprised he lived long enough to get killed. The beatings he received regularly only left him alive out of his attackers' general fear of you hanging whoever might kill him, I believe."

Kellerman nodded. "Now I remember. A toast to the death of Daniels, and a toast to the life of Ike Fletcher and a battle well fought."

The officers raised their glasses and cheered before downing their shots.

Sergeant Major Olinger refilled his glass and Kellerman's with the whiskey, while Hall pulled a silver flask of Hennessy from inside his shirt.

"Here, Cranston, Lockhart, have a brandy. You pair look white as sheets tonight," he said, and poured from the flask into their outstretched glasses.

"Thank you, sir," they replied in unison. After they downed the smooth brandy, a bit of color returned to their faces.

A comfortable silence lingered for a moment until Olinger, once again passing around the bottle, finally broke it.

"Sir, this was a test. We have a bigger fight ahead, and I am worried about it."

"I'm aware, Sergeant Major. I have set coordinates for our patrols to investigate at first light. I feel as if we are about to be hit on both sides at once. Don't ask me why I have that notion." He shrugged, palms up. "I just do."

Atticus Cranston spoke up. "Sir, my command was not needed in the fight, but they were positioned and ready, and followed orders. I wish I had more time to spend with them on the rifle practice is all, but at least they know how to listen."

"You'll have tomorrow, Lieutenant. The Apache won't be back for a day or two, and I suggest you use that time wisely."

"Yes, sir," Cranston replied, then downed the whiskey that the Sergeant Major poured for him.

"Watch your drinking, Second Lieutenant," Saul Olinger said, as he moved to the next man.

Cranston grinned. "Yes, sir."

Out in the rolling white sands of the desert, creatures of the night stirred awake, going about their nightly business unseen to the men at the fort. Coyotes howled mournfully to each other, communicating to their packs news about a mule deer or jackrabbit caught for dinner, and the evening birds called warnings and mating songs. Inside Fort Benjamin Grierson only a few buildings remained lit as the hours crept on toward midnight. Chan and Mrs. Zimmermann flitted around the infirmary fussing like old hens and arguing over the appropriate treatments for the few men who needed attending.

Constance Courtenay stepped out of her quarters while Mrs. Zimmermann was distracted and slipped out into the night, a heavy book tucked under her arm and a Colt .45 buckled around her waist—a new accessory from the armory she had all but demanded after the Apache attack was over.

She made her way across the parade ground and, to her relief, saw that a light still shone in Captain Joe Kellerman's office. She thought he may be as unable to rest as herself. A rapid movement behind her froze her in her tracks, and she lowered her hand to the gun before turning to see what was running up. Major Mouser had follower her, and she waited for him to catch up, bending down to scratch his ears and earning a heavy purr. "You can't sleep either, huh, little lad?"

The cat stretched lazily and yawned, then weaved around her legs, following her as she began to walk again. She stepped into the small alcove that covered the door to Kellerman's office, where a bored-looking young private stood outside the door. She smiled at him. "Is the captain in?"

The orderly looked her up and down lasciviously and it made her skin crawl, but she ignored it—as a woman working in a men's field, she had grown used to unwanted looks and comments.

"Yep, hold on a moment, ma'am." The orderly rapped firmly on the door and then stepped inside. She heard Kellerman loudly and crossly ask, "What now?" and it made her grin a little.

"Just a lady, sir, the arcee-ark-ah—"

"Archaeologist," she murmured, and the man turned to glare at her through the door.

"The bone digger-upper woman, sir,"

"Send her in," said Kellerman.

She heard the frantic sounds of rustling and clinking, as Kellerman cleared his desk and a chair.

Inside, the structure reminded her of a tomb or prison cell. The dingy excuses for windows were guarded by heavy bars, and the room was surprisingly small and sparse.

Connie waltzed inside as though she had been there a thousand times, Major Mouser right on her heels.

Kellerman stood briefly behind the desk and pressed his thighs to the hard surface so he wouldn't fall, as the ringing in his ear and dizziness persisted. Were he honest with himself, his whiskey consumption may have been a bit excessive combined, as it was, with allowing Mrs. Zimmermann, after many protests, to give him a very small shot of morphine to take away the pain of the torn, burned skin on his face while Chan ruthlessly fussed at it with stinging remedies. According to Chan, the stinging meant it was working.

Constance smiled warmly. "I thought you might be up. I promised to bring you some of my texts on the European endeavors across the southwestern territories, so I selected one of my favorites for you to read during your recovery. How are you feeling, Captain Kellerman?"

She looked fresh as a prairie rose in her pale pink silk blouse and canvas pants tucked into high leather boots, but Kellerman noticed the gun at her hip and thought the attack had shaken her more than she let on. Good, she finally understood the dangers he tried to impart when she arrived. Better yet, she was armed to fight those dangers.

He sat back down carefully and gestured to the seat across from him with a smile of his own, head reeling from the movements. "Just fine, Miss Courtenay. A little like I was shot in the face, but thankful that the villain's aim was not more accurate. Two inches over to the left and I'd be dead as a Christmas goose."

"Oh, please, just call me Connie, will you? You're making me feel like an old spinster with your insistence on the use of 'Miss' all the time. I have little concern for the rules of modern niceties, especially here in the middle of nowhere." She laid her book on the desk. The cover was green and embossed with gold lettering.

"I'll agree to it in this room, Connie, but in front of my troopers I must use the rules of decorum appropriately, lest they think I may approve of their own indiscretions. Drink?" He reached for the bottom drawer of the desk this time and selected a finer bourbon sent for him once every few shipments by request of General Sherman, a luxury he saved for special occasions or extreme upsets.

"Yes, please," Connie said, as Major Mouser leapt into her lap and curled into a tight ball, rolling over to reveal his white belly.

Kellerman watched this as he poured carefully. "Cats won't do that with me—especially not that particular cat." He pushed her glass across the desk, and she picked it up with her slender hand, tan from the sun. Taking a sip, she smiled, then to the captain's surprise downed the whole shot, and he refilled it for her with a grin.

"Well, felines have a special affinity to me, and I can tell you why if you promise—and I mean swear on your heart—that you will not mention it to Mrs. Zimmermann." She stared into his eyes intently, and he couldn't help but notice how brilliantly blue they were, like the ocean he once saw glimpses of, as a boy of thirteen, before the army took him away to this dull landscape. He'd never forgotten the way the water looked placid in the distance but crashed with fury on the shore. It reminded him that even the calmest of men could break into violence when they come against an obstruction.

"I swear it on my own heart," Kellerman said. "Mum's the word."

"It is the goddess Bastet. She is my guardian in this world."

Taken aback, Kellerman only replied, "I see."

Connie smiled. "I know it may sound preposterous to you, but during my travels in Egypt the goddess found me, at the ruins of her temple in Alexandria. She is the daughter of Ra, and a warrior goddess who is fierce in battle and fights against evil. Protector of women, and cats, of course, since she is cat-headed herself. Early depictions showed her as a lion-headed figure, but in the second millennium she was represented as a black cat, sometimes protecting a litter of kittens, as she is also the guardian of fertility and children. Out of desperation I prayed to her in the rubble of that temple when a group of men, wielding knives, tried to—well, you can imagine their intent."

Kellerman nodded.

"I could not understand their language, but I did recognize the danger, and although my martial-arts training took hold and I fought like a wildcat, it was only me, alone against five. I prayed, and begged her, and a massive piece of limestone suddenly shifted from the top of a lone standing pillar and fell upon the men with great force. Killed three instantly and trapped the limbs of the other two. I ran until I found my uncle and left Egypt soon after with my dignity intact although . . ."

She paused, her eyes downcast. "I had taken many blows to the stomach and the stab of a scimitar—you know, that long curved knife the Arabians carry. I hadn't felt it until my uncle screamed at the blood. The doctors told me I would live but could never bear a child. Although I lost my chance at motherhood, I gained a friend and protector in the goddess, and she keeps evil far away from me wherever I go."

Speechless for a time, Kellerman sipped his whiskey and thought before deciding what to stay. "I am right sorry about your—inability to bear a child. But I suppose I am happy that you found your goddess, if she keeps you feeling protected and strong. You are an interesting woman, mis—Connie. There is more to life than having babies. I haven't got a single one myself. That I know of."

She laughed lightly, "How old are you, Captain?"

"Forty-two, I think. Please call me Joe, if we are skipping formalities."

"I am thirty-five—I suppose too old for a baby, anyway, though someday I may take in a ward the way my uncle took me."

"You seem as adept as your uncle at all this bone digging, if not more so, and certainly more adept than that Berryman character. Universities won't accept a woman professor?"

She smiled sardonically. "Nope, not a chance. It's fine. They can't stop me from publishing my finds and doing the field work."

A silence fell for a time. "And who is your God,

Joe?" She finished her whiskey, and Kellerman poured her a third.

Another moment's silence, then Kellerman said, "We don't talk much these days." He pulled open the drawer where his bourbon lived and removed the old rosary, one he hadn't used since arriving at the fort and little before that. "Catholic, but I am out of practice. My father—" The drink had taken ahold of him, and he was speaking more freely than he would normally have felt comfortable with, but it felt good to let it out to someone other than Saul Olinger. "My father was a scoundrel. His name was Peter, too, and that is why I use my middle name—I can't stand to hear his name called as my own. He had a thick leather strap and a giant Bible, and those were two of his tools for raising up a child. My dinner depended on my memorization of verses, and a wrong answer meant a beating with the strap and an empty belly. If I stepped out of line, which to him meant trying to defend my mother when he beat her senseless in a rage, my punishment was to kneel on dried beans for hours holding that giant Bible aloft in front of me." He held his arms out forward, palms up, to show her.

"One time, when I was about eight, I dropped that Bible, and he responded with his worst brutality yet. I won't tell you more, as I can't bear to think on it. A childhood like that takes the shine away from faith, and yet my mother still encouraged me to pray and attend the church, so I did—until the night my father beat her to death. I suppose, now, my faith lies more in good whiskey and competent soldiers than anything else, but you never forget how to say a prayer, and I drop a quick one once in a while, as I keep hoping someday God will listen."

Connie stood from her seat, a tear running down her cheek. Major Mouser leapt off and, looking offended, proceeded to groom himself irritably. She thought for only a second and then rounded the desk, taking Kellerman's face in her hands. He knew he should stop her, but he didn't.

"May Bastet protect you from evil all the rest of your days," she said, her voice breathy. Her hands were warm and soft, and her eyes sparkled in the light of the oil lamp, and he drew her down to his lap and kissed her deeply, and she fell into his arms with a sigh. Then, she murmured against his skin, her lips tickling his throat, "What is that smell?"

CHAPTER 36

Dawn broke bright and clear, a watercolor painting of pink and yellow to the east that reflected upon the Tinajas Atlas Mountains and the various outcroppings of rock scattered across the desert. The blue trim upon the white stucco of the fort glowed in a dreamy light as the early morning duties began.

Mrs. Zimmermann was feeding her chickens and criticizing her hens for their poor output, when Constance appeared behind her looking bright-eyed and yet somehow exhausted. Had she come in from the parade ground instead of her quarters? Frowning at the woman, Mrs. Zimmermann decided she didn't want to know, and asked her to help with building the stove fire up good and hot for corn pone and salt pork.

In the west, the sound of war drums had begun, and their hollow sound carried across the sand dunes and set the men at the fort on edge. The camping Lipan by the boarded-up sutlery had packed up and left in a hurry, off to a safer destination, if such could be found.

From the shadows, a figure watched the troopers and civilians scurrying about their morning activities, selecting the next target. The professors argued with each other on their way to the trenches, and Berryman glanced around furtively, looking for something or someone he did not find. Here and there a soldier would stop and scan the buildings around him, feeling uneasy, as though he was being watched. Finally, having come to a decision, the shadow stalker turned to slip away back to the hole until the sun set that evening.

Lieutenant Hall checked in on the stables and walked through to ensure the horses were all receiving their proper attentions at the hands of the soldiers—and a handful of molasses oats each, as a celebration for their job well done the night before. Sergeant Chestnut held his hoof an inch from the ground and walked lamely, but thanks to the intervention of Mr. Zimmermann and a further visit from Chan, who had applied one of his smelly potions, the purple and black swelling in the fetlock had darkened but not traveled more than a couple of inches up the rest of the leg, and the sorrel seemed more concerned about the oats than his injury. Pleased, Hall made his way to Lucifer, who glared at him from the rear of his stall and refused to move. "Have it your way," Hall said, dropping a handful of the sweet oats into the feed bucket. "You weren't even out fighting the villains with us last night, lazy man that you are. Know well that you haven't earned these yet, but as a man of fairness, I'm including you in the gifting. Enjoy them, you menace."

Soon after the lieutenant had finished overseeing activity in the stables, the bell rang and the soldiers filed out to hit the mess hall, the lieutenant splitting off from the enlisted men as he headed for the officers' mess. All the chatter he overheard was about the Apache, and the story had grown so embellished that now there were supposedly fifty warrior braves instead of twelve. *Let them have it*, Hall thought. *If it encourages them to be vigilant now, and victorious in the next fight, then I don't care if they claim to have shot down a hundred Indians each.*

Lucas Dean chose a seat between Lieutenant Cranston and Professor Fernsby, watching his associates like a hawk as they shuffled to their chairs on the opposite side of the table. Nicky Barnes had mostly sobered up, but he and Frank were already lamenting the death of Ike Fletcher—a man they didn't even like—as a reason to receive hazard pay for their stint. Only Adam Louis remained calm and collected, understanding that they were playing the long game.

"Tell me, Professor, outside of your confinement in the closet, how goes your excavation?" Dean said, smiling at the old man.

"Quite good, quite good. I have started to find gold coin loose in the earth among the relics, and surely, that means the casket of treasure is near enough. I hope Captain Kellerman doesn't pull our help away today in preparation for more war, as it will slow us down tremendously," Fernsby said with a tinge of worry.

"Well, say there, Professor. We can help you out," Dean said, pointing at himself and the surviving Trey-Treys with a flipping motion of his index finger.

Fernsby slapped the man's shoulder cheerfully, "Old chap, I hear tales of your gallantry during the fight against the Apache and would be delighted to have a man of your fine esteem providing help to our cause."

"Whatever you need, boss." Dean grinned. "Your wish is our command."

"And here, we have a helmet worn by some poor fellow way back in 1538, the red plumes that would have adorned it are of course long disintegrated, but you can see the excellence of the work put into shaping and designing the high quality of armor by the Spanish in those days. The attention to detail certainly played a part in their ability to conquer. Though they lost this particular— Oh look, another skeleton! By Jove, I believe it is all there!" Professor Dankworth was overseeing the archaeology work of the remaining Trey-Treys and lecturing them on history and antiquities as they put their backs into excavating the trenches, and he pranced about like a cancan dancer, using his toes to point toward various areas of interest. Nicky Barnes had a throbbing headache and would have happily plugged the babbling professor right between the eyes if it weren't for Lucas Dean's watchful eye and a drive for riches. Once the gold was in hand, maybe he'd shoot the old man and Dean both, a thought that made him snicker.

A few feet away, Fernsby used the tray Tobias Zimmerman built to sift sand, letting the earth fall through the screen and reveal small and broken relics hard to spot by the human eye.

Constance Courtenay worked inside the tent, labeling and examining the finds, and packing some into crates filled with straw and red velvet, preparing them for a safe journey back to England when their time here had come to a close. As she turned a femur over in her hands and looked for identifying marks to jot on the tag tied to it, something gave her pause. Using an eye loupe, she bent close to the bone and let out a little gasp. Then she went to the other skeletal remains and saw they, too, showed the same. Excited, she burst from the tent and called, "Professors, come here, I've made a fascinating discovery."

A few moments later, the older men had come to join her side, and she passed her uncle the loupe first.

"Tell me I am not imagining things, uncle, as it seems there are tool marks on the bones that show where the flesh was systematically removed like meat. I think that these were victims of cannibalism."

Berryman scoffed, but Fernsby examined the femur and declared, "By God, you are correct, dear. Stripped the meat from the bones in a hurry by the look of it. Here, take a glance Jules."

Dankworth groaned and held his lower back, in pain from bending over the table and crates, but eagerly took his turn looking over the specimens before insisting Berryman do the same.

The consensus was that the remains showed evidence of being butchered, and a closer look at some of the broken pieces suggested that some of the largest bones had been cut up into slices and the marrow pried out.

"This wasn't in the letters left in the vault by Alvarao Antonio. He mentioned that starvation drove them to eat their horses but not each other, most certainly," Fernsby said, stroking his white beard in contemplation.

Dankworth chimed in, "The shame of cannibalism would have been great, and perhaps he thought he would bring dishonor upon his family. You know how worked up the Spaniards get about that sort of thing. It makes perfect sense to me that he would hide the truth."

"Superstition," offered Constance. "That paints a better picture about the superstition over a curse on this site. Perhaps he spoke of the cannibalism to someone, and they spread a rumor. Many things are lost in translation over the span of centuries."

A tall shadow darkened the tent flaps. "Knock, knock," Kellerman called before ducking to step inside. He had found the Chinese ointment smelled less significant, but the bandage remained in place and forced his campaign hat to sit at a jaunty angle. His golden mustache and a few long curls that fell from his hat shone brightly in the sun, but he looked tired, pale and had dark purple shadows beneath his eyes. "I came to offer my apologies for leaving you with only the pistoleros today, but with the patrols out and my second lieutenant in need of more time to train his command—well, you understand, I hope. Your man Chan should return to your service this afternoon. He has been a boon to our wounded and refuses to leave their sides at the moment." He caught Connie's eyes and winked, and she gave him a knowing smile that only Berryman noticed.

Fernsby flapped a hand. "Please, please, keep him as long as you need him. Healing the men who bravely fought off those terrible villains is far more important than bringing me tea and easing my rheumatisms."

"Thank you for your generosity, gentleman and lady. I will leave you to your work, but you should know that the attack yesterday was only a test of our defenses. In the next day or two, we anticipate full war bands of Mescalero and Chiricahua to hit us hard. To that point, please join Second Lieutenant Cranston again this afternoon for further training on your offensive skills. I can't promise you will have the safety of the storage room again."

Fernsby offered a salute as though he were enlisted, and Kellerman returned it halfheartedly, with a puzzled smile, before exiting the tent and stepping into the rapidly heating day.

CHAPTER 37

A brief funeral was held for Ike Fletcher and Private Daniels. Tobias Zimmermann provided plain wooden boxes and crosses, and the two men were planted in the fort cemetery with little fanfare. Fletcher was placed next to the grave of Dick Freedman, and the remaining Trey-Treys took a moment to remove their hats and bow their heads in prayer as the pine coffins were lowered into the ground. It may have been kinder to send them home to their families, but Father Staszczyk knew little about embalming, despite acting as the funeral director and morgue keeper in addition to his priestly duties. Besides, Ike had no kin that Dean could think of, and Daniels had been cast away from his family when they found out what he had done to earn the sentence. Hot corpses traversing the desert was a horrific affair even with the embalming, and sending them back to Yuma without being embalmed would only torment the driver.

Satisfied with his work after the two men were buried, Father Staszczyk made his rounds and spoke with soldiers in need of prayer and guidance, including a quick trip to the infirmary, though it seemed half of the troopers were atheists, a struggle he couldn't seem to overcome. He prayed for them anyway, in private. Salvation was at hand for those who would accept it.

The night and morning had dragged on into midday, and the priest found himself to be exhausted beyond measure as the adrenaline of the events wore off. He reasoned that a nap would suit him fine, and if any man needed his ministrations, they would knock, surely. It would certainly not be the sin of sloth for a man of sixty to rest. He lowered the wick in the oil lamp of his close quarters, bare of all but a simple bed, chest of drawers, and a crucifix that hung beside a painting of the Blessed Virgin. He lifted off his cassock and removed his leather shoes, wiggling his toes with relief as his feet ached. Tucking into the lumpy bed he began to read but quickly drifted away to the peaceful nothingness of sleep.

Father Staszczyk walked into the desert, a strange glowing light hovering in the sky. In the hazy vagueness of the dreaming conscious, the army fort lay behind him, but not as it was. Instead, it had become the gleaming phantasm of a fine Spanish fortress with brilliant red and yellow banners flying wildly from the parapets in a high wind he couldn't feel. He continued toward the light, terrified yet called to it as a moth to flame. After what may have been minutes or days, he neared the source of the light, and there stood the Virgin Mary, her blue robes dripping in puddles of cloth around her delicate feet clad in gold brocade shoes. A sparkling crown of stars plucked from the heavens circled her head, and the light of her being illuminated the twilight sky above, mixing with the moon and stars that hung in the misty cobalt hue. She was but a girl yet emanated the wisdom of all worldly knowledge. The father fell to his knees before her in supplication, and she bid him rise with a gesture of her hand.

"They are coming, son. You must join the fight, but you will not be the sole victor. Salvation will come on a dark horse when all hope feels lost, and you will be there to witness. Your role will be bloody, yet you will save a life that needs to continue forward on its path, and with faith in Christ, you will not falter."

"Mother, I am weak and old. I will serve God until my last breath is taken and I leave the earth forever to join the embrace of Christ. Am I to sin with violence and become a warrior, and die in the throes of battle— is that what God has chosen? I am afraid."

The Virgin beamed a beatific smile, and the father was filled with euphoric peace. "My son, be not afraid," she said. "To defend another is not a sin, and though your body is aging, your mind and soul remain young and strong. I am with you always."

Before the father could summon a reply, the vision faded and every trace of brilliant light disappeared, leaving only a heavy, darkened sky dotted by stars and the soft glow of a full moon. Shaking, the father fell to his knees and wept, covering his face with his hands.

"Father Stac—Staxy . . . Padre! Wake up!" A concerned solider shook the sleeping priest, gentle at first and then with vigor when the gray-haired man did not stir. Staszczyk bolted upright in a state of alarm and took in the scene, a patrol of mounted pickets was watching him with faces painted with deep disbelief. "How the hell did you end up out here, sir? If you'll pardon the language, Father." The soldier unscrewed his canteen and offered it to the dazed priest who accepted it eagerly and took long pulls of water to ease his parched throat.

"I— Where am I? I laid down for a nap in my quarters." His Slavic accent was thick but easy enough to understand, as he made it a point of speaking slowly and clearly.

The man took his canteen back and scratched at a peeling bit of skin on his throat, his fair Irish coloring not compatible with the Yuma desert's white sand, which reflected the brutal sun like a mirror and made hats win only half the battle of warding off sunburn. "Well, the fort is thataway"—he pointed, and the priest looked to see Fort Benjamin Grierson rising from the dunes at a fair distance—"so if you weren't kidnapped, and I don't believe you'd be alive if you were, then you must have been sleepwalking."

Private Howard Smythe piped up from atop his horse. "I've done sleepwalking afore—that's why the army says I'm a deserter. My attorney tried to tell them I was just wandering off in my sleep and got lost, but they wouldn't allow it, and now look at me. They even tried to say I accosted a lady, but I sure don't recall it and can't be responsible for what I may have done while not awake, can I? Do priests get court-martialed for wandering off? 'Cause you may be in a whole world of trouble if they do, on account of how ill-tempered the army is."

Corporal Edgar Wayne, now helping the father up to

his feet, turned and glared at the private. "Shut up and mind your manners. He's a man of God. Sorry, Father. Ignore that heathen rabble. Are you injured anywhere?"

Edgar Wayne had arrived at Fort Misery as a corporal, but that rank was the result of his demotion for the punches and kicks he'd landed on a captain when he'd caught the officer beating a horse. A professional soldier at heart, the stripping of his lieutenant stripes had cut deep. After a look at the paperwork and a brief interview, Captain Joe Kellerman quickly assessed that the new arrival was a welcome addition and assigned his duties accordingly—and, so far, had not been proven wrong.

Father Staszczyk patted himself down. He was barefoot, and his feet were sore and skinned from sharp rocks, but he was otherwise unharmed. "No, I'm fine, outside of my feet."

Wayne looked down and saw the priest's bloodied soles and toes, and winced. "All right. Can you ride a horse?" he asked, gripping the father's arm and guiding him toward his Morgan.

"Not really, though I do understand the basic principles of horsemanship."

"Well, Padre, you're about to become a regular expert. I'll help you up, one—two—three!"

A few minutes of grunting, lifting, and shoving later, Father Staszczyk was on the Morgan, as Corporal Wayne held the reins and led the horse back toward headquarters on foot. Before he left, he instructed the remaining pickets with a parting warning.

"Finish the patrol and head back. You'll likely cross paths with the Navajo and his men to the east. Listen to him—he understands the behavior of the Apache better than any of us. And Smythe, if you decide to sleepwalk yourself off into the desert, I'm sure the Apache will have a wonderful time waking you back up."

"So, you believe you experienced an apparition of Our Lady and now are hellbent on riding into battle against the Mescalero, is that the sum of it?" Captain Joe Kellerman stood alongside the cot where Father Staszczyk lay, having his bloodied and battered feet treated by Chan, who had cleaned the wounds and was slathering on some mysterious green substance. The Father had demanded his cassock and was present in all his priestly glory, despite the gray dust that covered him, and clutched a rosary in his hand.

"It is not a case of belief alone, Captain. I speak only of fact. The Blessed Virgin has appeared to me, and I must now follow her guidance or face the consequences." Staszczyk was grim, irritated by the reluctance of the captain, and everyone else for that matter, outside of Mrs. Zimmermann, who allowed that it was quite possible and was insistent he should write the Vatican immediately.

"What if the fact is that you had a dream and were walking in your sleep, and then I send an old man— begging your pardon, Father—to fight the Apache and then have to explain to the army and your superiors why I let a priest get murdered under my authority."

"Faith is required. And I will write down a letter detailing this miracle and leave it with my belongings, so if I die, you are cleared of responsibility for all my actions. You can try to talk me out of it until you are out of breath, Captain Kellerman, but I will not take no for an answer. If you refuse to let me learn under the tutelage of your second lieutenant, then I will take what I can from the armory and join unguided." The more agitated he became, the heavier his accent grew, and his words came out fierce and clipped.

Kellerman sighed. "Father Stay—Stack—"

"Staszczyk," Chan supplied.

"Thank you, Mr. Chan. Father, this is a bad idea, and I could have you thrown in the hole for insubordination until the notion leaves you, but I can't say the army would look any more favorably on my tossing a civilian man of God in a cell than it will on that civilian man of God dying by an Apache hand."

The father smiled. "I won't die—that was promised. But I must learn a few things as quickly as I—ouch"—he glared at Chan, then continued—"learn a few things as quickly as I can. So tell me where to start, and I'll be off as soon as this man sees fit to stop tormenting me."

Chan grinned, "If it does not hurt, it is not working. Pray to your Jesus. I hear he is good at healing."

Kellerman groaned. "All right, Padre. Second Lieutenant Cranston's lessons first, and then Lieutenant Hall's tutelage, but I am telling you right now, neither of them is going to like it any more than I do."

CHAPTER 38

"I don't like it, sir." Second Lieutenant Atticus Cranston frowned deeply, rubbing the back of his aching neck and thinking he badly needed a drink.

"It's a direct order, Second Lieutenant. There's no way around it unless you want to go inform the captain about your insubordination yourself. I'm certainly not going to tell him." Sergeant Major Saul Olinger stood beside Father Staszczyk, having delivered the priest to Cranston for bayonet and rifle training.

The priest was five paces away and watched the line of men charging the dummies with their bayonets and loosing war cries, and noticed three men of a similar age to himself, only one of whom seemed incompetent at the task. He surely would do better. After all, his was on a mission from God.

Cranston closed his eyes and counted down from ten. "Sir, I won't go so far as to disobey Captain Kellerman, sir. But God help me, I already have three graybeards, and now you've brought me a fourth. And I sometimes use unsavory language, as do my troopers—I hope he knows that."

Olinger grinned. "Treat him as you would anyone else. That seems to be what he wants so make sure he gets it. Here." He pulled out a tarnished flask and passed it to Cranston, who accepted it immediately and took a swig that made his eyes water. "That'll improve your attitude on our new trooper."

Cranston let out a little wheeze. "Sir, what was that?"

"Rum, a gift from Lieutenant Hall's secret stash."

"That's good, sir."

"Sure is—and Atticus?"

"Yes, sir?"

"Lay off the drink a little, you're hitting it pretty hard."

"Yes, sir."

"All right, Father Staszczyk, join the line—there between Mr. Dankworth and Mr. Fernsby—yes, that's it, right between the professors. Remember the Apache fight at a distance until they are certain they can approach for the kill. You'll need the rifle accuracy more than the bayonet, but if it comes time for close combat, charge in without hesitation or you may find yourself at the wrong end of a blade."

The priest took his position and clumsily picked up the Sharps. Cranston's shoulders slumped, but he wasn't about to let Joe Kellerman down, and he dove in to assist. If Fort Misery had taught him one thing it was perseverance in the face of chaos.

CHAPTER 39

The twilight brought a dramatic array of colors worthy of any painter's canvas, as lapis blue, sparkling with early stars, pushed down on the twisting lines of pink and yellow that gently swaddled the sinking sun. Once more, a light rain fell upon the denizens of Fort Misery and a heavy wind made the rooster atop the stables spin like a child's top, as Lieutenant Hall and Corporal Lockhart made their evening inspections of the horses and tack, *tsk*ing an unoiled saddle here and a rough looking coat there, but pleased by the livery duty's efforts overall. A weary patrol returned and handed off the torch to the fresh men and their horses who would take it up for the night, a nervous air surrounding all, as memories of the previous evening's attack weighed heavy in their minds.

Although supper was near, they could still hear the shouts and shots of Atticus Cranston's ongoing instruction echo across the parade ground, as the mission to whip the weakest links into shape continued with vigor.

"They've got him training the priest, sir," Corporal

Lockhart said, gesturing in the direction of Cranston's booming voice.

"I heard. Bully for him, I say! Every man here should be prepared to fight back, as our post seems to attract the worst of villains despite being planted smack in the middle of nowhere."

Lockhart laughed. "Yes, sir. We sure do seem to draw them all in." Then in a quieter tone, "I wish that the Apache would consider staying home from time to time."

"Are you afraid, Corporal?"

"A little, sir. The fort cemetery seems to expand so often that soon it'll stretch halfway to Yuma."

"Corporal, I will share a story with you to boost your courage, one I came up with myself in a moment of pure brilliance and inspiration. Are you paying attention?"

They had reached the end of the stable hall and stood in front of Lucifer's stall. The huge horse made his way to them and watched intently, either curious to hear the tale or looking for an opportunity to bite while one of the men was distracted.

"Yes, sir."

"Very good. Once upon a time there were two male hares, living in the desert. The hares did not get along as the first, a handsome hare, with majestic dark long fur, named Jim, would often eat all the edible parts off the limited supply of sparse bushes and plants before the other hare, called Flopsy, and a far less interesting-looking creature, with a dull brown coat, would get the opportunity. Flopsy was always afraid and too timid to confront the mighty Jim. One day, the meek, dull hare had decided enough was enough, and formed a plan. He would attack the beautiful strong hare to force his hand on sharing the vittles once and for all, and Flopsy, being weak, recruited help.

"Who? A rattlesnake! After an easy truce between snake and prey was formed, they planned the assault on Jim for dawn the following morning. The snake slithered, and Flopsy hopped, until they reached the warren of Jim, entering while the stronger hare was still sleeping contentedly, with a full belly and dreams of lady hares. Once inside the den a battle ensued and Jim dispatched the snake with a quick chomp of his large teeth. Alone, Flopsy spoke to Jim, saying, 'You eat more than you need and leave me with none, and I have had enough. It is time to settle this like men.' The two hares engaged in fearsome combat, Jim had the upper hand nearly the entire time, of course, but the rattlesnake had bitten him, and the venom began to take effect, so in the end both hares died from their wounds, never to search for shrubs again. It wasn't long before a happy coyote came along and ate all three creatures, and left contentedly."

Corporal Lockhart stared at Hall, waiting for more, but the lieutenant was beaming at him with a big smile and said nothing further.

"Is that—the full story? Sir?"

Lucifer eyed Hall with a look of sheer disgust and then turned away with his tail swishing, no longer curious about the humans.

Lieutenant Hall rolled his eyes skyward. "Yes of course it is. What more could you possibly need?"

"Well, I—quite frankly, sir—I am struggling to see

the moral and how it applies to our current predicament with the Apache. In fact, I am not entirely sure it made much sense, sir."

"Didn't make sense! Why you—" Hall took in a deep breath and pulled out his snuffbox. "You know what? I should have understood that you do not have the capacity to understand my highly complex metaphors. Never mind. Just remember this instead, Corporal. You do not need a complete absence of fear to be brave. Courage depends upon your actions, not your thoughts."

"Now that I understood—thank you, sir."

"Anytime. Pinch of snuff?"

CHAPTER 40

Deep in the shadowy desert, near a cluster of jagged rock formations shaped by millennia of water and wind, a spot that sheltered wild creatures in search of rest or a place to birth their young, the Mescalero had laid their camp. Roaring, tall fires inside the circle of wikiups and a scattering of piñon pine created a toasty refuge hidden from the keen eyes of Union pickets who looked east from Fort Benjamin Grierson and saw nothing but miles of sand. The men danced with complex movements around the flames, as sizzling sparks flew up to gambol with glittering rain. A solid drumbeat marked the steps of their moccasin-clad feet, and they moved as gracefully as ballerinas while they chanted the songs of war. Their copper chests gleamed in the firelight, and with each step that trampled the earth, they called upon the spirits to embolden them to victory against the white army men, who sat isolated and afraid.

The warriors that had died were cast from their minds. If their bodies remained when the full band staged the next raid, they'd retrieve them, but to think on death now would bring bad luck, and those men had died honorably in battle and were gazing down upon them with gifts of strength.

In two days, the warriors would strike again, in far greater numbers, and relish the riches held by the walls of the fort. They would take their women, if any existed, and claim many scalps. Then, with their bellies full of food, a cache of firearms, and a fresh surplus of horses, they would raid down into Sonora and deliver the Mexicans a reckoning, too.

In the cool night air to the west of the fort, a band of Chiricahua spoke animatedly around a campfire, speaking of how their assaults would honor Geronimo and bring about the Light of the Great Spirit, leaving peace and harmony on a land soaked in white blood. The youngest of the group, just turned eleven, curled close to the Elder's side and listened to stories of defeat and victory, loss and pain, completely enthralled. These men, too, planned to raid the fort in two days' time, but for tonight, leisure and stories were in order—until, eventually, a deepening chill drove everyone inside their wickiups, as the moon rose high in the sky, bright and clear. Tomorrow would be a day of dancing and drumming, when they would paint their skin and decorate the horses with sacred symbols, but tonight was for rest and meditations on the mission at hand. They knew the fort could be taken easily and had no qualms about the threat of losing the attack, ready to reclaim their territory and burn the white man's buildings to the ground.

As quiet overtook the camp, all remained peaceful

until an owl hooted somewhere off in the distance, a bad omen. The Elder returned to the fireside and began to sing in a heavy voice made no less powerful by age, praying for the spirits to change the sacred winds to blow in their favor and making offerings that he cast into the fire, one by one.

CHAPTER 41

Frederick Mann finished his stable duties and stepped out into the dark night, stretching his tight muscles with a groan. He liked working with horses—they understood him, and he, them—and the kinship was gratifying. Mann had struggled to communicate with his fellow-men for years, as they were often cruel and boisterous, completely unlike his brothers and sister at home, who were loving and kind, even when they doubted his claims of being the Messiah. His mama especially had coddled him, and when she passed away, his father suggested he join the army to escape their small town in Kentucky and see more of the world, perhaps giving him a new perspective—and, his father hoped, that would undo his conviction that he was Jesus returned. He had once tried to enter a seminary, but they refused him and labeled him a lunatic unfit for entry until he resolved his crisis of identity. So the young Mann had packed his books and clothes, and willingly signed the rolls, but a few weeks in, he realized that the army was not a vocation suitable for the son of God—and that was where the trouble began.

He fled in the night, hoping to set up shop somewhere more suitable, where no man was expected to carry arms and fire against a designated enemy with whom he, as an individual, had no quarrel. Selling fruit, linen, or apothecary goods sounded ideal and would allow him to embrace his role as the Christ, until God saw fit to reveal him to the world and the end times would finally arrive.

Instead, he became an apprentice for a horseshoe fitter, a man aptly named Hector Cobb, who dabbled in animal medicine on the side, and with Mann's skillful approach to all creatures great and small, suddenly, it seemed everyone in the dusty New Mexico town where Mann had settled after weeks of running was inquiring anytime they had a poorly dog or unwell canary bird. He did what he could to help and refused payment most of the time, accepting trades of bread and fresh eggs in exchange. This blissful arrangement only lasted three months before two stern-looking Army officials arrived with a court-martial summons and dragged him away in chains.

The trial had been swift, and the insanity plea failed in spite of, or perhaps due to, Mann's testimony that he was the One Christ and should thereby be given freedom to return to his nonviolent vocations. Much like Lieutenant Hall, the jury consensus was that he was faking it to get out of his duty to the army.

Sighing at the memory, Mann hung his head a little and headed back to headquarters to splash water on his face and rinse his hands before joining the rest of the enlisted men for supper. His stomach rumbled at the thought of hot food, though in truth Mrs. Zimmermann's selection of vittles were less than appetizing. *She tries, dear woman*, he said to himself, *and I am grateful for a full belly*. He had tried to re-create the miracle of loaves and fishes many times, but failed miserably, and he still had not turned water into wine. *Keep at it*, he insisted to his weary mind. *God the father will grant me the miracles needed in due time, I am sure.*

Mann headed to his bunk area and felt the hair on the back of his neck grow hot and the hairs there rise, a sure sign of trouble unseen. He slowed down pretending not to notice and then stopped short. Three men were in the gloomy corner of the hot room, and they all wore grins that were anything but friendly.

"Hello," Mann said softly, before starting toward his bunk yet again and hoping that they were only there to perhaps throw harsh words at him, words he had heard a thousand times. To his misfortune, the men approached him instead, with sinuous slinking movements like serpents.

"Why, hey there, Jesus man. Ain't you just pretty as a picture, now they've made you clean up," said the smallest of the three, a wiry middle-aged soldier with frizzy blond hair that was balding on the top. His oversized buck teeth gave him an odd lisp when he spoke.

Mann nodded but offered no reply. The next shady character came around behind him, this soldier larger and dark of eyes and hair, his face misshapen, as though he'd been in an accident or his mother had struggled with his birthing. One eye sat far higher than the other, and his nose was flat and held one enormous, upturned nostril while the other was barely a slit.

"What's the matter, Jesus boy, you skeered of us?"

Mann cleared his throat, "No, not scared. 'Yea, though I walk through the valley of the shadow of death, I shall fear no evil.' But I am trying to wash up for dinner. I know the cook lady doesn't take kindly to grubby soldiers, and I've been working with the horses all day." His tone was light and clear, but a waver in it gave away the fear growing in the pit of his heart.

The dark-haired man grabbed Mann by the arm and dragged him to the wash basin, and then with the blond on the other side they shoved him face first into the washbasin of water and held him there, struggling to escape, until his lungs burned and he was certain death was imminent. Finally, the largest of the trio—an imposing figure, whose shaved head and sinister grimace suggested he wasn't the friendly type—yanked him out by the hair. The man's face was covered with smallpox scars, and his eyebrows were patchy, as there were hard ridges of flesh where the hair couldn't grow.

"Well, look at that, all cleaned up and ready to go," said the short man, laughing at his cruelty. "We have a little surprise for you though, Jesus, and it seems your daddy—that's God, right?—seems he should be able to intervene at any time, if'n he feels like it."

Private Frederick Mann was yanked hair first onto the floor, and then the beating began in earnest. The first kick landed in his ribs and he held in a yowl of pain, but by the time the blows turned his face and body into a purple-and-yellow mishmash, he found he could no longer maintain self-control over the agony and unleashed choked screams between gasps of breath.

So, this is how I die, Mann thought, detached. *I suppose there are worse ways to go.* Crucifixion was surely painful enough for any man to suffer. The beating continued for what felt like hours, and then the final piece was added. Someone had made a crown, by weaving the heavy spikes of the barrel cactus that grew around the desert tightly with hay, and jammed it hard onto Mann's head, before propping his battered and broken body up in the corner like a child's discarded dolly.

"Wooo, boy! Don't want to stop, but I'm gettin' hungry—ain't we all hungry, boys? So, all done, for now. Think about this, Jesus boy, the next time you get to feeling inclined about spreading your blasphemy across the fort."

Laughing and praising each other's brutality, the three men headed to the mess for supper. Frederick Mann remained crumpled in the dark corner and didn't move until in a blurry state of concussed consciousness, he felt the prickling feet of a hairy tarantula investigating the back of his neck. He lurched forward and regretted it, as the pain in his ribcage became an explosion of agony and made it near impossible to draw breath. Weakly flailing a limp hand at the spider, he successfully scared it off, and it scurried up the wall with quiet swishing sounds, no longer interested in the activities of humans. A long time passed as he waited for death and slipped in and out of awareness, at times seeing visions of his mama and siblings, the kitchen of his childhood home, a cooling apple pie, and once he thought for certain that he heard the sweet singing of a canary.

After what seemed to be hours, he tried to open his eyes when he heard the sound of heavy footsteps walking across the hardwood floor toward him, but he found them too swollen. Then he heard the muffled cries of a man and felt rough hands on his shoulders—until, at last, the horror his body had suffered could go on no longer and he blacked out, seeing and hearing no more.

CHAPTER 42

Supper had been hearty. Mrs. Zimmermann put forth her utmost effort to nourish her charges and declared that "food and the Lord most quickly heal the soul," as she laid out the best of her stock. She had finished the meal off with peach cobbler, topped with tinned milk improved by a bit of sugar stirred in.

"You've outdone yourself, Mrs. Zimmermann. I do declare we are the most spoiled post on the frontier," Sergeant Major Saul Olinger said, with a wink at Joe Kellerman, having watched the captain carefully scrape a small green spot off a piece of beef in his serving of stew.

"Hear, hear," added Lieutenant Hall. "Although I think the beef had gone off—"

Joe Kellerman glared at him and kicked him in the shin under the table.

"Lieutenant Hall! My beef is never 'gone off,' though the army sends me their dregs. I slave away in that hot kitchen to ensure the quality of every dish! Why, the sheer impudence of such a statement! Captain Kellerman, did you hear him? Did you hear him imply that my beef had gone off?" Mrs. Zimmermann flushed with anger and hovered a heavy serving spoon in one hand and one of the cast-iron pans that had been scraped clean of cobbler in the other—very near to Kellerman's head as she spoke.

"Ma'am, I believe he meant to say that the beef stew had gone *awfully underpraised* this evening, as we were all so enamored by the quality of your peach cobbler. The lieutenant and I second the Sergeant Major's sentiment and agree you are a gift from God to us rabble here at Fort Misery. Wouldn't you agree, Second Lieutenant Cranston, that Mrs. Zimmermann's stew and cobbler were nothing less than ambrosia this evening?"

Atticus Cranston smiled brightly. "Yes, ma'am, it was a meal as fine as any served at West Point."

Around the table the praises of the cobbler were lifted high in a happy, noisy chatter, and satisfied, Mrs. Zimmermann lowered her spoon and retreated to her kitchen.

"You're trying to get yourself killed, James. Never insult a woman's cooking while she's holding a heavy cooking pan. For that matter, never insult a woman's cooking, least of Mrs. Zimmermann's."

"I suppose it was a risk, but she was standing closest to you, sir."

"Atticus," said Kellerman, "although it was the correct action here, I worry you're getting far too adept at lying smoothly. Are the other officers a bad influence, Lieutenant?"

"Yes, sir. I am learning."

The men laughed, and as the dinner table chatter

slowed down and everyone prepared to leave, off to their duties or beds, rushing footsteps thundered down the hallway causing the three officers and Lucas Dean to leap up from their seats with hands poised to pull their revolvers. Corporal Wayne rushed into the doorway and slammed to attention, out of breath and looking stricken. "Sirs, Private Mann has been assaulted and—and— well, you better come quick."

Captain Joe Kellerman was the first into the bunkroom and demanded the gathering crowd of enlisted men stand back as he made his way to the corner where Frederick Mann lay unconscious but breathing.

"Someone, get me some light," he barked, praying that the private's injuries were only worsened by the shadows. Private Billy Burt lifted an oil lamp from beside his bunk and hurried to bring it, holding it aloft so that Mann was cast into a full circle of illumination, and the sight made the young soldier sick.

"Permission to step away, sir," Burt said.

"Hold steady, Private," Kellerman said, but to little effect, as the young soldier passed the lantern to Lucas Dean with a frantic shove before violently retching all over Professor Fernsby—as a scholarly civilian, the most innocent bystander of them all. To his credit, the professor yelped from shock and disgust, but did not chide the boy and, instead, took him by the arm to guide him away from the brutal scene. "There, there, lad. Chalk it up to a new life experience that will stretch your knowledge—learn by doing I always say. Although—if someone could perhaps be so kind as to fetch us a few rags and some water . . ." He looked around expectantly, but no one paid him any attention, and for the time, he decided to just wait with the still sick soldier until help could be found.

"My God," Kellerman said, stunned at the level of depravity, a barbarous act even by the standards of Fort Misery. He bent down to check Mann's pulse and found it strong and even, a promising sign, he imagined, though he was no surgeon. "Corporal Wayne, bring a litter and tell Mrs. Zimmermann to prepare a bed in the infirmary for an incoming trauma, instanter!"

"Yes, sir."

As Wayne left at a run, Lieutenant Hall entered and when the corporal bumped into him, instead of his typical sharp remark, Hall looked only ahead, his handsome face worried and grim. He joined Kellerman and gasped, rage sending adrenaline coursing through him, which made his heart race at a gallop. Hall had taken a shine to the soldier who called himself "Jesus." He had found him to possess a natural ability to communicate with horses, and although strange and rather obstinate with the playacting of insanity, insisting he was the Second Coming, Hall could not imagine why anyone would go so far as to beat the man nearly to death.

Momentarily forgetting his rank, he knelt and pushed Kellerman out of the way, tapping Mann's cheek to wake him and wincing at the touch, as the swelling felt rubbery taut, and his fingertips came away bloody.

"Spooky, wake up. This is your lieutenant speaking, and I demand you awaken and look at me, you scoundrel. Look lively," Hall yelled sternly, inches away from the private's ear for maximum effect. When that did not bring the desired response, he again tried to slap Mann's cheeks, this time with force, inwardly hating the action but needing to get the man conscious again. The beating was severe enough to warrant fear of him slipping into a coma, if he wasn't in one already, or dying from internal bleeding.

"Private, this is a direct order. Wake up and look at me. You cannot let your commanding officers down by dying at the hands of rogue villains, do you hear me? The disappointment I would shoulder from your dying is unconscionable, and I won't allow it. Downright undignified. Get it together, soldier!"

"James," Kellerman said, in a low, measured voice. James Hall had shared stories of the private he nicknamed "Spooky," and it was clear that the lieutenant held an affection for the boy as though he were a younger brother. The waver present in Hall's voice suggested he was seconds from descending into a rage born of pain, and that wouldn't do in front of the other enlisted men, who still watched with wide eyes.

Finally, after a few hearty slaps and loud oaths from Hall, Frederick Mann opened one eye as far as it would go—no more than a slit. "Sir, sorry, sir," he said, the words thick and slurred.

Hall let out a deep breath of relief and wiped his sweaty forehead with the back of his hand, leaving a trace of blood behind. "Thank God. There you are, Spooky. Nothing to be sorry for, since you didn't die on me, poor chap. I am here, the captain is with me, and Mrs. Zimmermann is about to receive you for care. All will be well soon. All will be well. Don't fall asleep again. Tell us, do you know who did this to you. Do you remember?" Hall asked, his tone returning to that of the professional soldier he indeed was.

"I, I . . ." Just then Corporal Lockhart and Tobias Zimmermann arrived with the litter and demanded to have their path cleared. "Mrs. Zimmermann says I am to supervise and make sure the boy arrives in one piece, and to be careful loading him up."

"As always, Mrs. Zimmermann is right," Kellerman said. "Be cautious in how you handle him. God knows what he looks like on the inside." They laid the litter down alongside Mann and, with a series of careful movements, managed to get him situated onto it with only a small amount of groaning in pain—and Kellerman wondered if the trooper were stoic or too badly hurt to complain. Tobias took one end and Lockhart the other, and Hall accompanied the somber procession as parade marshal, speaking firmly to Mann, though it seemed he had fallen unconscious again, and bellowing at soldiers who dared get in the way.

Once Frederick Mann was transferred to an infirmary cot, Mrs. Zimmermann flitted about the room fetching towels and warm saline to rinse the wounds, morphine for the pain, and gentian violet to apply where needed. The horror of the crown of thorns had been removed only after the initial shot of pain killer and a forced double shot of brandy, the cacti spines left angry red puncture wounds that dribbled thin bright blood and required irrigation. Chan was summoned to assist and immediately went to the medicine chest that he now stored in the infirmary and began drawing out vials and pastes and potions. To the great alarm of Mrs. Zimmerman, who was uncertain about Chan being in what she considered part of her territory, he also unrolled a set of sharp cutting and poking tools that he rinsed with alcohol.

Constance Courtenay had helped her Uncle Fernsby into fresh clothing and also cleaned up a very embarrassed Private Burt, who had been given the rest of the evening off, though he would not sleep. For his part, Mann had stayed awake since the transfer from litter to gurney and seemed determined to remain conscious and somewhat talkative even though passing out again may have been a mercy.

In the hallway outside, the officers convened, shaken up by the brutal event but still aware of the oncoming threat of Apache bands set to arrive any minute.

"He won't reveal his attackers, says he must 'turn the other cheek,' " Hall said, infuriated and deep into a bottle of Hennessy. He passed the bottle to Atticus Cranston, who readily accepted, took a drink, and handed it to Saul Olinger. Joe Kellerman had nipped down bourbon and was pacing and chain-smoking, his head throbbing from both stress and the bullet graze.

"We will talk him out of that notion when he's recovered some," Kellerman said. "Even a crazy man surely wants to seek retribution."

"Will you hang them, Joe?" Olinger asked without emotion. "Or pack them back to Yuma for trial. We put up with violence given the nature of our post, but this was beyond the pale, we can't—won't let it pass with impartiality."

Joe Kellerman sighed and locked eyes with his NCO. "Attempted murder, plain and simple—of course we will serve justice. And what timing it is, to have the Apache at our door, expected directly, and some religious zealots trying to murder a deserter who has thus far been bothering no one excepting Lieutenant Hall and Corporal Lockhart, since they're the ones in charge of him. Surely the crown of thorns means they were agitated at his proclamations of being the Second Coming. What else would fire them up so bad?"

As if summoned by the mention of blasphemous concerns, Father Staszczyk entered the hall looking for all the world like the walking dead. His stilted, wooden steps carried him slowly and he bent at the waist, clearly nursing a sore back. His right arm hung limply at his side, yet still carried a rosary and small crucifix in his red and swollen hand, a Bible pressed against his ribs by his left elbow.

"Officers," he said with warmth, although with each step he winced in obvious pain.

"Father Stac—Stizzy-cack—"

"Staszczyk," Atticus Cranston said, looking at the old priest with a hint of guilt.

"Thank you, Atticus. Father, what's happened to you?"

"Oh, nothing, nothing, Captain Kellerman. I suppose I became somewhat overwrought during my desert vision for a start, and then the second lieutenant was kind enough to include me in his drills today. I worked with a rifle and must say they're surprisingly heavy."

Olinger and Kellerman looked askance at Cranston, who cast his eyes downward, his recently improving calvary mustache not thick enough yet to hide his blushing face.

"And following that, the lieutenant"—the priest gestured to Hall, and his shoulder made an alarming pop that made everyone cringe—"was charitable enough to train me in horsemanship. Corporal Lockhart, too, showed me the way to rattle a saber—huzzah!" Staszczyk grinned and took another step, stumbling. Four men reached to catch him, but he brushed them aside. "Oh, don't mind me, I'm fine. Nothing a hot bath won't fix— although where I'd find one at the fort, I don't know." He frowned and righted himself, adjusting his collar and cassock. "Listen to me prattling on about myself while one of my flock is suffering. I have heard rumors of the nature of the assault. Are they true?"

"Depends, Father. What were the rumors?"

"That they mocked Christ's suffering on the cross and beat him near to pieces."

"In that case, yep, you have the right idea. I'm sure he will be very happy to see you. He thinks, or at least claims he thinks, that he is the Messiah. A Second Coming of Christ, born and raised in Kentucky," Kellerman said flatly.

"Oh my," Father Staszczyk replied. "Well, you don't hear that every day."

CHAPTER 43

The patrols returned near midnight with nothing to report, but Ahiga was unsatisfied. What did the white men know about tracking Apache, or spotting omens for better or worse that the desert and sky gifted in plentiful numbers if they only knew how to see them properly. A small shift in the sand or the wisdom carried on the sounds of a nightbird could foretell doom or fortune, yet the calvary pickets on their mounts only sought the obvious, bonfires and drums, wickiups in the distance, or the thrumming of voices carried across the dunes. Bah, they couldn't see in the dark, not if they used only eyes and ears to seek the enemy. Yes, the Apache were coming, no doubt, and it took a little investigation to uncover that secret. But his worries were darker and more ominous, as many signs informed him that there was trouble brewing right under their noses, inside the post.

Although Ahiga felt no kinship for the recent arrivals and least of all the private who delusionally called himself "the Christ," the savagery of such an attack was sickening and disturbed all at Fort Misery during a time when their full concentration was needed to fight off the impending war parties. The Apache saw the fort as an easy target, where they could leave with horses and provisions, and possibly women, too. But at least the Apache had a clear motivation, as they acted to reclaim stolen land and return it to their people—although they were determined to create entertainment along the way.

The attack on the Christ man and the two murders, one on the fort grounds and another off, were the start of a grotesque pattern that set Ahiga's hair on end. Sick kills made by a depraved individual, slaughtering merely for fun, who was as yet unmasked and walked among his fellows like an ordinary trooper—or civilian. A man who could slit another man's throat in silence was a "bad hombre," as he had heard Lieutenant Hall call people of that ilk before. Honorless killing with no incentive—no Indian would choose to butcher a man, then leave without at least finding a way to earn the reverence he deserved as the respected victor. Only out of cowardice or sport would a man do that, or a hidden agenda, perhaps—he was determined to find out the reasoning.

Hidden inside one of the dig tents with no lanterns lit to illuminate the midnight sky or call unwanted attention from the soldiers on night watch, Professor Oliver Berryman spoke in hushed tones to his associate. Berryman's clipped Austrian accent grew stronger the more passionate he became. Gesticulating wildly, angry, the professor was jabbing at the crates, now packed full of

antiquities and relics, and pointing toward the trenches—
and his partner in crime found it irritating.

Berryman's beetle brows drew together. He sneered,
dressing his companion down and making clear his agitation at the lack of progress in what he now considered
a pressing issue. Luckily for him, the dampened moonlight meant his condescending face couldn't really be
seen by his companion, who was losing patience with
Berryman's monologue.

"She's an uppity wench," ranted the professor at a
whisper. "Why, she has the idea that her endowments
give her an intellectual advantage, but the silly woman
is far out of her league. I am sick of her," he jabbed the
air with a finger. "You understand why I would want
her gone, anyway, but more importantly, taking her
out of the equation deals a heavy blow to her arrogant
uncle, who will lose his will to continue and either hang
himself, leave for England, never to think of this voyage
again—or refuse to bow down and keep searching for
de Toro's cache."

Berryman paused for breath—in the dim light his
companion unconcernedly observed the old man turning red as a beet—then continued: "If it is the latter,
then it will be up to you to take care of him, and you're
to make him suffer. Suffer, I say! Once the foolish
woman and Fernsby are eradicated, then it is just down
to Jules. God, I hate that idiot! Do you know he once
had the audacity to chide me for attempting to seduce
the Courtenay woman? As if I am inferior to her! Jules
can be dealt with, too—harshly. But hold off on him
until the gold is unearthed, because I have no intention
of trying to manage the brutes assisting us on my own.

Wait until the treasure is in my grasp, then put him down. We're so close, and I want the goods brought up, then I need them all gone—*gone!*"

Following his animated outburst, he glanced around nervously with a scornful expression, as if daring anyone to have heard him. He saw nothing that stirred, and the night remained quiet outside of the light pitter patter of rain on the tent.

Taking a deep breath, Berryman then arranged his face in a crestfallen countenance and put on what he believed would be the performance of a lifetime, when the moment had arrived: "Despite our terrible losses," he said, in a voice feigning pity, "it seems I will have to carry forward, honoring the memory of my fallen colleagues by shouldering the full burden of our endeavors. They would of course want it to be done that way. I can hear them now saying, 'Never give up, Berryman. Be our champion.' Meanwhile, here I stand before all of you, a wretched creature, devastated by the loss of my dear friends." Here he paused and placed a hand on his heart, tears welling at the corners of his eyes. "Yet stoic and strong, I alone shall remain to salvage the archaeological mission and ensure their names—Dankworth, Courtenay, and Fernsby—go down in history books, praised and admired, even after the great tragedy that befell our inseparable team of brilliant intellectuals in these heathen lands. Oh, woe is me to think their accolades will come posthumously. I wish I could give up, but the pursuit of wisdom must never cease, and I shall not falter." He slumped his chin to his chest as if overcome by grief. After a slight pause, he cackled, "Not bad, eh? I've been rehearsing."

Berryman's associate said, "Bit wordy, if you ask me. But the performance was decent. Anyway, what about the rest of this stuff in the crates. If you take off separately with nothing but the gold, won't it be noticed?"

"Fear not, the crates are already addressed to the British museum and a few universities, and as far as anyone knows I will have fled to isolation, overwhelmed by my grief, taking the gold along to pay for a time of recovery in some far-off land. Or the treasure will become lost entirely on the ship home. I haven't decided yet—genius is fickle, my girl. It takes a while to sort out the appropriate way to handle capers such as this one. Besides, don't overestimate these people at the fort—I doubt they think too deeply."

"I'm not a girl. I'm barely human," came the flat reply.

Berryman flicked his hand, "Yes, yes, fine. I don't care if you're a hippopotamus, your work thus far has been superb although I must say it turns my stomach. Speed it up, that is all I'm asking. If not—"

The associate grinned. "If not—what? What is it you think you can do, Ollie?"

Being addressed as Ollie was enraging, and Berryman raised a hand to lash out with a slap but caught himself in time. The movement had not gone unnoticed, and he became uneasy, a fine sweat breaking out on his forehead and upper lip. "If not—it is simply that we won't have a chance to get it done in time. The soldiers prattle on endlessly about another expected Apache attack. Though I certainly won't fight them."

"Is that all? Calm down, I'll get it done."

Lucas Dean couldn't sleep, an affliction that had tormented the gunfighter since he was a boy. He wandered the fort with a lit cigarette, thinking about the treasure buried in the sand underfoot, but mostly worrying about the Indians. It had seemed like a good idea at the time to enter Fort Misery and make nice with the captain, keep eyes on the gold, and not attempt surviving in the desert on nothing but meat and water, but it was a choice he was rapidly coming to regret. Ike and Dick dead, Nicky guzzling whiskey and drunk most of the time, and Frank—the man had turned weirder than ever.

Part of the reason Dean walked the fort in the wee hours tonight was Frank—he'd found a tarantula, named the giant spider Rosie, and was keeping the dang thing in a pail beside his bunk, feeding the creepy creature grasshoppers and huge horseflies, an arrangement the spider seemed quite fine with, probably due to the steady supply of rations.

When Dean asked why he wanted a pet tarantula, Frank's only reply was that "she seemed lonely." And when Nicky threatened to stomp the beast under his bootheel, Frank informed him that he could shoot him between the eyes just as easily as the spider ate her flies.

The upshot was that Dean's gang was falling apart at the seams. The Trey-Treys had joined the soldiers, and he knew their gunwork had helped fight off the Apache scouting party attack—outside of poor Ike, whose spirit had hopefully traveled up not down after he died, and that miserable private, who most definitely took stairs down—but Dean wasn't confident in how well this particular post of the U.S. Army would handle a full war band. Having seen the state of the troopers, he figured they were largely wannabe outlaws, with bad attitudes and poor aim. To his own surprise, he trusted the officers, sure enough, but there weren't near enough of them.

Of course, the murders were ever present in his mind, too, especially the killing of Dick ,who was old and not bothering anyone, and had been the father figure he'd never had. Then there was the matter of the treasure. Was it truly cursed or did the bogeyman of a killer just want them to give up on trying to seize it out of superstition, so they could take it for themselves? Fort Misery did seem to live up to its reputation of being a haunted, bad luck piece of land, and he couldn't wait to light a shuck east and never look back.

As Dean made his way back to the bunks, hopeful that maybe the spider had fled to buggier hunting grounds, he glimpsed Constance Courtenay, her dark hair loose over her shoulders, sneaking quietly through the shadows, heading toward the officers' quarters with a fluffy orange cat following behind. The woman was clearly avoiding being spotted by any of the posted guards, sticking to the shadows, and Lucas Dean grinned. She was a beautiful woman, so it didn't surprise him a man must have taken a shine to her, and he wouldn't share her little secret. Every once in a while, he found that he was capable of being a gentleman.

CHAPTER 44

Captain Joe Kellerman stood at the window in his office, watching the night pass slowly as the moon rose higher in the sky and cast a pale blue glow across the fort. He swirled whiskey in his glass, having already had too much but not ready to give it up yet, and looked for any sign of movement in the dark desert beyond the soft yellow rectangles of light that were cast out of the headquarters building. Light rain fell, and somewhere in the darkness an owl hooted—something he immediately thought of as a bad omen, thanks to the Navajo's teachings—and he watched Private Nelson walking back and forth on duty, yawning and looking bored.

A boring night was much needed, but the threat of the Apache lingered, and it would be a long time before Kellerman could sleep peacefully. He expected Connie to come, a whispered promise made in passing while they sat down for supper, but he saw no trace of her. Falling in love was a terrible idea, so maybe it was for the best if she'd fallen asleep alone, yet he couldn't help but feel a sense of longing in her absence.

"Foolish man," he said aloud to himself. "This is the

last thing you need." He downed the whiskey and poured another, giving up the window and picking up the book she'd left him, *The Ulster Journal of Archaeology, vol. 8*, then settling behind his desk to read.

A quarter of an hour had passed when he heard a sound at the door, like something scratching. Rats, he thought, not even glancing up from his place on the page. The scratching sound grew more insistent and he lowered the book, looking to see if there was a pesky rodent visible, and as he did a series of thumps began rattling the door in its frame, *thump, thump, thump thump, thump!* Kellerman stood, pulling his .45 Colt from the holster and belt that hung on the hatrack, cautiously approaching the door with quiet steps. He jumped when he heard the frantic, creaking mewing sound, and then lowered his revolver. Just the darn cat, he thought, and swung open the door laughing, "You scared the heck out of me you little rascal . . ."

The words died on his lips as Major Mouser flew into the room, fur puffed out like he was a moving tuft of cotton, and completely covered in blood.

Joe Kellerman picked the cat up and for once the terrified animal didn't resist, and instead buried his head against the captain's chest to hide his face. "What's gotten into you, Major? Something attack you?"

He inspected the clinging cat thoroughly, but there were no injuries to be found. All the while a sinking feeling deep in his gut grew stronger, until he began to feel nauseated and spooked. Then he saw something that sent a piercing stab of ice right through him. Tangled on the cat's bloody paw was a heavy lock of long dark hair.

CHAPTER 45

The bugler had been sobered up and the alarm raised, and with the widely dispersed men searching the fort, it didn't take long to find her. Constance Courtenay had been impaled upon one of the spikes Tobias Zimmermann had used in the construction of the practice dummies, the burlap and straw removed so that only the pole remained. It was a small mercy that it seemed her impalement and most of her disfigurement had come postmortem, and that the particularly vicious torture of her being skewered would not have been felt. Like Corporal Pierce, her throat was slit, and her scalp partially removed creating a patch of skull surrounded by her lovely thick hair.

Captain Joseph Kellerman was a hard man living in a hard era, as were all the soldiers garrisoned at the fort, many having committed serious crimes of their own. But to a man, they turned from the sight, some unable to look again. The capacity for anyone to demonstrate such hate, such violence, was unthinkable, and not a man among them knew quite what to do at first.

Kellerman stood, halted, staring, rage and sorrow

building to a level of apoplexy that he feared would kill him. Finally, Ahiga broke the tension, demanding Frank Abilene's grubby frock coat and draping it over Connie's body. Thankfully the old professors were still abed, and it was only the enlisted men and Lucas Dean's pistoleros who saw the gruesome tableau. Snapping back to life, Joe Kellerman bellowed, "Get her down. Take the post down," and proceeded to begin the process himself with the help of Ahiga and Saul Olinger, who made short work of lifting the wood from the earth, laying the woman gently on the ground.

Joe Kellerman removed his shirt to cover Constance's face while the coat hid the rest, then they stood together in silence, deciding on the next course of action. Sergeant Major Saul Olinger then took the captain by his arm. "Joe," he said, "look at me. Here, come on, look at me."

After a long moment, Kellerman turned his gaze from the dead woman to Olinger, who angrily asked, "What is happening to us?"

There was no reply but the whistle of the wind, and on it carried the sound of heavy drums from across the desert.

CHAPTER 46

At dawn the rising sun made an optimistic promise of a beautiful day, streaks of brilliant watercolors across a sky broken only by swirling wisps of white clouds placed as if by a painter's delicate strokes. But the stunning display was lost upon the residents of Fort Benjamin Grierson, who saw nothing but melancholy and misery in the landscape surrounding them, as they wallowed in the exhausted detachment of shock and grief.

Nearly all of the enlisted men had taken turns helping the archaeologists with the trenches and recovery of relics, and they had marveled at the wit and beauty of Constance Courtenay, who was clever about the work and quick to reprimand the men, when needed, in a way that sparked laughter and was never cruel. She had been as willing to labor and get her hands dirty as any of the troopers, and during Second Lieutenant Cranston's training, proved herself handy with a gun and a blade. The soldiers had joked that the feisty young woman would be the first gal ever to become a cavalry officer for the U.S. Army if she put her mind to it, an idea hammered home by the way she freely tossed back shots of whiskey while telling stories of wild adventures.

And now she was dead. Killed in a terrible way, to boot.

Father Staszczyk did what he could, trying to lift the men's spirits with talk and prayers but found his efforts to be mostly futile. To reach out for the mercy of a God who allowed such atrocities was bleak and reassured none but the truly devout. Mrs. Zimmermann had spent the morning in her bed, deep in her own prayers, and planned only a simple breakfast, of cornmeal mush and salt pork, that she could lay out with minimum effort and would be just filling enough to feed those who, despite their sadness, still lived with an appetite to eat. None had slept, none had answers for why such a horror was foisted upon them, and all were waiting for the next onslaught of misery that was just around the corner. In quiet moments, the war drums grew louder, as ominous as the thunder that accompanies tornadoes, and patrols went out to ascertain how much time they had until the Apache made their move.

Captain Joe Kellerman was grim and silent. He had allowed himself to feel the tendrils of budding love for the first time in a decade, and the punishment for doing so had been hard and swift. Had he condemned Connie simply by caring for her? he wondered, or was this the work of the ancient blight said to be laid across Fort Benjamin Grierson—with the added curse of digging up a dead conquistador's gold? He resolved, either way, that from that point forward, he would not entertain the notion of romance.

Lieutenant Hall saw this questioning despair in the

captain and tried to ease it with a hand on the shoulder, and an offer of snuff, and Sergeant Major Saul Olinger too had attempted to draw the captain into conversation. In the end they left Kellerman be, as men do.

After the terrible discovery of Constance, the officers had lit lanterns and organized a hunt for the killer. Hall, Olinger, Cranston, and Joe Kellerman had questioned everyone present at the fort, but found no traces of a murderer, no obvious signs or clues as to who'd done it. Even the vilest criminals who'd chosen the hell of Fort Misery over Yuma Prison were disturbed by the brutal murder of an admired woman.

There was no telegraph at the post, and Kellerman considered sending a courier to Yuma to request a marshal to investigate the string of murders but knew that with the Apache nearby, it would be sending a man to his death to try it, and he couldn't spare a full troop. Attack was imminent, and there was no stopping to mourn. They had to prepare for battle, all the while wondering who the killer in their midst was, and when he would strike next—and who would be his victim.

The true anguish had come with informing Professor Fernsby about the fate of his niece. Mrs. Zimmermann and Father Staszczyk had done their best to clean the woman up and give her dignity in death, but there was no hiding the worst of it, and although they insisted Fernsby not look at her body—Lieutenant Hall even trying to physically restrain the distraught archaeologist—he had refused to agree with their requests. Now he had not been seen again since retreating into his quarters just before sunrise, and Kellerman, fearing the man would hang himself, used his authority against the protests of

Fernsby's fellow professors, to station a man inside the room with him and to make sure there were no guns within reach. Chan flitted in and out, dividing his time between bringing soothing teas to the professors and tending to his wards in the infirmary. He was clearly devastated but, like a soldier, pushed through to do his work.

As the day moved on, hot and dry, Captain Joe Kellerman set two privates the task of covering the bloodstains in the sand, hiding the worst of the crime. As they worked, and having done all he could for the time being, he retreated to his office to lay out battle plans for the fight ahead, the pain of his heart buried deep like the bloody stains, but with whiskey and resilience in place of the pure white grit of the earth.

CHAPTER 47

Ahiga followed the tracks of moccasined feet in the sand, gazing down at them from his horse. He raised a hand to signal the pickets behind him, *stop*. They obeyed, and he slipped down from the paint pony and left, becoming like a snake with glittering eyes and approaching near to the Mescalero Apache camp. He watched as the warriors sharpened their axes and talked, laughed, preparing to take down the fort on the way to Sonora. The Navajo scout watched patiently, absorbing as much intelligence as he could, interpreting the Athabaskan words as he understood them, and when he had seen and heard enough, returned to his patrol.

"They'll come at dawn. They believe the sun will light their way to victory as they seize the fort and supplies. Any white man caught alive will be their slave as they raid Sonora, forced to fight or be tortured." He shrugged. "Personally, I would choose the fight over Apache ideas for fun torture techniques, but white men are crazy. They do not see it as torture. To them, honor hurts all the same. Anyway, tomorrow at dawn is the attack, and that is the important part. Something about women, too, but there's only Mrs. Zimmermann now."

Corporal Lockhart said, "Thank you, Ahiga, for your thorough report."

Ahiga nodded, his copper skin glowing beneath the noon sun. For the occasion of a fight, and to mourn the death of Miss Courtenay, he'd painted the top half of his face black, improvising with soot and the small amount of Navajo white paint he kept. He proved a small advantage to ward off wandering troublemakers, as to most white men he looked like an Apache warrior, and where there was one there were likely to be many. The Navajo and Apache, in their own tongues, Dine and Inde, respectively, were cousins, but they had warred with each other for centuries. As the Indian Wars raged in the American West, it was not uncommon to find a Navajo scout, or an occasional Apache scout, on army posts, especially when there were opportunities to spy on each other. Many years after the Yuma desert had eaten away at the fort and Devil's Rock, and the Indian spirit had been tamed down to reservations of land, Navajos would join a war to fight against the Japanese threat by speaking Athabaskan to each other over wires for a different branch of military, the United States Marines. But if the Fort Misery scout Ahiga had been told on that sun drenched day as he tracked Mescalero for Captain Joseph Kellerman that his cousins would be dubbed Windtalkers and be granted Medals of Honor by a United States president someday for speaking their language, after Japanese enemies dropped destructive weapons from angry flying machines bigger than thunderbirds, he would have laughed.

For today, his primary concerns were staying alive and keeping the soldiers in one piece. He felt little loyalty to the U.S. Army as whole, but his options were few, and once a Navajo had set his mind to protecting a man or a post, his aim would stay true until death. It was the only honorable way to proceed. It was the Spaniards who had dubbed them Navajo. To their own selves they were simply "the People," the Dine. No matter. Let others call them what they wanted, it couldn't kill their spirits.

As the Indian Wars raged, it was the Comanche who were feared more than any others, and as a general rule, none would go out of their way to spy or report on them—since they were the Lords of the Plains—choosing instead to squabble among the smaller, tamer tribes. Ahiga was thankful that the attack would only come from the Apache on this occasion, as he did not feel the enlisted men at Fort Misery could take on a large Comanche battle and win, at least not now.

Ahiga mounted his horse and clucked lightly, gesturing to the west. The patrol moved out, circling the post to track for any further threats.

CHAPTER 48

The hammering noise pounded into Captain Joe Kellerman's already throbbing head as he began surveying the progress being done in anticipation of the Apache hordes.

It was unfortunate for his headache, he thought, that hammering was a heavy part of the current activities, but there was nothing to be done but grin and bear it, since it was mainly his idea.

As mallets swung to each man's own working rhythm, the booming *Thunk Tink, Thunk Tink* combined with their bellowing blue oaths over occasional smashed fingers and turned into a sort of song, with their good-natured laughter rounding out the overall tune. The *Thunk* men were stronger and working as speedily as possible, while the *Tink* men were slower and more delicate with their swings, yet still getting their work in neatly enough for the keen eyes of their overseer, Tobias Zimmermann, who now and then used his hammer as a gavel to get the emphasis into his commands. At that very moment, he was yelling, "Put. Down. That. Damn. Board. Nelson!" above the chatter and noise.

Zimmermann had rounded up a solid team of troopers

plus the pistoleros Adam Louis and Frank Abilene, and thanks to his stern leadership, and a full understanding that Captain Kellerman would hear about any irregular behavior, every last one of them was agreeably engaged in sawing, holding up, and nailing to fulfill the goal of placing boards across the windows of the headquarters.

Working with thick, heavy planks, the men were removing or reinforcing window shutters as needed to create the defensive measures Kellerman and Zimmermann had come up with to give them a fighting chance. The idea, if it worked as they hoped, was that the exterior walls would reveal only small holes, around seven inches across by five inches high, though no one was making exact measurements, given the press for time.

In this way, when the framed miniature windows were completed, the men inside could see out easily enough and aim as many as three barrels out the small rectangles at a time, or even shove out a bayonet, if needed, while the approaching Indians on the outside would have a harder time aiming into the holes for direct shots and surely be unable to see a man bellying up to the window until it was too late.

It was a medieval style of defense, but Fort Misery was a medieval sort of place. In fact, Lieutenant Hall had asked Tobias Zimmerman if it were possible for them to build a trebuchet in a hurry, and the idea was still being floated around. Flaming projectiles would likely make even the Apache pause.

Given how dark the small openings would make the buildings, Tobias pointed out the need to station lanterns carefully to avoid a calamitous fire should a wounded or panicked trooper kick one over, and he was engineering small tin lampshades to hide the glowing lamplight from the open nooks while leaving enough light to see both feet and ammo.

"Good work, Zimmermann!" Joe Kellerman said, shouting to be heard over the din. "You should get the rest of the civilians in here working. As far as I know, they aren't busy with the second lieutenant yet."

"Sir, I do believe they've now all taken to ground. If you can find them and get them out of their nest, I'll be happy to have the help."

Captain Kellerman hadn't anticipated Fernsby being of any use following the brutal murder of his niece, but he didn't expect the other pair to hide out, too. Not now, with the hours to attack counting down. It didn't surprise him that the old professor still had not surfaced from his quarters, but now it seemed Dankworth and Berryman had joined him there, as the men were nowhere to be found.

While Kellerman was checking on work, the other officers called a brief and informal meeting in a storage room to discuss their plan of getting the professors up and moving again before the Apache arrived.

"Keeping a watch for the dead, I suppose. They're British—you know how intent good old Queen Victoria is about everyone keeping keen to their rules. I suppose they may be wanting white lilies or some other floral pretties, perhaps even silk fabric for the shroud," Lieutenant Hall said. With his flowing black hair and beautiful blue eyes, he had the perfect visage—exactly what one would expect of a soldier well-schooled in Victorian mourning customs.

Second Lieutenant Atticus Cranston thought it over

for a long moment and added, "We have the father, so maybe they won't care about all the other typical supplies so much, being in this country and all that. Meaning all the stuff that we don't—well, can't get here. We can still stop clocks, and cover the mirrors, and open windows if they ask." Flushing a bit. "I read a lot."

Hall nodded. "Yes, you're likely right. You're learning to be like us older officers, wan of the world and its frivolities. Of course, it goes without saying you've learned the most from me, Atticus. Haven't I trained you well?"

"Yes, sir," Cranston said.

The sergeant major side-eyed Cranston and Hall, shaking his head at their babbling nonsense. "Well, this is all lively and lovely, Lieutenants, but may I offer a simpler and more probable solution?" He stretched his arms above his head with a groan, already tired and knowing the hours ahead were to be unbearable.

Hall grinned, "Sir, please do."

"They're afraid of getting murdered by the same fella that killed Miss Courtenay, Corporal Pierce, and the Trey-Trey . . . what was his name?"

"Freeman, sir. Dick Freeman," Cranston said.

"Yes, that one. So the old men are probably hiding in there, and of course, the most obvious solution of all is that the captain should go talk to them. I'll suggest he do this now. In the meantime, Cranston, you and Lieutenant Hall head over and help Tobias keep our band of scoundrels in check."

* * *

Joe Kellerman knew that the professors weren't dead since he had not only posted the trooper to keep watch but also saw Chan darting in and out. But all the same, he felt like he was about to walk into a morgue. Sighing, he removed his calvary hat, held it to his chest and nodded for the trooper on guard to knock.

Chan opened the door, quickly appraised the captain's head wound, then said, "I'll tend to you soon. Mr. Jesus Mann still needs more help. You'll be fine." As he went to leave, Chan pulled on Kellerman's shoulder so that he could better whisper into his ear, "Get rid of Berryman, right away."

That was all he said before slipping out the door and letting it bang behind him.

Chan telling Kellerman that he'd tend to him soon reminded him of the wound on his head, as he had completely forgotten about the thing. Remarkably, Kellerman's injury, just a scrape, had healed right up, and since the silly looking bandage was off, all that remained was an angry scab. If he were to admit it, which he would not, he thought it made him look tough and was not entirely displeased with the scar it would leave. Although now that Chan had reminded him, he realized it did still sting. Undoubtedly, he would be in for another round of smelly oils and pastes.

Professor Fernsby was lying on one of the twin beds, the covers loose but drawn across his legs. The elderly man looked peaked, and he had a book open in his hand, his other groping at crumpled handkerchiefs that littered the bed and side table. "Forgive me, Captain, I've been in rather a state. It'll all be gone with me, I do promise you," he said gesturing to the traveling trunks packed to varying degrees that lay scattered around the room.

"I completely understand," Kellerman said. "So you're leaving us now, then?"

The professor stood. He was off balance and looked even thinner and paler than when he'd arrived, a walking cadaver, for sure, if ever such a thing were possible. In place of his usual crisp tan explorer kit, he wore thin blue linen pajamas and no shoes, revealing age-spotted skin with yellowing nails. His hair was a wispy halo, and even the stubble of growth along his jaw looked white and patchy. "Yes, it is time for me to depart, as soon as I can arrange transportation. I must take Constance home with me. I know that won't be easy, but money can buy just about anything, even in Yuma. We plan to take her there to have her . . . made comfortable"—the old man choked up and quickly daubed his eyes—"and then head on off back to England."

"I see," Kellerman said. "And the other professors," he made the inquiry to Fernsby but was watching the other two out of the corner of his eye. Julius Dankworth had taken up another bed and was curled on his side napping, or doing a very good job of pretending to, his face toward the wall. But Berryman sat crouched like a gargoyle on the bottom corner of Fernsby's bed, his face a mask of irritation and something dark that Kellerman didn't like. Avarice, maybe.

Berryman leapt to his feet. "I will remain of course, to see to it that Mr. Fernsby and his dearly departed receive their fair share of the wealth, once it is secured. Archaeologists must always stick together—it is our professional code. We'd never abandon someone in their hour of need."

"I see. And Mr. Dankworth?"

The man didn't stir, and Fernsby went to rouse him, but Berryman stayed his hand, "Let him sleep. Poor old chap was up all night helping those—highwaymen, during the hunt for Courtenay's killer. He spoke to me after you'd gone to bed and said that he planned to stay and finish the dig all the same. Fret not, Fernsby, old friend. We will find the fortune and deliver your share."

His smile was hard and unpleasant, and Kellerman took a careful measure of the man, wondering why Chan wanted him gone. "Well, in that case, I do believe Mr. Fernsby should be allowed time to grieve in peace and quiet, so Professor Berryman, Professor Dankworth, Second Lieutenant Cranston will be expecting you on the parade ground." He stepped out the door and took glance at the growing morning sun. "Don't dawdle now—time is of the essence."

CHAPTER 49

In the infirmary, Chan was applying a stinging golden tincture to wounds on the pale skin of the soldier he called "the Jesus Mann" and making pleased sounds as he daubed more here and there, nodding at his own handiwork.

"Jolly good! You look like a brand new man," Lieutenant Hall said, taken aback by how well the private, Frederick Mann, had recovered in such a slight span of time. "My word, Chan, I daresay that you are truly a magician. I've never seen the like of such a thing in all my time!"

Chan grinned and held a finger up. "Ah, thank you, Lieutenant, but remember, all your time has been small." He held a second finger up an inch apart. Then, as he spread his fingers very wide apart, he said, "Chinese time has been loooooonnggggg. If we did not know how to do this all that time, how do you think we would have had any time to build an empire, build our Great Wall, or learn to perfect cooking dumplings? It all takes time."

Frederick Mann offered Hall a crooked smile with

cracked lips, "Thanks be to God, and to China." His voice was weak and raspy, and his right eye was still swollen nearly shut, only a sliver of glittering blue showing in the slit between two heavy purple rose hips. The cactus wounds were deep, but they'd scabbed over easily enough, it seemed, and a ring of garnet marks made it look like he wore a beaded necklace around his forehead the way Hall had seen some fancy ladies of the evening do in the city of New Orleans. The purple, yellow, and green of his bruises was present but fading at the edges, and the darkest areas of red where there had been the scuffed torn skin shaved off by bootheels now were pale pink.

"How are your ribs, Private? Worst thing for a man to get dinged in a battle."

"It hurts when I breathe, but Dr. Chan says it won't kill me. I know about how sometimes a man has his rib bone puncture a lung if he breathes too deeply, but doc says it won't happen to me. Right doc?" Mann frowned, clearly still not feeling assured about the safety of his lungs in their proximity to the bones that hurt.

"I keep telling you I'm not a doctor. Not in this country, not in my old country. Well, maybe could be in old country, but not here. Just Chan. And your lung is fine."

"Hurts to take a deep breath, doc."

"Chan. Yes, it will hurt for long time. Keep drinking your tea, *fang-feng* and rosemary, for the lungs, then for bones you get the *yin-han-huo* and *gu-sui-bu*. Good as new soon."

Mann reached for his cup with an unbandaged arm, grimacing with each sip of the green steamy murk.

"You getting all the plants that you need from the

desert, doc?" Hall asked, only half joking, as he knew the Mexicans made all sorts of concoctions out of desert roots and shrubs.

"I have everything I need to grow fresh over again from seedling up to man if I want, right here." He proudly patted the top of an enormous black and cinnabar enamel case on wheels, so tall Hall wondered how the man could reach the top.

"Any man comes in wounded by Apache, I can fix them. Just don't let the Apache fix me first, okay?" He grinned and threw his hands up as though he'd been shot through the heart by an arrow.

"Sure thing, doc, we'll try."

Saul Olinger and Joe Kellerman were assessing the state of the armory security and the organization of its goods within. "Make sure Hall has a key for this box here. He tends to forget and misplace it about right when we need him to—" They were interrupted by a frantic Private Wesley, who came scuffing to a stop in front of them with a crisp salute.

They saluted him back. "What is it, Private?" Kellerman asked, praying it wasn't their expected Indian guests come hours ahead of schedule.

"Professors, sir. One of the professors is real dead. Sir."

Olinger and Kellerman shared a look, and Saul did his best to maintain a straight face while saying, "Real dead? As opposed to sort of dead or half-dead or maybe dead?"

"Sir, yes, sir."

"Which professor is it," Kellerman asked, alarmed.

"Professor—uh, Professor Julius Dankworth, the First, sir."

"Had Professor Julius Dankworth, the First, told you, when he was pre-dead, that you should address him with that title?"

"Yes, sir."

"Well, Private, maybe there's a son we don't know about, but from here on out, he's Julius Dankworth, the Last."

Olinger chuckled, and then Kellerman winced at his own dark humor. "Private Wesley, that joke is to remain classified and confidential, and you do not have the clearance to repeat it. Understood?"

"Yes, sir."

"Good. Take us to him."

"He was fine, not, oh, two hours ago! He said he needed to lie down after being up most of the night after the discovery of poor Miss Courtenay." Professor Oliver Berryman was frowning at the corpse of his former colleague with an air of complete disapproval. Julius Dankworth remained in the bed where he'd been found, rolled over onto his back and staring skyward, as dead as he was ever going to be. Berryman had notified the trooper who stood as their sentry, after dressing himself in the shared quarters and finding that the old man was stiff as a board when he tried repeatedly to prod him verbally and physically to do the same.

Professor Fernsby sat in a corner chair, still in his thin blue linen pajamas, head in hands, heavy tears jerking his shoulders.

Looking around the room, Berryman sniffed. "Well, it seems that I am the only one of my fellows who chose to dress for this occasion." He smiled dryly and searched the faces of the sentry trooper, two officers, and Chan, who'd arrived shortly after the private went to fetch someone in authority. Then, seeing no acknowledgement for his obvious bravery, he rolled eyes and snapped, "For God's sake, Paul, pull yourself together. We're going to end up eaten by savages, if you don't get over it and join in whatever the army wants from us."

"Apache are not cannibals, eating another man's flesh only for witchcraft. And witchcraft is bad medicine," Ahiga helpfully chimed in, from directly behind Berryman, making the professor jump and spin like a frightened cat.

"Good grief, where did you come from?" Berryman shrieked, clutching his chest.

Ahiga frowned and then put a thumb back over his shoulder. "The door."

"Ahiga," Kellerman said, "can you please go tell Private Wesley that we need Father Sch—stack . . . that we need the padre, again. Then will you let Second Lieutenant Cranston know he's down two men thus far from his collection of civilians. One, permanently."

"Yes, sir," Ahiga said, then slipped away as silently as he'd arrived.

"Sir, do you think he does that on purpose?" the sentry trooper asked as he watched the scout's exit.

"What, use moccasined feet to slip behind and scare white people?"

"Yes, sir."

"Yes, I imagine he does. I would, too." Kellerman then joined Chan, who was gently crossing Dankworth's wrists in front of each other so that his elbows would fit in a coffin by the time he was stiff enough to be placed in one.

"What do you think, doc? Apoplexy? I hope you say something natural, because we don't have time for anything even a little unnatural at this precise moment."

Chan looked perplexed, "I am not a doctor. The Jesus Mann calls me doctor—now you all do it?" He waved his finger in the air. "Stop that! And sure, could be his heart went *boom*." He looked over to the still softly sobbing Fernsby, flanked by Berryman who was studying them in return, and the sentry, a towheaded young man, who seemed deeply embarrassed.. Chan cleared his throat, hurrying to leave. "So sad. I'll just go check on the living."

On the way out the door he stood up on his tiptoes to whisper in Kellerman's ear, "For now, say it was natural. After all, arsenic is very natural, indeed."

CHAPTER 50

Despite the all-around lack of sleep and pervasive bad feelings, as the noon sun rode out in full golden finery, with a few light clouds tracing behind to serve as a dainty skirt, only one person at Fort Benjamin Grierson truly felt tired. She'd wriggled down into her hidey-hole shortly after sunrise and stayed there, fearing discovery by one of the troopers, given the number of boots on the ground searching for Constance Courtenay's murderer. Now, the dinner bell was ringing, meaning it was high time to come out and find something to eat. A little fresh air wouldn't hurt, either. After the last tones of the bell faded, the heavy canvas that served as a trapdoor lid flew open just as she reached up to flip it open. Oliver Berryman looked down, gleeful, eyes shining like a rat who just found out that the farmer's grain stores had no cats on guard.

"There she is, my glorious Estrella! You truly are a star. You've terrified them just as much as I had hoped."

The young woman smiled, but covered her mouth

with her hand as she did so, flapping with her other hand to gesture that Berryman should move back so she could crawl out one-handed on the makeshift tent poles she'd dug in as a ladder.

"Oh, stop that, silly girl, beautiful girl. I know what you look like. I've known all along, haven't I?" Berryman said. His dark eyes looked magnetic to the young woman peering up at him from the hidden portion of trench they'd kept under "his" tent, though he only slept in it the first night.

She climbed out, and Berryman thought her as hideous a creature as the earth had ever seen emerge from beneath soil. What kind of God allowed this one, he wondered, hiding his inner dialogue with a feigned smile. Surely, one of the old Sumerian demons or perhaps a nicer, newer God, who declared she was to be punished by this face.

The young woman sat coyly at the edge of the trench, filthy. Her hair was dark brown and now was tangled, where blood had flown toward her own scalp while she'd been taking away the others'. Berryman reached down, and she recoiled from his touch.

"Silly creature, you really have to get over all of that if you plan to become my dear lady wife," he said, trying again. She relaxed a little and allowed her head to fall against the palm of his hand, making him the one wishing to recoil. "There, there, you've done so well. Last night your work was perfection."

Estrella leapt from the trench with graceful ease and stalked away from him with her arms crossed, and said over her shoulder, "I bet you liked that, seeing that beautiful lady dead. She wouldn't let you near her while she was alive, though, would she?"

As she turned toward him to spit out the words "would she," he slapped her across the face with the full force of his hand, the heavy rings he wore leaving rips and dents across her cheek and tearing her mouth. The cleft palate she'd been born with was deep, and the extremity of it, and the staggering cost of having it repaired with any decency had been something he'd used to gain hold of her since he'd found her begging in East Indian gutters for coins and crumbs.

A girl birthed into a lower caste, who would certainly never attract a large dowry in the future, even if she had been born a beauty, she and her mother had been banished from the family dwelling after her mother gave birth to triplets—two stillborn and the girl he now called Estrella.

Berryman found her shortly after her mother had died, and though she'd been nothing but a sickly street urchin in rags, she could hold and use a knife better than many men he knew. Bad men had taught her that, he later learned.

The professor had need of an innocent-looking young person to do his dirty work—getting his hands bloodied wasn't his style. And he believed it possible she would stab him for his coin purse when he found the girl while searching for the one he thought looked the most primed for violence.

But after a few false starts and lost coins, he chose her, and when he offered her more coin in exchange for a small favor, her face changed from innocent to calculated cruelty and rage born of hunger, then shifted into curiosity and perhaps even hope.

Estrella could remember the moment as if it were only days ago, not years past. The tall, skinny white man with a funny accent did not ask her for anything repulsive and had instead bade her go to the tented side wings of a brightly hued merchant's stall and await another white man, who would be leaving with a satchel full of rolled parchments. She was to follow the man, until they went past a dark empty alley, and then slice the back of his knees with her knife, and when he fell, she was to slice his throat or stab him in it until he stopped yelling. Either way was fine. Then the man paying her would run up and steal some of the papers and get away fast.

Many years later, when they could speak in each other's languages more easily, she'd come to find out that the papers were said to be the very gold treasure map they were here for now, but that the ones stolen in India were false. Now, he had the real ones, and she knew it would mean soon they could wed, and she could live out of the shadows once again.

Ashamed by what she'd said, she wiped her face silently, eyes downcast.

Berryman smiled and took her face in his hands, gently this time. "You know better, dear. You're the only woman for me. Now, here, eat. I'll send for you when the time is next right. Soon enough, we'll be on our way." He handed her a napkin stuffed with hearty slices of corn bread and salt pork, and gave her the canteen he'd refilled that morning at the seep.

Estrella took her food and returned to eat with her feet dangling into the trench, watching the canvas walls of the tent for approaching shadows and looking forward to the day she could bask in the sun.

CHAPTER 51

Atticus Cranston received the news about the death of Professor Dankworth with a drawn-out sigh, one that his range assistant for the day, Lucas Dean, felt deeply. Dean was not too aggrieved over the loss of another one of the professors. Although the death of Miss Courtenay had truly been a horror, fewer archaeologists roaming around, now that the treasure was almost unearthed, was fine. However, the ragged group of troopers he was helping the second lieutenant hone were nothing to boast of, and with the Apache, the strength was going to lie in suppressing fire. Even if the old coots couldn't shoot well, they could fire enough rounds to give some fella a rethink about charging straight into the fight.

Cranston dismissed the troopers when the dinner bell rang and sent them on their way, hanging back and looking over the straw dummies, now one less than before, and examining the holes. He noticed that Dean was waiting for him, and said, "They are getting better, I daresay. Not by much, but better all the same. Look at this here." He pointed to the chest of a dummy and noted the fresh black paint had been punched through neatly by five rounds in a cluster.

Dean smiled and pointed to a lower cluster on the next target. "Gutshot this one—that'll hurt."

A shadow crossed Cranston's face, and he was quiet for a moment, then said, "I did that to a man, you know. And the worst part is, I never thought twice about it at the time."

"He surely earned it. They usually do."

"He'd been notified," Cranston said, nodding. "Do you think—as with Miss Courtenay, Corporal Pierce, and your man, of course—do you think when a man murders to cause pain intentionally like that, he was born purely evil, or that a devil got into him just for a moment?"

Dean eyed the young redheaded lieutenant to see if the kid was testing him, but the question seemed genuine and almost pained. "Well, now, I suppose it largely depends on the man, but I can't say I have ever seen a newborn baby who was evil, have you?"

Cranston smiled. "No, but I have called one or two evil. My sister had a baby whose screams could break glass when he was hungry and mad about it."

"Yep, they'll do that." Dean smiled. "But since I get a feeling you're including yourself into this philosophical question about whether or not a fella was born bad for gutshooting a man, I can safely say two things: Shooting a man in the belly is not the same as what happened to Miss Courtenay, and if you were the one pulling the trigger, you had a mighty fine reason for it."

"You don't know me that well, Mr. Dean."

"I suppose not, but I've known a lot of very terrible

men, and I know you are not one of them, Lieutenant. Come on, we should eat. The Apache may not leave us another chance."

Cranston frowned. "I sure hope our last meal won't be green salt pork."

Lucas Dean laughed, rolling a cigarette as he walked. "I agree with you there."

"Don't tell Mrs. Zimmermann I said that."

After Atticus Cranston had downed what he hoped wouldn't be one of his last meals—although he had told Mrs. Zimmermann it was very good indeed—he made his way back to the parade ground to have a quick look over the dig site and make sure none of the troopers were taking advantage of the day's distractions and pilfering antiquities. The afternoon had brought in billowing iron-colored clouds and distant lightning, and the air was thick and stiff, as the desert waited for the heavens to open again. Were Apache better or worse at fighting in the rain? Cranston wondered.

He'd have to remember to ask Ahiga. The scout had answers for every Indian question, though sometimes he seemed to make it up. Thunder rumbled and the wind picked up again, fluttering the empty tents as he neared the site. The trenches sat dark and deserted, yawning like open graves, and the thought of it gave him a terrible chill and a sudden uneasy feeling. Cranston stopped and appraised the area. He felt as though someone was watching him closely and whipped around to look behind. Nothing stirred but the rising wind and metallic clang of the flagpole some forty yards away. He took another step forward and kept his hand on his holster, ready to draw. Sweat beaded on his light mustache and dripped salt onto his lips as he took another step, nearer to the tents now. Something wasn't right, he thought, but the trenches seemed undisturbed outside of a single shovel and pickax that had been left carelessly on the pathway of earth that provided a bridge between the tented workspaces and the actual holes.

He walked all the way onto the site, scanning every inch of terrain carefully in hopes of finding the source of his misgivings, which deepened with every step. Finally, he arrived at the last tent in the line that formed the encampment and stood silently for a moment, listening. The tent poles creaked gently, and the canvas made a flapping sound like a trapped bird. In the distance, the banging noise of construction had resumed, and he heard the distant voices of two men bellowing in disagreement, followed by a wild hoot of laughter. The feeling of being glared at by someone unseen intensified, and he warily looked at the closed tent flaps in front of him.

Shaking his head he said aloud, "You're losing it. Cracking up," and then pulled up one of the flaps roughly, fully expecting to find someone inside. Nothing. "See," he said to himself, as he lowered his hand from his pistol and walked over to the stack of heavy trunks, locked and labeled carefully.

The professors kept their keys hidden somewhere with their personal belongings, as Kellerman had suggested they do and had taken the most valuable possessions to the officer's quarters. Cranston absentmindedly checked the padlocks to make sure they were not cut, and then his eyes drifted to the artifact sorting tables. Odd, he thought, seeing that several bones and a valuable looking piece of jewel-encrusted gold were laid out as though someone had just been at work. They'd used the tent as an impromptu interrogation room earlier that very morning, a place to interview suspects separately following the discovery of Miss Courtenay. Nothing had been left out of place then, he was sure of it.

One of the professors must have gone back to work again—how careless to leave out what looked like important finds in a fort positively teeming with thieves. Cranston frowned, he'd take it to their quarters, and probably get chided for touching it, but that was better than it being sold into a carnival in a few years, when some light-fingered trooper found a way. He turned to search for an empty crate and saw a flash of movement, as his entire world went black.

CHAPTER 52

Dusk had come in hard, delivering a storm, as Sergeant Major Saul Olinger took another worsening brief from the scouts and made his way to Joe Kellerman's office. Beyond the small window gap, lightning split the sky in angry flashes of light.

"Break of daylight, Joe, that's all we've got. Ahiga reports that they show no signs of changing their minds, come rain or shine," Olinger said, neatly reaching over the desk to retrieve the whiskey, which he badly needed.

"If they refuse to stay home, I sure wish they'd take a nice trip somewhere far to the east once in a while. I bet the Apache would love Boston, for example." Kellerman smirked, lighting his cigarette, adding, "They could try out ice cream—might like it."

The door flew open, and a pale and unusually panicked-looking Lieutenant James Hall burst in without knocking, his hand on the neck of an even more panicked looking Private Wesley, who had been assigned orderly duties for the night.

"He wouldn't wa—" the young private squeaked out, and Hall tightened his grip.

"I wouldn't wait, you reprobate. Atticus is in the infirmary! He was attacked."

Second Lieutenant Atticus Cranston lay in the infirmary bed, white and still, his ambitious yet thin copper mustache stuck out starkly against his nearly bloodless face. "Just a boy still," Saul Olinger whispered to Captain Kellerman as they stood on either side of the bed, watching and waiting.

"Second Lieutenant Atticus Cranston, wake up. That is a direct order." Kellerman's attempt found no reply.

Mrs. Zimmermann gently cradled the back of Cranston's head with a towel soaked in blood and rainwater, but both dripped from the young officer onto the bed and floor.

"We need to get the uniform off, he's sopping wet." Her voice was eerily even, the tone of a person holding on to their hysteria by a hairbreadth. "Doctor Chan is bringing something to stop the bleeding, he says. He went to fetch it."

"They found him next to the weapon—it was this contraption," Lieutenant Hall said, showing the heavy wooden square frame Tobias Zimmermann had built the professors, upon request, shortly after their arrival. The corner was stained with blood, and the sight made Kellerman's stomach roil with rage.

"Why him? Where was he?"

"On the bloody cursed dig site for reasons unknown, just before the first tent in the line. No witnesses to be found, the rain washed away the tracks—although Ahiga has just gone to look, and he may find something. That scout is more effective than a Pinkerton most days, I daresay. Seems unprovoked. Atticus is well liked by the men here, even the worst of them, and it doesn't match the modus operandi of the butcher who killed the others. Either he or the killer would be dead," Hall said. Then: "The killer, most assuredly. I raised this man at my own knee to be a fine officer, did I not?"

Saul Olinger looked anxiously at his time piece, shifting his weight restlessly. "Joe . . ." he said.

"I know," Kellerman said, then: "Lieutenant Hall, I need you to go lay down a command. No one is allowed to travel about freely alone until I say otherwise. Take the sergeant major with you, have the corporals further the order down the line. No muster—go man to man—and then round up the civilians and get them in head-quarters, in any room that will not inconvenience Mrs. Zimmermann."

"Put them in the reception. Keep them away from my kitchen and this infirmary," Mrs. Zimmermann said.

Saul Olinger and Lieutenant Hall flashed to attention and saluted, leaving with last lingering looks at their fallen comrade, who still had not stirred. Head-wound damage was often fatal. For the unlucky, it brought something worse than death, turning a man into a drooling child again or taking their mind in other ways, if they survived infection.

Captain Joe Kellerman began carefully removing his second lieutenant's soaked uniform, his mind racing. All the trouble had begun with the arrival of two separate groups, the archaeologists, and the pistoleros. Victims in both parties made it harder to narrow down the likely suspects, though it didn't seem like the old men were capable of or would cut up their own—

Jealousy? Was one of the elderly professors so enraged by his shared affection with Miss Courtenay that he became a madman? Before the captain could ponder further, Chan bustled into the room, his long black braid soaked with rainwater and a small jar clutched tightly in his fist. "Okay, sorry, I got it now. Mrs. Zimmermann"—he made a little bow toward the woman—"would you be so kind as to roll my medicine chest over here. I left it secured with the Christ Man."

Mrs. Zimmermann scowled at the deranged Private Mann's nickname, as she always did, but gently placed Cranston's head on the pillow and left with a curt, "Yes, doctor."

"Still not a doctor, just Chan," he called to her back, as she scurried to the other end of the ward, where Private Mann was resting behind a tacked-up sheet curtain to block light.

Chan turned Cranston's head and pulled away the towel, with a disapproving "tut-tut" sound.

"How bad is it? Will he wake up?" Kellerman asked, busying his own hands with the shaking out of the second lieutenant's heavy uniform coat before placing it on a waiting chair.

"It is bad, but I will do everything to fix him. First, I need to get the bleeding stopped, so I have this."

Chan uncorked the jar and began liberally applying a gray-looking powder to the wound. The substance became alarmingly saturated with blood but coagulated into clumps that to Kellerman's untrained eye looked promising. Then the odor hit.

"My God, Chan, do you have anything in your magic kit that won't reek up the entire Yuma desert?" Joe Kellerman said, covering his nose with the back of his hand. "What the heck is that?"

Chan beamed, his eyes sparkling in the low light. "My own special blend. I made it years ago, and it has never failed me. Took some trying, but I perfected, and that is why I was happy to come to great states of America, patent and sell to Americans. You people always fighting someone. It is secret recipe, but I can tell you some. First thing is boiled donkey skin, but only some parts. Second thing is squirrel fur, then the herbs—so, Chinese yam, a little ginseng—"

Kellerman raised his hand. "You know what, doc? I am very sorry I even asked. Just cure my officer, and we'll call it square."

A woman's scream rang out from the other side of the infirmary, followed by "MOTHER MARY PRESERVE US!" As Mrs. Zimmermann ripped the curtain down, clearly aghast, a confused but improved-looking Private Mann could be seen sitting up in his bed, peering out from the long hair that fell over his eyes.

"Sea monster! Or . . . a squid! A demon! Captain! I don't know how, this young man has been plagued or attacked by a creature in this bed—the end times! It'll be the end for us all, Christ preserve us!"

Chan looked up from his ministrations on Atticus Cranston, as Kellerman ran to Mrs. Zimmermann's side, frowning for a long moment, then beginning to cackle. "Mrs. Zimmermann, dear lady, it is not the end times with your devil man. No, he's not here."

Kellerman stood by her side, studying the patient. He

saw no obvious cause for the woman's shriek and near hysteria. "Ma'am, I don't see anything," he calmly said.

Private Mann leaned forward, his expression wounded. "I just asked if after she was done helping the doctor, she would come change the dressing on my shoulder, sir."

The private bent as far forward at the waist as he could, and Kellerman saw the trouble, rows of angry looking purple and red circles puffed up in neat rows on the wounded man's back, and a set of three on his unbandaged shoulder. "Oh," Kellerman said, befuddled. The marks did remarkably look like the suckers of a sea creature, the kraken he'd once seen in a traveling show come to Fort Misery, in the rain perhaps. He shook his head to clear it. Impossible—

Chan called out again, "Mrs. Zimmermann, that is from me! It is not a devil squid! Ancient Chinese treatment, I put hot cups on his skin to draw out the bad *qi* and heal faster."

"At ease," Kellerman said, and Mann laid back down and tucked the blankets up to his throat again. "You have to admit he is coming along remarkably fast, Mrs. Zimmermann."

Harrumphing about being surrounded by heathens, she ignored the captain, a sure sign of her distress, and rolled the medicine chest to Chan.

Kellerman smiled at Mann but only received a hollow look in reply. Sighing, he returned to Cranston's bed. If they survived the dawn, he'd tell the story to Saul and James—they'd appreciate it.

"Is there anything I can do to be of further assistance, Chan? As much as I would like to remain here, I am afraid the Apache won't be willing to reschedule due to sudden illness."

The bleeding had indeed stopped, thanks to the odiferous and downright horrifying mixture, and now Chan began cleaning the area with a pale green tincture.

"No, nothing you can do now, Captain. The nurse and I will attend him and send for you when he wakes. If he wakes."

His last words hit like a punch to the gut, and Kellerman nodded stiffly, then left, hearing the conversation behind him fade away.

"Doctor, I am not a nurse."

"And I am not a doctor. Give me the white oil please, nurse. No, the other white, white one . . ."

CHAPTER 53

Corporal Lockhart and Corporal Wayne were accompanying three of the pistoleros to headquarters when Kellerman arrived, passing through on his way to survey yet another crime scene, much to his displeasure. "Where are the rest?" he asked sharply.

"Sir, Lieutenant Hall went to collect the graybeards."

"Where is the sergeant major?"

"At the graybeards' trenches, sir, to meet with the Navajo scout."

Lieutenant James Hall had rounded up an enormous, floridly red-faced private named Curtis O'Donnell to accompany him as he escorted the archaeologists to theoretical safety. Lucas Dean joined them, while Adam Louis offered his gun and wits to Sergeant Major Saul Olinger, who had taken the young private Billy Burt as his second. The officers shared a knowing look, wondering if they were being taken into a trap. In the end, they decided to risk it and split into their respective parties, keeping a close eye on the two shootists.

The sergeant major and Private Burt found Ahiga trailing a path on his light feet, unaccompanied and in the dark, while working his way up from the last tent in the row at the dig site. As they waited for him to finish, to avoid disturbing his dutiful work, the rain came down in heavy torrents that felt like ice to Olinger, and he knew that his bones, far older and wiser than those of the young private beside him, would be stiff and aching tomorrow. He made a grunt of displeasure to himself, and Private Burt started.

"Sir?"

"None of your business. Stand up straight, you young whippersnapper, dang scoundrel. If I see you slouch again, I'll give you a boot in the rear."

Private Burt snapped to attention. "Yes, sir."

Adam Louis chuckled, and Olinger glared at him but, seeing that the man was pushing forty, decided he was allowed to live. For now.

After what seemed like perhaps a full ten minutes in the freezing rain, Ahiga finally joined them, his Henry cradled in one arm protectively. "Sir, looks like a man was hiding here, but he's gone. The rain has made a mudslide to the trenches. Even Navajo can't see through such a thing."

"No, but you can apparently see in the dark," Olinger said, his own lantern flickering dimly, as the scout spoke out of inky blackness.

Ahiga nodded. "Of course. I have told all of you many a time that white men are blind at night—something wrong with your eyes. Come follow me with your fire. Don't slip in the mud."

They followed him to the farthest tent in the line, far

from where Second Lieutenant Cranston was discovered according to the report, carefully pulled back the entrance and went inside. The room smelled of wet canvas and something foul, the odor of death and stale filth.

"What is all this?" Olinger said, approaching the pit in the earth that ran beside an unfurled roll of tarp and a few flat boards, with rough cuts, that seemed to have been scavenged from Tobias Zimmermann's workshop.

"That's what I said, more or less," Ahiga stated dryly.

"How did they get in and out of here without being discovered by the sentries? Or you? And where have they gone now?"

Adam Louis peered at the pit and wrinkled his nose.

Olinger watched the gunman out of the corner of his eyes, wondering if he was associated with the recently vacated pit.

Ahiga shrugged. "Many people in and out of this place all day and most nights, sir. Many footprints everywhere. Who would see unless they were looking? Late at night, if someone was quiet, they could slip by in the dark, since your white men cannot see. Or because your sentries were asleep." He cast a sidelong glance at Private Burt, who flushed but didn't duck his head for fear of the promised boot up the rear end if he bent his neck.

"You didn't see, oh, mighty owl?" Olinger asked, growing testy.

Ahiga shrugged again, but his eyes darkened. "Sir, do not invoke the night birds—bad medicine. And sure, I probably did see, but I see many in and out, like I said, but I never saw an extraordinarily suspicious man. They're all suspicious."

"Yes, I suppose they are. We'll request a pair of sentries to watch the area until we need them back for the Apache. Come, we have to report back to the captain before he thinks we've disappeared."

As they filed out of the tent, Ahiga spoke quietly to Olinger. "Sir, how is the young second lieutenant faring?"

"I don't know, Ahiga. He's out of the fight for now."

The scout nodded. "He's a good man, Atticus Cranston. The spirits of this place will protect him. They see what is in his heart."

"I sure hope you're right."

"Professors, sorry to disturb you." Lieutenant Hall stepped into the dimly lit room and seeing that only the obnoxious Oliver Berryman was awake, he sighed internally. "You need to come with us right now, captain's orders. Please bring any belongings you may need for the night and morning. The Apache are incoming, and I can't promise we'll send a man to be your concierge anytime soon."

Berryman glared. "Where are we going?"

"Headquarters, sir, with the other civilians. Second Lieutenant Cranston, who I have been shaping into a fine officer and, as such, is not a man prone to unawareness, was badly injured by a person unknown. Until such a person has been identified and the threat is over, you'll have to stick together where we can guard you. I am quite sure that Mrs. Zimmermann will have hot coffee ready."

Oliver Berryman rolled his eyes but moved over to

the limp form of Paul Fernsby and jabbed him, more roughly than Hall thought necessary, into waking. It didn't appear that the old man had actually been sleeping, but he lay still simply limp with grief. "Yes, yes. I'm coming," he said, his voice tired and holding nothing of the pretentious bravado he'd arrived with such a short time ago.

The place will do that to a man, Hall thought. You can go ask the bleached bones of deserters in the desert how fast they were worn to nubs by jolly old Fort Misery.

"May you all please exit so that I can change my clothing in private, for God's sake," Berryman snapped, pausing by a heavy traveling trunk with the lid closed but unbuckled.

Hall bristled. "Terribly sorry, old chap. You're not to be left unattended for a moment further. We're all men here, no one is interested in your—in you. Hurry now, sir, time is fleeting." His handsome face lit with a smile, but it held menace. James Hall was an imposing figure on his best day, and as he stood now with his hand lightly resting on his saber, Oliver Berryman decided not to push it. The professor quickly moved to a tub chair in the corner instead and picked up his oilskin, hat, and put on his leather boots. The hat and oilskin were wet and the boots muddy, a detail noticed by both Lieutenant Hall and Lucas Dean, who had stood away in the shadows watching, his back against the wall and mouth silent.

The professor abandoning the trunk after a hissy fit piqued Dean's interest. Why would the old man not even open it in front of them all? He casually strolled behind the lieutenant to be nearer that side of the room, smiling. He approached the trunk, "I can help you out, Professor. What do you need out of here?" he said. "I do believe we're asked to be on our way in an awful hurry."

Berryman lurched forward. "Don't touch that! Nothing—I don't need anything. I changed my mind." He turned to see Paul Fernsby putting a shirt on at a snail's pace and nodded in his direction. "He'll need help. Go right ahead."

Lucas Dean lingered for a moment, his fingers tracing the trunk lid, and Lieutenant Hall and Private O'Donnell, now joined by professor's suicide watch sentry, Private Frank Katz, all stiffened. The shootist surveyed the scene, and seeing that he was outnumbered, laughed lightly. He put his hands up, and said "Okay, just a helping sort of man, am I."

As he walked away from the chest, he stopped and sniffed the air, made a face, and then crossed the small room to assist Fernsby, who was also soon aided by Private Kratz, who helped the old man with his hat and coat.

Belongings gathered, they prepared to leave, and then Fernsby stopped. "Wait a moment," he said, shuffling to his bedstead. He took a photograph case from beneath the pillow and tucked it into his coat. "My niece, a portrait we had made in Vienna. Forgive an old man's sentimentalities."

Hall felt an uneasy prickle on his back as the five men exited, like he was being watched, and he turned to scan the empty room with narrowed eyes. Nothing stirred outside of the light pattering of rain on the windows and roof, but something was wrong. Maybe it was the death and dying associated with the place, he thought, but he doubted it.

"Lieutenant?"

"Yes, yes, proceed. I'm coming."

Captain Joe Kellerman had just crossed the parade ground when he saw the Navajo scout and Sergeant Major Olinger, accompanied, Kellerman noted with a trace of alarm, by one of the shootists. "Well?" he asked, his voice harsh.

Lightning split the sky in an angry display behind his head at the same time as thunder crashed across the desert, and in the flash of light, he looked grim and strained. A bad sign about the second lieutenant, Olinger thought, but he avoided the query for the time being and merely replied, "Sir, Ahiga found a hideaway in one of the tents. There were no remaining tracks to go after, thanks to the rain. Looks like someone was lying in wait, and when the second lieutenant was alone, attacked, then moved out of the location for reasons unknown. That's all we have, for now."

For a long moment Kellerman studied Adam Louis, who stared off into the desert and watched the spectacular storm as it grew, unbothered by the tension and topic of conversation. Finally, gesturing at Louis, he said, "Where was he?"

At that, Louis shifted his gaze with his strange feral eyes to the captain and smirked. Rain dripped from the brim of his sombrero and caught in his ungroomed mustache, but he did not move to wipe it away and instead kept his hands unnervingly near to his waist where a bowie knife and Colt sat waiting for action.

"Sir? Oh, Mr. Louis—yes, sir. He was with us at the time of the discovery, and before that he was with Lieutenant Hall and myself until we split into patrols. We're escorting him back to headquarters now, where I imagine the lieutenant has already arrived."

The captain nodded curtly. "Very well, then. Let's deliver Mr. Louis, and then we can check in on Second Lieutenant Cranston."

Back at headquarters, the soaked, tired men were gladdened to see Mrs. Zimmermann arriving with two pots of hot coffee and a stack of cups on a silver tray.

"Ma'am, you are an angel. I have never seen a lady quite so beautiful and magnificent," Lucas Dean said, flirtatious in his tone and smiling graciously. Tobias Zimmermann walked into the room and wrapped his arm around his wife, planting a kiss on her temple.

"Isn't that the truth, Mr. Dean? However, next time a simple 'thank you' will suffice," Tobias said, smiling far less graciously. Mrs. Zimmermann rolled her eyes and went about pouring the coffee, a bitter brew that made the professors grimace upon their first sips.

"You're quite welcome, gentleman. Terrible night to be outside, terrible night for the Apache to make their moves on us. A terrible night all around. Rest assured that the Lord will provide for us in the end. We must simply keep faith." Then, as she delivered coffee to

Kellerman, she said softly, "Captain, he hasn't awoken, but the doctor says his heartbeat is strong."

Joe Kellerman gave a thin smile. "Thank you, Mrs. Zimmermann. No coffee for me just now. I must be on my way to check on him." He gestured to Hall, "Lieutenant Hall, help our guests get settled in," and then turned to the professors and pistoleros, noting that Fernsby sat in a state of dishevelment with downcast eyes, and he wondered if the man's grief could temporarily be cast aside when the Apache were at their door or if he would lay down and die. "The night will be long and tomorrow longer. You gents should try to rest. I am afraid the accommodations here won't be very comfortable, but the lieutenant will have the privates bring bedrolls. This is for your own safety—better off with sore backs than dead."

Berryman grunted. "Surely you can provide us cots—that's really the least you could do, given this inconvenience."

Kellerman stared at him. "No, the least I can do is keep you alive."

The professor glared back but, looking around at the disapproving faces of everyone else, said no more.

"Sergeant Major, follow me," the captain said, and together they left, Tobias Zimmermann following close behind. "Tell me your thoughts on the Fey-Feys, and the attack on Atticus," Kellerman said, as they passed through the narrow hallway on the way to the infirmary.

"I saw nothing to indicate they are responsible. They're creepy little fellows, no matter how you tear it, but there has been nothing yet to make an outright accusation of crime that I am aware of—though perhaps Lieutenant Hall will report otherwise. We're watching them closely, sir," Saul Olinger said.

"Tobias, thoughts?"

Tobias Zimmermann had sold his gun as a bounty hunter and spent time as an outlaw, before settling down with his wife for a quieter life of carpentry and occasional hangman duties at the fort. He now wore his Colt high on his hip and had entered defensive mode, ready to fight anyone who looked at him crooked. "Well, sir, can't say I have been at ease since they arrived. But three murders, an old professor dropping dead, and now Atticus contribute greatly. As I've told you, they're known outlaws, so of course I expect them to be after trouble, but what that trouble is I can't say, and outside of drunkenness and being creepy, as Mr. Olinger said, I've yet to see anything to accuse them of." He sighed. "Only a fool or madman would choose the middle of an Apache war band attack as their time to strike, and Dean is arrogant and criminally inclined, but no fool. So, on that account, we should have nothing to worry about for the next ten or twelve hours, at least."

"Quite so. And the professors?"

"Captain, Fernsby is destroyed. I am worried he'll run out into rifle fire at dawn. The other man, Berryman, is such a nuisance he's practically begging me to plug him, and of course . . ." Tobias trailed off.

"And of course, two of the party are now deceased," Kellerman said, his voice flat. "Doctor Chan seems to believe that Professor Dankworth was murdered by arsenic poisoning, but as of yet I haven't heard why he believes it to be true. He has cast aspersions on Blackberry while making the claim."

"That's Berryman," Olinger said, then, frowning: "Berryman is a real piece of work, but it seems improbable that he would murder three out of four using physical violence. Poisoning I can believe. He strikes me as the type."

"They say it's a woman's weapon, poison," Kellerman said.

Tobias grimaced. "For God's sake, don't give Mrs. Zimmermann any ideas."

They had just reached the infirmary and went in quietly, Kellerman disappointed to see another patient. "Private . . ."

"Clarke, sir," Olinger supplied.

"Private Clarke, what seems to be the trouble?" The trooper was tucked into a bed, drenched with sweat that plastered his black hair to his head, and shivering so violently his teeth chattered.

"Sir, I got sick with somethin', but the doc is helping me," Clarke said, his voice raspy. Bill Clarke was in his early thirties and had chosen service at Fort Misery over imprisonment for committing several crimes, his rank having been stripped down from corporal to private after his prosecution.

"I see," Kellerman said, just as Chan bustled into the room and went to Clarke's bedside. "Here you go, Mr. Clarke. Take down the fever. Drink it up." He gave the private a small cup of tea filled to the brim with herbs, and for once, it was a pleasant smelling concoction.

Clarke took it with his thanks and began sipping,

shivering to such an extreme he nearly spilled it and had to use two hands to lift the steaming potion to his lips.

"Get well, and recover yourself in a hurry, Private Clarke. I'm already down three men."

"Yes, suh-suh-sir."

Chan turned to Kellerman. "Good news, Captain. Your second lieutenant is getting his color back. His heart is strong, pulse excellent. He will surely survive. He won't be able to join the fight in the morning, but survive, he will indeed, I believe."

He led the way to the bed that held Atticus Cranston and patted the young officer on the knee. "Now he just needs to wake up, that is all. Then we know he is healthy, though I suspect he will have a terrible headache."

"Thank you, doctor," Kellerman said. The man was right, Cranston's cheeks were returning to a normal color, and his breathing seemed steady and even. "Is there anything you need? At first light, we can expect a hell of a battle. I will ask Mrs. Zimmermann to give you the key to the physician's room where Miss Courtenay"—he paused, gathering himself—"where Miss Courtenay was sleeping. You and Mrs. Zimmermann will both be better off there when the raid starts. I'm going to need the pair of you to care for our wounded. And, if the battle is lost, my advice is don't let the Apache take you alive. Mercy is not a concept they cotton to or even seem to be familiar with. Mrs. Zimmermann certainly cannot be taken. Do you understand?"

"Oh yes, yes, I understand. Mr. Atticus says I am a natural with the Sharps rifle and saber, however, and if you can equip me with both tonight, I will defend the nun nurse, come"—he paused to think—"hell or high water, as Americans say."

Tobias Zimmermann laughed with a wheeze.

Kellerman and Olinger grinned, and Chan politely gave them a confused smile. "Is this offensive to her?" he asked, feeling a bit pained over having in fact addressed her, as such, to her face. He admired the woman. She was stern, strong as iron, and highly determined. Crazy perhaps, but remarkable.

Tobias smiled. "She's my wife. She is a sainted figure here, but she is not a nun."

"Oh, I see. And you have children?"

At that question, the carpenter's face fell. It was a sore subject. "We did, yes," he said quietly.

Eager to change the subject, Kellerman said, "Doctor, you can speak freely in front of us all—I trust these men with my life. You told me, before Mr. Dankworth died, that I needed to get rid of Berryman, and then, afterward, something about arsenic poisoning. Explain it to me, please. My entire fort seems to be under a curse, and I need answers to an increasing list of questions."

Chan fussed with the end of his long black braid, possibly one of the few times since his arrival with the expedition, as Fernsby called it, that he had appeared flustered.

"Well . . . I began treating Julius shortly after we arrived, for diarrhea, pain in the stomach, then headaches. The day he died his fingernails were the final clue, you see some types of poison will cause the fingernail to get white stripes, like a zebra, and little dots, too. I became suspicious of—"

"AHHHHHHHHH!"

Atticus Cranston woke up with a bone-chilling scream, making Private Clarke let out a startled cry, while everyone else nearly jumped right out of their skins.

The second lieutenant tried to spring up from the bed and looked around dazedly, shouting incoherently as Kellerman and the sergeant major moved to his side and firmly attempted to restrain him so that he wouldn't fall. Cranston began taking wild swings and clobbered Saul Olinger in the face with surprising strength. "Get off me, villains!" he cried out.

"Atticus! Cranston! For God's sake man, it's us— you're safe. You punched the sergeant major," Kellerman said firmly.

Cranston lost his strength and laid back down, panting for breath and wide-eyed, blinking like an owl.

"Bully good shot, Cranston," Olinger declared, pinching his nose and upon seeing the blood on his hand wondering if it was broken. It wouldn't be the first time. "But remind me to provide you with latrine duty in the near future." He smiled, then winced. Chan quickly handed him a surgical sponge, saying, "Please don't bleed on my floor, Sergeant Major. Very hard to clean from the wood."

"Thanks for caring, doc," Olinger said dryly.

Cranston had recovered himself a bit but still gasped like a fish out of water, as Chan, grinning, returned his attention to the younger man. "Welcome back, Mr. Atticus. How does your head feel?"

Sputtering, he replied, "I— It hurts very badly. Captain, I was attacked, and I don't know by whom."

"You've had us worried. You took a bad hit to your skull. Did you see anyone near you? Ahiga says not only were you bashed, but the villain unknown must also have dragged or carried you into the rain. Small wonder you didn't drown like a turkey."

Cranston shook his head and then grimaced with a yelp. "No, sir, I didn't see a soul. There was a skull and a trinket on the tables, in the archaeology tent with all the trunks. I was trying to pick them up for safekeeping, since no one was around and—I don't remember anything after that. A bad smell, is all—very bad. How long have I been asleep, sir?"

"About three hours or so, since we found you, but how long you were out of commission before that you have to tell us."

Chan drew up a dose of morphine. "This will ease the head pain and help you rest," he said, approaching with the syringe.

"I can't rest, the Apache will be here," Cranston said, and then yelped. He tried to reach back and feel his head wound, but Chan swatted his hand.

"Second Lieutenant Atticus Cranston, you're not fighting the Apache in this condition. Listen to the doctor," Kellerman said. "That's an official order."

"Not a doctor, just Chan. Listen to the captain. You lost blood, you scream when talking, Apache only going to"—he pantomimed lancing, firing a rifle, and war dancing, making the sounds to accompany all three. "You'd be killed."

"All right, all right, a small dose," Cranston said,

wincing again. "Captain, I went to the dig, because it occurred to me—"

"Captain, bad news," Lieutenant James Hall stormed into the infirmary, with Mrs. Zimmermann following at a run, and Father Staszczyk behind her. "Chiricahua are almost here, ten minutes out if we're lucky."

"Damn it all! Get the bugler out of bed."

CHAPTER 54

Thunder shook the earth, and the moonlight blended with the stars and planets to create an eerie purple in the sky, illuminating the Yuma desert in soft, pale shades that shifted as clouds swirled in angry formations. Everyone at Fort Benjamin Grierson assumed their battle stations and sat in relative silence waiting for the incoming attack.

Ahiga and Captain Kellerman peered out through the boarded windows of the headquarters, watching for signs of life. "I thought you said dawn," Kellerman said.

"There will be more at dawn—the Mescalero will come. These are Chiricahua, and they moved past us, so we all believed they'd gone past and maybe on to Sonora. I am not a spiritualist mind reader or psychic, sir. How should I know they meant to come back?"

Lieutenant Hall picked up the bottle of whiskey from between his feet and passed it to Kellerman, who downed a swallow before passing it to Ahiga, who declined.

"Ahiga, remind me to add 'sass talking the captain' to the list, if we survive this," Hall said, stroking his beard as he peered outside.

"What list, sir?"

"The list of your faults."

"Yes, sir."

"Captain, half the troop is drunk by now. They were planning to spend a few hours sleeping it off."

Kellerman nodded, "Yes. I am not worried, Lieutenant—a drop of liquid courage will only serve to improve them, I suspect. The Chiricahua are busy listening to Geronimo and won't go down easy."

"That scallywag, I've heard he has about four wives." He toed the soldier beside him. "What say you, would you want four wives?"

"No, sir."

"You don't like women, then?"

"Uh, I love women, sir. Four just seems like a lot of them."

"Damn right, it is. Here, have some snuff in honor of women. Always remember, I'm watching you and your behaviors toward beautiful ladies, you scoundrel."

"Yes, sir."

Inside the infirmary, Chan and Mrs. Zimmermann sat armed and drinking. The fort was eerily silent as everyone listened for the incoming hoofbeats and yells of the Apache as they drew near, and it was setting Chan on edge.

"I meet your husband. Well, not 'meet him'—come to know him. He loves you very much, I think."

Mrs. Zimmermann poured a double finger of bourbon. Her revolver had been checked for ammunition and now lay atop her gray skirts, waiting for action.

"Tobias, yes. Twenty years of marriage. He's a good, respectable man." She passed the bourbon to Chan with a nod. They sat beside Cranston's bed; the young officer was snoring loudly and unaware of their presence.

Private Clarke sat atop his own bed cradling a rifle, and Private Mann seemed to be drifting in and out of sleep.

Chan set his carbine down and drank the bourbon before taking some to Clarke. "Here. Good for fevers— or so I hear from U.S. Army men." He winked, and Clarke took an enormous gulp, making Chan snatch the bottle back in a hurry. "Okay, okay—that much maybe not so good. You need to have aim on the rifle."

"You don't have any children, nurse?" Chan asked, returning to his seat.

Mrs. Zimmermann froze, then downed her drink and poured another. "I lost three, just infants. Two sons born sleeping, a daughter who lived three days. No more came after that, and that was God's will. I cannot question it."

Chan studied her, saddened by her obvious pain. She was not a beautiful woman, and in her fading youth iron streaked her hair and the weight of a hard life clung to her thin shoulders, bowed beneath a light shawl, but he saw the good inside her shining as brilliantly as a mountaintop sunrise. "I am sorry your God did not allow the blessing of motherhood to your own children. However, you are now an excellent mother to these"—he thought of the words he had learned during his time at the fort— "troops of raggedy scoundrels."

Mrs. Zimmermann, clearly beginning to feel the effects of her bourbon, chuckled and then broke into laughter. "Cheers to my raggedy scoundrels. May the good Lord help them save our souls from the Apache tonight." She raised her glass, and Chan toasted her, grinning.

Sergeant Major Saul Olinger and Corporal John Lockhart were posted up inside the enlisted men's mess, flanked by troopers on all sides who eagerly watched through the windows inside the darkened building. Soft light flickered from Tobias Zimmermann's modified lanterns and allowed them to see their feet and the occasional rat who ran squeaking from corner to corner in search of crumbs.

"Ready, men! Show them who we are!" Olinger cried, and within minutes the yipping of Apache was upon them, as bullets and arrowheads flew into the thick stucco exterior of the building amid the dull roar of thundering hooves.

CHAPTER 55

"Wait for it, unless you have a clear, fatal shot," Tobias Zimmermann called over to the young private Billy Burt, as the Apache warriors approached, terrifying in their warpaint that in the soft flamelight of the exterior lanterns lit their faces like a masquerade from hell. "Don't give away your position with a wasted shot, see, they're waiting for us to fire so that they know where we are," he continued. Zimmermann and Burt peered out from the boarded windows alongside six other troopers. All were quiet as mice inside the narrow hallway that led between the reception and infirmary.

Moments later, someone opened the fight with a shot from the enlisted men's mess and an older warrior on a palomino flew back from his saddle with an anguished cry of pain, leading to a barrage of return fire. The Chiricahua circled, regrouping, and their mounts faded into darkness, then came back again.

"Fighting shadows," Captain Kellerman said to Lieutenant Hall, as they took turns firing. Out in the darkness, the Apache took occasional hits but had no intention of leaving and did not raid inside the fort.

"They can't see us and we can't see them, what is the point?"

Ahiga spoke, "Exhaustion, sir."

"What?"

"They will exhaust us by first light. Not too far away now. Then they can raid the fort when we are tired and half dead, and morale is low."

Captain Kellerman grinned. "Well. The morale is always low in our little patch of hell on earth, so they certainly won't take the wind out of our sails, isn't that right, Lieutenant?"

Hall fired a shot and without taking his eyes away from his targets, declared, "Quite so. Bully for Fort Misery—you can't demoralize the downtrodden!" Another shot, then loudly, "Do you hear that, you ruffians? The Apache wish to take away your morale!"

A raucous explosion of laughter echoed through the room amid the gunfire, the pistolero Nicky Barnes made a sound akin to a dying donkey, a strange laugh for a stranger man.

"You men chose hell—you going to let the Apache send you off to heaven instead?" Hall bellowed.

Cheering came up from all sides with cries of "Hell, no!" and "Never!" And with renewed enthusiasm, the troopers began firing again, as the onslaught of lead and arrowpoints beat like hail against the building's exterior, the Apache fired up. Lightning split the sky, illuminating the bodies of warriors dropped on the sand and a dead pony soaked red with blood. As the boarded windows were worn down by incoming assault, bullets whizzed by like angry hornets, and Nicky Barnes yelped as a shot slammed into his left bicep.

"Barnes, you alive?" Kellerman called.

"Yes, barely. I can still shoot but am going to bleed out fast." The shootist had turned the color of curdled milk and sat cross-legged on the floor, attempting to tear a strip of his shirt to use as a tourniquet.

"Private Harper!"

"Sir?" Harper hurried to the captain's side.

"Help Mr. Barnes. Get him down to see Mrs. Zimmermann and Doc Chan right away."

A portly, fair-haired soldier serving his time for robbery with violence, Harper had proven himself to be useful and good-natured but slow with a firearm. The private saluted Kellerman and then hurried to Barnes's side, helping him to his feet and then leading him off to the infirmary, the pair ducked over low as they went.

"Tell them I need him back, instanter!" Kellerman yelled.

"Yes, sir!"

"Captain, sir." A dark-haired trooper with startlingly blue eyes approached Kellerman at a run.

"Yes?"

"The sergeant major requests reinforcements in the enlisted mess, sir," the blue-eyed soldier said, shortly before a bullet tore into the man's chest, piercing his heart and killing him before he hit the floor.

"Damn it!" Kellerman bellowed, then: "Keep it together, lads! Fight the devils back!"

"Sir, yes, sir!" came the replies.

"Ahiga, you're with me. Saul needs reinforcements." Kellerman turned to Hall. "Hold it down, Lieutenant."

"Of course, sir. I never fail."

Ahiga carefully stepped onto the porch of the head-quarters building and scanned the parade ground and surrounding buildings. Angry sheets of rain sliced the night, carried on heavy gusts of wind, as thunderclaps rolled in one after another, the storm so intense that Ahiga wondered if a rare tornado was imminent. The Apache had yet to breech through into the fort and continued to dance in and out of the surrounding shadows in their hope of exhausting the army before dawn. After establishing that there were no scouts to be found, Ahiga nodded for Kellerman and the small troop they'd gathered to cross to the enlisted men's mess and quarters where Olinger requested their presence.

Whispering, Captain Kellerman asked, "How sure are you that we're clear?" He had his Colt ready and carried his rifle across his shoulder, opposite the saber.

"Quite sure, sir."

"Only quite?"

"No more than quite is possible, sir."

Kellerman nodded then turned to the troop. "No noise—don't make a sound—just run."

They crossed the ground quickly and entered the building to see what the trouble was.

"The trouble is," Sergeant Major Saul Olinger said, thumbing his revolver and firing over and over out of the window and into the night, aiming for suppressive fire more than a hit, as the shadows and heavy rain had him at a disadvantage, "I lost four in about a minute, and I have one that needs the infirmary but no one to spare to get him there."

"Who is it?"

"Private Smythe. Took an arrow into the thigh and has been carrying on about it ever since."

Kellerman looked around the dim room and spotted the private moping in a corner, his entire trouser leg was black with blood, and the injury was obviously severe.

"Saul, he seems to have good reason for complaint."

"Maybe, but that doesn't mean it is any less tiresome."

As arrangements were made and two men took away poor Private Smythe, the first hints of dawn began playing out across the desert. Night creatures went into their dens, and soft light glowed beneath the blanket of stars meeting in the middle and making an impressive tableau, enhanced by the sparkling rain. In the early hints of light, the horrors of the raid began to show more clearly. Dead and injured Apache and their horses were scattered across the desert, while inside the fort, troopers in various states lay or sat in bloody uniforms, cradling injuries, if they were still alive at all.

"Dawn is here," Ahiga said flatly, pausing to reload, his thick black braids now soaked with sweat and blood—whose, he couldn't say. "More bad news is coming,"

"Thank you, Ahiga." Corporal Lockhart said, dryly.

"You're welcome, sir."

CHAPTER 56

Inside the infirmary, Chan and Mrs. Zimmermann were making short work of patching up the troopers the best they could. They were able to send four men back out to fight, but a few were down for the battle and would not survive the day.

"It is the gangrene," Mrs. Zimmermann said to Chan, as they tended Private Smith, who distracted himself by nibbling on the dried salted beef he washed down with cold coffee as they cleaned the wound. "We can get them past the injuries fine enough but I lose more to infection than anything else. Whatever you have in your arsenal to keep the pus away I'm more than grateful to try."

At the mention of pus, Smith made a face and choked a little on the beef he'd dunked in coffee to soften it up, but recovered and went right back to eating all the same. Breakfast such as it was, had been rounded up in a hurry from the storeroom, and Mrs. Zimmermann had done what she could to ensure men received their food at their stations. She reminded the orderlies to instruct the men to thank the Lord for their meals and their lives, and the message was passed on but loosely followed.

Lieutenant Cranston was weak but had ordered his bed pressed against the wall and window, where he could watch through a crack in the boards with his rifle in hand. He was unsure about having the strength to pull the trigger or hold the gun up very long, but he planned to try. The battle had tapered off, and the desert was eerily quiet, giving those in the fort time to recover their breath and recoup—but not relax. Many dead Apaches lay out in the sand, but the heavy rain made it hard to see exactly how many there were in the dim light. The living warriors had pulled back and were shadowy figures, pacing on horseback, plotting.

Cranston didn't like it, and wished he knew what they were saying, or plotting, but the pounding headache with each movement he made kept him from tracking down Ahiga or his fellow officers to find out.

"I wish I knew what they're up to out there," Lieutenant James Hall said, to no one in particular, though he was flanked by Corporal Wayne and Lucas Dean, as they all watched from behind the boarded windows, now peppered with bullet holes. An ax was embedded in one of the planks and the handle swayed in the heavy storm winds, creaking and pinging from occasional balls of hail.

"Ain't easy to say what they're thinking at any given time," Dean said, yawning. He bent down and picked up his coffee. It was growing cold and bitter, but it was in that moment the best coffee he thought he'd ever had. "Say, anyone checked on those professors recently?"

Hall frowned. "I forgot all about them. Corporal Wayne, check on the civilians, and report back, instanter. I hope they're still alive, The captain will be quite unhappy with us if they got themselves killed."

"Yes, sir."

"We're fine, Corporal." Paul Fernsby sat cross-legged on his bedroll, tucked into the corner of the wide hallway between the reception and Kellerman's office. The hall was dark and secure with only two tiny high windows that had remained untouched by the battle. A lamp flickered dimly at his side, and he clutched a tin cup of coffee as though it were a life raft. Oliver Berryman paced up and down, a Winchester clutched in his skinny arms and a sour expression on his face, his mind on the fate of the gold and Estrella.

"There is more fighting to come, sirs. The scouts say we can expect another war band at any moment, and the first Apache are still lingering, though we chased the scoundrels off for the most part."

Fernsby brightened. "Jolly good show! I knew you boys would do it. I'm afraid Professor Berryman and I have not proven much help, but I thought we would do well to keep out of your way, and cover our rear ends, as you Americans are fond of saying."

Berryman stopped and scowled. "Speak for yourself, Paul. I am ready and willing to fight the savages as needed. I have been simply waiting for my grand opportunity.

Timing is the key to any great battle, you know. In fact, when Henry the First was—"

Corporal Wayne raised his hand, "Thanks, Professor. Please continue to cover your own—you know. If there is nothing else you'll be needing, I have to be on my way."

Fernsby grinned for the first time in days. "Really, we're fine. Thank you, Corporal."

CHAPTER 57

Amid the rumble of thunder, the sound of a drum began to rise, accentuated by the high musical tones of yips and war cries. Captain Kellerman and Sergeant Major Olinger watched, with resigned, grim faces, as two dozen Mescalero charged at a gallop out of the gloom with their lances and rifles raised, painted faces made terrifying by the rain that caused rivulets of red and black to pour down the warrior's chests and onto their horses like dark blood. Lightning ripped across the sky in violent displays of power as the rising sun struggled to shine from behind the black clouds. "Maybe they'll get hit by a lightning bolt," Olinger said.

"We aren't that lucky," Kellerman replied, taking a heavy nip from the bottle of whiskey planted at his feet, washing it down with coffee, and then shouldering his rifle. "Hold your fire!" he called, as the assembled troopers prepared themselves, focused and rigid in their positions.

A tense moment passed, and when the Apache had come in close enough to make for better targets, Kellerman bellowed, "FIRE!"

The room exploded with gunfire and steel-colored smoke, the acrid tang of gunpowder burned throats and eyes in the enclosed space, but not a single man paused in his duty. Immediately, two Apache dropped, one hit between his eyes a split second after launching a lance that stabbed the exterior wall with a heavy thump. A horse screamed and collapsed, its rider leaping off in the nick of time to avoid being crushed, and pained cries came from wounded Indians, as blood splashed from their wounds. Realizing their error, the Mescalero scattered in three directions to regroup and change their approach, as four of the surviving Chiricahua rounded the back of the fort with plans to enter from the rear.

Two buildings away, Lieutenant Hall saw them go and cursed. "Of course, this morning they have chosen to be friendly. God forbid they fight among themselves for a while. Corporal Wayne, go tell Mr. Zimmermann we need to be rid of sneaky scoundrels coming upon the rear. Mr. Dean, find your men and go with him. Make it clean and quick before the rest of them get any bright ideas."

Frank Abilene followed Tobias Zimmerman into the shadowed overhang of his workshop, as Lucas Dean and Adam Louis watched from inside the building a few feet apart, ready to signal. The workshop sat feet away from the small shed used as a temporary morgue, and the scent of sawdust and leather mingled unpleasantly with old blood and decay. The men sat silent, guns drawn, listening for the first hint of approaching Apache, and soon it came. A soft whickering of horses, then a low guttural sound, and Lucas Dean raised his hand to show he saw them through the workshop window, a gesture Adam Louis repeated for the men outside. The first warrior came on foot, axe in his hand, and the man's eyes widened with surprise when Tobias Zimmermann neatly put three bullets through his heart.

A second Apache rushed the building, dropping to one knee as he prepared to sight his Winchester, but before he could raise the gun to his eyes, Adam Louis plugged him, and he dropped, facedown, on the floor. Dean's and Abilene's hammering revolvers made short work of the two remaining warriors, the berserk cry of a young Apache cut off mid-yell by Dean's bullet to the throat, his eyes conveying rage as he struggled to pull a bowie knife from his waistband with his left hand while trying to fire his Colt with his right. But although Abilene gutshot his companion, the man went down screaming and managed to fire off several rounds, nicking Dean across the thigh, causing him to let loose with a barrage of curses.

The fight over, Tobias Zimmermann looked over the corpses to make sure none were still breathing. "That was easy," he said, satisfied. "You boys sure come in handy, in a pinch."

Dean nodded and then turned to scan the headquarters as the sound of shouting, gunfire, and distressed horses increased to a fever pitch even the thunder barely drowned out. "We better go see what we still have on our plates," he said. As the men made their way back across the parade ground, carefully watching for any signs of a threat, Dean looked longingly toward the dig site, which sat abandoned and unattended. As far as he knew, the treasure hadn't been found yet, but surely, they were close, and a pity it was not to have a chance now to hunt it out while everyone was distracted. Maybe, he mused, there will be an opportunity if they get the professors working on the cleanup crew—that is, if they even survive the day. He cut his eyes to Louis, who was staring out at the parade ground, and Louis nodded.

They'd be ready when the time came, one way or another.

CHAPTER 58

Second Lieutenant Atticus Cranston killed an Apache from bed and, pleased with himself, let loose a victorious whoop. The boarded windows had been shot to pieces, and rain soaked his bedclothes, but he held his position, commanding the troopers who lined the walls, and although deeply exhausted and fighting off a beast of a headache, cheering on their efforts with great enthusiasm.

Captain Joe Kellerman was making his rounds and laughed to see his lieutenant with feet propped up in the bed, commanding his soldiers like a king from a royal litter. Nicky Barnes stood to the other side of Cranston, taking measured, careful shots with a Colt, his left arm bandaged heavily with white gauze and held in a sling against his chest. Mrs. Zimmermann and Chan were huddled down in the far end of the room, where there were no windows, tending to the worst of the wounded who lay or sat crammed into beds and on the floor within the limits of the narrow space, as far removed from the line of fire as possible.

The gunfire was slowing, and Kellerman peered out,

Colt drawn, to see where things stood. The ground was peppered by heavy areas of blood, where men had been wounded or died, and there were marks in the sand where they'd either crawled off half dead or been dragged by their comrades away from the fight. The drums had ceased, and the war cries quieted. The battle was nearly over, and Kellerman felt a wave of relief despite the losses he'd not yet been able to tally. The garrison still stood, and that was the important part for now.

As the morning sun shifted, he watched a few straggling Apache mount their horses and fire toward the headquarters, only to be met with a returning hail of bullets that sent them scrambling off into the sheets of rain and out of sight.

"Bully, sir! I think we've done it. Every man jack of them has turned tail and run!" Cranston said, grinning at Kellerman, as the receding shapes of the Apache riders faded and were joined by a handful of others.

"I never had any doubts, Lieutenant. You have all done well," he said, then cheekily, "Every 'man jack' of you."

Chapter 59

A ragtag group of exhausted troopers staggered outside into the rain, ready to assess the damage to the structures and collect their dead. Then, if fate—and Kellerman—were kind, maybe they'd be given leave to sleep.

Lieutenant Hall joined Kellerman and Saul Olinger in Kellerman's office, the three officers sipping hot coffee, courtesy of Mrs. Zimmermann, and passing around Hall's bottle of Hennessy.

"The men need sleep, but they'll have to take it in shifts. James, set the burial detail, and ask Father Stacls— Stackse—"

"Father Staszczyk," Hall said, his voice tired, dark purple shadows showing beneath his eyes.

"Thank you. Have him say blessings for the dead. Ahiga can say his, too, and both can comfort the surviving troopers as they need. I want the men working in pairs still. We may have sent the Apache packing, but we haven't found our murderer."

A sharp knock at the office door, and Hall quickly hid his expensive cognac between his knees, as Kellerman called, "Yes, come."

Tobias Zimmermann was escorted in by a very young and frazzled-looking orderly, and plodded to a bucket chair and collapsed into it with a tired grunt. He gratefully accepted the cognac and took a long gulp before passing it back to Hall. He rolled his right wrist, and the bones within it cracked loudly, making everyone but him wince. He rubbed the creaking wrist with his left hand and, after a time, released a deep sigh.

A moment of silence passed as Tobias took out the makings and carefully rolled a cigarette, taking a long draw. "You know, Joe," he said watching the steel smoke of his exhalation spiraling and twisting into shapes he tried to identify—one looked like a rabbit. "I was once a man only a fool would cross, an outlaw at large, and proud of it, until I gave that life up. I chose to become a bounty hunter, since that seemed more—civilized. And of course, I was a good one, then, too. But I hung up my guns for the sake of my sanity and the love of Mrs. Zimmermann, of course. Yet here I am taking on Comancheros and Apache, hanging men at my gallows, all for you in the middle of nowhere. And now I am looking at a lot of work to be done to fix the damage from this battle, all the while knowing we will have another one any day now." He shook his head and took a long pull of his drink.

"And I am lucky to have you. Fort Benjamin Grierson is sturdy, Mrs. Zimmerman is a living saint and tending to the wounded, right now with the tenderness—and meanness—of a loving mother, and you haven't missed a shot. You aren't saying you want to leave me, are you?" Kellerman asked with concern.

Tobias sighed and reached for more drink. Downing

it, he said, "No, just tired. I suppose, and wanting to tell you my position is all your fault because of that charm you have. What next?"

"What's next is a mass grave, tending a full infirmary, and a manhunt. I'm hesitant still to send out a dispatch with a wire for Pinkertons or a marshal, not that they'll give us any. Attacks, I'm used to, but the murders are something else. These murders. Anyway." Kellerman took the Hennessy, and seeing the remains were low, opened his drawer instead, pausing briefly to finger the rosary beside his bourbon and thinking of Bastet as he pulled the bottle out.

"James, you earned it. I drink to forget. Don't waste your precious mama's gifts on me," he said, passing the bourbon to Hall and opening his own bottle instead.

"You're thinking of her," Hall said.

"A little, yes. She was one of a kind."

Major Mouser leapt into Kellerman's lap, making him jump. The blood had been groomed from his fluffy orange fur, and his face was cranky as ever.

"How did you get in here?" Kellerman asked, surprised. The cat settled into his lap and began kneading his legs and purring. "What do I do now?" Kellerman said, frozen with a glass in the air staring at the orange fluffball on his lap.

"I daresay he likes you," James Hall said, grinning. "Stroke his back. Scratch under his chin a bit."

"If you say so," Kellerman said, petting the cat who settled his weight deeply, in contentment, and began to purr loudly.

"Well, isn't that something." Olinger smiled. "That cat has hated everyone but Miss Courtenay, yet here he is. They say animals are messengers from the dead, you know."

"Who's they?"

Olinger waved his glass. "Oh, you know—them."

Further speculation was interrupted by a knock. "Yes, yes," Kellerman said, and Ahiga stepped in, looking the orderly up and down with disapproving eyes of flint.

"You are raggedy," Ahiga said. "You have the honor of watching over the captain, who is a noble man, and yet you stand here looking like this?" He flicked a loose button on the private's coat, then scowled at the man's crusty shoes and dirty hems. "Navajo would flog and shame you in front of the whole tribe, then we—"

"Thank you Ahiga," Kellerman interrupted. "I appreciate your concerns, but given what we have been through, I must ask that you leave the private in peace."

The orderly was shaking slightly but tried to look stern. Of course, looking at the Navajo scout who cradled his Henry in his bulging bronze arms and bore scars across his broad chest, the thin nineteen-year-old private had no impulse to say anything much in reply and kept his face neutral.

"Yes, sir," Ahiga said, and, with one more critical glance at the orderly, closed the door.

He entered the room and quickly assessed the inhabitants. "Sir, you're missing one. Lieutenant Cranston still in the infirmary?" Ahiga asked. He looked concerned. The scout had a soft spot for the second lieutenant.

Kellerman gestured to a chair, but Ahiga shook his head and remained as he was.

"Yes, but you'd be proud of our young second

lieutenant, Ahiga. He made a private roll his bed against the window and lay there shooting and barking orders like the West Pointer he is," Kellerman said, grinning. "But doc says he has to stay in bed until his head wound heals."

"Bully for Atticus," added Hall. "I've taught him all I know. He's a testament to my wisdom and to the very might of Fort Benjamin Grierson."

Ahiga looked relieved, then: "We have a doctor now?"

Chan bustled around the infirmary, ignoring the spurts of rain that came through the cracked windows. He figured a fresh wash of water energy never hurt, unless it soaked his patients. Bad energy filled the little hospital, newly built though it may be. Besides most of the men needed a bath. More patients brought more unpleasant odors, and Chan produced small herb sachets from his medicine case, giving one to Mrs. Zimmermann. Held under their noses, the tangy blend of lemon balm, rosemary, strong mint, and ginger helped mask the smells. Then he opened a tin of menthol to swipe beneath their noses as well. The nurse looked askance but turned her face from the men, and he did it anyway.

Working together, he and Mrs. Zimmermann and the Jesus Mann moved the worst cases in their brass beds away from the walls and into the driest areas, pinning privacy curtains around them with help from the long arms of Privates Conner Johnstone and Daniel Williamson, both lanky farm boys who had been caught for desertion before choosing the hell of Fort Misery over a sentence at Yuma. By the third time, Williamson vomited. Chan sent him to find a superior to assign him elsewhere. "You fought well, Mr. Williamson. Look— barely bullet holes here, eh? I imagine captain will have work for you." He smiled and bowed deeply to sweeten the suggestion, secretly thinking he could take no more vomit.

"You sure you don't need me no more, doc? I ain't mind it here. I like helping."

Mrs. Zimmermann passed by with a tray laden with medicine and bandages, and quipped, "Trooper, doc's saying you and your weak stomach should get out. Go on, no one needs to clean up after you."

Williamson flushed red beneath his tanned face, and he ran a hand through his blond hair.

"Been that way since I was a kid—can't help it," he said sheepishly. "Sure, I'll go find the captain."

Chan clapped his hands together, "Good man! Off you go!"

CHAPTER 60

Restored by brandy and whiskey, the officers broke off their meeting and stepped outside, taking in the grim scene before them. The rain had lightened, and the sun broke through the clouds, casting a warm glow over the scene. Dead Apaches littered the sand, and nearby lay half a dozen horses, one paint pony still alive but braying in pain and confusion over his predicament.

Hall grimaced, then, taking time to kneel and stroke the dying horse on the head and neck before pulling the trigger, ended the horse's misery with a swift bullet. Duty done, he holstered his Colt and said to no one in particular, "I hate that, you know. The horse doesn't deserve it and can't understand."

Kellerman surveyed the dead, their bronze skin turning the color of ash. Many appeared to be just boys still, their eyes staring at the sky with mouths wide open, perhaps one last prayer to their God, as life fled from their mortal shell. Inside the fort boundaries, he knew a few of his own young men lay in similar tableaux. Senseless, he thought, but shook the feeling off.

"Lieutenant Hall, choose a few horses and men to

drag both the bodies and horses out into the desert.
The Apache can handle their own dead this time. If not,
the vultures and coyotes will think it's Christmas come
early. Saul, stick with me. We can assign details as we
come across them."

Hall snapped to attention, with a crisp salute. "Yes,
sir." He glanced at Olinger. The older man looked
drawn and exhausted. "And hopefully we find time to
sleep. You look done in, Sarge."

Paul Fernsby made his way to his quarters, hand-
kerchief held to his nose to block out the growing
stench of dead troopers and spilled blood that made him
gag, doing his best to avert his eyes from the ungodly
lines of dead men being laid in a neat row, in preparation for burial. A paunchy middle-aged private named
Martin Harris accompanied him, seemingly unfazed by
the gruesome sight, and opened the door to the professor's room with a grunt. "Here we are, sir," he said.

"Yes, thank you. There's no need to supervise me.
I'm quite all right unlike those poor chaps laying out
there."

"Captain's orders, sir. No one to be alone."

As Fernsby entered the room, two things struck him
at once, Berryman's trunk was open and seemed empty,
and an unpleasant odor filled the room that had nought
to do with the massacre victims outside. Curiosity
piqued, Fernsby peered into the trunk and saw blankets
covered with filth and no artifacts within. He frowned—
why did Berryman create such a fuss about no one
opening it, if all it contained was linens? A question for

another time, he thought, as he gathered his pith helmet and boots. The men assigned to assist him at the excavation were otherwise occupied, but there was no reason he couldn't get back to work. Surely, the treasure was near at hand. He needed something to distract from his grief. He chided himself for moping about and making the officers fret. He wasn't suicidal, just in shock and pain over the brutality of his loss. Getting back in the swing of things would surely hold the key to starting life anew, without his niece—though the thought of her murder sprung fresh tears to his eyes. Onward, onward, he reaffirmed, and then away from this god-forsaken land once and for all.

The rain had mostly subsided, and a detail had begun the backbreaking work of digging a mass grave for the fallen troopers, the work overseen by Corporal Wayne. Joe Kellerman checked their progress and then made his way to look in on his wounded warriors, greeted by a cheerful Chan at the infirmary—now filled with noise, as the bullet hole–riddled boards that remained intact were being pried from the windows, and occasional moans and groans from patients filled the air.

"How's our second lieutenant, doc? He ready for action yet?"

"Not yet," Chan said, grinning. "He's a stubborn man, tried to get out of bed to leave and"—Chan made a motion with his hands—"*bang*, onto the floor."

He pulled back the curtain. Atticus Cranston jumped, shirtless but dressed in his pants, a look of irritation on his face. "Doc won't let me out, sir," he said, sliding his eyes to Chan, as if to dare him to mention his collapse.

Kellerman shrugged. "Doc's orders, Cranston. But you did a superb job fighting Apache from your bed. That West Point training paid off."

CHAPTER 61

Although everyone at Fort Misery was exhausted, Tobias Zimmermann recruited soldiers to make repairs, and the sound of hammering and sawing echoed across the desert. The Apache corpses had been dragged far out and the exhausted escorts of the dead given leave to sleep for a few hours to recuperate. Mrs. Zimmermann did her best to prepare a hearty lunch to replenish the tired soldiers' energy, and the grave detail worked diligently, even as the rain renewed with vigor.

At the dig site, Fernsby was back at work, sifting through the muddy sand, joined by Berryman, who had disappeared for a time but would answer no questions as to his whereabouts. As the men worked diligently, they drew an audience, the surviving Trey-Treys, who watched with hungry eyes as the older men lifted artifacts into small wooden boxes and carried them into the tents.

"We find ourselves with nothing to do," Lucas Dean said, offering a hand up to Fernsby, who struggled to climb from a trench with a small piece of aged armor that looked like a bit of sword dulled by time. "Mind if we offer a hand?" He smiled warmly, buttering the older man up. Berryman overheard and stiffened immediately, but Fernsby was naïve and grinned. "Oh, what a kind offer. We could use an extra set of hands. I'm not quite myself now, you see. The loss"—he choked up—"the loss of my Constance has wounded me, and I feel I have lost strength in mind and body. I hope to finish this quickly, then move on. We won't stay, but I cannot disappoint the President. This is highly delicate work, but perhaps you can assist me in the labor under close, close supervision."

"Most certainly, Professor. I am your humble servant. Nicky will help, too," he said, climbing into the trench and gesturing for Barnes to assist Berryman, who scowled as though he'd smelled a dead skunk.

"I don't need help," he said, but Barnes didn't take no for an answer and swaggered up to the old man menacingly.

"Well, you've got it," he said, dropping his hand to his Colt.

Frank Abilene surveyed the scene and then wandered off, saying, "I'm gonna go see if the gravediggers need a hand. Holler if you need me."

Dean called after him, "You can be sure we will—the very instant your assistance is required."

The sun had risen and set for two days following the Apache raid, as the storm began to ease and give way to puffy clouds upon a cobalt sky. Twelve dead had been buried, prayers said, and life at Fort Benjamin Grierson slowly, tentatively returned to its rhythm. The professors worked diligently on their excavation, though Fernsby lacked his previous enthusiasm and was simply going through the motions in an effort to find his treasure, while Berryman was fidgety and bad-tempered, leading Joe Kellerman to be suspicious of the man and his motives. The Trey-Treys had taken over assisting the labor, as the troopers continued making repairs under the stern guidance of Tobias Zimmermann, who barked orders and cursed in outrage, threatening boots up the rear and hangings as a matter of course.

Inside the infirmary, Kellerman and Lieutenant Hall pulled up chairs to the bedside of Atticus Cranston, who continued to protest his ability to return to duties.

"I feel fine," Cranston lied, the head wound still sharp and sore.

"No, you don't," Hall said firmly, pouring a large glass of whiskey and handing it to the young second lieutenant. "You've no need to put on airs for us. The worst of it's over, and you did a fine job of fighting off the Apache from your bed. A man recovering is worth more than a half-dead officer in the field." He held out the bone box. "Snuff?"

"Olinger is dispatching a scouting party down south, and Corporal Wayne's on the way to Devil's Rock—in hopes of raisins, as Mrs. Zimmermann informs me the army is opposed to her plum duff and determined to starve us all," Captain Kellerman said. "There's nothing for you to do, Atticus, but rest and get well again."

Frederick Mann wandered over to the officers, still stiff and bruised, but smiling broadly. "Hello, sirs," he said, then: "Might I trouble you for a drop of that whiskey?"

Hall looked the private over, then poured a glass.

"You scoundrel, it would do you well to return to duty at the stables. Lucifer has been looking for a man to kick. Are you healed?"

Mann downed the shot and swayed a bit on his feet from the movement. "Thank you, sir. And yes, I suppose so, sir. Though Mrs. Zimmermann and Doc Chan say I'm still feeble. It's been quite boring in here. We don't have a great many books on hand."

Chan marched up and placed a hand on Mann's shoulder to steer him back to bed. "What did I tell you? Longer you lie down, faster you get better. Come, leave the officers alone—you're going to fall, and then, what will we have to do, heal up a broken arm? I'll find you a new book, if you behave." He steered the private back to bed and moved on to his other patients, all of whom had a remarkably good prognosis, despite their hacking coughs and scabbed wounds.

At last, he made his way back to Kellerman, his expression serious. "Captain, I need to speak with you. I believe Oliver Berryman may try to murder Paul Fernsby."

"Why? For what purpose?" Kellerman asked, rubbing his hand over the itchy scar where the bullet had grazed his head.

"This I do not know. Perhaps to seize the treasure for himself. When we were departing London, I saw a few men following us—watching him—and he became nervous and hid belowdecks until the ship left the port. He may owe a few debts. I've seen him gambling and losing. All speculation, of course, but I'm certain that he poisoned Julius Dankworth, and I fear Mr. Fernsby's life is in peril."

"And what of the gunmen, the Fey-Feys?"

"That's Trey-Treys, sir," Cranston said.

"Thank you, Cranston. What is your speculation of them? Are they working with him?"

Chan thought a long moment. "I don't believe so. But they may have their own purpose in mind. In Yuma, the professors were very drunk, and Berryman lost a small fortune in a card game, but Fernsby covered the expense to avoid conflict. Even if the gang has no interest in lost treasure, they may have a desire to take Fernsby's cash. He flashed it around foolishly, though I warned him against it."

"I see," Kellerman said. "Well, I think we should head to the excavation and see what everyone is up to. Lieutenant Hall, let's go play at being Pinkertons." He stood and stretched his neck, making it crack and pop. Cranston tried to stand, but Hall pushed him down and handed him the bottle of whiskey.

"Stay here, Atticus. We'll send for you if you're needed. Don't waste the whiskey," Hall said sternly. Cranston frowned but cradled the bottle close. "And Lieutenant, watch your drinking."

Chapter 62

Lucas Dean and Frank Abilene were hard at work shoveling the loose muddy earth, as Fernsby and Berryman supervised. A few more relics had been removed, but there was yet no great cache of treasure to be seen. It was hot, thirsty work, and Nicky Barnes had gone off to retrieve canteens of water for his fellows, as the sun beat down heavy upon their backs. Captain Kellerman and Lieutenant Hall arrived just in time to see Fernsby carefully carrying a wooden box filled with something interesting into a tent, muttering to himself with excitement. Professor Berryman, however, was nowhere to be found, a fact that immediately made the officers suspicious.

"Why, hello, officers!" Lucas Dean cried out cheerfully, his sombrero pulled low over his sunburned face and the top buttons of his shirt undone to let the air in. "Come to help with the excavation?"

Kellerman smiled thinly. "No, we'll leave that to you. We need a word with the professor."

Dean gestured to the tent where Fernsby had just disappeared inside. "I don't know where the other one is, but Professor Fernsby has been teaching us quite a bit about Spanish conquistadors. More than I ever needed to know, in fact."

James Hall pulled aside the tent flap, and the two men stepped inside the cool dim space. Laid out on the table were pieces of human bone and glinting bits of armor and weaponry, and Fernsby was writing down information on tags that he tied to each piece.

"Professor Fernsby, we're glad to see you working again. How are you this fine day?" Hall said, reaching for his snuffbox in preparation. "Have a pinch, sir—it'll do you good." He extended the box to Fernsby, who, after a pause, accepted it.

"Nearly ready to move on, my friends," Fernsby said, then his face clouded. "I can't stay the full time. I hope you're able to send for my transport early. You surely understand."

Kellerman met the man's gaze with pain of his own, a brief moment of shared grief. "I understand. If the scouts come back with an all clear, I'll send a dispatch to Yuma. But what of the treasure?"

Fernsby brightened. "We found a casket today that I suspect contains the gold, but the excavation is fragile, and we must take our time, despite our enthusiasm."

"I see," Kellerman said. "I need to speak with you about a—well, a delicate matter, as well, I suppose. Would you join us in my office? I won't take much of your time."

Fernsby shifted nervously. "I suppose so. I must admit I'm not fully comfortable leaving Mr. Dean and his men unsupervised with the goods. And I have no idea where Berryman has run off to. He disappeared a while ago."

"In that case, we can speak here." Kellerman pulled over a wooden stool and bade the older man to sit.

"What is this all about. Did you find who murdered my Constance?" Fernsby said, his voice cracking upon his niece's name.

"Not yet, but we will. It has been brought to my attention that your own life is in danger, and that the death of Professor Dankworth may not have been accidental—and that a member of your party may be responsible."

"A member of— You mean Oliver?" The professor reached inside his vest pocket and produced a silver flask, taking a swig. "Gentlemen, I met him at university— when we were still boys, really—but twenty years of working at our various excavations kept us apart, and I only knew him from correspondence and the papers he published. It wasn't until we made it all the way here to America and the Yuma desert that I began to see signs that perhaps he—well, perhaps he wasn't all that he seemed. I paid off his gambling debts at a tavern, you know. He was about to be dragged into the street by a tough-looking fellow—dentist I think he is, Holliday. A few bad hands at poker that I thought nothing of until I saw him trying to sneak out through the kitchen. His bad temper, too, is something to contend with—but not abnormal among academics, frankly. Why would you believe he killed Julius, though, and how? Chan said the death was natural."

Kellerman grimaced. "Chan didn't want to add to your worries, but he told me that Professor Dankworth was showing the symptoms of arsenic poisoning, that it built over time, say one ship voyage and a trip west across the country. How you avoided the same fate, I can't say."

"I see. Is there any hard evidence? You cannot accuse the man of nefarious intent without proof."

"No, not yet. But for your safety, I'm assigning a trooper to stay with you at all times, and to keep an eye on the Tree-Tree men, too."

"Trey-Trey, sir," Hall interjected.

"Yes, them. We also need to find Professor Berryman. I don't like him being unaccounted for. Any ideas?"

Fernsby thought, then said, "No, I can't rightly say."

"The gold is near, darling. A little while longer, and then we'll be free of this place—and rich beyond our wildest dreams."

Oliver Berryman was crouched in the abandoned sutler's building, speaking to Estrella, who lay out on a blanket, stiff and cold with exhaustion despite the cloying heat inside the abandoned building. She smiled sadly. "And then we'll be married?"

"Yes, dear. You can have surgery and live as a true bride. You'll be the toast of London society. We may have a problem with those gunfighters. I suspect they're after the same profits as we are. You need to be careful. They're not as dim as the rest of the denizens here." He handed her a bundle of food and a canteen. "Be a good girl. It isn't long now."

* * *

Professor Fernsby was busily working when the sand slipped away from beneath him and he dropped a solid ten feet down into a pit, landing with a heavy thump on a heavy wooden box. A flurry of shouts rang out above him as the younger men, worried the old fella had at best broken his hip or, at worst, his neck.

"Professor, you all right?" Lucas Dean called down, peering over the edge. Soon his face was joined by others as a group cautiously looked into the pit trying not to slide in on their knees.

"Someone get a rope, the perfesser is down there!" a trooper cried out.

"Dead?" came a reply.

"Dunno yet," the first man said.

Fernsby coughed, the wind knocked out of him. "I am not dead. I'm quite fine, I think. One moment, please." He looked around, the area was dark and appeared to be a man-made structure of some kind. Wincing, he rolled to his side and then crawled onto his knees.

"Nah, he ain't dead. You get the rope?"

"Remarkable!" Fernsby cried, dusting off his hat and gazing around, as the sun shifted just enough to allow his adjusting eyes to see where he was. "A tomb, perhaps? No." He looked down at the wood he stood on and saw it was a heavy, casket, bigger than the initial discovery, already retrieved, that he thought might contain the treasure. That one had fallen beside him and split open and revealed itself to be empty outside of loose sandy soil and a few relics.

"Say, you up there. Someone bring me a sketchbook and pencil, please," Fernsby called, and Frank Abilene soon appeared with the request.

"You want us to come down with you?"

"Not yet. Just lower that in a bucket. Yes, there's a good lad. My God, boys, I think we've done it! Someone, find me Berryman!"

Nicky Barnes was watching the abandoned sutlery with narrowed eyes, smoking a cigarette and considering. He'd watched one of the professors, the rude one, enter the building but the man hadn't come out yet. The heavy afternoon sun must have been making it roast inside, but a rainstorm was gathering yet again. What was the old coot doing in there? Barnes wondered.

"What is he doing in there?" a voice said, and Barnes nearly jumped out of his skin, dropping his cigarette down his shirt and hopping in a panic to squash out the burning coal.

"You're so spooky!"

Ahiga stood at his shoulder, calmly cradling his Henry like a baby in the crook of his arms. "Yeah, so white men tell me. You are out here being spooky, too. I have been watching you, watching him. So what's he doing in there?" Ahiga asked.

"Darned if I know—that's why I'm watching him. Odd behavior is all, if you ask me."

"Hmmm."

They stood in companionable silence for a few more minutes, as the wind picked up and the storm drew in closer, threatening rain yet again, as monsoon season seemed determined to hang on to all of its glory. At last, Oliver Berryman exited the building, looking around furtively, before hastily making his way back toward the parade ground.

Barnes stiffened and Ahiga said, "Ah-ah," to stop him before he followed the professor. "Not now. He's nervous, and a nervous man looks around too much."

They watched him go, then Ahiga said, "He went in with food did he not? Canteens?"

Barnes brightened, "You're right, you spooky cuss. He's got someone in there."

"Maybe so, yes."

"Well, hell, man, let's go take a look-see."

"There you are, Oliver! Look down here—we found it!" Fernsby called up to Berryman, when the professor joined the circle of men around the caved-in pit. "Come join me, old boy. By jove, we've got it now!"

Lucas Dean lowered Berryman on a rope, the drop was short enough but still, having something to hold kept him from snapping a leg. He looked around at the structure. "What have we here, Paul—a tomb?"

"At first I thought not, but look at the casket. It's a sarcophagus." The men studied the wooden box, heavily carved and decorated with bright pigments that created a face akin to a Spanish conquistador.

"What did the map say, exactly?" Berryman said, frowning.

Fernsby flipped through his sketchbook and read. "'The heart of gold can be found where Conquistador Don Esteban de Toro lies in his final rest, treasure to be had inside the greatness of man.'"

Fernsby and Berryman shared a look. "Could we have been mistaken? Is *he* the golden treasure?"

"Only one way to find out," Berryman said, then called up, "You, boys, send down tools and lanterns, instanter! We may need a few of you down here with us, too."

As the work began again in earnest, rain broke out once again, thunder crashing, lightning scrawling across the desert sky like a demented god's warning.

While the storm raged, heavy rain providing covering noise, Nicky Barnes and Ahiga quietly opened the door of the unused sutlery, Barnes with his Colt drawn by his side. A bad odor hit their faces and made them wrinkle their noses, old decay and the dusty must of an abandoned structure. It was dark inside, but they could see a woman, asleep on a Mexican blanket, a canteen and scattered remnants of food beside her. The room was otherwise empty and silent. Ahiga put a finger to his lips and Barnes nodded, understanding the silent communication, and just as quietly, the two men stepped back out into the storm.

"Could be a Lipan gal he's captured in there. I haven't seen him in the company of an unknown woman before tonight," Barnes said. "Not that there's any spare ladies around the fort."

"I'll get the captain. Make sure she doesn't leave. Keep out of sight in case Berryman comes back."

Barnes crouched, nodding, and rolled a fresh cigarette as he settled in for sentry duty.

Ahiga found the captain at his desk, his collar ringed with sweat, as he concentrated over the stack of paperwork before him with pen in hand, scribbling here and there as needed. The orderly was nowhere to be found, and the scout tapped on the open door.

"Yes, Ahiga, what have you to report?"

"The Berryman professor went into the sutler's store. He entered with food and canteens in hand, then exited alone, no food or canteens, and made his way back to the parade grounds."

Kellerman looked surprised. "I assume you took a look after he left?"

"Yes, sir, and there's a young girl with black hair wrapped up in a blanket, sound asleep. Barnes is keeping an eye out to make sure she doesn't leave."

"He has a castaway, then, but why? Is she a Lipan girl? Lord knows they've caused us enough trouble in the past."

"No idea, sir."

Kellerman rubbed his hair, making the sides stand up, a sure sign of his disquiet. "Well, the good news is the scouts returned with an excellent report. The Apache have retreated and are licking their wounds. We can send for the professors' wagon. I've just signed the papers to authorize it, in fact. Let's get rid of them. I'm still waiting to hear from the other patrol if we have had any luck with supplies at Devil's Rock before Mrs. Zimmermann threatens to put me in the stewpot. Let's go to excavation and see what can be seen, shall we?"

With a longing look at his bourbon, he stood, then

hesitated and downed a shot, holding the jug up to offer it to the scout.

"No, sir. Thank you. sir."

"Good, watch your drinking."

"Yes, sir."

CHAPTER 63

Night had come in quickly, desert winds and cool rain bringing relief from the unrelenting heat. Joe Kellerman and Ahiga arrived at the dig site just after the heavy casket Paul Fernsby had fallen onto had been lifted and placed inside a tent. With Oliver Berryman barking instructions, a ragtag assembly of helpers lifted the lid, and when the contents were revealed, there was a moment of stunned silence.

Finally, Fernsby broke the tension as he peered at the large heavy-bodied skeleton in armor that lay within. Time spent inside the grave had left blossoms of discoloration in green and purple across the armor and bones, yet the feathered plumes of the man's hat were in near mint condition.

"This must be the fallen conquistador," he exclaimed, smiling. "They honored him as divinely as they could, it seems. Look here." He pointed to the brass breastplate on which lay a golden approximation of a human heart, thin and flat and hammered to the armor beneath. "The treasure we have been seeking all this time—it was simply him. Well, financial loss aside, this will be a glorious find all the same. Think of it! 'The Golden-Hearted Conquistador de Toro'—museum visitors from around the world will come to view him in all his glory."

Fernsby shook Kellerman's hand enthusiastically. "Thank you for allowing us to disrupt you during the excavation, Captain. I am sure you now see why it was of such great import. Even though we are left without material riches, we found something truly remarkable for the tomes of history! Why, just think, your fort will be on a historical registry list for people to visit!"

Kellerman blanched, "No! Don't you dare, Professor Fernsby. Stick him in your museum, and leave it at that. I don't care where you say you found him, but don't you dare mark it down as in the middle of my parade ground."

He started to say something else, stopped, and then took a deep breath. "I've sent for your transport. Please let Lieutenant Hall know if you require assistance from my men to pack up and prepare for your return journey." With that, he ducked out of the tent, the rain already heavy enough to start running rivulets off his shirt. He sighed, looking at his torn-up parade ground. At least they'd be gone soon, and they had given the men something to do with the task of filling it in and smoothing it down again.

CHAPTER 64

When the last of the finds dug up by the professors were packed into boxes and it became clear they wouldn't have enough transport space, Lucas Dean offered the use of his own wagon between the fort and Yuma. Fernsby wasn't looking forward to his long trip back across the west, or to London, but was determined not to leave anything behind, including his niece's body, and readily agreed to the help. It was the opinion of Captain Kellerman that having the Trey-Treys escort the professor's antiquities away might lead to robbery, but it wouldn't be his problem once he was watching their backs fading into a dust cloud, and he decided to say nothing. As of yet, Lucas Dean and his men had done nothing that could force the Army to hold them, so whatever their intentions were, or had been, were not his concern.

The more worrisome questions centered on Oliver Berryman and his apparent ward, as when Ahiga and the others had returned to search the sutler's building, they found it vacant and hadn't seen the young woman since. Barnes swore up and down that he never saw the woman leave, and Kellerman was beginning to think the men had imagined her, based on the shape of a blanket in the shadowy building. In the meantime, Oliver Berryman was often seen to be moving furtively around the wagons and excavation packing, and under orders from Kellerman, Ahiga kept him under surveillance.

The night before the professors' departure, Mrs. Zimmerman provided her finest, for a farewell dinner at the officer's mess, the room still riddled with bullet holes but otherwise standing fine. The officers were in high spirits, celebrating Lieutenant Cranston's release from the infirmary, and the Trey-Treys were talkative, telling tales of derring-do, whiskey loosening their tongues. But Oliver Berryman remained unusually quiet and kept leaving the table to "check on things."

The fourth time Berryman left the room, Joe Kellerman, wondering exactly what the professor was up to, excused himself to follow the man, skulking along behind him until they reached the roofed wagon port beside the stables. Kellerman waited a long moment, then turned the corner behind the professor, to a shocking scene unfolding before him.

An emaciated young woman, with coarse, matted hair, was helping Berryman transfer boxes from the wagons to different wagons, each crate painted with a dark mark on the side. A strange creature, who looked ready to bolt—yet fierce—she also seemed to be removing items from the boxes and secreting them in her clothing.

Ahiga appeared out of the shadows at Kellerman's side, whispering, "I believe that's the young woman from the sutlery, Captain. See the knives? I bet she's our killer."

Clothed in grubby dark broadcloth trousers and a man's coat, around her waist there was a collection of knives, the smallest blade as slender as a pinkie finger, the largest a bowie knife, everything tucked into a leather cord she wore as a belt.

"Who is she? And where was she this entire time?"

"The hidden hole of the tent, then in the sutlery, under rocks, who knows. He hid her well."

Kellerman drew his Colt, preparing to step out and confront the woman, and Ahiga shifted his grip on his Henry. If it came down to it, he'd shoot her before chancing a knife fight. A blast of thunder roared overheard and blocked out their whispered voices and the sounds of their movements, and they may have had a chance at surprising her, but then Oliver Berryman made a most fatal mistake. The cadaverous professor materialized from the back of a wagon and passed out the pried and hammered golden heart through the tent flap to pass to the woman.

Kellerman seized the moment. "Oliver Berryman, drop it. Open your hands, put them where we can see them, and step out slow. You're hereby held under arrest by my authority as an officer of the United States Army until such time as the U.S. Marshal Service comes to collect you." He pointed to the woman. "You too. Hands up, lady."

After a long tense moment in which the professor seemed to consider making a run for it, he broke into a grin and raised the hand not clutching the relic heart.

"I am but a lowly archaeologist, Captain. What could

the army or a marshal want with me? You're obviously making a terrible mistake here. I was simply rearranging some of our finds for travel, and I'm offended you think otherwise."

"Step down easy," Ahiga said, his Henry pointed at Berryman's chest, while he also watched the woman from the corner of his eye. Ignoring Kellerman's order, she had begun to slink away from the wagon, into the shadowy light thrown from the stables.

Soon a crowd had gathered, and Lieutenants Cranston and Hall, after briefly assessing the scene, flanked the captain and scout, guns drawn. Nicky Barnes came from around the stables with a rifle, the rain thrumming on his hat yet leaving a lit cigarette clamped in his teeth untouched.

Not liking his odds against the armed men, Oliver Berryman gave it up. He dropped the heart, which hit the earth with a thud, and then slowly raised his palms open and skyward. Kellerman and Cranston were on him immediately, each grasping an arm, concerned the man would reach for a hidden gun or bolt, and Corporal Wayne brought a set of leg manacles from the nearest guard post, clamping them against the man's legs to keep him from running.

"Really, is any of this necessary? We need to settle down and have a conversation, for heaven's sake. Where is my dear man Fernsby?"

"Quite so, it is necessary. You're a sneaky little—" Hall had turned briefly away from watching the young woman to see the manacles go on, and to his astonishment, she had instantly disappeared. "Where is she?"

"What? Where is who? Already?" Kellerman bellowed.

"The woman!"

"Lieutenant Hall! Cranston! Corporal Wayne! Apprehend her!"

And so it was that the men went in pursuit of the escaped young woman, but she seemed to evade them at every turn, akin to a rat, disappearing into places too small for even the thinnest troopers to follow, though they all made their best efforts, being riled by the arrest—even though they weren't all entirely sure why it had happened or why they were chasing her.

Oliver Berryman was marched past the fort's gallows, the majestic structure so lovingly maintained by Tobias Zimmermann, beautifully framed by moonlight and the rain that turned the wood silver, a loose hemp rope creaking on the wind. Berryman shuddered. "You won't hang me here, you ruffians—over what, a small theft? The might of the entire English army and the Queen would be on your back within minutes."

"You think so?" Kellerman said, grinning. "Hey, Lieutenant Hall, Berryman here informs we'd get to meet the queen if we hang him. Are you up for it?"

"Oh yes, sir. I'd be jumping for a chance to meet ol' Queen Vic! I daresay Mrs. Zimmermann would faint from excitement if Her Majesty paid a call, particularly if she complimented the plum duff, perhaps, on a day it was subpar." Then Hall frowned with the crushing weight of disappointment. "But I imagine he will get his fair trial in Yuma or beyond, not here. Real pity, I say."

CHAPTER 65

Fort Misery's temporary holding cells were most often filled by men accused of petty crimes—drunkenness or punching a commanding officer—yet they stood with windows that faced the gallows in perpetuity, in case a man needed reminding about the consequences of crossing Captain Kellerman. Having already chosen hell, it was a rarity that soldiers were further sentenced to death at the fort, but when they were, they were allowed to read with the priest or Mrs. Zimmermann.

The rooms were damp, cobwebbed, and held a strange odor, no matter how often Mrs. Zimmermann scrubbed, a task she undertook believing it her duty to keep it comfortable for what she considered redeemable sinners.

If a man or two was in the clink, Father Staszczyk and a reliable trooper were given desks to keep eye on the criminals until such a time as Kellerman freed them, or a warrant officer arrived. Mostly, the arrestees slept off their problems and were released in the morning, with a stern warning.

But Professor Berryman fought like a wildcat, trying

to break his way out of the heavy manacles and to escape the cell before the door swung shut, until finally Atticus Cranston, still cranky from his injuries and suffering a headache, said, "Sir, I can just shoot him. How much trouble would it be?"

"No trouble at all, Lieutenant. Would you care to?"

Cranston had unholstered his Colt when Berryman cried, "Fine! I yield! I still don't know why you thugs think I'm a criminal. I'm but a scholar, for God's sake!"

Kellerman nodded. "You sure are. A criminal, that is. Mr. Oliver Berryman, you're hereby arrested for the attempted murder of Second Lieutenant Atticus Cranston, the murder of Julius Dankworth—"

"The First," Cranston chimed in.

"Thank you, Lieutenant—the murder of Julius Dankworth, the First, attempted theft of priceless relics that your partner, yourself, and the president of the United States have informed me are quite important, and are for now under suspicion of kidnapping and possibly more murder via being an accomplice to the young lady we're seeking. Now, shut up and cooperate, or I will most surely allow the second lieutenant to shoot you, as I believe it will aid his recovery."

With that, the cadaverous professor was unceremoniously dumped on his butt into the dim cell with no further physical protests and, manacles unshackled, the cell door slammed shut with a bang.

Outside, the men of the fort could hear him carrying on about English rights, but they all studiously ignored him. Finding his wayward companion was their only priority.

Chapter 66

Professor Fernsby was animated, having suffered too much excitement from the arrest and manhunt, as he stood resting one hand on a cane and using the other to point at the labeled cases being loaded into the extra wagon that had arrived in record time, with no threat of Apache or Comancheros. "Oh, if only my Constance were here. These discoveries will land us on the map!"

Lucas Dean and the Trey-Treys stood watching, disappointed at the lack of riches but hiding it well. "You don't intend to sell any of it, Professor Fernsby?" Lucas Dean asked. His startling green eyes had lost some of their sparkle. "It would bring a small fortune."

Fernsby placed a hand on the man. "No, my boy. Not yet time. The advancement of historical discovery matters more than a few pounds. But do tell me—is this the life you really want? Following around old coots in hopes of gold to run away with in the night? Don't take me for a fool. I know why you've been hanging about this place."

Dean had the grace to look uncomfortable. He toed his boot in the sand and rolled a cigarette, finally replying,

"I suppose not. When I was a boy, I wanted to find the bones of dinosaurs and dragons, but those were only a myth."

"They're not a myth anymore, Mr. Dean. Well, at least in that we know they're likely still around somewhere," Fernsby said to the younger man, his eyes bright. "But human history is far more interesting and important than old lizards, I'd say."

Silence fell as Fernsby watched over the work. Then, reflecting, he said, "Come with me, to London. Constance was my assistant, and I am lost without her—but an American outlaw like you may be just the ticket. Think of the adventures we can have, Lucas. I can tell you're smart. You're going to die in some fool gunfight, and for what? Come with me. Let me teach you. I'm an old man, sure, but my brain"—Fernsby tapped his head—"my brain is sharp as ever. And you may be my brawn. Your Wild West shootist skills will be a novelty over there—they'll keep me protected, too, I would imagine. Losing my niece to brutality has put me into a mind of shock. I have come to understand that intellect is not a sword or shield. You'll be rewarded handsomely for your work—steady, honest pay."

Lucas Dean thought about it for a moment and looked over at what was left of his gang. The last surviving Trey-Treys, eyes greedy for treasure to be dropped. *What a way to live,* he thought. *I don't even like these men. We never accomplished much—certainly will never be on par with the great outlaws like Jesse James. History is going to forget us. We can be sure of it.*

"All right, then, we'll give it a go. Mainly on account of how I suppose I would like to see something new.

No hogwash, though, you understand. Let's just see how I like it first."

Fernsby smiled. He hugged the reluctant Dean, who stood stiff with a look of horror. "I have always believed in you," the professor said, leading Dean to believe the old man may be brain damaged and a little drunk, but sparking a warm feeling in his chest all the same.

Ahiga sidled up to Nicky Barnes, this time not making him jump. "This is okay with you, spooked white man?"

Barnes laughed beneath his badly groomed mustache. "Works out just fine. I'm tired of the Trey-Treys. Frankie will find his own way. He does better alone anyhow. He's plain crazy that way."

CHAPTER 67

The storms had yet again gathered in full force, with soldiers rushing to complete their duties, but the scouting party trying their hardest to find the girl was nothing but increasingly frustrated.

"I bet she wandered off into the desert. She'll be dead in a day, I reckon," Corporal Lockhart said, frowning at the rough terrain beyond the fort.

"Thank you for your optimism, Corporal Lockhart," Hall said.

"Yes, sir."

The men continued their circular search of the premises, not a stone unturned or room unlooked at, all the while wondering if she truly was a violent murderer, which made the job unnerving.

After trying everywhere else, the party led by Hall headed to the graveyard, looking for areas of disturbed dirt that should be well settled, a process that made the superstitious Lockhart shiver, as he feared incurring the attention of angry dead.

"Gentlemen," James Hall called, raising his gauntleted hand. "What's this?" He pointed to an older corner of the cemetery, where a simple white cross bore black paint that said:

JOHN N HAMER – U.S. Calvary – DIED A HERO
1858–1875

There was an odd disturbance of the earth where the man's grave lay. Looking it up and down carefully, Hall used his saber to gently poke the middle, where a belly would most likely be, and he wasn't much surprised when the dirt cried out in pain.

"Found her!" Hall called, keeping the saber point where it was. "Come on out, ma'am—careful now." He retracted the blade a bit, and slowly, with stiff movements, a woman squirmed out from under the dirt. She was filthy, covered in mud, and her stench made some of the nearby troopers raise their neckerchiefs to cover their noses.

Bawling, she began: "He made me—it's all his fault. Please don't kill me, though I deserve it!"

Hall shushed her and dropped to one knee, reaching his hand to cradle her chin. "There, there, we won't kill you—yet. Who is the 'he' you speak of?"

Estrella looked up at the handsome cavalry officer, a beautiful man, she thought, but as Oliver had told her, the most beautiful men are all criminals and adulterers. She sniffled, for good measure. "Mr. Oliver. He is to be my husband."

Hall looked at Kellerman, who had joined them, followed by Cranston. "Is that so?" Kellerman asked. "He abused you into a life of crime—is that it?"

A pause from her to think, then: "Yes, oh very badly

abused, as you say. But Oliver is my fiancé, he protects me from harm, and in return I help him with . . . projects."

There was a tense silence as the gathered men took in the emaciated young woman, until, at last, Kellerman again said, quietly, "Is that so?"

Cranston turned to Lockhart. "Fetch us Mrs. Zimmermann and Doc Chan, will you?"

"The Jesus Mann is ready to be out of my infirmary. please return him to duty as I cannot take anymore. Earlier he tried baptizing the Major Mouser."

"The cat?"

"Yes. With water. It—went as expected."

Lieutenant Hall laughed and headed over to the bedside of Fredrick Mann, who still sported bruises and a sling, and now had the recent addition of numerous cat scratches. "Captain, I'm taking Private Mann back to the stables. Keep me abreast of —" He nodded toward the woman, who sat hunched on Chan's table.

While Mrs. Zimmermann and Chan made a fuss over her, horrified by her overall condition, Estrella watched furtively from behind her lank hair, looking for weaknesses in the soldiers, so gallantly clothed, and in her helpers, as they tried to clean her up.

"Does your lip bother you, young lady?" Chan asked, lifting the ragged drooping edge gently with a tongue depressor.

"Yes, it bothers me."

"Well, no trouble at all to fix it, madame. Get you in good shape first, and then I'll have it good as new. Little surgery is all but not hard. Now tell us why you came to hide here on the Fort of Misery all this time. It was for the professor?"

Estrella paused to consider her options. She could try honesty, and maybe the men, and lady, at Fort Benjamin Grierson would take her on as their own. Maybe she would wed the handsome lieutenant who'd smiled at her so kindly, or the younger one with copper-colored hair. The captain clearly did not like her, but that was fine. She was lonely all the time and ashamed for it. But—no, she was a murderer, a trained assassin. And worse, as Oliver had never let her forget. She needed to find him first and listen to his guidance.

"Where is Oliver? Let me speak to him," she said, refusing to look Chan in the eye.

Chan looked to Captain Kellerman, who shook his head. "Absolutely not. Young lady, you need to tell us why you're here and what you have done before I will consider that. You're in a lot of trouble, as far as I, and the U.S. Army, are concerned."

She snapped her head up to glare at Kellerman with a rage that made his spine tingle. She looked like something out of a penny dreadful horror story. "No, just kill me, then."

The captain pinched the bridge of his nose. "Negative, ma'am. Not an option at this time. Speak to me."

Her captors believed they'd disarmed her, taking the knives from her waist, but she kept two daggers, one tucked at her bosom and another in her shoe. She calculated if it was better to attack them or slit her own throat, and, for the moment, decided neither.

"You know what I am?" she asked, angry.

"Have no idea, ma'am. That's why I'm asking."

"Dirt," she spat. "Just dirt. But Oliver is to marry me when we leave this place, despite my flaws."

Kellerman felt genuine compassion for her in that moment. She was pitiful to look at, and he wondered what could drive a woman to end up in her state but feared he knew all too well how she'd been treated. Of course, she believed the professor was her only chance. "Not true, ma'am, neither that a man cannot love you, nor, I am afraid, that Oliver Berryman will take your hand. Are you willing to take a noose for the old man, who has, by your own account, abused you?"

She was silent. Chan moved off to his medicine chest, feigning disinterest in the proceedings, though Kellerman knew he was up to something.

"You would have been a welcome guest here at the fort. All he had to do was tell us you existed," Mrs. Zimmermann said, lying a little, only because the girl was clearly deranged and would have required a bath and delousing. "My dear child, I've met many a lost lamb in my day—I say this to you as an honorable Catholic woman. Why, just last year we had a darling one who stayed with us a time. God will always forgive a repentant sinner."

Kellerman pointed a finger at Mrs. Zimmermann. "She speaks the truth. Mrs. Zimmermann loves trash."

That was met with a glare he studiously ignored.

Chan returned with a small white china cup filled with a pale steaming liquid. "My dear heart, you drink now, ease you. I can't imagine, even as a young lady, your joints are not sore—am I right?" he said, smiling broadly.

Estrella eyed him suspiciously, then nodded and took

the cup. She raised it to her lips with a smile, then threw the liquid into Kellerman's face, temporarily blinding him. In an instant she was on her feet, hissing and snarling like a cornered beast, her knives flashing. A raucous cacophony of shouts was raised as Kellerman turned the air blue with oaths and tried to blink away the painful concoction, while Chan and Mrs. Zimmermann leapt back to avoid the slashing blades. In an instant, Estrella was gone from the room.

"Damn it all! Shoot her if you have to!" Kellerman roared, sending the private on duty who'd wandered off to speak with his bedridden comrades, rushing out after her. "Chan! What is in that? Stings like the devil, and I can't see a thing!"

Chan grimaced. "Well . . . Supposed to work as a truth potion to calm her down, she made it a blinding potion, but that is not my fault. Here, here—we rinse. You'll be fine."

CHAPTER 68

Lieutenant James Hall was giving Private Mann a list of suitable chores that could be performed with one arm when he heard the shouts echo across the fort. "Now what?" he said, rushing out to look. Six harried troopers were chasing the young woman, who bounded like a hare across the parade ground toward the stables. Hall drew his Colt and waited, but at the last minute she changed direction and was gone.

"Oh, for the love of—" the lieutenant yelled. For such an unhealthy creature, she somehow had the ability to move like smoke, disappearing and reappearing into thin air in a blink. It was giving him the willies, and he wondered if she was possessed of some witchcraft found at one of the professor's ancient tombs.

He holstered his pistol with a groan. "Private Mann."

"Yes, sir."

"See to your list. I'll be back. When Private O'Connell arrives for his duties, inform him that he is to assist the wagon loading and feed the brays. I want these god-forsaken archaeologists gone in a hurry."

"Yes, sir."

* * *

Lieutenant Hall took off at a run in the same direction as the woman, heading for the holding cells and Father Staszczyk's quarters. Off to visit her lover, he supposed.

He was joined by several soldiers at the jail, where they stumbled upon a horrific scene. The priest was nowhere to be found, but the private assigned to guard duty lay on his back, half in and half out of the open doorway. The man's salt-and-pepper hair was coated in thick red blood, and his pale eyes stared skyward with a permanent look of horror. "Dead," a private said, as though it were not apparent.

"Careful. Be prepared to fire," Hall told the men as he stepped over the corpse, gun drawn. The storm created a riot of sound on the roof of the building, making it hard to hear any movement inside, and he started as lightning and thunder shook the earth. The floorboards creaked beneath the men's heavy boots as they entered the dim room, only to find the holding cell that contained Berryman open and empty.

CHAPTER 69

"Terrific," Joe Kellerman said, his eyes ringed in a red bandit mask of inflammation and blisters. He had met his men at the cells at the moment the escape was discovered, enraged triply by the murder of Constance, the escape acts, and the blinding attack. "Move out. Find her, find him—dead or alive matters little to me at this point. I give you full authority to—"

"Captain!" Private Harris interrupted him, huffing and puffing after a dead run to seek help. "Come quick, sir, they've got the good perfesser, and they gonna kill him!"

The sun was sinking through the iron clouds to the west, filling the Yuma territory with deep shadows, periodically relieved by flashes of lightning. Captain Kellerman and Lieutenant Hall, and a dozen or so soldiers approached the stables with determined but cautious steps. They reached the wagon port, where the driver who'd come to collect the professor stood in the corner, hands skyward and face sour. The man quickly pointed before returning his hands up, and there in the corner, Estrella held a gleaming silver blade to Paul Fernsby's throat. She was surrounded by gunmen, yet the blade over the jugular of the old man who had gained affection from the men of the fort stayed everyone's hands.

Kellerman scowled. "What's the meaning of this? Let the man go, he's done nothing to you."

His words were terse, but he made no motion toward raising his Colt, knowing full well it would be an immediate death for the professor.

Estrella said nothing, just glared with malice and tightened her grip. Fernsby gulped saliva, nauseated, but afraid vomiting would trigger his death.

Oliver Berryman was noticeably absent, and Kellerman and his officers watched for the man with their peripheral vision. Ahiga, Nicky Barnes, Lucas Dean, and Frank Abilene stood silent in a cluster at the entrance to the hallway of the stables, still as statues, calculating their chances for getting off a shot before the madwoman slit Fernsby's throat, but all four, despite skill and speed, felt those chances to be low.

Lieutenant Hall tried. "Ma'am," he began, smiling brilliantly at her. "I'm very sorry that you've been hurt and put through hardship," he lied. Hall thought her evil incarnate. "But killing an old man will never ease your pain. I— We"—he gestured to the assembled men— "have all seen combat. It seems on the surface a small thing, but I assure you that a lifetime of nightmares is all it brings." This part was true, particularly for those who'd served during the War Between the States and seen, firsthand, the horrors of the battlefield. "You just drop that knife now so that I can help you."

Estrella looked at him. She found him to be very beautiful, but he'd never fool her. She thought, *All they'll do is kill me.* "No," she said, flatly.

The driver spoke, unprompted. "Hey there, ma'am. Which if it weren't too much to ask, I would like to take my son and go away, for a bit, you see. I don't know what yer quarrel is with the army and the old fella, but it ain't involve me nor Bob none at all, do it? Yer a right purty lady, which if it ain't too much for me to say. Maybe you and Bob can get together back in Yuma someday, he does need a little wife, and a son."

If only for a moment, Kellerman thought he'd happily plug the old muleskinner and his son, the pair grinning like persimmon-eating possums at the madwoman before them and likely making a bad situation worse.

Sure enough, she tightened her grip and dug the knife into Fernsby's throat, drawing beads of crimson blood. "No one leaves."

Oliver Berryman chose that moment for his grand entrance, coming out from behind the farthest wagon.

"Oh, gentlemen," he said, smiling, "I do thank you for this wonderful performance of empathy toward my ward, but flattery will land you nowhere. She knows she's hideous, don't you, darling?"

She looked wounded, but nodded all the same.

"But it matters none, and do you know why? She can kill anyone, and I do mean anyone. Why, if I wanted to kill the queen, or your president, I would send her and it would be done. No fuss, no muss."

She nodded again, and Fernsby let out a whimpering sound.

"Now, all we ask is a wagon, some relics to sell—including the heart—and we will happily be on our way. Isn't that right, dear?"

"That's right," she said, and Kellerman noticed that she was so cowed she had lowered her gaze. He could use that. Thinking, and wishful for bourbon, he squinted his burning eyes.

"Berryman, you scum. You call the young lady hideous. You made her sleep in filth, and yet she is what to you besides a killer?"

"She's my . . . girl."

"Your bride?"

"Perhaps, someday."

Estrella bristled. "Some day?" she asked, pained.

"Well, of course, dear. I won't have enough money to fix your face and provide a home until all of this nasty business is done."

"The doctor here says I'm easy to fix."

Berryman frowned. "The doctor is a liar," then: "Wait, are you talking about Chan? My dear girl, he's nothing but a servingman with an overinflated ego. Look at yourself in the mirror. It will take a small fortune and proper English surgeons to repair you."

Estrella was nearly incandescent with rage, but the target of her ire had shifted to Oliver Berryman, and Captain Kellerman seized that opportunity.

"Ma'am, Doctor Chan is a brilliant physician. Why he has cured my second lieutenant via bat excrement, that is the man who I do believe you tried to kill?"

She returned her gaze to Kellerman's, and he saw the madness in her expression.

"The copper-haired man? I didn't try to kill him. Oliver said it would be too provoking. We just knocked him out."

"I see," Kellerman said. "But you killed the others?"

"Yes."

"Why?"

She shrugged. "He told me to do it."

"You went to Mr. Dean's camp and killed the man, and took his scalp?"

She cocked her head toward Berryman. "He said to make it look like the Apache, and so I did."

"Their belongings, from the wagon?"

"Scattered."

Berryman was becoming increasingly agitated, though somehow still under the impression he would skirt the law.

"Why did—" Kellerman paused and took in a breath. "Why did you brutally kill Miss Courtenay?"

At this Estrella smiled. "She was very beautiful, wasn't she?"

"She was."

"If we did not kill the other ones, then the fortune would be divided, do you see? Just this one is left." She dug the knife into Fernsby, who looked near to a faint. "But why should the pretty lady die pretty? If you're dead it stops mattering."

"ENOUGH!" Berryman roared. "She is insane—she has no idea what she's saying. Captain, believe me, yes, we did knock out your redheaded man, only because he was interfering." He chuckled. "Come now, why would I allow this gruesome creature to attack the others? It is only the riches I'm after. Let me go, and I'll trouble you no further."

"What of the woman?"

"What of her? Hang her, shoot her, it matters little to me. Freedom and a few treasures to sell, that's all I ask."

To the heart of the wounded, lonely woman, his words were daggers. "Oliver?" she said, her voice soft like a child's.

"Just kill him. Don't you see the ruse?" Berryman spat, gesturing at Kellerman. "We'll both move on. Honestly, what did you think would happen? That I'd love you? YOU?"

There are people who can be pushed to their limits and walk away, but for some, the damage turns their minds incapable of reason. Estrella may have lied to herself about the love she felt for the aged professor and his motivations, but the lie couldn't override her emotions. With a cry of fury, she shoved Fernsby to the ground and charged at Berryman, slitting his throat from ear to ear, a fountain of blood spilling to his feet as he fell.

Horrified, even the most seasoned troopers briefly froze with their mouths agape, and that was all it took. Knife still covered in blood, Estrella leapt from one target to the next and now stood with her arm wrapped around Lieutenant Hall, blade to his throat the way it had been for Fernsby. Kellerman raised his Colt then paused at the look in Hall's eyes.

"This is ridiculous. You're a woman, everyone will

be easy on you, they won't hurt you," Kellerman said, lying.

"They always hurt women," Estrella replied.

"Who is they?"

"You."

"Me? I've never hurt a woman."

"YOU!" She bellowed. "All of you!" She dug the knife blade into Hall's flesh, but he remained stoic, hunched backward to accommodate her shorter height.

Lieutenant Hall knew he was likely to die as Berryman had, choking on his own blood in the dirt. The sun had fully set, and the lamps were not yet lit, so the room had grown dark and close, only the bright blazes of lightning revealing the movements of the soldiers. Fernsby was curled in the corner, clutching his chest. The Englishman carried no pistol or blade, but fury was a strong antidote for overcoming weakness of any kind. His beautiful Constance gone at the hands of this woman, the fault of Berryman, a man he had trusted as a fellow gentleman, and now the impending doom of the calvary officer became too much to bear. He rolled to his knees and in the flashes of light saw the captain shaking his head almost imperceptibly, warning him to stay down. He'd just risen to his feet when the sound of hooves came pounding through the stable hall toward the brutal scene. Every head, even Hall's, turned, and the men watched a flickering light approach through the darkness.

A massive black horse with what at first seemed to be a headless rider jumped through the doorway, Ichabod Crane incarnate, the glowing flame of his lamp blinding those who tried to see the mysterious horseman.

"Unhand him, she-devil! Lilith!" a voice boomed. Stunned, Estrella had loosened her grip on Hall, who seized the chance to drop his weight and fall to his knees, fumbling for his gun. The massive horse snorted into his face with the sound of outrage, and a silver blade flashed from the darkness and was immediately followed by a sickening *thwack* sound and a heavy plop.

Hall, scrambling away, and Kellerman both opened fire, as Lucas Dean and his men frantically tried to see their target without shooting at bystanders but found themselves blinded by the fiery explosions of the officers' guns.

The horse skidded to a stop with a word from the rider, the wagon port once again falling silent apart from the heavy rain and rumbling thunder. A voice came from the dark, as the lantern was raised barely enough to reveal the shadowy face. "Lieutenant Hall, sir? Are you all right?"

Private Frederick Mann sat atop the majestic and unruly horse named Lucifer, a bloody saber in his good arm and lit lamp in his bad one. The bad-tempered beast he rode bareback was perfectly calm, and all present would later swear they saw the animal smile.

"Private Mann?" Hall said, shaken.

"Sir, yes, sir. Sorry for the commotion, but the demon woman was going to murder you." He patted the horse. "Luce said so, and we came to save you."

"Thank—you, uh, Private."

"Yes, sir."

Spooked and about done with the bloody scene, a

few men hurried to light the lamps. Estrella's severed head lay a foot away from her corpse. The woman's face was oddly peaceful, and though she'd been vicious and horrid in life, it was the opinion of all gathered that perhaps Saint Peter had welcomed her, anyway, with a chance at some happiness for the very first time.

Private Mann looked at her, and at Berryman, then dropped his saber. "I don't like it at all, sir. I won't promise to ever hold a weapon again, but you're just about the only man who's been kind to me, and it wouldn't have been right to let you die that way."

Hall simply nodded. As Private Mann steered the menace of a horse away and back into the shadowy stables, Joe Kellerman called after him, "Private"—Mann paused but did not turn—"we'll never forget this."

Mann nodded, still facing away, then continued his path.

Fernsby bent to retrieve something from Berryman's splayed feet and picked up the heart that he'd tried to steal yet again, it seemed. "It's only valuable attached to de Toro's armor . . . you idiot," he said, with a frown.

The officers had started to reorganize their thoughts just as a frantic figure appeared at the doors. Second Lieutenant Cranston, pale and panicked, took in the scene as he said, "Sorry, sirs. What did I miss?"

CHAPTER 70

"Which if you're ready, we can depart," the wagon driver, Mr. Belcher, said, glancing around the fort nervously and thinking it was an accursed hellhole he'd never return to, regardless of the payday.

"Yes, yes, one moment." Professor Fernsby, sporting a small gauze bandage on his throat beamed at Captain Kellerman and Lieutenants Hall and Cranston as they gathered to see him off.

"It has been a pleasure, officers," he said.

"Has it been?" Kellerman said, eyebrow raised.

Fernsby sighed. "No, not at all. I hope to never see the likes of this place again."

"Pinch of snuff?" Hall said cheerfully, holding out the box.

"One for the road, most certainly. I am afraid you've created a bad habit in me, James."

"Oh yes, sir, if there is one thing the U.S. Army is exceptionally talented at, it is creating bad habits."

Fernsby smiled. His heart was heavy, as he'd left the body of Constance behind to a burial at the fort cemetery, after admitting it would be a bad idea to transport it.

Yet . . . "I think you would have loved each other, Captain. For a lifetime," he said sadly.

Joe Kellerman placed a hand on the older man's shoulder. "You may be right. But that wasn't what fate chose, for any of us. We'll see her again someday, you and I."

"Me sooner than you, most likely, but do try to stay out of trouble?"

Kellerman grinned. "I'll give it a shot."

Belcher looked skyward at the encroaching clouds. "If it ain't too much trouble—"

"Yes, yes. I am coming. Where is Chan? I want to say goodbye. And please, officers, do give my regards to the sergeant major."

"Here I come, and then you go, go, go." Chan stepped from behind the officers, grinning, looking fresh and rested in contrast to the rest, who were half dead from stress and fatigue.

"My most brilliant man," Fernsby said, clasping the short Chinese man on his arms. "You're sure you want to stay?"

"Yes. The Fort of Misery needs me for now, then someday I will be famous, too, as America is land of opportunity, and"—he looked side to side, then raised a palm and stage whispered—"they all think I am a doctor."

Fernsby laughed and then shook hands one last time with the officers and his former servingman before ambling up into the wagon beside the driver. They'd arrived to create havoc on the parade ground with three men, a lady, and a Chinese servant, and a single wagon with a small number of trunks, yet the professor left without them, and with three wagons full of loot.

As they watched the dust clouds fade into the distance,

Kellerman felt a sense of relief. "Do you think he'll be all right?" he said to Hall and Cranston, who had both participated in the send-off, mainly to ward off the monumental task of filling in every trench the professors had created.

"The professor? Yes, I think he'll be just fine, sir," Cranston said.

An odd sentimentality had struck Kellerman. "I grew to like the old coot."

Hall piped up. "You've always been tenderhearted, sir," he said, deadpan.

Kellerman glared at him.

"Captain!"

Sergeant Major Saul Olinger came striding up with something enormous, white, and furry cradled in his arms, struggling beneath its weight.

"What the heck is that?"

"A dog."

"Where did you find a dog?"

"It found us—*she*'s a real pretty thing." Olinger placed the dog, who unfurled into a white shepherd-type canine with pert ears and sparkling black eyes, on the ground, and she licked the sergeant major's face enthusiastically with a bright pink tongue. "Oh yes, she's a pretty girl, such a pretty baby," Olinger said, meeting the dog's affection for him with equal enthusiasm.

"Saul, that 'baby' is at least a hundred pounds and likely a rabid wolf," Kellerman said, feeling his headache return.

"Yes, but look at her—she's just a little girl, baby girl, lovely rabid wolf—oh yes, yes, she is . . ."

Cranston and Hall shared a bemused look as the sergeant major continued to coo at the huge beast.

Thunder cracked across the sky, making Kellerman glance up into the distance. He blinked. Surely, he couldn't see what he thought he did—an approaching caravan, sand flying into the air despite the damp earth. He groaned. "Oh no. Now what?"

A wildly out of control coach seemed to lead the charge, careening toward the fort as the sky erupted into a fury of lightning behind it.

James Hall took out his snuff. "Likely nothing good, sir. Care for a pinch?"

**TURN THE PAGE
FOR A RIP-ROARING PREVIEW**

**The Wildest Western You'll Ever Read—
Believe It or Not**

**In this rollicking stand-alone novel from the
bestselling Johnstones, fact and fiction collide in
the jaw-dropping story of Jesse James's little-
known, disaster-prone brother.
They call him Calamity—for a reason . . .**

Calvin Amadeus James, aka Calamity, isn't an outlaw
like his notorious brothers Jesse and Frank.
He's worse—due to the bad luck that follows him
everywhere he goes. Every job he takes—from army
scout to gambler to cowboy and rail worker—ends in
catastrophe. No matter what he does, Calamity James
always seems to be on the wrong side of history . . .

The Great Chicago Fire of 1871?
Calamity placed the lantern next to the cow that
kicked it over. The gunfight at O.K. Corral?
Calamity stirred up trouble in Tombstone
right before it all went down.
The fateful saloon shooting of Wild Bill Hickok?
Blame it on Calamity James. Some folks say he's
even responsible for Custer's last stand at Little Big
Horn—but Calamity swears it ain't true.
He's just a magnet for bad luck, who's trying to find
his good luck charm—a pretty dancehall girl
known as Clumsy Catherine.
But somewhere along the way, he foolishly joins the
James–Younger Gang with his outlaw brothers.
And that's when Calamity's infamous bad luck
gets a whole lot worse . . .

National Bestselling Authors
William W. Johnstone
and J. A. Johnstone

CALAMITY JAMES

The Unbelievable, Untold Story
of Jesse James's Other Brother

On sale now, wherever Pinnacle Books are sold.

Live Free. Read Hard.
williamjohnstone.net
Visit us at kensingtonbooks.com
Western

PART ONE

BEING AN INTRODUCTION TO THE PRINCIPAL CHARACTERS IN THIS NARRATION

1842–1851

Chapter 1

He was born in the cabin his father's congregation built. It burned down that night.

At least his mother was used to hard luck. Anyone who came to this earth in Kentucky, even those born into money and good stock, knows all too much about misfortune. As a child, Zerelda Cole's father broke his neck in a riding accident, her brother would kill himself in 1895, and between her birth and her brother's demise, she would witness more torment and tragedy, more brutality and beastliness, than a writer of myriad penny dreadfuls could dream up. Giving birth to an illegitimate child fathered by a soon-to-be minister just continued Zerelda's string of foul luck.

This is not to say that Calvin Amadeus James was born out of wedlock. Even those who could not fill a flush at a table or bet on the right horse to win at Kansas City's agricultural fair eventually will see something work out. No, Cal was born on January 28, 1842, one month after Robert James married Zerelda, whose daddy had been dead since she was two years old, and her mama, after remarrying, had left that young but tough girl with her grandpa Cole. And even though the fire that left the new cabin in ashes and just about everything the newlyweds owned was consumed in the blaze, one of the blessings was that Robert James's family bible was lost, too. The parents of Cal, a pink lad of five pounds, seven ounces, would not realize this at first—indeed, there were many tears and questions to the Lord of why, why, *why?*—but well before Cal reached the age for schooling, both Robert and Zee—Zee being what most folks called Cal's mama—realized that the loss of the cabin, and the family bible, was a blessing from the Almighty.

That bible was the only written documentation to prove that Calvin James was ever born into this family. Zee didn't even call for a midwife to birth her first baby. That was all left to Zee and her praying husband, and the baby entered the world bawling and pink and healthy.

Yes, sympathy should be given to Cal, for his father and mother decided, since Robert was about to graduate from Georgetown College and enter the ministry—though he was already practicing his sermoning but not his baptisms at the cabin those settlers had put up—that they would be better off giving up the infant. Robert paid a young couple to take the newborn as their own. It would work out for the best, all parties agreed, because the woman, Charity Marmaduke, just lost her own infant child to an outbreak of diphtheria, and, more important, she and her husband, Obadiah, were headed west.

Robert wiped his eyes and did some serious praying and begging for forgiveness as the Marmadukes rolled down the pike with the sleeping infant in his new mama's lap, but Zerelda was of sterner stock, and she just spit the juice from her snuff into the grass. As fate would have it, Zerelda would get in the family way again and give birth to a strapping young fellow. By then, the Reverend Robert James was preaching the gospel. They named him Alexander Franklin James, who entered this world, on January 10, 1843, on their farm near Centerville, Missouri—which eventually changed its name, as towns were fond of doing in those times (especially when it came time to get a post office), to Kearney.

But we shall come back to the James family in due time.

Obadiah and Charity Marmaduke were, like Cal's true parents, natives of Kentucky. Blue grass ran through their veins. Their grandparents, if you believe the stories Obadiah told in the taverns and after barn raisings, had traveled to Kentucky with Daniel Boone. And even if the closest the Marmadukes ever got to Daniel Boone was following the trails he had blazed, Obadiah did have a case of the wanderlust that afflicted Dan'l and other explorers of our wondrous western frontier.

The Marmadukes settled in Iowa, and, oh, how Charity doted on that baby boy, even though he had a habit of crying and keeping both new mother and new father awake all night. Charity once confided to a friend that she hardly slept a wink on the journey by wagon from Kentucky. But she was a young woman with a baby boy to hold and she was not one to complain. At least, for the first couple of years.

They kept his name, at least Calvin, which, as most Calvins will tell you, got shortened to Cal. They even told the Jameses they would keep his middle name, Amadeus, and it was penciled into their bible, too, but the lead faded, and worsened after the roof leaked and soaked that Good Book.

We should point out that by the time the boy was five years old, calamity followed young Cal with such frequency that not only friends of the Marmadukes but the Marmadukes themselves thought there might be some truth to the rumor quickly spreading that a Kickapoo woman had put a curse on the newborn—despite the fact that it's hard to find a Kickapoo in Kentucky. Or Iowa. In fact, after years of investigation, we have never found proof that any Kickapoo ever set foot in the state that has given us Daniel Boone, Jim Bowie, and Kit Carson.

And certainly not Iowa.

Folks started calling young Cal, a tall, good-looking, and fairly smart lad, "Calamity," because bad luck just seemed to follow him, though, more often than not, bystanders—and not that strapping youngster—seemed to get the worse of things.

Like the horseshoe-pitching contest on the Fourth of July when Cal was five or six years old when all the boy had to do was come close and he would have won the fat sow for a prize. Instead, he busted out the windowpane at the Market House—which was behind Cal. The owner of the Market House, a generous sort, shrugged it off, even though glass was right scarce around Flint Hill.

Iowa on the Mississippi River was a fine place to be in the 1840s. The pig market was sound, and cholera was kept in check, at least more than it was down south in Saint Louis and New Orleans, where folks boarded steamboats all the time to escape that infernal plague. There were tanners and hunters, coopers and grocers, merchants dealing in dry goods, queensware, boots, nails, iron, stone, steel, nails, Jewett's Patent Carey Ploughs, medicines, dyes, putty, saddles, tin. There were more lawyers than one could shake a stick at. There was a congregational church on Columbia Street, but Mr. Partridge often opened up the hall above his store for other religious services. And the *Burlington Hawk-Eye* came out at least once a week, most times. In fact, Mr. Marmaduke read about the war against Mexico in that newspaper, and considered going, but decided against it.

There wasn't a dentist, the nearest one being a steamboat ride down to Saint Louis, but you could get a tooth pulled by just about anyone who had a keg of whiskey and a pair of pliers.

"Maybe I should have gone to Mexico," Obadiah was heard to say at Drury's groggery in the dreary winter of 1846–47, when Iowa was still celebrating its admittance into the Union. "I could have died a hero at the Alamo."

"That wasn't the Mexican war, feller," the man next to him said.

"Sure, it was," Obadiah said. "Mexicans slaughtered Crockett and Bowie and all them others."

"That was the war for Texas," the stranger said. "Then Mexico and Santee Annie got riled and that's why we marched to Mexico. To free Texas agin and get all the rest of 'em places. Like Californie."

"You don't know nothin', mister. So quit yer brayin'."

That resulted in Obadiah having to work his way to Saint Louis and back as a stevedore to get a busted tooth pulled.

Obadiah could have kept on stevedoring but complained that the work was too hard and that the Mississippi River was a right frightening place to be traveling. And sometimes the river stunk worser than a pig farm.

In short, the Marmadukes had landed in a place that was full of opportunities, for this was the West (at least at that time), and a fellow could make his mark in this wild, new, free country.

Unless your name happened to be Obadiah Marmaduke.

Especially after Obadiah gave up on being a stevedore. Well, that job did require a willingness to sweat for hours, and you ought to be able to carry a fifty-pound keg down the plank and up the bank without dropping it three times.

Speaking of dropping, a pail of nails slipped out of Obadiah's hand and fell on the construction boss's right foot, and so Obadiah was unemployed as soon as Mr. Clavean stopped hopping around and cussing up a storm. The nails didn't weigh anywhere near fifty pounds, but five pounds on your big toe when you're not expecting it hurts just the same.

Old Fullerton gave him a chance at selling dry goods, but Obadiah was color blind and couldn't tell a bolt of blue gingham from the pink one, and he broke two silk parasols trying to show Mrs. Bettie McDowell how to open one. Those were the five-dollar parasols, mind you, not the fifty-cent ones.

He tried selling bottles of Wistar's Balsam of Wild Cherry, which, he said, reading from the slip of paper he was given and twenty-seven cents in advance, could prevent the consumption killing fifty thousand folks a year and also remedy any liver affections, and asthma and bronchitis, not to mention things like chronic coughs and weak lungs, or even bleeding lungs. Problem was, Obadiah realized he liked the taste of the wild cherry and drunk up three bottles without selling a one. Chillicothe George, who was running that deal, broke one of the empty bottles over Obadiah's head.

Thing was, Obadiah Marmaduke had been quite successful back in Kentucky. That's how come he could afford a wagon and mules to take his family all the way to the Mississippi and cross it into Iowa Territory, which entered the Union on December 28, 1846.

So poor Obadiah took to drink and then, as so often can be the case, he took to cards.

Glory be, for a while he thought his luck had changed.

Obadiah Marmaduke won a sternwheeler in a poker game, and everyone said that the Marmadukes had it made now, for the *Hawkeye* was one of the finest vessels on the Mississippi, a double-engine mastered by the able and fine Christian captain, Silas S. Throckmorton. Two nights later, bound for Oquawka, New Boston, Bloomington, Rock Island, Davenport, Galena, Dubuque, and Potosi, the *Hawkeye* went up in flames just like the James's cabin. Some folks said they had seen young Cal poking at a fire near the boat landings—though he might have just been warming himself, as it was February and the temperature was well below zero—but most just chalked it up to a stevedore who had been careless with pipe or cigar.

This was about the time that Obadiah began to think about his son who really wasn't his son, and began to believe that the Almighty had turned His back on a poor struggling, kindhearted, and hardworking (at least in his own mind) soul who had had a lovely wife, who had been distraught over losing a young son, then thrived at first with Cal, but now was disheveled, dismayed, and disillusioned.

Once, after Cal had been playing with a dog and one, either canine or kid, had torn up half the butter bean plants, Obadiah had sighed, found the jug of Carmichael's corn liquor, and said, "I swan, Charity, but that boy is a jinx or a curse."

"Hush your mouth, Husband!" Charity barked back, and Obadiah obeyed.

But later—after Charity stepped on a nail and had to find the Indian woman who could cure such injuries, and the Indian woman (who was not Kickapoo, but Otoe) would not treat Charity unless that boy of hers was out of sight, so Charity told Cal to go to the river and fish, and after the nail wound was treated, and though no fish were caught, Grover Denton drowned in the Mississippi that day, albeit his boat capsized a good two hundred yards downstream from where Cal was wetting his line—"Maybe," Charity suggested to Obadiah, "'taint Cal whose causin' us this mess of bad luck. Maybe it's just Iowa is a curse to us."

Which got them to thinking.

After all, it wasn't like Burlington, Iowa, was some

sort of paradise, not after struggling to survive for nigh a dozen years. Charity conceded that she missed Kentucky. She even told her husband she might could settle for Missouri.

Little did she know that Missouri was about to come to their home.

CHAPTER 2

Charity Marmaduke was putting out the fire when, over the towering flames and popping of grease in the skillet in the chimney, she heard a man's voice call out, "Halloooo, the cabin."

She had just screamed at young Cal, because when the skillet got all blazing, she asked for the flour, and the young lad, about eight years old, handed her the sugar by mistake. Fire, in case you are not much at cooking, reacts to sugar a whole lot differently than it does to flour. Much shrieking and some profanity followed as flames leaped toward the roof and smoke caused both mother and child to cough a bit and shriek in alarm a lot more. Charity found the flour herself, thus tragedy was averted.

Strangers were uncommon at the Marmaduke cabin—a little ways out of town—but not unheard of. Still, Charity, fanning herself with a smoky-smelling towel, left the fireplace, which served as the winter and summer kitchen, since the summer setup had been destroyed by an angry cow Cal had been trying to milk.

"Don't open that door, boy!" Charity snapped, when

she realized what her son, her adopted son, was about to do. She dunked the towel into a bucket of water—which Cal had brought in to throw on the fire in the skillet before his mother had screamed, "No!" and later would teach him that oil fires and water do not mix well at all, same as oil fires and sugar, and such an act might could have burned down the entire cabin and, possibly, mother and son, with it.

A muzzle-loading rifle leaned in the corner near the door, but Charity did not go for it. She simply looked through the peephole in the door, pulled back, rubbed her eyes, then tried for a better view.

Recognition was slow to come, but come it did, and Charity stepped back.

"Who is it, Mama?" Cal asked, then coughed, because smoke remained heavy. The fireplace had never drawn worth a fig, even when it was burning oak, not grease.

Well, she needed to open the door anyway to let that rancid smoke out of their home. Rubbing her eyes, she looked at Cal, then peered through the hole again. Maybe she had been seeing things.

She hadn't.

"Stay—" No, she couldn't let the boy stay inside this smoky cabin that stunk of burned grease and scorched bacon.

So she opened the door.

"Come along, Cal," she said. "Leave the door open so the smoke'll go out. And"—she stepped outside—"company's here."

The man held the reins to a good horse. He removed

his black hat and bowed slightly. The wind blew the linen duster.

"Preacher," she said softly. "How are things in—?" She almost said Kentucky, but Robert James had written every Christmas. The letters were always signed by him, not his wife. They were short, simple, usually with a verse or two of Scripture.

"Missouri?" Charity finished.

The Reverend Robert Sallee James bowed, and put his flat black hat atop his head.

"Fine, Missus Marmaduke," the preacher said. His eyes quickly moved from the woman to the boy.

God was good, he thought with a smile. The kid looked more like his daddy than he did his ma. The preacher's wife was a good woman, a fine mother, worked harder in gardens than anyone the preacher had known, and could milk a cow without complaint. And was fat and mean and ugly.

"Cal," Charity said, turning to the tall, strapping handsome kid. "This is— This is . . . a preacher we knew back in Kentucky. The Reverend James."

"Preacher." Cal nodded.

"Calvin," the preacher said. He must have gotten some smoke in his eyes, the boy thought, because he brought a knuckle to his right eye, then his left, and sniffed a bit before his Adam's apple went up and down.

"Why don't you bring your horse to the corral?" Charity suggested. "Cal, go fill a bucket with water from the well, and then get some grain for the preacher's hoss."

Cal did as he was told, and with the horse drinking and snorting up some grain, he walked over to the stump that served as a thinking chair in the front yard. The preacher was sitting, but Cal, without even being ordered, drug the rocking chair off the porch and brought it so that his mother could rest. Then he put his hands behind his back and just stood there like that knot on a log folks was always talking about.

The stranger, Cal learned, was the minister at New Hope Baptist Church in Clay County, Missouri. He had two sons, Frank being the oldest, seven years old, "just about a year younger than you, Calvin." The man's clear eyes smiled at young Cal, who thought this preacher was a real preacher and knowed things better than anyone who didn't know the gospel from cover to cover, because most folks thought Cal was a good year or two older than he actually was.

"A young son—Jesse—he'll be three when September comes along. And a precious little girl, Susan Lavenia. She's just a couple of months old now." He looked around. "Is this strapping young lad your only child?"

"Yes, Reverend," was all Cal's mama said, and she changed the subject. "What brings you so far from your congregation—and your family?"

The preacher sipped water Cal had brung him.

"I'm called to preach," he said. "We have a fine new church at New Hope—made of brick—but I ride the circuit for the Lord."

He preached on and on about all he had done in Missouri. Luring some Baptist college to the nearby town of Liberty; it had just opened its doors this year of 1850. He had married many young couples, saved hundreds of souls, preached far too many funerals, and shown the unenlightened the Light.

"And my family has a fine cabin on a creek in Clay County. We have a fine farm. Growing hemp for cash. And food to eat. They'll be fine without me. The Lord called me to Missouri, and I've preached and saved many souls. But now,"—he pointed west—"now there is a great migration to California. Gold fever is luring many folks westward. Gold can bring deviltry with it, and I must fight the devil with all my might. So I am bound for California. For how long, I do not know."

"How far away is Californie?" Cal asked.

The preacher smiled. "As far as it takes us to get there."

"You goin' alone?" Charity asked.

"I go with the Lord." Smiling, he pointed south and west. "I'm to join a party in Independence, Missouri."

Charity stared at the reverend for a long while. After glancing at her son, she looked Preacher James in his sparkling clear eyes.

"Ain't this a fer piece out of your way?"

This time, the preacher did not answer.

"Cal," Charity said, "go get that skillet, and take it to the crick and wash it good. We don't want the preacher to think we'll serve him burnt bacon on his journey west to save souls and such."

The boy didn't want to go, but he did.

"Scrub that skillet good," she told him, and then waited for the Reverend James to speak his piece.

Which Charity related to her husband when the worthless oaf came home that evening.

* * *

Obadiah Marmaduke's mouth stayed open.

He was sober, bringing home all of his twelve and a half cents he had earned doing a few odd jobs in town. He scratched the stubble on his cheeks. He was sure he was sober. He didn't recall going into any saloon, and besides, most of the grog shops wouldn't let him inside, anyway.

"Say that agin," he requested of his wife.

"The preacher wants to take Cal with him."

That's what it had sounded like the first time.

The man's sore head shook slowly. He found the cup of coffee, which wasn't really coffee but was all they could afford, and drank about a quarter of it down.

"There's a train—wagon train—they are to join in Independence. A number of Missourians are going."

"We ought to go!" Obadiah sang out.

"We're not going to California," she told him. "I'm too far from Kentucky as it is, and there are wild Indians between here and that gold—if there's any gold left by the time we could get there—and California is full of Mexicans, I hear, who don't speak a word of English."

"Like Kentuckians do!" Laughing at his joke, Obadiah slapped his knee.

Charity's eyes stifled his hilarity and left him groveling and staring at his worn-out boots.

"What's the preacher want with Cal?"

The woman sighed. "Forgiveness," she whispered.

"Huh?"

"He feels he committed a sin. Which"—she shrugged—"I guess he did. I guess we all did. And he wants to get to know his son. That's the best I could get out of what he was saying. He'd say this, then bawl for thirty or forty seconds, then spout out some Scripture, then cry some more, and then he would talk about that woman he married."

Obadiah leaned forward. This might be something worth hearing.

"Well, between tears and torment," Charity said, "what I taken from his talkin' is that this Zerelda James ain't the most forgivin' and kindly Christian women you'd expect to be a preacher's wife. She yells and threatens. She don't like him runnin' off here and there all the time to preach—even if that's what a preacher does."

"Maybe he just wants gold," Obadiah suggested. "I heard on the riverfront that the newspapers say that the gold won't never run out. That it's like pickin' apples off an apple tree. That there's more gold than there is ants in California, and a body can't help but get rich there. Maybe we should—"

"We're not going anywhere," she told him. "Till they run you out of town."

He pouted. She sighed after two minutes and leaned over and patted his hand.

Looking into his wife's eyes, Obadiah whispered, "Do you think he'll tell Cal the truth?"

"Do you think he should?"

He studied his feet, then looked around the cabin, then stared at his wife again. "He's handy to have around, ain't he?"

Charity sighed and shook her head.

"We were young and foolish and heartbroke." Her

head bowed, and she sniffled. "But he is a good boy. Handsome. He's just . . ."

"Unlucky."

Her head shook. "To us." Her eyes met his again. "He almost burned down the cabin this morn."

"Did the preacher mention, ummmm . . . you know—maybe offering . . . some money—for getting his son back?"

She would have slapped him, but she recalled the Reverend James's words about forgiveness and charity and love.

The hard part, of course, was telling Cal the truth.

Which is why they lied: California was the land of dreams and gold, and the future—their future—lay in that wondrous place. It would be an adventure. Riding—though from what Charity had heard, it was a whole lot more walking than riding to get to California—across the great West, seeing those never-ending plains and then the greatest spectacles in all of America—the mountains, the glorious Rockies and Sierras, so high they touched the clouds. Waterfalls and rapids. Sunsets with every color on the palette stretching across a never-ending sky. And the Pacific Ocean, blue and calm and wondrous.

Cal's eyes brightened at his future. In California, no one would know how much bad luck he brought with him. He would have friends. And maybe he would keep friends. Maybe his luck would change in California. He probably could find some gold, too. He'd be helpful, for once.

"When do we leave?" he shouted.

"Well,"—his mother reached out and patted his hand—"you're going out with the Reverend James." She waved her hand around the cabin. "We have to sell our place, you see."

He saw—he saw his mother's eyes. He said, "I see."

But he told himself that California would be an adventure. And there was something about the preacher that he liked and respected. Cal's ma had taken him to services, maybe not every Sunday, but lots of times, and he had enjoyed the singing. He could belt out "Rock of Ages" like everyone else, and there was much satisfaction in saying amen. And he sure liked that concept of forgiveness.

So he forgave his mother, silently, and asked the Almighty to do the same. Then he climbed up to his bed to pack up his clothes and such, and get ready for the trip west.

Visit our website at
KensingtonBooks.com
to sign up for our newsletters, read
more from your favorite authors, see
books by series, view reading group
guides, and more!

Become a Part of Our
Between the Chapters Book Club
Community and Join the Conversation

Submit your book review for a chance to win exclusive
Between the Chapters swag you can't get anywhere else!
https://www.kensingtonbooks.com/pages/review/